BONED

A survivor at a major Australian television network, the author has witnessed the excesses of the eighties, limped through the belt tightening of the nineties and been bemused by the bonings of the noughties. He or she continues to forge a successful small-screen career.

For obvious reasons, the author prefers to remain anonymous.

BONED

ANONYMOUS

PENGUIN
MICHAEL JOSEPH

MICHAEL JOSEPH

Published by the Penguin Group
Penguin Group (Australia)
250 Camberwell Road, Camberwell, Victoria 3124, Australia
(a division of Pearson Australia Group Pty Ltd)
Penguin Group (USA) Inc.
375 Hudson Street, New York, New York 10014, USA
Penguin Group (Canada)
90 Eglinton Avenue East, Suite 700, Toronto, Canada ON M4P 2Y3
(a division of Pearson Penguin Canada Inc.)
Penguin Books Ltd
80 Strand, London WC2R 0RL England
Penguin Ireland
25 St Stephen's Green, Dublin 2, Ireland
(a division of Penguin Books Ltd)
Penguin Books India Pvt Ltd
11 Community Centre, Panchsheel Park, New Delhi – 110 017, India
Penguin Group (NZ)
67 Apollo Drive, Rosedale, North Shore 0632, New Zealand
(a division of Pearson New Zealand Ltd)
Penguin Books (South Africa) (Pty) Ltd
24 Sturdee Avenue, Rosebank, Johannesburg 2196, South Africa

Penguin Books Ltd, Registered Offices: 80 Strand, London, WC2R 0RL, England

First published by Penguin Group (Australia), 2008

3 5 7 9 10 8 6 4 2

Cover and text design by David Altheim © Penguin Group (Australia)
Cover photographs by Gregg Segal/Getty Images (woman);
George Doyle/Getty Images (background)
Typeset in 12/16.5pt Fairfield Light by Post Pre-press Group, Brisbane, Queensland
Printed and bound in Australia by McPherson's Printing Group, Maryborough, Victoria

National Library of Australia
Cataloguing-in-Publication data:

Anonymous.
Boned.
ISBN 9780718105006 (pbk.).
I. Title.
A823.4

penguin.com.au

To the good guys . . . there are a few

'The TV business is a cruel and shallow money trench, a long plastic hallway where thieves and pimps run free and good men die like dogs.'
Hunter S Thompson

'What happens to all the good women then?'
Anonymous

PROLOGUE

Kate Corish unlatched her balcony door with a practised elbow. In one hand, she juggled a short black and a Zippo lighter. In the other was a can of Red Bull (sugar free), two pens and a notebook. She had two tightly wrapped newspapers shoved under each arm and an unopened packet of cigarettes clenched between her teeth.

It was 6 a.m. and already Kate's mobile was ringing insistently from deep inside the pocket of her faded grey trackie daks. The pants were so old now that the elastic was brittle. Only the generous curve of Kate's hips kept them from slipping right off. As a result, the phone was vibrating somewhere nearer her knee than her upper thigh.

With both hands fully occupied, Kate was forced to let the caller go through to message bank. Bugger them anyway. People who called this early needed to learn a bit of patience. Plus there was the small matter of conducting a coherent conversation at this hour. Kate estimated she was still several hundred milligrams of caffeine short of forming a simple sentence.

The phone exhaled a short, hopeful electronic chord as Kate continued to manoeuvre herself and her morning provisions onto the balcony. The next stage was the trickiest. Pressing her

Pilates-honed butt against the reinforced glass, she pushed the sliding door open until the gap was just wide enough for her to squeeze through sideways.

So far so good. Confidence up, she executed a wobbly pirouette. The move was designed to deposit her neatly and gracefully into her outdoor reading chair. But that was supposing Kate kept her balance. Which she almost never did. On this occasion, she managed to catch one foot in the hem of her sagging trousers, trip over the metal door runner and catapult herself inelegantly into the outside world.

She cursed as she stubbed her toe on a large terracotta pot. A pen slipped from her grasp, skittered across the tiles and plunged off the verandah, heading for the street below. Kate dumped her cargo onto the teak outdoor table and peered over the railing. All clear. One of these days her clumsiness was going to cost someone an eye.

Twelve floors below, Sydney was yawning awake. An endless conga of headlights streamed over the Bridge and into the CBD. Ferries plied the shark-grey harbour while commuters hurried towards Milsons Point station, their chins burrowed doggedly into winter coats. It promised to be a spectacular August day, but until the sun reported for duty the temperature would remain stubbornly in single figures.

Kate took some comfort in knowing she wasn't the only person awake and working this early. She lit a cigarette and took two long, appreciative drags before moving on to her coffee.

Her ritual had scarcely changed in her nineteen years as a television journalist. Up at dawn. A hastily sculled short black. Then a long and careful inspection of the nation's newspapers, usually accompanied by half a dozen cigarettes. Occasionally, vanity, fear and the pleas of her personal trainer would convince her to trade the fags for nicotine gum. But Kate's resolve only ever lasted until the next big story. Or the next big row with her Neanderthal boss.

The Red Bull was a relatively recent addition to her morning drill. As Kate edged into her forties, she found she needed more than a single cup of coffee and a lick of mascara to get out the door. Age was a bitch.

She worked the cling wrap off the first newspaper, opting to go tabloid first. For no good reason, except perhaps an unaccustomed bout of loneliness, she'd shared the previous evening with a bottle of sixteen-year-old Lagavulin Scotch. As a result, she was feeling slightly queasy. And, at more than a hundred dollars a throw, a little guilty too. The *Financial Review* would have to wait until her brain kicked into gear.

Monitoring the news on ABC radio with one ear, Kate flattened the *Daily Mail* across the table. On the other side of the world, Israel and Hezbollah were busily killing one another and threatening to draw the rest of the Middle East into the madness. British police had thwarted a terrorist plot that might have been the next 9/11.

The ABC led with the fighting in Lebanon. Kate would have gone with the latest terrorist threat, which had a lot more traction with the Australian audience in her opinion. But both stories had been pushed off the *Mail*'s front page.

'Fuck!' Kate exclaimed as she read the day's lead story. Her right hand reached for the ring hanging on a gold chain around her neck. She sat back and squeezed her eyes hard shut. She felt like she'd just been kicked squarely in the guts. Hard.

A photograph of Kate took up most of the front page .It was an unflattering paparazzi shot, taken at the wrong end of an industry awards night. Channel Eight's biggest star looked slightly the worse for wear. She would have liked to blame a dose of antibiotics or headache medication for her dishevelled appearance. But the truth was she'd just let her hair down for once. And she'd been caught. Naturally, the publicity girls would be furious with her. But that was the least of Kate's troubles. She was far more concerned by the headline: NOT TONIGHT, KATE!

Kate's shock turned to anger as she scanned the copy. The facts – if indeed they were facts – were straightforward enough. She was going to be dumped as host of her network's flagship current affairs program *Australia Tonight*. She might hang on for a few more weeks or months. But she would not be at the helm in 2007.

The article went on to quote audience sampling data. Female viewers found her intimidating, probably because she was single and childless, Kate surmised. A decade ago, she was admired for being gutsy and career minded. Now it seemed that her decision to put work ahead of love and family was viewed with suspicion, especially by other women.

But that wasn't the worst of it. According to the data, it wasn't just women who were switching off Kate Corish. Men, the *Mail* reported, considered her aloof. They had another way of saying that in the boardroom. In executive speak, Kate wasn't fuckable any more. And she knew only too well that was fatal for a woman in commercial television, no matter how impressive her resume.

Kate took a generous swig of Red Bull and almost brought it straight back up. She puffed out her cheeks and forced the liquid down with two determined gulps. It tasted bitter. Clearly, taurine and a stomach full of unmetabolised Scotch did not mix. Kate pushed the can aside and opted for another cigarette instead. Smoking always helped her think anyway.

She was sure the research material had been leaked. And by someone who was dangerously well placed. This wasn't the sort of stuff that made its way into a network press release.

Only a handful of executives had access to viewer survey

information. And for good reason. The station didn't want the world to know if one of its stars wasn't shining so brightly. And the bean counters certainly didn't need well-performing celebrities realising how much they were really worth.

After two decades in the game, Kate was pretty good at picking fact from fabrication. And this story felt uncomfortably like the truth. That was plain even before she got to the lame assurances of the network's chief executive officer.

The newspaper had collared Billy Simpson on his way to the football. The inset photograph showed him grinning inanely above a Bulldogs scarf. There was a second man in the picture, standing a little behind and away. Kate recognised the figure straightaway. *Fucking boys' club*, she thought. Simpson's feeble response filled her with a white-hot anger.

CEO Billy Simpson described Kate as a brilliant journalist and a real team player. 'She's run the hard yards for this network,' he said. 'Kate Corish is very much a part of our future vision. There's a job here for Kate as long as she wants one.'

Of course, Billy didn't say *what* job – probably a forced transfer to Special Projects. Everyone in the business knew what that meant. Special Projects wasn't nicknamed the departure lounge for nothing. Kate was as good as gone.

First Jessica. Then Jana. *And now me*, thought Kate. There had been whispers that Naomi was in the line of fire. Women were always fair game in television. But in all her years in the industry, she had never witnessed this much blood-letting.

Or perhaps she'd simply chosen not to acknowledge it before.

The truth startled her. Television had always been like this. Of course it had. The only difference was that this time *her* head was on the chopping block. When Kate started out there had been dozens of women working alongside her, both on the road and behind the scenes. Some had been her age. Others had been five and ten years older. Now there was only a handful left across the entire industry. Those few survivors were being picked off one by one.

Discarding the newspaper, Kate hobbled back inside for another cup of coffee. Her toe was still smarting from its earlier run-in with the potted palm. And her hangover had hunkered down for a lengthy stay. This was about as bad a start to a day as she could imagine. And not even the slightest warning from her favourite online astrology site. Surely crippling herself and losing her job on the front page of the newspaper was worth a tiny mention.

'Load of bloody rubbish,' Kate grumbled as she made a beeline for the coffee machine.

The kitchen was sleek, modern and spotless. Kate didn't mind admitting it was the kind of clean that came from lack of use rather than any strong commitment to hygiene. The apartment was more a pit stop than a real home anyway, somewhere to change clothes and refuel.

Stone, steel and glass. Kate had seized on minimalism with the same gusto that she'd embraced shabby chic three pay rises earlier. She'd cheerfully handed over a small fortune to an interior designer who minced his way through her apartment and discarded anything that suggested personality. By the time he'd finished there wasn't a whole lot left. A termite colony and an acid bath would have achieved much the same result. And cost less.

Over time, Kate had added some personal touches, guiltily rescuing a few of her favourite souvenirs from storage. A rug from Afghanistan with its confronting patterns of tanks and guns. Black-and-white tapestry pillows from Bosnia. A Saddam Hussein mantle clock from Iraq. A wood carving from the Maldives. But no matter what she did, the place still felt empty.

The home phone rang as Kate twisted the dial on the coffee machine to the shortest, strongest and blackest option. She let the answering machine pick up. It was the executive producer of *Australia Tonight*.

'Look, honey, I don't know where they get off printing that shit. I'll call that fat slut television writer this morning and find out where she's getting her fucking information. None of it's true of course. But even if it was, you know I've got your back.'

Kate shuddered. Words of support from the most treacherous bastard in the business. She was in deep trouble all right.

The next call was as brazen as it was predictable.

'Megan Halliday here. I'm keen to follow up on my report in the *Mail* today. I'd love to hear your side of the story. What are you planning to do next? Are you hoping to stay in television? You can catch me on my mobile.'

The woman's gall was breathtaking. Not a scintilla of doubt that Kate was on her way out or that her sources were anything but entirely credible and accurate.

'Fat slut,' Kate muttered under her breath, guiltily borrowing the boys' club vernacular. She wondered if Megan would be quite so pliable if she knew what the network suits called her behind her back.

Just as Kate was thinking of yanking the telephone jack from the wall, she heard a familiar and welcome voice.

'Hi, Kate. It's Sandra Cook. I hope you don't mind me ringing. But I know you're an early riser. I just read the newspaper. Is there anything I can do? Or if you just need someone to talk to, call me. I can't believe this crap is still going on. Anyway. Don't let them get to you. Bye.'

Sandra was a class act. This was one call Kate would return . . . eventually. She was too dazed right now. Kate Corish never showed weakness. Not even to her allies.

Kate limped towards the bathroom, careful not to place too much pressure on her bunged-up toe. A couple of Panadeine were in order, as much for her mood as for her variously aching body parts.

She bolted down the tablets and splashed some water on her face. Her stomach lurched menacingly with the sudden movement. Kate lowered her head and leaned forward, hands firmly gripping either side of the basin. After a few minutes, the nausea passed. She cautiously lifted her head and gazed wearily into the bathroom mirror. She didn't look like a woman who'd just got back from holidays, even with the tan.

Her blonde hair was matted and dull. It had once been her proudest asset. But nowadays, its lustre owed more to the genius of her colourist than to good genes.

The blue eyes were familiar enough, if a little less piercing for the previous night's excesses. But they were surrounded by crows' feet and heavy dark circles. Forty years of gravity marked her face, from the single deep frown line that cleaved her forehead to the jowls that dragged at her features like lead weights.

Kate pressed her fingers flat on either side of her face and stretched her skin out and upward. She looked better. Younger. As she let her skin slide back into place, she could certainly understand the temptation of cosmetic surgery.

Thank God for good lighting technicians and make-up artists, she thought. As a television star, Kate was assigned a team of people whose sole professional responsibility was to make her look gorgeous. From what she could see in the mirror, they were clearly very skilled at their work.

When exactly had she started looking so old anyway? She didn't feel any different from her twenty-year-old self, except maybe in her ability to bounce back from a big night. Then again, how long had it been since she'd been wolf-whistled passing a building site? Five years. Maybe more.

She was still attractive. Even with a hangover. But she was no longer a young woman. And she'd wed herself to an industry that celebrated and rewarded youth.

'Nineteen fucking years.' Kate pushed her face closer to the mirror, until her nose and forehead were touching the glass, clouding it with her breath.

Where had the time gone?

ONE

Kate Corish sat straight-backed and alert opposite the news and current affairs chief of Australia's most powerful television network. She'd spent the best part of a week deciding what to wear for this moment. But her carefully chosen ensemble of navy blue Country Road power suit and white Adele Palmer shirt had obviously failed to make an impression. She felt invisible.

Five minutes had passed since a whippet-like personal assistant had ushered Kate through to Bruce Mawson's office. So far the great man had barely looked up from his paperwork. All he had offered by way of acknowledgement was a half-raised hand, a grunt and a nod towards the chair she was now occupying.

The delay was rattling Kate's already fractured nerves. She could feel a heat rash erupting beneath her pink Chanel scarf. And what the hell had got into her legs all of a sudden? They were jiggling up and down like rubber jackhammers. She pressed her palms down hard on her thighs to stop the shaking. But all that did was leave a sweaty smear on her new skirt.

Still, she knew there were hundreds of young wannabes who would trade places with her in a heartbeat. An audience with Bruce Mawson was a rare event, especially for a college student.

For a start, the more lowly jobs in television tended to be filled by the nieces and nephews and sons and daughters of the people who already worked there. Plus the recruitment of station lackeys usually occurred much further down the food chain.

Kate had snagged this interview through a combination of resourcefulness and outright cheek. She'd asked one of her mates – a trainee producer with a second cousin in engineering – to slip her resume into the internal mail. She figured that way there was a better chance the envelope would make it on to Mawson's desk. And it seemed she'd guessed right because here she was, sitting across from her mark, waiting for him to look up and start firing questions.

The only positive about being so thoroughly ignored, Kate thought, was being able to stare at him without the slightest fear of being caught.

Bruce Mawson looked more like a cowboy than a television boss. He was wearing jeans – the worn kind, not the dark, stiff type usually favoured by executives affecting the casual look. His stubble was a day's shave overdue. His barbershop hair was sticking out every which way, its wayward spikes and kinks matched only by the extraordinary convolutions of his thick white eyebrows.

His feet were crossed lazily at one end of the desk. He was holding his reading material a little too far from his face, betraying a measure of long-sightedness. The fingers of his free hand were curled around his belt loops, and occasionally made short excursions north to scratch his ample belly. Mawson wasn't so much sitting on his chair as reclining against it. Clearly, the guy was as relaxed as Kate was tense.

Pulling at the cuffs of her textured silk shirt, Kate scanned the office. The room was big of course, with a conference table at one end and a casual lounge area at the other. It was also very dark and overtly masculine, like one of those English gentlemen's clubs.

Or how she imagined they'd be, anyway. A couple of Chesterfield leather chairs and a mounted moose head would have fitted in perfectly.

Photographs covered the walls. Mawson had been snapped with all the station's celebrities and a few big international names as well. The gallery was an impressive who's who of Australian television – Roger, Don, Sandra, Mike, Caroline – all mugging chummily for the camera.

But Mawson himself was the star turn in the largest and most prominently placed of the photographs. The picture had been taken during his reporting days. Kate guessed he could only have been in his early twenties. About the age she was now. He was standing by the side of a dirt road, one arm draped casually over the shoulder of a long-haired cameraman. The background was nondescript. They could have been anywhere from a war zone to a country golf club. Kate wondered why this moment was so significant that its memory dwarfed the snapshots of Prince Charles and Mother Teresa that flanked it.

Finally, Mawson leaned back in his chair and lobbed what he had been reading towards the furthest corner of his desk. Kate immediately recognised the head shot clipped to the front page. A friend had said the photo made her look like a young Michelle Pfeiffer. Glossy, shoulder-length blonde hair. Big blue eyes. Straight white teeth.

Mawson had been reading her carefully typed job application, presumably for the first time. It occurred to Kate that she'd scored this interview on the strength of a single flattering photograph. With only a few weeks of work experience at a country newsroom to her credit, her resume was flimsy at best and an unlikely catalyst for a job interview with someone like Bruce Mawson.

Good looks were the diplomatic passport of the television

industry and a handy short cut, Kate knew that. Why else had she been waved straight through to Mawson's office? Still, she refused to feel guilty. Even if she was hired on the basis of her looks, he'd soon find out her brain was actually her most impressive asset. At least that's what she kept telling herself.

'So, you're in your last year of college?' Mawson swung his scuffed RM Williams to the ground and reached for a cigarette.

Kate nodded, suddenly uncertain whether she should be addressing this man as Mr Mawson, Sir or Bruce.

'And you think that qualifies you to apply for a job in the most successful television newsroom in the country?' Mawson's eyes narrowed to a squint.

Kate squirmed. How was she going to answer that one? If she said no then what was she doing wasting Mawson's time? But if she said yes she'd sound way too egotistical. Silence wasn't an option either. That would just make her seem stupid.

Mawson had resumed his preferred position, feet up on the desk and hands behind his head, waiting for her answer.

Kate gulped. 'I'm looking for a very junior position, of course, something where I can learn the ropes.'

'Good. Because if I employ you, don't expect to see the pretty end of a camera any time soon. You'd be a shitkicker. Nothing more.' Mawson took a deep drag on his cigarette. 'You're a good looking girl, Kate. But I don't need another bit of fluff who just wants to get her mug on television.'

'No, sir.' There was no longer any question how the man should be addressed. 'But I really do want to be a journalist. Not a TV star.'

Mawson arced his cigarette towards the jammed ashtray, sending little grey snowflakes fluttering onto his desk top. A two-pack-a-day habit Kate guessed. She'd give up way before reaching that point.

'So what do you hope to do here once you've got some miles up?'

This time Kate had an answer ready to go. Like an actress learning her lines, she had practised this one in front of the bathroom mirror a dozen times already. She'd still been running it through her head as Whippet Woman escorted her up the glass elevator and through the station's executive suites.

'I'm a big fan of Sandra Cook,' she replied carefully.

Sandra was one of the network's biggest stars, co-hosting a weekly current affairs show that was pitted against *60 Minutes* on Sunday nights. Sandra had started in the newsroom and after more than a decade of big scoops and even bigger scalps had been rewarded with an anchor job. She was also generally acknowledged as the first woman elevated to an on-camera role for reasons other than window dressing.

'I know I'm a long way from this yet. But I'd like a career like Sandra's. Reporting from war zones. Nailing those big interviews. My other role model is Diane Sawyer. The American networks are still way ahead of us when it comes to producing strong, intelligent and passionate female reporters. I'd like to think my career could be just as long and distinguished.'

Mawson raised one unruly eyebrow. 'Diane Sawyer?' He paused for a moment. 'She was a good sort when she started out.'

'She still is, isn't she?' Kate shot back, immediately regretting the impulse. Backchatting your would-be boss was not generally considered a high-percentage interview technique.

Fortunately, Mawson didn't seem to notice. 'Yeah, I suppose so – not bad for forty, or whatever she is.' He stifled a yawn. 'Do you have a boyfriend, Kate?'

All Kate could manage was a limp, 'No.' Principles were a luxury she couldn't afford today.

'Good, because if you work here, you'll be on call twenty-four hours a day. Seven days a week. No excuses.'

'I'm fine with that,' Kate said firmly. Romance wasn't on her radar anyway. There was plenty of time for that after she'd established her career.

Mawson stood up and gestured towards the door. 'Okay. Let's see what you've got, kiddo.'

Kate followed him down a central flight of stairs and then along a surprisingly shabby passageway. Moving from the executive floor to the station's backblocks was like inadvertently wandering into the servants' quarters. The polished parquetry and art works had disappeared, replaced by particle-board flooring and chipped walls. Every few metres, on both sides of the corridor, there were doorways, like the cabins on a ship. The rooms, not much bigger than broom cupboards, were stacked full of complicated-looking machinery and monitors. Kate recognised the set-up as edit suites.

'ENG arcade,' Mawson volunteered.

Electronic News Gathering. Kate had heard the acronym before. This was the engine room of any television news operation, where minutes and hours of footage were chopped, stirred, beaten and reheated into easy to digest, bite-sized portions, ostensibly reflecting the events of the day.

It wasn't quite eleven o'clock so most of the suites were empty. But in a few hours time these rooms would be pumping, as editors spooled through tape cursing cameramen for missing the crucial shot and abusing puffed-up reporters for insinuating themselves into every frame.

Mawson strode ahead, giving Kate little time to absorb what was around her. She hurried to keep up, all the time collecting visual clues, sweeping her surroundings much like a speed reader scans the pages of a book.

At the far end of the corridor, a former edit suite had been converted into a makeshift dressing-room for Channel Eight's second-tier newsreaders. The room was dominated by a huge mirror surrounded by Hollywood-style lightbulbs. A narrow benchtop was strewn with make-up, sponges and heavy-duty cleansers. Maybe two hundred ties cascaded down the length of one wall, creating a technicolour waterfall of fabric. Directly opposite was a large colour chart and calendar. It was filled with tightly handwritten notes, presumably recording the tie and shirt combinations of the various male presenters each day.

Kate's stomach did a little flip-flop. She had told Mawson she wasn't interested in being a television star. But the idea that one day she might be sitting in this tiny room, getting ready for a news bulletin, thrilled her more than she cared to admit. She wanted to be a serious journalist. Passionately. But she had to admit she wouldn't say no to a little fame if it came her way.

The cramped dressing-room marked the end of ENG arcade. From there, the corridor dog-legged. Immediately ahead, Kate glimpsed a cavernous and brightly lit space she instantly identified as the main newsroom. To the right was another dingy passageway. Mawson stopped and motioned her towards it.

'They're about to put a news flash to air. You might as well watch.' He pushed open the nearest door and waved Kate inside. His expression didn't change as he added, 'After all, I know how keen you are to learn the ropes.'

It was a good-natured enough dig. But that didn't stop the colour rushing to Kate's cheeks.

She concentrated on the scene in front of her. Five people sat side by side at a long benchtop, all staring up at a bank of monitors. Two of the screens were taking direct feeds from the United States. Everywhere buttons and dials blinked for attention. It looked like the flight deck of a jumbo jet. But it only took three people to get a large passenger plane off the ground. Kate wondered what everyone here did.

She recognised the director, of course. He was a big man with a salt and pepper beard and cheeks even pinker than her own. He was the conductor of this symphony. Everyone in the control room knew their jobs. But like disparate elements of an orchestra, they needed someone to bring them together.

His assistant sat to one side of him. She looked like she'd taken the job straight out of high school. To his right, a slightly older woman was poring over scripts at her computer terminal. She was the news producer most likely.

As for the other two, Kate was clueless.

'Vision switcher. Audio operator,' Mawson explained, nodding at the final two members of the crew.

Like the edit suites, the control room wasn't built for entertaining. Even with her back pressed hard against the wall, Kate received a sharp jab in the belly every time the director reached across the control panel to flick a switch or a lever. A metre away, Mawson was holding the door open with one foot so as to position most of his bulk in the hall outside.

The room hushed as the director intoned, 'In five, four, three.' The final two numerals were delivered silently. But everyone in the control room nodded their heads to the imaginary beat of the countdown.

The news flash graphic appeared on the screen, accompanied by urgent, pulsating music. Then a familiar face filled the central monitor. It was the network's weekend newsreader and number two presenter. His hair was the colour and texture of coir with a complexion to match. Watching at home in her lounge room, Kate had always thought of him as Mr Beige. She had never been especially taken with him. His chin was ill defined. And he smiled like a Grimm Brothers' wolf.

'Good morning and amazing news just coming through from the United States. Baby Jessica has been rescued from that abandoned backyard well. We cross now to live coverage from America's NBC network.' The beige one paused awkwardly, his brow furrowing in temporary confusion. 'The reporter is Dan Molina.'

As the director cut to the US feed, the newsreader jumped out of his chair and angrily yanked the microphone off his lapel.

'Who wrote this fucking shit?'

A girl around Kate's age began to speak. 'Sorry, I don't see what . . . ' Her voice tapered off as angry splotches of red broke through the presenter's thick pancake make-up.

'You can't expect me to pronounce names if I don't see them first. It's not like the fucking guy's name was Jones or Smith. It's fine for you. You're not the one who ends up looking like a complete cunt in front of thousands of people.'

In the control room, the director wisely cut sound from the floor. The newsreader's tirade continued on mute. The young woman was cowering beside the news desk, dangerously close to tears.

Kate guessed the girl was a junior. A shitkicker, as Mawson would say. What was she letting herself in for, she wondered, as she followed the news and current affairs chief out to the newsroom.

Walking into the barn-like space, Kate felt like a prize heifer being paraded for the benefit of the local cockies. She sensed dozens of male eyes browsing her curves. Every man in the room, it seemed, was weighing up his chances at stud.

The newsroom wasn't exclusively male but coursing testosterone was as much a part of the office landscape as the choking cigarette smoke and jabber of the police radio.

A quick head count revealed six women. All of them were sitting at their desks, hunched over computers. Despite their oversized shoulder pads, they seemed to be trying to make themselves as small as possible. Not one looked up as Kate passed by.

The men had no such reservations. Clearly, no one had ever told them it was rude to stare. They were standing around, leaning against walls and desks, legs apart, talking and laughing a little too loudly. They were giants. Masters of the universe – as large and as idle as the women were little and busy.

She followed Mawson out of the room and towards the fire stairs. The stairwell ended two flights below at the loading dock. The area was crammed full of props Kate recognised from the network's various studio productions. There was a kitchen, far larger and better appointed than the one she avoided every night in her college share house. Jammed next to it was the game wheel from a recently axed evening variety show. The thing looked decidedly drab and unglamorous away from the set, those glittery pie-shaped promises of cars and cash looking as tragic as a drag queen the morning after Mardi Gras. Palm trees, lounges, gym equipment . . . even a couple of motorbikes. The place looked more like a clearance warehouse than a television station.

Thick black curtaining obscured the entrance to the studio area. Mawson pushed the material aside and gave the heavy soundproof door a firm shove with his shoulder. Kate followed him through a maze of back screens, picking her way around cables and discarded polystyrene cups.

Finally they reached their destination – a compact news set. So Mawson wanted to assess her presenting skills after all. Kate wasn't too surprised. The bloke had singled her out on the basis of an attractive head shot. He'd at least be curious as to how her assets translated to the screen.

'I'm going to watch from upstairs,' he told her as he headed back in the direction they'd just come from.

'You just sit there, love, and we'll get the lighting right.' The studio director was a stout, grandfatherly type with cheeks stained purple by years of whisky consumption.

Kate patted down her hair and checked her outfit for creases. She closed her eyes and willed her neck muscles to relax. Her interview hadn't been a disaster, exactly, but neither had it been remarkable. She guessed she still had a chance of a job in the new year, if she could just bring her nerves under control.

'Get a load of that!'

Kate's eyes flew open. She glanced around, trying to identify the source of the voice. The studio was empty. Obviously, the microphone up in the control room was open.

'Yeah, baby,' another voice drawled. 'I'd screw that – beer or no beer.' The remark was followed by a long low wolf whistle. Kate scowled. Even college girls knew about that old newsroom tradition. Whoever was first to bed the new girl earned themselves a case of beer.

Kate felt the skin around her neck start to prickle. The damned rash was coming back.

'Fuckers,' she thought angrily. Or maybe she said it out loud because the microphone was hurriedly switched off. The studio was mausoleum quiet again.

Kate quickly checked herself in the lens of the studio camera. Good. No flyaway hairs. And her make-up remained understated and in place.

Without warning, someone flicked a switch and the studio was bathed in a sea of lights. They glared from above, in front, behind – Kate could see nothing except the autocue, a giant screen in front of the camera with a script ready for her to read.

She quickly scrolled through the text. It was the same script Mr Beige had stumbled over up in the newsroom.

'Dan Molina,' she practised under her breath. The name really wasn't difficult to pronounce.

Kate nodded that she was ready and the autocue started to roll.

'This is the Channel Eight morning news. Good morning. I'm Kate Corish.' Kate could hear the hesitation in her voice as her tongue wrestled with the first few words. Like a motor reluctant to start on a cold morning.

But by the time she reached her name, the words were flowing easily. Her performance wasn't professional exactly. But it was still a fine effort for a rookie. At least Kate hoped that's what Mawson was thinking upstairs.

Up in the control room, three men appraised her abilities.

'Do you think her eyes are too blue?' Mawson asked, scratching his stubble with genuine concern.

'Mawson, shit, I wasn't looking at her eyes, check out her tits.' Reg Carter was the toupeed and middle-aged director of news. As was always the case when Carter assessed or spoke to a woman, he adjusted the contents of his underpants. The habit had earned him the nickname Ball Scratcher from the women in the office.

'Yeah, I did notice that talent . . . I'm just wondering if she comes across too cold. Will it unnerve the punters?'

Mawson studied Kate's image on the monitor in front of him. Down in the studio, Kate was sitting forward, elbows on the news desk, fingers linked under her chin. She was staring into the camera, smart enough to realise her audition wasn't yet over.

'Well, I don't know about you guys but I'd give her one.' The chief of staff, Mike Ripley, sucked back hard on his twenty-third cigarette of the day. His face was so round, the action gave him the appearance of a deflated puffer fish.

All three men paused, considering this. Ripley and Carter exchanged salacious looks, both imagining themselves in bed with Kate Corish. Not for a moment did they entertain the possibility that she wouldn't want to open her legs for them.

In the studio, Kate continued to smile into the camera. The men nodded to one another. The girl was fuckable all right. The blonde with the sensational tits would be offered a job at Channel Eight.

Kate was starting to wonder if she was supposed to find her own way back through the maze of corridors, when Mawson finally reappeared at the studio door.

'Okay, kid, you've got a start.'

Kate wanted to punch the air or at least grin but the chief's expression made it clear that wasn't the appropriate response.

'The news director's name is Reg Carter. He runs the newsroom. He hires staff. He fires staff. And any decision he makes, he's got my absolute backing. So if you ever try to go over his head again, your career is over. Do you understand me?'

'Yes, sir.' Kate nodded, trying but not quite managing to appear contrite. She was way too excited to feel the sting of the reprimand. In any case, she had her foot in the door now. She couldn't imagine needing to call on Mawson again.

There was a clear hierarchy in television news that Kate had chosen to ignore. At the top of the tree was the head of news and current affairs. Bruce Mawson watched over all Channel Eight's news programs from the evening bulletin to the breakfast show and the weekend magazine programs. He was responsible for the overall look of the shows. He chose the hosts, pulled out the chequebook when the big stories broke and generally ensured that the network was producing the kind of news and current affairs that people wanted to watch.

The day-to-day decision making fell to the shows' various executive producers. In the case of news, the man in charge was the news director, Reg Carter.

After an enjoyable half-hour ogling his latest recruit, Kate's new boss was wandering around the newsroom, moving from desk to desk and generally alarming his legion of young assistant producers. Reg Carter's little excursions always made staff jumpy. A single tap on the shoulder could mean the end of a career. And a couple of times a month, it did.

Carter was tall, skinny and squinty eyed, with a small Hitleresque moustache. The fluff on his upper lip was nowhere near as lush as the rug on his head. As a manager, he was invariably described as cold, even sadistic. He was reptilian in looks and nature, and none of his staff would have been surprised to discover scales under his neatly pressed Pierre Cardin shirt.

He smiled with thin, chafed lips as he made his rounds. He was well aware of the effect he had on his junior staff. In this office, fear was considered a legitimate management strategy. It was certainly effective. Carter's newsroom out-rated its commercial rivals two to one. And he'd been running the joint for more than a decade. Most news directors were lucky to see out their two-year contracts.

He sauntered past the main production areas and over to the bank of preview machines lined up a few metres behind the main news desk. Four junior producers were hard at work, watching and transcribing enormous stacks of video tapes. Their eager heads provided the busy backdrop for the day's news breaks.

Some of the tapes had been shot by camera crews earlier that day and the previous night. Others contained news bulletins and stories from around the world, beamed in by satellite during the early hours of the morning. All the material needed to be checked and evaluated to decide what would make the cut for that evening's bulletin.

Carter's quarry was seated at the end of the row. Matthew Keaton was a clean-cut young man in his early twenties with an open friendly face and the sweet eagerness of a puppy.

'Matthew. How are you?'

Given the latest rumours of staff cuts and Carter's unsettling presence, Matthew was feeling rather less than well. But instead of throwing up, he managed a faint, if unconvincing, 'Good.'

'I just encountered a friend of yours – Kate Corish,' Carter's right hand headed south towards his groin region.

Matthew pushed his headphones down to his shoulders. He was uncertain of the correct response and waited for his cue. Sending Kate's resume through the internal mail system wasn't a sackable offence. But it wasn't playing by the rules either.

After a few deliberate moments of silence, Carter added, 'Very impressive.'

Relieved, Matthew replied, 'Smart too.'

'I didn't say she was perfect.' And with that, Carter slithered away to his office and the ministrations of his well-disposed and lovely young secretary.

Kate jammed her Girl Power compilation tape into the cassette player of her 1974 VW beetle and bunny hopped across two lanes of traffic. She could scarcely believe her luck. A job straight out of college! That just didn't happen any more. Not with the unemployment rate at eight per cent and rising.

The relief was overwhelming. She'd be able to approach her final exams knowing she only had to pass. There was no need for any last-minute academic heroics to land a job. And, unlike everyone else in her year, she wouldn't be spending her last long summer worrying about the future. Life was good.

The first song blared through the car's tinny second-hand speakers. Eurythmics. A huge dumb grin spread across Kate's face. This sister was doing it for herself all right. She pounded the steering wheel with both hands and sang loudly and hopelessly out of tune, unaware that her right indicator was still flashing and causing all sorts of confusion in her wake.

By the time Kate reached her mother's place in the leafy labyrinth of Sydney's upper north shore, she had joyously slaughtered Helen Reddy, Cyndi Lauper and what would have been the best of Gloria Gaynor, if left unaccompanied.

'How did you go, sweetheart?' Dianne Corish called from somewhere at the back of the house.

The rambling old building was way too big for just two of them. It had been too big seventeen years ago, when her father died. And it seemed even emptier now that Kate had moved out of home to go to college. But Dianne refused to budge.

'It's my home. More to the point, it's your home too,' she would protest every time her daughter presented her with glossy brochures on some new harbour-front development. Kate suspected she'd be burying the woman in the backyard, next to her sixth-grade guinea pig and two traffic-challenged cats.

She eventually found her mother in the kitchen, busily stacking a dozen home-cooked frozen meals into an esky. Each foil plate was individually wrapped. A sticker on the outside identified its contents. Beef Stroganoff with rice. Veal Marsala with carrots and peas.

'Mum. You don't have to cook for me! I'm big enough to look after myself.'

'I'm not going to have my daughter living on two-minute

noodles every night of the week.' Dianne sniffed as she clipped the lid on the esky and plonked it at Kate's feet. 'So how did your interview go?'

Kate beamed. 'I got it. I start as an assistant producer at Channel Eight next February.'

'That's wonderful,' Dianne said in a tone that suggested nothing of the sort. 'And you can always go back to your studies at the end of the year, if that's what you want to do.'

'Mum!' Kate cried with exasperation. 'I graduate as a journalist at the end of this year. I don't need to go back to my studies.'

'You never know. You might change your mind and decide to study law after all.'

'How many times do I have to tell you? I don't want to be a lawyer.' Kate had been arguing the point with her mother for the best part of three years.

'Well, it's a pity. Your father wanted you to be a lawyer, you know.'

'I was four years old when Dad died. I doubt he was hoping for anything more from me than a good night's sleep.'

'He did always say that the media was the circus of the twentieth century,' Dianne said. 'But that's very nice about the job. If it's what you want to do.'

'It's what I want to do, Mum.' Kate fixed her mother with a look that made it clear there would be no further discussion on the subject.

'The scarf did the trick,' Dianne offered, trying to make up for her earlier lack of enthusiasm.

Kate smiled at the thought. She didn't have the faintest notion how to accessorise. It was her mother who had suggested and knotted the scarf around her neck that morning. The woman was a pain in the arse. But, Kate had to admit, she did try.

Dianne hurried on, settling for a more neutral subject. 'You need to take the meal out of the freezer to defrost in the morning. And then put it in the oven for half an hour.'

'I know. I know. But really, you shouldn't be cooking for me.'

'Well, at least I won't have to worry about you so much next year, if you're moving back here for work.'

Kate didn't have the heart to tell her mother she'd be finding her own apartment the moment she got back to Sydney. That discussion could wait for another day. She was in way too good a mood to waste energy on arguing. And guilt.

I'm going to be a journalist for Channel Eight, she told herself. And her stomach did a little somersault for possibly the zillionth time that day.

TWO

Kate scanned the newsroom, anxiously fingering her temporary visitor's pass. It was 9 a.m. on her first day and the place was already buzzing. Once again, Whippet Woman acted as her chaperone. But this time there were no executive elevators or solicitous enquiries about whether she'd like tea or coffee. Instead, she'd been summarily escorted up two flights of stairs and then deposited (or, more accurately, dumped) at the entrance to the newsroom.

A heat rash prickled the skin around Kate's neck. Now she'd moved out of home there were no cleverly positioned scarves to help disguise her nerves. Still, on this oppressively humid February day the scarf would only have ended up abandoned anyway, draped over the back of her lounge alongside her pantyhose and newly purchased Covers jacket. To think the outfit had cost her the equivalent of two (as yet unearned) pay packets. And she wouldn't be wearing it until at least Easter.

Money was an issue now that Kate had moved into her new apartment. The rent was more than she could comfortably afford. But she loved the place. It screamed sassy career girl. And it was right in the heart of Sydney's nightclub district. Her mother had been horrified, of course. But whether Dianne Corish was objecting to her daughter's decision to strike out alone or her choice of address, Kate wasn't entirely sure.

Kate's 'apartment' was actually the poky top floor of a tiny inner-city terrace. Steep narrow stairs opened up to a little landing. To the right there was a small sitting room with an even smaller balcony attached. Directly behind, a short hallway led to two bedrooms. The second was just big enough for a guest but hopelessly undersized to accommodate any permanent inhabitant. As a result, the place was let out as a one-bedroom. Kate had fallen in love with it and her landlords, Al and Ben, pretty much on sight.

Al was handsome, gym-honed and in his late twenties. Judging from the ute parked on the street outside, he was also a trades-man of some sort. 'You can have the flat just because you look like Michelle Pfeiffer,' he said. 'But remember, I expect to be introduced to loads of stunningly attractive young men.'

Kate must have looked disappointed because Ben draped a sympathetic arm around her shoulder. 'Oh, sweetie. You know all the good ones in this town are gay or taken. And this gorgeous man is both.' He grinned. 'I think it was the car that threw her, Al. You are such a tease.'

'Geez Louise. Can't a queen drive a ute any more without being accused of being straight?'

Kate had quickly settled into her modest apartment. Ben and Al provided a considerably more welcoming and nurturing environment than the Channel Eight newsroom appeared to be.

Kate's eyes jumped from one stony face to another. But for Mr Beige, no one looked especially familiar. Kate wasn't a big Beige fan. Not after witnessing his little temper tantrum the previous year. But that didn't stop her from being hopelessly starstruck. In fact, she was finding it hard not to stare. Her eyes kept darting back towards the station's second-string but still very well-known newsreader. Kate took a few mental notes for her mother's benefit. Dianne Corish had a little crush on the Beige one and would no doubt be demanding details when she called that night.

For his part, Beige was leafing idly through a women's magazine, oblivious to Kate or indeed anyone else around him. He wasn't a handsome man. But he wasn't ugly either. He was just . . . neutral. His appearance failed to elicit any emotional response at all. For reasons Kate didn't quite understand, he seemed enormously credible as a result.

Unlike the self-absorbed Beige, Kate was acutely aware that people were watching her. But no one was willing to interrupt what they were doing to introduce themselves or even make eye contact.

It was shocking luck that Matthew was rostered off today. A friendly face would have taken the edge off her first-day nerves. There was no point dwelling on what ifs though. Kate was just going to have to look after herself. She gave the place another quick sweep.

The newsroom was a large open-plan space, without obvious partitions. But the borders and the hierarchy were as clear as if it were a school playground. The reporters were the alphas of the pack. They were bunched in one section of the room, awaiting the day's assignments. Kate recognised most of their faces, if not their names. They were probably only six or seven years her senior. But their confidence made them seem many decades older. Kate couldn't imagine ever being so self-assured.

In another area, a team of assistant producers (aka shitkickers) feverishly typed away preparing the day's news breaks. They were uniformly young, attractive and impeccably groomed. And, Kate guessed, supremely ambitious as well. How she would get herself noticed in their company, she had no idea.

The sports journos congregated in one corner, throwing a foam football around and loudly debating Australia's batting inadequacies in the Bicentennial test. Nearby, camera crews slouched about, trading jokes. Unlike everyone else in the newsroom, they were sensibly dressed for the muggy conditions in shorts and T-shirts.

The epicentre of activity was the main production desk, a horse-shoe-shaped arrangement that looked like the flight deck of the *Starship Enterprise*. Kate decided to head in that direction.

Sitting in the command position was the line-up producer. On the wall opposite, four television screens continuously monitored the output of rival stations. With a flick of a switch and the push of a button, the screens flashed up incoming feeds from all over the world.

The line-up producer organised the day's images and events into a sensible working order and then sweated it in the control room as the evening bulletin beamed live into lounge rooms around the city. Kate knew it was a job that required nerves of steel. And for the first time in Channel Eight's history, a woman was sitting in the pilot's seat.

'Hi. I'm Kate Corish. I'm starting today as an AP.' Kate offered her hand to a vivacious butterball of a woman who looked to be in her late twenties.

'Welcome on board. My name's Gillian.' The introduction was accompanied by a wide smile and a little shake of tight, shoulder-length brown curls. *Thank God*, Kate thought. *I've stumbled onto someone friendly.*

'Just let me track down Reg. He'll want to know you're here.'

Kate waited, feeling a bit more relaxed. She instinctively liked Gillian. But she couldn't help wondering at her eclectic dress sense. She'd teamed a tan suede vest with a pastel-pink pussy cat print

T-shirt and Liberty print calf-length skirt. The whole ensemble was pulled together with a maroon tassel belt of the kind normally used to cinch school gym tunics.

Kate peeked over the work station to catch a glimpse of Gillian's feet. She was half-expecting bobby socks and jackboots. But the reality was a pair of what looked to be new season Sergio Rossi pumps. The woman was wearing three hundred dollars worth of shoes on her feet when the rest of her outfit looked like it had been rescued from a seventies clothing bin.

As Kate pondered the puzzle of the designer footwear, a commotion broke out a few metres in front of her.

'Well, fuck me,' a gravelly voice boomed. 'You've got to be fucking kidding, haven't you?'

Kate flinched, momentarily taken aback by the stream of invective.

'Our esteemed chief of staff,' Gillian commented deadpan, nodding towards the source of the racket.

The chief of staff area was a tiny three-sided room, no larger than an average bathroom and surrounded by large glass windows. Two people crammed into the space, along with four telephones, two CB radios and a telex machine.

A pasty looking man was leaning halfway out of the COS booth. His face looked a bit like a scrubbed potato that had sat at the back of a cupboard for a few weeks – it was heavy, slightly pock-marked and squishy looking. What was left of his hair was the colour of bruised fruit. It hung in loose, greasy strands across his forehead. Neglectful genes had completely forgotten to craft him a chin. Kate judged him to be about ten years her senior.

His nicotine-stained fingers clutched a phone against one spongy, almost feminine thigh, pressing the mouthpiece into the brown gabardine of his trousers, though not firmly enough to prevent the caller from hearing what he had to say.

'Christ, has she taken her cunt pills today or what? Bolshie bitch is saying she can't deliver on the police informant story for another day.'

Kate was shocked. But no one else so much as looked in the man's direction.

'She can suck my dick if she doesn't get that yarn up tonight.' The COS was now staring directly at Kate, as if challenging her to react. 'I don't care if she doesn't eat, sleep or shit. She's already had a week on it. We need it NOW. End of story.'

With that, the man ducked back into his booth, slammed the phone back onto its hook and began barking orders into the CB radio. Another argument flared almost immediately. The camera crew at the other end of the two-way were more interested in grabbing a morning coffee than filming the smouldering remains of a western-suburbs high school.

The atmosphere was overwhelmingly male and combative. And the chief of staff had just announced himself an appalling and foul-mouthed pig of a man. But to Kate's great surprise, she found she didn't particularly care. Maybe because she was caught up in the excitement of actually being in the newsroom. Whatever the reason, she instantly decided she'd make peace with her feminist sensibilities some other time.

'Reg!' Gillian called across the room to a man who bore more than a passing resemblance to a praying mantis.

Kate recognised her new boss instantly.

'Good morning.' Kate smiled and held out a firm hand, forcing the news director to abandon his suddenly ticklish crotch area.

'Good to see you again, Katie,' Carter said, directly to his newest employee's chest. 'Did you meet our chief of staff yet or did you just hear him?'

Kate arranged her features to suggest that an introduction would be a rare and tremendous privilege.

'Katie Corish, meet Mike Ripley.'

Ripley poked his head around the glass and held up his hand. Once again, he had a phone attached to his ear. From his expression, the conversation wasn't going well.

'Okay. Let's get you straight out on a story,' Carter said, temporarily tearing his gaze from Kate's bosom. 'You're not going to be much use to us in the newsroom until you know how things work on the road. Jonesy. Jonesy. Get over here.'

A hulking figure peeled away from the reporters' huddle and lumbered over to Carter and Kate.

'This is Katie, our newest recruit.' A man Kate knew instantly as Geoff Jones favoured her with a big toothy grin. Her stomach responded with a nervous lurch.

Geoff Jones had the cookie-cutter look of the successful male television reporter. He was part Dudley Do-Right, part American gridiron player. And, Kate decided, pretty damn cute, even if Matthew was right about his many conquests in the newsroom.

'Hi, I'm Kate.' She stressed the single syllable, hoping Reg Carter would catch on.

Geoff took her extended hand and held onto it a fraction too long. Kate was horrified to feel her cheeks flushing schoolgirl pink. Flustered, she turned to Carter, waiting for instructions.

'Geoff's going to take you out on the road today and show you how it's done.' Carter allowed himself a quick scratch of his nether regions. 'He's one of the best we've got. So take it all in, Katie.'

Geoff gave her a slow wink. 'Looks like we're going to be a team, Kate.' He emphasised her name, letting her know he'd been paying attention. It wasn't hard to understand why he was so successful with the ladies.

A half-hour later, they were on the road. Kate stared intently out the crew car window, watching Sydney's sprawling suburbs whiz by. She could scarcely believe she was off to cover a real city story. Her work experience had all been out in the bush, where abattoir closures and issues of parallel parking passed for news. But today was a murder – a double axe murder, no less.

From the front seat, Geoff checked the rear-view mirror. Kate Corish was some hot piece of arse all right. Crammed into the back seat as she was, her skirt had ridden up to expose a well-toned thigh. And though her white short-sleeved shirt was demure enough, she'd left the top three buttons open.

Holy shit, thought Geoff. The chick is wearing bloody lingerie. He had to knock this story over quickly. With a little sweet-talking at lunch, he reckoned he could nail her tonight. He was going to enjoy this one and not just because there was a case of beer riding on his success.

'Do you like going out to nightclubs, Kate?' Geoff asked, slipping a tape into the cassette player.

'Not too often,' Kate admitted. 'The drinks are way too expensive. That's if the doorman lets me in.'

The first few bars of 'Faith' filled the car and Geoff started grooving in his seat. 'I tore up the dance floor at Rogues last night to this one.'

'What's the story today, anyway? Did you get much from Ripley?'

Kate checked her notes. Before heading out, she'd jotted down the scant details the chief of staff had managed to glean from the police radio.

Two dead – female in their mid-twenties. Multiple wounds – possibly an axe. Bodies discovered by a neighbour and close friend who had been looking after one of the women's children. Attack occurred sometime during the early hours while the victims were in bed asleep.

'Lesos,' Geoff commented with a sneer.

'Pardon me?' *Surely, Geoff didn't just say . . .*

'Dykes. Muff divers. Lesbians. No great loss. I can't stand homosexuals.' Geoff continued twiddling his index fingers in the air to the beat of George Michael.

'Just because they shared a bed doesn't mean they were sexually involved,' Kate pointed out.

'Well, when I share a bed that's exactly what it means.' Geoff grinned wolfishly.

Right on cue, the next song kicked in.

'Boom, boom, boom (let's go back to my room),' Geoff sang lustily with more than a hint of invitation. 'And *that* is exactly what I did after I finished dancing last night.'

Kate fancied she saw the cameraman roll his eyes in the rearview mirror. The guy was certainly full of himself. But he was also successful and good-looking. And today that balanced the ledger somewhat.

The news wagon pulled to a stop just as Geoff's tape clicked over to its B-side and an Orchestral Manoeuvres in the Dark triple play. Their destination was a sad and ragged cul de sac many suburbs further west than Kate had realised existed.

The neighbourhood had the neglected look of another public-housing disaster. Each townhouse appeared exactly the same as the next. Flyscreens were torn. Windows cracked. Broken and discarded plastic toys littered unkempt gardens. Three doors from where they had parked, a property was cordoned off by blue and white crime-scene tape.

The cameraman grabbed the two-way. 'We're here, Ripper. Let you know when we've got something.'

Kate got out of the car slowly, uncertain exactly what constituted correct murder-scene etiquette. She was grateful when Geoff offered her a cigarette. It took the edge off her nerves. And it gave her something to do with her hands while her eyes checked for cues on how to behave.

About a dozen journalists were congregated on the nature strip at the edge of the police tape. They could have been waiting for a movie to start or the gates to open for a football match. Everyone was laughing and exchanging jokes and complaining far too loudly about being stuck in a housing commission shithole on a sweltering thirty-three degree day.

Kate tried to act as casually as everyone else. A double axe murder was just a day at the office for these people. As it would be for her one day, she guessed. But right now she couldn't stop thinking about those two bodies lying lifeless and bloody less than a hundred metres away from where she was standing. She was going to have to toughen up.

After a few minutes, Geoff stomped on his butt and knotted a narrow tie around his oversized neck. 'Okay, now to find this neighbour.'

'What neighbour?' Kate started to ask. But Geoff was already bounding down the cracked cement pathway to the nearest house.

Almost immediately, Kate realised what Geoff was up to. She was enormously grateful he hadn't insisted she tag along for the experience.

Of course. The bodies had been found by a neighbour. Now every news service in Sydney wanted that neighbour to relive the experience for the titillation and entertainment of its audience.

Kate had learned in college that the art of pressuring the bereaved into talking was called the death knock. She didn't particularly approve of the practice. It seemed . . . cruel. But Kate was realistic enough to accept it as part of the job. Although she did wonder if she would ever have the stomach to do it herself. Watching Geoff with his nose pressed hard against a grubby window, she wasn't sure if she was impressed or repulsed.

Five futile minutes of knocking later, Geoff returned, his tie loose to his chest. 'No one home.' He tapped a cigarette from his packet of Dunhill International. 'Where the fuck are they? It's not like anyone living around here would have a goddamn job.'

'If I lived here, I'm not sure I would have stayed around for all this.' Kate gestured towards the street. There were five police cars, all with blue lights flashing, two satellite link trucks, five television news cars and another dozen or so private vehicles that presumably belonged to the radio and print contingent.

'Guess you're right. Too many coppers. Place like this, just about everyone would have an outstanding warrant.' Geoff paused. 'So it looks like the end of the line for us. We'll leave the boys here to get the shot of the bodies being taken out. You and I can go and grab some lunch.'

'But what about the death knock?' Kate wasn't ready to leave a real murder scene just yet. So much for her reservations about exploiting the bereaved.

'No one home, love. We've gone as far as we can go on this one.'

'How about the people who live behind? Maybe they knew the victims,' Kate suggested.

Geoff frowned for a moment. 'What the hell. I guess it's worth a shot.'

A few minutes later, Kate was sitting in the back of the car, a headphone cupped over one ear. She'd been thrilled to discover she'd been right. The neighbours at the back were home. A car was parked outside and the front door was open. Now it was all up to Channel Eight's gun reporter to kick the goal.

The crew had fitted Geoff with a radio microphone so they could hear and record his conversation with the people who lived in the house. At worst, the Channel Eight story would include vision of Geoff offering his condolences to the neighbours. At best, he would talk them into an on-camera interview.

Through the cans, Kate heard a woman come to the door. She was crying.

'Madam. I am so sorry for your loss.' Kate couldn't make out the response but it wasn't the sound of a door slamming. So far so good. 'My name is Geoff Jones. I know this is a terrible time for you. But it would certainly help the police if you could talk to us and let the public know what has happened. I'm sure your friends, God rest their souls, would want you to do that.'

There was more muffled crying and then the sound of a door closing. It seemed Geoff had struck out after all.

Kate was surprised to discover she was actually disappointed.

She sighed, ready to give Geoff a supportive shrug of the shoulders. But Geoff wasn't looking despondent. Rather, he was jigging from one foot to the other and pumping the air with his fists. Obviously, he'd scored a touchdown.

Dropping his chin into his lapel microphone, he whispered, 'Ugly bitch wants to put on some make-up and brush her hair. Won't make any difference. But get this. She found the fucking bodies!' With that he gave the camera a furtive thumbs-up. The signal made Kate feel a little queasy.

Eventually, the front door opened again and Geoff composed his face into an expression of care and concern. The camera crew quickly set up for the interview.

'Tell me what happened this morning,' Geoff began. He sounded genuinely sympathetic.

Standing near the sound recordist, Kate searched the woman's face. She wasn't unattractive, but any beauty was hidden beneath a bad haircut and worn and baggy clothes. And though she was maybe only a couple of years older than Kate, poverty had etched deep, sad lines into her skin. The events of the last few hours had done the rest.

The woman spoke slowly at first but seemed to find confidence with every one of Geoff's encouraging nods. She had let herself into the house during the morning, worried that her best friend hadn't stopped by to collect the kids. There had been blood everywhere. One of the victims was still alive when she found them but died before the ambulance arrived. If only she'd gone to investigate earlier. She went on to beg anyone with information to contact the police. Her courage was extraordinary. This woman was so close to breaking point, but for the memory of her friends she was holding strong for the interview.

Geoff seemed to be winding up when he fired one final question. 'How does it feel to see your best friend chopped up into little pieces?'

Kate recoiled in horror. How could Geoff be so insensitive? The woman's bottom lip started to quiver. And that tiny tremor quickly became a tsunami that crashed over her entire body. After a few wordless minutes standing and sobbing, she doubled over, heaving deep and desperate breaths.

Geoff's index finger traced wide circles behind his back. It was the signal for the cameraman to keep rolling. He didn't need to worry. The crew knew better than to stop tape. Geoff waited until the woman had cried herself out before wrapping up the interview.

As the crew were packing up their gear, Geoff threw a comforting arm around the devastated woman.

'You shouldn't do any more interviews today. This is all the police will need. So if any other television reporters knock on your door just say no. You've done everything you can. You're with the highest rating network anyway. Understand?'

The woman nodded, newly applied mascara streaming down her cheeks. 'And one other thing,' Geoff added. 'Do you have a photo of the victims?'

The woman stumbled inside, returning with a tatty photo album clasped to her chest. Geoff prised it from her arms and riffled through the pages, scooping up a smiling picture of the deceased and popping it into his pocket.

As bodies and gear piled back into the station wagon for the return trip to the station, Geoff grabbed for the two-way.

'Ripper. We got tears.' In the cruel and parallel universe of commercial television news, it didn't get any better than that.

A few minutes before 6 p.m., Kate joined the team in the newsroom to watch the show go to air. Everyone was tense as the familiar theme started to play. A news bulletin is made up of a thousand tiny parts. And Reg Carter noticed if a single one of those parts failed. Often, the person responsible would be out of a job by the time the station logo appeared on the screen at the end of the half hour.

Carter sat in Gillian's seat at the head of the production desk. She was in the control room, of course, jockeying the bulletin to the finish line. Reporters and producers perched on desks around and behind him. How close they sat was determined by seniority. Kate found a free spot between the stationery cupboard and the coffee urn. It was the lowliest piece of real estate in the newsroom, a circumstance underlined by the fact that her nearest neighbour was the timid young girl who'd been bawled out over the Jessica McClure script.

On the wall opposite the production desk, each television

was switched to a different news service. Carter's attention flitted between monitors, constantly checking that his reporters and camera crews hadn't missed a shot or an interview. Their jobs depended on it.

The axe murder led every Sydney bulletin. Naturally, the neighbour was the centrepiece of Geoff's report. Kate watched as she bawled at the camera. Her distress pricked at Kate's conscience. After all, she was the one who had pointed Geoff Jones to her door.

Sitting in prime position next to Carter, Geoff happily accepted congratulations for his story. None of the other channels had landed an interview with the woman who had found the bodies. Geoff was a hero. 'How did you find her?' a producer asked.

Kate started to blush expectantly. 'You've just got to think outside the square, mate. Just think outside the square.'

She scoured his expression. There wasn't a trace of embarrassment on his face. The bloke really believed this was his success alone.

Kate's guilt at helping Jonesy find and then emotionally dismember the neighbour was replaced by bitter disappointment that her role in the day's events had been entirely overlooked. She knew she was being contradictory. And that her twin frustrations were utterly irreconcilable. But she was upset all the same. If she was going to sell out, she at least wanted to get the credit for it.

And to think she'd been tempted to sleep with the jerk!

THREE

'So what do you think?' Five months had passed since the axe murder yarn and Geoff Jones was still angling for a way into Kate's pants. Today's manoeuvre was his most inspired to date. He had decided to introduce Kate to one of the great traditions of Sydney news gathering – an early-morning coffee at Bill and Tony's in Darlinghurst.

It had taken all Kate's willpower to drag herself out of bed at 6 a.m. It had still been dark outside and bitterly cold – a circumstance cruelly highlighted by the high ceilings and polished floorboards of her little apartment. Not even the fluffy grey stray curled up next to her was interested in budging, even though the kitten visited quite often enough to know that if it followed Kate into the kitchen, it would be rewarded with a plate of smoked or red salmon.

Kate stomped and shivered her way to the bathroom. Worse again, she wasn't even getting paid for her efforts.

After an exciting few weeks chasing cop cars and fire engines, Kate's wings had been suddenly clipped. She'd been given a tantalising view of the world as a reporter, then banished to the coalmines. She spent her (paid) working days spooling through tapes and writing news breaks, just like all the other assistant producers. The only way to get out on the road was to team up with a reporter on her days off. And the only reporter willing to let her tag along was Geoff Jones. Kate knew his motives weren't exactly altruistic. But she appreciated the opportunity all the same.

Bill and Tony's was an unremarkable establishment but it had a reputation for serving some of the best coffee in the business – if you could just keep the liquid from sloshing into the saucer. A dozen or so wooden chairs and tables teetered uncertainly on a quarry-tiled floor, challenging customers' sense of balance. And Kate's in particular, given her hopeless lack of dexterity.

Being just a short stroll from police headquarters, the café attracted the heavyweights of Sydney crime reporting. Kate had already spotted a couple of well-known television roundsmen huddled and whispering in one corner. Over at the pinball machines, two more familiar faces pitted their skills against the Raiders of the Lost Ark game, their media credentials clipped importantly to their belts. Bells clanged as their index fingers jabbed furiously at the flipper buttons. Every so often, an electronic voice counselled them to 'Choose wisely'.

Kate smiled at Geoff. 'I like it. It feels . . . ' She paused for a moment, sipping at the strongest coffee she'd ever tasted, '. . . authentic.'

It was shaping up to be a slow news day. Geoff and Kate had started out just before seven at the police media office. Television reporters were only occasional visitors to the College Street headquarters. Unlike their hapless colleagues in print and radio, they didn't have to start their days at five in the morning. Thank God, Kate thought. Early mornings weren't in her repertoire.

A single, long desk ran around the perimeter of the room. Journalists sat a metre or so apart along its length, separated from each other by thin partitions. A few minutes before the hour and the half hour, the radio men turned into their respective booths and huddled over telephones, filing their twenty-second reports in a general mumble of baritone. Kate could just make out a lone female voice. Only the ABC would send a woman into this lion's den of testosterone.

In the middle of the room was a large rectangular table. At one end, three men were deep in conversation, smoking and playing gin rummy.

'He's gay for sure,' the youngest one said, discarding a queen. Kate guessed they were talking about Beige. His sexuality was hotly contested around town and a constant source of speculation between Al and Bill.

The next player picked up the card and began laying down his hand. 'That makes sense. I thought I could taste shit on his dick this morning.'

Kate almost choked on her Diet Coke. And she thought she was beyond shocking after so much time around Channel Eight's chief of staff.

Her face flaming red, she turned her attention to the other end of the table. Two blokes were signing receipt slips for one another. Kate wondered if she was the only one who saw the irony in crime reporters committing low-level white-collar crime at NSW police headquarters.

A policewoman scurried in, gripping a spiral-bound notebook.

'Okay, guys, I've got more on that bike fatal in Tamworth. The victim was a 25-year-old male. The fatality occurred in the main street at approximately 6.30 a.m. He was riding with members of his cycling club at the time. Sorry, that's it for the moment.'

One of the tabloid hacks reached for his phone and began dictating. He was clearly not going to be deterred by a paucity of facts.

Kate listened as he rattled off the next day's copy. 'It was horrible. One witness said, "I've never seen so much blood".' The hack's voice was flat. He was utterly disconnected from the scene he was describing.

Kate stared at him, appalled.

'What?' he sneered, as he dropped the phone back onto its cradle. 'There were witnesses and I think we can safely assume the scene was horrible. And unless every single one of his riding buddies worked at an abattoir, which is doubtful, rest assured someone there was seeing more blood than they had in their lifetime.'

At that moment, the policewoman poked her head around the corner. 'Guys, I've got a bit more for you. The riders were members of a local abattoir social club.'

With that bit of information, every journalist swung back into their booths. Now they'd be able to track down some real witnesses.

The bicycle fatality was a useful story for press and breakfast radio but it was nowhere near big enough to send a city television crew hurtling towards the north-west of the state.

So Geoff and Kate had wandered over to Bill and Tony's. Their first job – a press conference detailing the latest initiative to ease Sydney's traffic congestion – wasn't until mid-morning. For once, the government was actually abolishing a toll.

'I've been thinking . . .' Geoff ventured, stirring his cafe latte in what he imagined was a contemplative manner. 'How would you like to ask the questions at the presser today?'

Kate's eyes widened with delight. She favoured Geoff with a genuine smile. Its natural warmth immediately registered in his groin area. Maybe he was still in with a shot after all.

'You understand of course, I'll be putting together the report. But it'd be good experience for you to get into the media scrum, learn how to get your voice heard.'

'Geoff, that would be fantastic. Thank you so much. Do you have the press release there?'

Geoff pulled a scrunched-up piece of paper from his back pocket and unfolded it in front of Kate. The heading screamed 'Driving a Bargain'.

'Now, there are a few things you need to know about handling a press conference situation, Kate.'

Kate had long ago realised that Geoff's television-sized ego was not matched by an equally expansive journalistic brain. But if he wanted to cast himself in a mentoring role, Kate was happy enough to listen. The bloke had been around the block a few times, after all.

'First you've got to stake a good position for yourself. The camera crew should look after that. The last thing we need is the interview shot in profile. But keep right next to the camera. You don't want some radio fuck elbowing you out of the way. They're going to try and get right up close so the call sign on their microphones gets seen on the evening news. But always remember. We're television. We're the real stars. So don't let them push you around.'

Kate nodded, suddenly nervous about standing her ground against so many more experienced hands.

'Now you'll probably want to ask a question. Have a read of the press release. Everything you need to know is there. See where it says this initiative will save NSW motorists millions of dollars every year? The question you ask is how much will NSW motorists save through this initiative. And the pollie responds that NSW motorists will save millions of dollars every year as a result of this initiative. Get it?'

Kate looked at Jonesy blankly. She knew she had a lot to learn. But surely being a journalist involved more than simply eliciting statements already contained in a press release.

Geoff misinterpreted Kate's expression for beginner's confusion. Go easy on the kid, he thought. It wasn't like he'd picked up the concept straightaway either. He started again, this time speaking more slowly.

'Look here.' Geoff jabbed at a paragraph highlighted with a bullet point. 'See where it says the government's committed to providing NSW with a road infrastructure that will take us into the twenty-first century? You ask what kind of commitment the government has to our roads.'

Kate still looked gobsmacked. So Geoff hurried on. 'Look, the roads minister is out of town and some junior pollie is looking after the presser today. You'll both be wearing training wheels. Don't worry. You'll do fine.'

Strange, Geoff thought. He'd pegged Kate as being way smarter than this. Her obvious confusion had him thinking how attractive she was all over again. As they walked back to the crew car, he started humming 'Tonight's the night'.

He was still in a chipper mood when they arrived at the press conference forty minutes later. Around twenty journalists had made the trek to Sydney's outskirts to marvel at the city's newest on-ramp and to herald the government's soon-to-be-announced largesse.

Geoff stood to one side of the pack and lit a cigarette, watching everyone jockey for space. Just as he'd predicted, Kate was struggling to keep her foothold next to the crew. The kid would be lucky if she so much as opened her mouth.

Wedged between a safety rail and a sumo-sized radio journalist, Kate was coming to much the same conclusion.

The politician issued a short statement before taking questions. He was young, in his early thirties, and generally regarded as a rising star of the party.

'How much will NSW motorists save through this initiative?'

a female voice called from the back of the pack. The politician quoted the press release word for word in reply.

Kate had her question ready to go. But every time she started to speak, some louder and more aggressive voice cut her off.

'What kind of commitment does the government have to our roads?' the radio guy asked.

After a half-dozen or so questions and answers, the camera crews broke from the scrum and began filming the press conference from different angles.

Kate made the signal for her own crew to stay put. 'But we've got to get cutaways,' the cameraman hissed.

'Please. I just want to ask one question,' Kate pleaded.

'Whatever you say. But you can answer to the editor.'

As the other crews started packing up, Kate nervously cleared her throat.

'Why take the toll off a highway that services one of the city's richest electorates, while people out west have to put their hands in their pockets to use the M4 every morning?'

The politician stopped short, his ego deflating as suddenly as a pricked balloon. He hadn't been provided with an answer to this line of inquiry and he wasn't in a position to venture an opinion.

Kate tried again, uncertain if the politician had heard her properly.

'Most of the drivers using the M4 are just trying to get to work or get their kids to school. This highway leads out of Sydney to rich people's holiday homes.'

All around Kate, the press and radio contingent began to switch their tape recorders back on. The government's young gun was goldfishing helplessly.

One of the newspaper men jumped into the fray. 'By the way, doesn't your family have a beach house a few hours out of Sydney?'

He winked at Kate. 'And wait a moment, isn't your home just a couple of blocks from here? At least *you'll* save a few bob from this initiative.'

Humiliated, the politician stormed off, radio and print reporters trailing in his wake, firing more and more questions he was ill-equipped to answer.

Kate headed back down the ramp, trying but not quite managing to wipe the grin from her face. She couldn't believe it. She'd actually asked a question at a press conference. And because of it, she'd ended up delivering Geoff a far better story than the one contained in that self-serving press release. She couldn't wait to see his face.

She changed her mind the moment she glimpsed him waiting for her next to the crew car.

'What the fuck was that about?' Geoff demanded, his cheeks mottled beetroot red with fury. He was launching little globs of spittle at her black beaded cashmere jumper. 'How could you do that to me? I gave you a chance and you fucked me over. Ripley's going to have my balls for this.'

Kate stared at him, mystified by his reaction. 'I'm sorry, Geoff, I thought—' The crackle of the CB radio interrupted her. It was Ripley.

'What the fuck do you cunts think you're doing? I've just had that prick press secretary on the phone reading me the riot act. I send you on a simple story about a toll being lifted and you two go all Woodward and Bernstein on me. Geoff, you know the fucking drill. We give his man a clear run. He gives us the dirt on the opposition. I'm not losing a source for you two fucks.'

'Thanks a fucking lot, Katie.' Geoff jumped into the front seat and slammed the door, recklessly jettisoning his five months of intensive spadework. 'And don't expect me to cover for you either. You're on your own.'

The prospect of being on the receiving end of one of Ripley's famously savage rants filled Kate with terror. Whatever you do, don't cry, she told herself over and over again during the long, silent drive back to the station. But her eyes had already started watering.

'You two. Over here.' Ripley bellowed across the expanse of the newsroom. In another life he might have been a tenor. He certainly had the volume and physique for it.

Kate trailed behind Geoff, shoulders hunched, head down, wishing herself invisible. Reg Carter was waiting for them at the chief of staff area as well. This was not looking good at all. And so ends a short and inglorious career, she thought.

Kate knew Geoff was going to hang her out to dry. She probably even deserved it.

'Look, I had nothing to do with—' he began.

Ripley quickly cut him off. 'Yeah, mate, whatever. Look, the yarn's moved on since I last spoke to you. Lawsy's gone crazy on this rich man, poor man angle. He's agreed to an interview when he gets off air. It's the story of the day, mate.'

Ripley's pale eyes drilled into Kate's, daring her to call his bluff.

Reg Carter broke in. 'Good call, Ripper. And nice job, Geoff, although I'm surprised you let Katie handle the press conference.'

'Oh, I had her well and truly briefed. It was never going to be a drama.'

Kate looked at Geoff and then at Ripley. She wasn't sure she was becoming a better journalist at Channel Eight. But she was getting one hell of a lesson in television and office politics.

'Oh, and Katie?' Reg's hands automatically descended below his belt as he said her name. 'You've earned yourself a chance on the road. I'll add your name to the reporting roster from Monday. Don't blow it.'

'You should have seen your face when Carter told you. I swear I thought you were going to drop to your knees and blow it for real.'

'That's disgusting!' Kate shrieked, only just managing to gulp down her mouthful of beer. Somehow, Gillian got away with saying the most appalling things, just by shaking her angelic ringlets. The woman was like Holly Hobby on acid.

Kate and Gillian had decided to grab a celebratory drink at the local pub after work. The establishment was dubbed Studio Three by the many Channel Eight folk who drank there. Its greatest (and some would argue only) charm was its proximity to the office. But the owners had done their best to cater to the media crowd. The walls were covered with signed photographs of the network's biggest personalities.

'Are you excited?' Gillian asked.

'Probably more nervous than anything. I'll be working a lot more closely with Ripley now.'

'You'd best learn how to schmooze up to him. He assigns the stories. So it doesn't pay to piss him off. You know he used to be a used car salesman,' Gillian continued. 'When that didn't work out I guess journalism was the logical next step.'

'Too late, I think. The guy hates me already. Though I'm not sure exactly what I've done wrong.'

'You're female. And you're smart. Plus you're not going to need to sleep with him to move up the ladder. That pisses him off big time.' Gillian slammed down her beer by way of emphasis, soaking the cuffs of her cowl-necked jumper in the process. For reasons Kate couldn't begin to fathom, her new friend had woken up that morning and chosen to team baby pink mohair with a dark corduroy paisley pinafore.

'He wouldn't consider just leaving me alone to do my job?'

'Unlikely.'

'But why?' Kate drained her glass. She was headed for an almighty hangover and was surprised to realise she didn't care.

'Look. Who knows? His mother's a piece of work. Or at least that's what I've been told. Some wannabe model. Shunted him off to a posh boys-only boarding school when he was just eleven, even though the family lived in Sydney.'

'That's just some psycho bullshit excuse for acting like a cunt.' Kate almost gasped as the word left her mouth. The 'c' word was bandied about the office all day long. But she'd never said it herself. Not out loud anyway. Obviously, she was a whole lot drunker than she'd realised. Her cheeks reddened with embarrassment.

Fortunately, Gillian seemed not to notice. Her attention was fixed on the task of wringing beer from her sleeve.

'Maybe you're right. I just prefer to think there's a reason people behave like that. If they do it for no good reason . . . well it'd be like working with a band of serial killers or something.'

Kate lit a cigarette and grinned. From her experience, she wouldn't be the least surprised if Ripley had a stash of body parts in his freezer.

'Well, I'm not going to let him beat me. If I work hard, I'll be fine.' She tried to infuse the statement with a confidence she did not feel.

Gillian looked over towards the bar, judging how long she would have to wait for her drink. 'Of course, you'll be fine, Kate. You're too good not to be.'

Kate turned towards her friend, hoping for affirmation. But Gillian was already out of her seat, hunting the next round of drinks.

It seemed getting the gig was going to be the easy part.

FOUR

Kate pushed her nose to within a few centimetres of the bathroom mirror and aimed the eyeliner towards her bottom lid. She tried to channel the skills she had so stubbornly ignored at the June Dally-Watkins School of Deportment when she was fourteen. A little tuition in the art of good grooming had been her mother's idea. As she fashioned a wobbly blue line beneath one eye, Kate had to admit the ever-immaculate Dianne Corish might have been onto something.

She blinked a couple of times and tried again. Outside, she could hear the sounds of laughter as her colleagues made their way upstairs to the boardroom.

Tonight was a big night on the station's social calendar. It was Friday – the thirstiest night of the week in television. But more than that, it was mid-November. Official ratings would end for the year in just over twenty-four hours, marking the start of television's festive season. (Or its silly season, as the critics called it.)

And if that wasn't excuse enough for a drink, it was also Sandra Cook's last day at the network. The departure of a big-name celebrity meant that absolutely everyone would be there to pay their respects. Or, this being television, to be seen to be paying their respects.

Kate had been surprised and disappointed when she heard that Sandra was leaving the station less than twelve months after her own arrival. Working with such an industry legend was one of the reasons she had been so determined to get a job at Channel Eight in the first place.

Kate could trace her decision to become a journalist back to a single Sandra Cook interview in March 1979. Back then her career aspirations had extended no further than being the cruise director on the Love Boat. But that was before she chanced upon Sandra's interview with Idi Amin. She'd watched in awe as this glamorous woman coolly carved up one of the most dangerous men on the planet like a Sunday roast.

'You call yourself the King of Scotland, His Excellency President for life. You have awarded yourself a CBE – conqueror of the British Empire. And my personal favourite – Lord of all the Beasts of the Earth and the Fishes of the Sea.' Sandra's eyes didn't leave the face of the Ugandan despot for a moment. 'But *Time* magazine calls you a killer and a clown. From what I've witnessed that seems a fair enough assessment, don't you think?'

Kate gasped at the woman's audacity. She decided then and there that Julie McCoy was a flake and that she, Kate Corish, was going to be a foreign correspondent.

Now, almost a decade later, her idol was swapping television for magazines. According to prevailing wisdom, Sandra was smart to be leaving at the top of her game. Why wait around for the ratings to drop and be shoehorned out of your chair by someone younger and hungrier a few years down the track?

Kate checked her watch. A few minutes before six o'clock. The party would be starting and she was running late as usual.

She had taken extra care deciding what to wear that morning. Her mother's colour analyst had assured her she was a classic

'Spring'. And she'd chosen tonight's outfit on the strength of that advice. It was a dusty pink cotton dress with a full skirt and relatively discrete shoulder pads. A wide elasticised belt cinched her waist. She loved it. But mostly because the generous cut ensured she was a size eight.

Kohl. Blusher. Eye shadow. Frosted coral lipstick. Just a quick lick of mascara and she'd be done.

Kate tried to unscrew the cap, first with her hands and then with her teeth. But the damned thing was jammed hard. Cursing, she gave it one last almighty tug. The effort successfully liberated the brush. It also had the effect of spraying great blobs of liquid mascara suddenly and violently into the air around her.

'Shit.' Kate checked her reflection. Just as she feared, electric blue splatters now scarred her dress from bust to waist.

'Oh dear,' a brunette offered from a safe distance two basins away.

Kate recognised the girl as one of the newsroom's more attractive and ambitious production assistants, Jenni Parker. Jenni with an 'i', Kate called her.

'And your beautiful dress!' Jenni's tone sounded sincere. But since she was wearing a very tight and very short black and brown acid-wash leather skirt, Kate guessed she was fibbing. There was no way the owner of that skirt would admire her conservative outfit. Still, it was kind of her to pretend.

'Shit,' Kate said again, staring down at her damaged dress, at a loss what to do next.

'Hang on. I've got some Vaseline in here somewhere.' Jenni began rummaging through the biggest make-up case Kate had ever seen. 'If you smear a little Vaseline onto the mark, the stain will just sponge off. Amazing stuff, Vaseline. You can use it to make your perfume last longer too.'

Before Kate had a chance to protest, Jenni began dabbing at the mascara. A greasy snail trail of blue slime soon dissected Kate's dress, north to south-west.

'That's great, thanks, Jenni,' Kate stammered, glancing uncertainly at the gooey mess. 'Shouldn't you be getting to the party?'

'And leave you like this? No way, Kati.' Kate cringed as she heard Jenni adding an 'i' to her name.

The girl was decidedly Bambi-like (although Kate wasn't sure whether she was comparing Jenni to a fawn or a porn star). She seemed pleasant enough but Kate was in no mood for small talk. At this very moment she was supposed to be rubbing shoulders with the media elite up in the boardroom. And instead she was stuck in a bathroom discussing stain-removal techniques. If only she weren't so bloody clumsy.

Jenni failed to divine her new friend's mood and began jabbering away, a chummy, girls-own expression settling on her face.

'You've done so well. You are soooo lucky, Kati. Out on the road reporting already. How did you do it?'

Kate bit her tongue. According to newsroom scuttlebutt, Jenni sent a tape of herself playing at reporter to the boys upstairs. The show reel had apparently highlighted her breasts more than her reporting skills but someone on the top floor had deemed that cup size was a legitimate measure of talent. And so Jenni had landed the job.

'Well, I did work very hard for three years at uni getting my journalism degree.'

'I studied too,' Jenni offered eagerly. 'I'm a fully qualified aerobics instructor.' She handed Kate a flannel she'd retrieved from deep inside her make-up kit. What was that bag – the bloody magic pudding?

'Look, I'm fine, honestly. I really appreciate your help. But there's no point in us both missing the party.'

'Well, if you're sure, Kati . . .' Jenni was already halfway out the door, her earlier reservations about abandoning her colleague forgotten. Obviously, she didn't want to be stuck in this bathroom any more than Kate did. 'By the way, you might want to take another look at your eyeliner. It's really uneven. See you up there!'

Kate positioned her body under the hand dryer, arching her back so that the top of her dress was positioned directly beneath the air flow. She looked as though she'd been snap frozen while limbo dancing. Unfortunately for what remained of her dignity, the roar of hot air stopped her from hearing the bathroom door open. It wasn't until a pair of flecked grey Sergio Rossi sandals appeared in her line of sight, that she realised she was no longer alone.

'What the hell?' Gillian laughed.

'I'm afraid I've had a bit of a mishap.'

'I can see that. But you're missing out on the big farewell.' Gillian moved in a little closer to inspect the damp and discoloured patch on Kate's dress. 'It doesn't look that bad, you know. But why don't we sneak down to wardrobe and borrow a scarf or something? You can wear it while the material dries.'

Kate wasn't sure she wanted to accept fashion advice from someone wearing a flounced off-the-shoulder broderie anglaise sundress. But a trip to wardrobe beat marinating in a bathroom alone.

Gillian led the way through a rabbit warren of corridors and stairs to the basement of the building.

'Here we go,' she announced, pushing down hard on the handle and giving the door a push with her expansive rear.

'Oh my God,' the two women gasped in unison as they entered, both braking mid-stride.

The wardrobe department was an L-shaped space. So the other two occupants of the room weren't in direct view of the doorway. But an unfortunate positioning of full-length mirrors reflected an unlikely and highly gymnastic tryst in the furthest corner of the room.

A well-known quiz-show host was seated on a swivel chair. He was holding the petite and impressively flexible wardrobe mistress upside down. Her mouth was placed where the zipper of his pants would have been – if he'd been wearing any trousers. He was returning the favour at the other end.

They were clearly engrossed in their tasks. So much so that neither looked up. But even if they'd wanted to, their contortions were so complex that the manoeuvre would have been near impossible.

Kate and Gillian tiptoed back out the door, collapsing into fits of laughter at the other end of the corridor.

'Limber young lady, isn't she?' Gillian observed.

'A regular Russian gymnast. I think I'll manage without the scarf. I'm pretty much dry now anyway. I'm not sure the wardrobe mistress can say the same.'

Gillian coughed and snorted as she tried to stifle another round of giggles. 'Okay. I've got to grab my gear from the newsroom. I'll see you up there.'

Staring into the packed boardroom a few minutes later, Kate wished she'd stuck with Gillian. She felt hopelessly out of her league.

Everywhere she looked, she saw faces – famous faces. The kind of faces that usually belonged on the small screen or in the pages of *TV Week*. What had she been thinking? She didn't belong here.

'Hey, Dorothy. Pick your jaw off the ground. You're not in fucking Kansas now.' Mike Ripley lumbered by carrying a couple of drinks.

Pulling herself together, Kate plunged into the heaving and drunken crowd. Ahead of her, a young business reporter danced on the bar to the Robert Palmer track, 'Addicted to Love'. She had a cigarette hanging from her mouth. A chardonnay sloshed about perilously in one hand. Stilettos dangled from the other.

At ground level, her dance partner, a fleshy, middle-aged Lothario, was bouncing around and singing along. To underline the lyrics, he had unzipped his fly and was holding a small cocktail frankfurter to his crotch. His pelvis gyrated menacingly to the beat.

In a quieter corner, Kate spotted Ripley schmoozing the weekend weather girl, a woman whose stylist had channelled *The Bold and the Beautiful* to craft her look for the evening. An enormous helmet of dark wavy hair sat atop even larger blue sateen shoulders. Ripley was resting one chubby hand against her tiny waist. His body language was unmistakably masculine and proprietary.

Kate was appalled to observe the mating dance was mutual, although she suspected the woman's interest had more to do with the upcoming vacancy for a mid-week weather reporter than the quality of Ripley's conversation. Even so that was no excuse. The guy was married. He should have been off-limits.

Suddenly, a loud gushing noise claimed Kate's attention. A metre or so away, a dishevelled looking man was swaying alarmingly and relieving himself in a pot plant. After the mascara incident, Kate didn't want any more little accidents. She executed a swift defensive side step and headed to the far corner of the room, where she'd finally spotted a familiar and friendly face.

'You're late!' Tezza, her favourite cameraman, saluted her with a beer.

'Who are all these people?' she asked. 'And what's with the guy with the weener? I thought dance moves like that had been eradicated in the seventies, along with smallpox.'

'He's a big man in the sports department. Spent most of this year covering the golf overseas. Got nicked for touching up a young research assistant and had to lay low for a while. She's gone, of course, with enough cash to put a deposit on a house. But she'll never work in the industry again.'

As Kate watched, the man brought the frankfurter to his mouth and began to simulate oral sex.

'He's disgusting!'

'Stay tuned. You'll see a whole lot worse than that before the night is out.'

Kate looked towards the far end of the bar where Reg Carter was talking to one of the assistant chiefs of staff. The guy was maybe only a few years older than Kate, with a rapidly receding hairline and a fleshy, almost feminine body. She had dubbed him the 'tubby apprentice' for his rounded belly and cloying subservience to Mike Ripley.

The third member of the group was the newly christened 'Urinater'. But he had fallen asleep. Or maybe he had passed out. Kate wasn't sure which.

Tubby and Carter were slapping each other on the back, sharing a joke. The sudden burst of blokey laughter jerked the Urinater back to a reluctant consciousness. It was a narrow window of opportunity. He used it to throw up on himself.

Carter quickly reached for a serviette and tucked it roughly around his colleague's neck, covering the worst of the spew. He and Tubby then moved to the other end of the bar to continue their conversation.

'Told you it was going to get worse,' Tezza commented, taking a smug swig of his beer.

'Who *is* that?' Kate was horrified. But she was also looking forward to telling Ben and Al the story when she got home.

'You mean the guy with bits of vomit attached to his beard and a large wet patch across his groin?' Tezza was savouring his role

61

as the seasoned party veteran. 'Believe it or not, he holds a senior position in the news and current affairs division. Watch out for him at the end of the night. He rarely leaves these functions alone. Power can be quite the aphrodisiac.'

Kate grappled with the concept of willingly sharing her bed with a man soaked in urine and regurgitated beer.

'And speaking of office Romeos. Look who's headed our way. I think I might go scare myself up another beer.'

Kate followed Tezza's line of sight. Geoff Jones was barrelling towards her.

'Don't you dare leave me to—' she hissed at Tezza's disappearing back.

'So, gorgeous, how have you been getting along without me?' Geoff asked as he adjusted his tight fawn pants.

'Good, Geoff. And thanks for all your help this year. I wouldn't be reporting if it wasn't for you.' Kate wasn't entirely sure that was true but it was near enough to Christmas and it was the charitable thing to say.

'Any time, sweetheart, any time. Now can I get you a drink?'

'I'll have a chardonnay, thanks.'

As Geoff dutifully scurried off to the bar, Kate escaped to the sanctuary of the ladies' loo. Or tried to. She quickly discovered that the boardroom only had one unisex bathroom. And according to the more experienced partygoer, who had provided her with directions, it was nowhere near up to the task of catering for these kinds of numbers. It was little wonder a drunken executive might occasionally choose to take advantage of a potted palm.

Kate pushed the door open anyway. What did she care if there was a queue? After all, she wasn't in any hurry to resume her tête-à-tête with Jonesy.

The bathroom comprised two rooms, a narrow and inadequate

powder room leading onto a perpetually locked toilet cubicle. As Kate stepped inside, she almost collided with Sandra Cook. The guest of honour was trying to fix her make-up in the mirror. It occurred to Kate she'd been crying.

With the toilet engaged and the two women reluctantly occupying the same tiny space, Kate felt obliged to make small talk, however awkward.

'Sandra, I'm so sorry I didn't get to work with you. I grew up watching your reports.' Kate knew she was prattling but couldn't seem to stop herself. 'I was just twelve when you did that interview with Idi Amin.'

Sandra fixed her with an angry look. Too late Kate realised she had just reminded the woman of her age. If the veteran really was leaving the industry to make way for a new generation of reporters, the comment must have sounded almost bitchy.

She tried to recover. 'I'd really appreciate any tips you might have for a rookie.'

Sandra's face twisted with resentment. 'Fuck your university degree. Fuck how hard you work. If you don't have a penis, you don't have a fucking hope. How's that for advice?'

And with that Sandra Cook, Kate's idol of ten years, stormed out. Kate stared after her in disbelief, her legs buckling with the shock. Television certainly was a deceptive medium. Kate had spent half her life admiring someone who was obviously a complete bitch.

As the bathroom door swung closed, a telltale snorting sound came from inside the engaged cubicle. The occupant/s must have been waiting for the powder room to clear. Kate decided it would be quicker to try the bathroom downstairs. And a whole lot less embarrassing depending on who and how many people emerged from the toilet.

Just as she had guessed, the disabled bathroom on the ground floor was displaying the green vacant sign. Her ploy to ditch Geoff Jones had now become a journey of necessity. She pushed against the door.

Until that moment, Kate couldn't imagine her night getting any worse. Then again, she hadn't counted on walking in on a semi-clad Mike Ripley with his XXL patterned Bonds briefs down around his ankles. He was sitting on the toilet seat, chins up and eyes closed. A brunette head was bobbing up and down in his lap region. Kate didn't notice much else. A tiny anchor-shaped birthmark behind one ear. A pile of clothes discarded in a heap on the floor.

It had to be the weekend weather girl. When Kate had escaped the boardroom twenty minutes earlier, she'd been draped over Ripley, her tongue halfway down his throat. Clearly, the woman was committed to a career in meteorology.

Kate had heard the old joke: *you've got to give head to get ahead.* But she hadn't quite believed it. And even with the X-rated proof working urgently right in front of her, she still found the idea outrageous. She just couldn't conceive of any job that would warrant locking lips around Ripley's private parts. Suddenly she really needed that chardonnay.

Just as she started to back out, Ripley's ferret eyes flashed open.

'Why, Katie,' he snarled. 'Don't go. I'll let you jump the queue.'

Kate fixed him with a look of utter contempt before she turned her back and walked away, closing the door carefully behind her. He really was the vilest creature she'd ever had the misfortune to meet.

Mawson was just finishing his farewell speech to Sandra as Kate crept back into the boardroom.

'To Sandra,' he boomed, glass raised.

'To Sandra,' everyone repeated enthusiastically. Watching Sandra, there was no way of telling she was anything other than absolutely delighted by Mawson's tribute and the gathering in her honour. It was an impressive performance, given her earlier assessment of the industry and of the men politely applauding her.

At the back of the crowd, Kate spotted her old college friend and now colleague, Matthew Keaton. She rushed towards him, relieved to find some genuine company after her eventful and circuitous tour of the station's bathroom facilities.

'You won't *believe* what I just saw in the toilet, Matt. Our chief of staff was getting a little extra service from one of the girls.'

'Welcome to television, as Bruce Gyngell once so famously said,' Matthew replied with a grin.

'I don't think Ripley's ever going to forgive me for catching him with his pants down.'

'Worry about that tomorrow. Anyway, I've been looking everywhere for you. I have some good news. You've finally got some competition on the road. I'll be replacing Sean Scott as a reporter.'

Kate didn't know Sean especially well but she admired his style and his look. He wasn't especially large. He wore a normal-sized collar. And he didn't speak 'bloke'. That alone set him apart from the Geoff Jones clones. He was also a gifted writer and interviewer.

But Carter had sacked him anyway – ostensibly because he wasn't pulling his weight. Kate knew that wasn't true though. In reality, Ripley had simply stopped assigning Sean any stories. As Gillian had pointed out, it didn't pay to piss off the chief of staff.

Kate felt a cold chill run through her body but pushed it aside. 'That's fantastic news, Matt. Congratulations.'

'Well, I'm a little nervous about taking over from Sean. They're big shoes to fill. Luckily, no one here seems to realise just how good he is.'

Their conversation was interrupted by the tinkling of glasses. A big star like Sandra Cook merited more than a single speech.

Standing on a lighting kit, Reg Carter readied himself for his audience by making a quick adjustment to his manhood. After all, he was talking about a lady – and a good-looking one at that, even if she was over forty.

The room quietened as Carter began. 'Well, I've known Sandy her entire career. I was the one who hired her for a spot in the newsroom. And it was definitely one of my better decisions. That was her first gig in TV and she's since become one of Australia's most respected newswomen. When was that – a hundred years ago?'

The crowd chuckled. Kate knew Sandra would be biting her tongue. Drawing blood in the process, probably.

'You'll be a big loss to this network, Sandy, but we understand your need to move on and we support you in that. As I've always said, if I was in the trenches, I'd pick Sandy Cook to fight alongside me. No one finer.'

Sandra's smile was strained.

'So good luck in your future ventures and thank you for your years of service to this network.'

'Speech! Speech!' the boardroom roared.

Sandra stood up and turned slowly towards Carter, locking eyes with him.

'Reg, you old fart, if I was ever stuck in a trench with you, I'd shoot you myself!'

Sandra sat down again to howls of laughter. Kate almost found herself liking the woman again. It had been a long week and an even longer night. And the three wines Kate had tucked under her high-waisted belt were making her feel a bit tipsy. In any case, she had more than enough tales to entertain Al and Ben for weeks to come.

Gathering up her briefcase, Kate spotted Geoff Jones a few metres away, clearly drunk and staggering slightly. He had a dumb smirk on his face and was looking down lovingly to . . . Oh Christ. He had his penis out of his trousers. Worse still, he was offering it to that same poor AP who'd been Beige's whipping girl all those months ago. Young Alison was frozen, like a rabbit in the headlights. She really was too sweet-natured for television. No wonder the kid had decided to throw it all in for a round-the-world air ticket.

'Check it out, babe,' Jones was slurring proudly as Kate raced to Alison's rescue.

She quickly threw an arm around Geoff's shoulder. 'What happened to my chardy, sweetie?'

Looking down, Kate pretended to do a double take. 'Oh my God, Geoff. That looks just like a penis. Only smaller!'

Alison burst out laughing, the colour flooding back to her face. All Geoff could do was shove the offending appendage back into his perma-press trousers and storm off.

Turning to Alison, Kate added, 'I think Mr Jones just bought you an extra year's travelling . . . and first class at that. You should make an appointment with a lawyer.'

What a night, she thought, as she skipped out the door. She couldn't wait to get home to Ben and Al. Not that they'd believe a word of it.

A week later, Reg Carter called Geoff into his office.

'That incident at Sandra's farewell,' Reg began. Geoff looked sheepish. 'Mate, I know you were just having a bit of fun but it's causing all sorts of trouble with human resources. And it's cost us a few bob too.'

Geoff nodded, pale faced.

'We have to be seen to do something about it.' Reg paused to underline the seriousness of the situation. 'So we're sending you to Europe for three months. Take a look at how the Italians get away with it. I don't know. Just get the hell out of here until things cool down.'

The two men smiled. Blokes had to look after each other.

FIVE

STORY ASSIGNMENTS FOR 1 JUNE 1989	
Park Murder	Pratt
State Rounds	Keaton
Special Story	Jones
Tiananmen Reax	Beige
Warm Weather	Parker
Student Fashion	Corish

Different day. Same shit.

Kate groaned as she scanned the reporters' assignment page on her computer. Once again, she'd been allocated the light and breezy fluff piece that came after the weather. And this time, she was reporting on fashion of all things. Kate appreciated a new frock as much as the next girl. But her idea of special-occasion dressing didn't extend much beyond getting out the iron. She was absolutely clueless when it came to cutting-edge design.

What the hell had she done to deserve this? Other than catch Mike Ripley with his member thrust halfway down a young and ambitious throat. Despite Gillian's assurances to the contrary, Kate was convinced Ripley was trying to squeeze her out just as he had Sean Scott before her.

Her only consolation was that the weekend weather girl hadn't picked up the reporting gig. (God only knows what she *had* picked up in that bathroom.) The woman had quit the day Jenni with an 'i' was given the job ahead of her. The slight must have been terribly deflating, given her intimate knowledge of the boss's high-pressure systems. Hard to swallow, in fact. Maybe that had been the problem.

At least it was heartening to know that you couldn't just sleep your way to the top in television. Although it pained Kate to think that any woman would consider taking that route in the first place. Still, given the dross she was covering each day, Kate was starting to wonder if she shouldn't relent just a little and favour Ripley with an occasional smile.

Today, even Jenni had scored a passably interesting yarn. It was the first day of winter. But Sydney had experienced week after week of unseasonably high temperatures. La Nina. El Nino. Climate change. It was all fascinating stuff. Unfortunately though, the station's dedicated weather reporter had never heard of global warming.

'What are greenhouse gases?' she had asked Tubby, her breasts resting prettily atop crossed arms. 'I thought plants were good for the environment.'

Kate wished she'd waited around to hear the assistant COS's reply. Tubby's considered analysis of the phenomenon would no doubt have provided her with yet another excellent dinner-party anecdote.

Matthew's career was powering along. He'd been visiting friends in Canberra the day Assistant Police Commissioner Colin

Winchester had been assassinated. For the next two weeks, his reports led bulletins right around the country.

No sooner had he returned to Sydney than the state roundsman was felled by a bout of chickenpox. Five months later, Matthew was still based at Parliament House. Word had it his predecessor's face was so badly pockmarked he'd probably never get back on air, at least not on commercial television.

As Matthew was so fond of saying, he'd been fair hit up the arse with a rainbow.

Geoff Jones had been assigned the day's 'special' story. Or at least that's how Ripley described it in the computer system. Way too many people at the network had computer access. And when the newsroom had an exclusive, the information was guarded like the crown jewels.

No one wanted to tip off the station's top-rating current-affairs program *Australia Tonight*. The two shows might have been on the same network but they were bitter rivals nonetheless. The other commercial stations weren't providing much competition in the news and current affairs department. So the journalists at Channel Eight had started fighting one another for ratings supremacy. There had even been a few cases of duelling chequebooks, with one Channel Eight program upping the ante for the next. Mawson was happy enough to let the rivalry run. It kept his people hungry.

Kate figured if Geoff had been assigned to the 'special' story, it couldn't be too earth shattering. But she'd still swap places with him in a heartbeat. Or with any of the other reporters for that matter.

The murder of a vagrant in an inner-city park had naturally fallen to the police reporter Andy Pratt. And Beige had scored what Kate considered the yarn of the day – a piece on the local Chinese community's reaction to the latest events in Tiananmen Square. Right now in Beijing, a few thousand students were inspiring millions to demand a better life. And it looked like they were going to get away with it. Kate wondered if Beige could even find China on a map. He was the quintessential talking head. No brains required.

Nowadays, everyone in the newsroom referred to Channel Eight's aspiring anchorman as Beige. Tezza had been the first to seize upon Kate's nickname. Within a few weeks, everyone was using it. Poor old Beige wasn't happy about the development but the bloke didn't have the imagination to figure out how or why he'd earned his new moniker.

Still, he was in a far better position than Kate. She didn't care what her colleagues called her. She just wanted to cover a real story. It rankled that students were making history on one side of the world but on her beat they were making frocks.

Of course nothing was ever going to change if she accepted her lot in silence. Kate took a deep breath and marched over to the COS desk. Polite but firm she reminded herself. She didn't want to get railroaded. But she wouldn't get anywhere by screaming like a banshee either. Only the male reporters got what they wanted by raising their voices. Their female colleagues just ended up with a reputation for being difficult.

Ripley and the tubby apprentice were leaning back on their chairs, swapping stories from *Penthouse Forum*. Kate didn't wait for the men to wrap up their little session. Ripley would relish reading about dripping juices and horny shafts if he thought Kate was listening. She could almost hear his tongue stroking the words. It was a sickening thought.

'I'm sorry to bother you.' Kate tried to sound apologetic but she couldn't erase the scorn from her voice. Embarrassed, Tubby shoved the magazine back in its brown paper bag. 'I want to talk to you about the stories you've been assigning me.'

Ripley tried to meet her gaze but ended up fiddling with the dials of the CB radio instead. He found Kate Corish way too intense for a good-looking broad. Her eyes just about bored a hole in his head.

'Last week it was a beautiful baby contest. The week before that it was a fundraiser for the RSPCA. And if I never attend another tree planting, it will be too bloody soon.' Kate tried to inject a little chuckle into her delivery. She had to keep the tone light.

'I'd do a great job on the Tiananmen Square story. My dad was a human-rights lawyer so I have some contacts I could use.' That was a lie. Her father had been dead nearly twenty years. But she was sure she'd make a better fist of the yarn than the lacklustre Beige. 'Maybe someone else could cover this fashion parade?'

'Who do you suggest? Pratt perhaps?' Ripley sneered. 'The frock decamped along the runway in an easterly direction.' Tubby laughed at his boss's joke.

'What about Beige? He did a bit of fashion reporting last year.'

'That wasn't fashion reporting. It was a flirt piece with Elle McPherson.'

'She's a fashion model. So his report must have been about fashion and modelling.'

'No, Kate. It was about how charming Beige is. We turned the pillow-biting poonce into a ladies' man. After all that hard work, I am not going to send him mincing out to report on frocks. Anyway, fashion is a chick story. And since you fit the description, you're it.'

Ripley pushed his melon face so close Kate could smell his cigarette breath. Her stomach lurched but she wasn't about to give him the pleasure of pulling away. There was only one way to deal with a bully. She had to stand her ground.

'And do you know what?' Ripley continued, his voice coated in sarcasm. 'You did such a good job on the Bicentennial celebrations last year, what with all those kids, animals, period costumes, blackfellas dancing and fucking tall ships, you've carved out a bit of a niche for yourself, I reckon.'

With that, he retrieved his gentlemen's magazine and started flicking through the photographic spread.

Kate wasn't especially surprised by Ripley's reaction. Gillian had warned her about typecasting early on. 'Haven't you noticed that all the police roundsmen are rough around the edges cop types, complete with cheap suits, crap ties and dodgy grammar?'

She had noticed of course. She'd also noticed if there was a story involving a humidicrib, there would be a young female reporter standing sympathetically beside it.

Kate wanted to argue the point but Ripley's greedy eyes made it very clear the conversation was over. Her complaints were no match for the buxom charms of Miss June.

'You're a bloody marvel, Kate. Keep up the good work!' Tubby added with a daffy Freddo Frog kind of smile. Kate searched his face for any trace of irony. Nothing. Maybe that's why Ripley had taken to him. He agreed with Ripley without engaging a single neuron of his own.

Clearly, there would be no decent stories issuing from the COS booth any time soon, Kate thought as she trooped back to her desk. She was just going to have to make her own luck. Pull something out of the hat just once to crack through to the next layer.

Right on cue, the phone on Andy Pratt's desk started ringing. It was ten o'clock and the lazy prick still hadn't shown his face. Police reporters kept their own hours and their own books. Every night it seemed they were out with the coppers. Or at least that's what they claimed on their expense forms.

Kate leaned over to answer her colleague's phone.

'Kate Corish here. How can I help you?'

'I need to speak to your police reporter. Pratt, that's his name, right?'

'I'm sorry. He's not here at the moment. But I'm more than happy to help you and pass on any information.'

'The information I have is sensitive. Who are you anyway?'

'I'm Andy's research assistant.' Kate bluffed, reaching for her pen and Spirax notebook. 'If you just fill me in on the basics, I can get Andy to call you back as soon as he gets in.'

The woman on the other end of the line paused. Kate was surprised when she didn't just hang up. 'I own a gentlemen's estab-lishment in the city. You've heard of Mickey Morgan, I assume?'

Morgan was a notoriously corrupt cop who worked out of Kings Cross. He was untouchable. Or seemed to be.

Kate was silent for a moment. Maybe only one per cent of the cold calls that came into the office amounted to anything. The major-ity were from the chronically lonely and the impossibly deranged. There was the woman who believed her clothesline was possessed. Or the man who claimed to have invented a cure for baldness. Some stories sounded promising but lacked the hard evidence needed to get them across the line. Other times, callers would embellish the truth to pique a reporter's interest. It usually turned out that the real story wouldn't engage a pre-school show-and-tell class.

So the odds were stacked against her. But there was something about this woman that felt like the real deal.

'Maybe you'd prefer to discuss this in person,' Kate suggested. 'Andy won't be back until this afternoon. But if you like, I can bring him along to meet you. Just for a chat. No pressure.'

'Pratt can't show his face around here,' the woman snapped angrily. 'Someone might recognise him.'

'What about me? Could I come and talk to you instead?' Kate held her breath against the silence.

'I guess so.' The woman was thinking aloud. 'Just don't look like a reporter. Dress like you work in a bordello not a boardroom. The name's Irene by the way.'

The meeting was set for the following Sunday. Three days away.

Kate left a handwritten note on Pratt's desk and headed out to do her fashion piece, a little bounce in her step. Student design didn't seem anywhere near so dull now that she'd lined up some real investigative work. She couldn't wait to brief Pratt.

A full day passed before she finally clapped eyes on the network's elusive police reporter.

'Andy, I think I might have a story for you.'

Pratt lit a cigarette and squinted at her through the smoke, barely acknowledging he knew she sat next to him.

'I took a call yesterday from a woman called Irene.'

'Kate, this better be quick. I'm working on something here. And I have a shitload of calls to make.' Pratt was thumbing through a black leather Filofax crammed with mysterious pencilled initials and phone numbers.

'Well, this woman owns a brothel and I agreed to meet her on Sunday to research a story for you. She wants me to be the go-between, in case you get recognised.' The words were spilling out of Kate's mouth with no regard to sense or order. She really should have rehearsed her spiel. A bit late for that now though.

'A woman owns a brothel. Now there's a lead. Knock yourself out, kid.' Pratt said, picking up his phone and dialling a number.

'But there's more—'

Pratt cut her off. 'Mate, I haven't got time for this. If you want to waste yours, be my guest.' And with that he swivelled around in his chair and gave his full attention to whoever had just answered the phone.

Kate watched him for a moment. The police reporter was hunched over his desk, one hand cupped importantly over the telephone receiver. After the initial greeting, the conversation was conducted in a dramatic stage whisper. Pratt looked up and waved her away impatiently.

'Stupid,' she told herself as she collected her briefcase and jacket from her desk. Stupid for not practising what she had to say. And stupid for believing she could come up with a story that would pique the interest of a seasoned hand like Andy Pratt. She wished she hadn't set up the meeting. But she was pretty much stuck with it now. She couldn't just stand up Irene. And given all the secrecy, she doubted she could simply ring the brothel and cancel either. What a nightmare. Worse still, she had two whole days to stew about how badly she'd misjudged the situation. Maybe she wasn't cut out to be a journalist after all.

She was still feeling painfully sorry for herself when she switched on the television the next morning. The news was full of the massacre at Tiananmen Square. A British correspondent called Jonathan McTavish was in the thick of the action reporting on the army's brutality and risking his life to film the hundreds, maybe thousands, of casualties at local hospitals. Kate didn't budge from her lounge for the entire day as she flicked obsessively between the radio and television coverage.

There was an Australian TV journalist there too, filing reports from a hotel balcony. He was doing a fair enough job but Kate liked to think she'd be on the ground dodging bullets.

Of course, she couldn't expect to be reporting from war zones just yet. But there were plenty of stories that needed telling at home. Her meeting with Irene probably wouldn't amount to anything. But it was worth finding out.

By the time Sunday arrived, Kate was excited again. She found some gel in her bathroom cabinet and scrunched her usually sleek shoulder length bob into a Madonna-style tousle. A black lace ribbon held up one side, giving her hair a mussy, wanton look.

She'd called Matthew for advice on what to wear.

'You don't think I actually frequent those kinds of places do you?' he teased. 'You should probably be speaking to Ripley. He'd have way more experience than me on the subject.'

Kate answered him with silence. And Matthew knew her well enough to imagine the killer glare that accompanied it.

'Okay, okay. You need to look fuckable. But even more than that, you need to look available. Visible underwear. Ultra tight pants. Bedroom hair. I don't suppose I can come around and give you a hand getting ready?' He wasn't surprised to get a stern knockback.

Kate eventually opted for a red bra under a see-through midriff top. Daily sessions at the gym had earned her a flat, taut stomach. Finally, here was an opportunity to show it off. She rounded off her ensemble with a pair of black lycra aerobic tights. Not ideal but Kate had nothing else. The fuckable, available whore look wasn't something she generally strived for.

Finally, she needed to find the right shoes. Kate rummaged at the very back of her wardrobe for the high heels she had bought for her graduation. She hadn't worn them in a very long time.

Reporting didn't lend itself to stilettos. Or to shortish, body-hugging skirts for that matter. Although Jenni seemed to manage all right. Kate learned her lesson the first day she flew in the station chopper. Luckily, she was wearing a pair of sensible bum-covering cottontails at the time and not a G-string. Because as she discovered, there is simply no way of executing the one-metre leap into the passenger seat of a helicopter without offering the world a protracted gander at your undies. From that day on, Kate's workday wardrobe consisted entirely of pants, jackets and sensible shoes.

Kate slung an oversized white belt around her hips and checked the mirror. Prostitute? Maybe more Bananarama meets Porky's Revenge. But it was close enough.

Bernstein hopped onto her bed, swishing his tail and shedding fur malevolently. The fluffy grey stray had long ago decided to move in with Kate on a permanent basis. Now the sweet little kitten was a spoiled cantankerous teenager. He knew he was about to be abandoned for the day. And he was mightily ticked off about it.

'Sorry, Bernie. I've got a better offer.' Kate swooped him into her arms for a conciliatory cuddle. He pulled away, legs straining against her chest, back arched angrily. Damned cat did a better line in guilt trips than her mother, she thought, as she grabbed her bubblegum-pink quilted ski parka and hobbled out the door. These shoes were going to give her blisters for sure. She just hoped it would be worth it.

Fifteen minutes later, Kate was parking her trusty VW beetle directly in front of the address she'd been given. She forced herself out of the car, lit a cigarette and stared up at the grand old terrace. Nerves were setting in. She wished she could simply drive away.

But Matthew would be grilling her tomorrow about her big scoop and there was no way she was going to admit to chickening out.

Kate reached the top of the stairs and pushed the door open, almost losing her balance in the process. She was hopelessly out of practice at affecting a confident and feminine teeter. Thankfully, the place was empty. Ten o'clock Sunday morning wasn't exactly peak hour in the bordello business. So what little dignity she had remained intact. She rang the little brass bell and waited at the desk.

Irene appeared a few moments later. Kate watched as the woman walked towards her. Strawberry blond hair – professionally coloured. Manicured nails. Her outfit was simple but well cut – the kind of clothes that looked thrown together but would cost a fortune at any eastern-suburbs boutique.

She was certainly well turned out. But life hadn't given Irene an easy ride. Her skin had been hammered into leather by too many late nights, too many cigarettes and, by the smell of her breath, too much brandy.

Still Kate could tell she had been a great beauty in her day. She was a little plump now. But once upon a time, those curves had been dangerous. And that smile! It was wide and genuine and lit up her entire face. Kate hadn't expected a smile like that after their terse telephone conversation.

Irene was just as curious about her visitor. Even in her present get-up, the girl was clearly from the same moneyed class as most of her clientele.

Kate extended a professional hand. Given that she was wearing fire-engine red underwear and it was clearly visible, the gesture seemed faintly ridiculous.

'I hope they're paying you well in that joint because you'd earn big dough here.' Irene took a long drag on her menthol cigarette.

'Thanks for the compliment, Irene.' Kate took a risk. 'And I imagine if I pursued this profession you'd be the kind of woman I'd want looking after me.'

Irene narrowed her eyes. She knew Kate was trying to flatter her. But she liked it all the same. 'Let's go inside and talk.'

Kate followed Irene through the beaded doorway and into a salon-like lounge room.

'Can I get you a drink, honey?'

Kate had yet to discover a more effective method of bonding with talent, even this early in the morning. 'Yes, scotch if you've got it. Neat,' she said.

'Straight scotch – an unusual choice. More a man's drink I would have thought.'

'It's my dad's influence. I've never been much of a beer or wine drinker.' Kate wasn't sure she even remembered her father drinking scotch. But there had always been a bottle of whiskey and a heavy crystal tumbler positioned on the sideboard when she was growing up. It was as if her mother was still waiting for Alexander Corish to come home.

Irene poured Kate a double. Her own serving was even more generous. 'So, Kate, let's get down to business. Like I told you on the phone, I can serve up Micky Morgan and a fair few other coppers who've been squeezing me dry here. My back's against the wall so I'm figuring my best shot is to go public.

'If Chris Masters was still at *Four Corners* I'd be calling him. But he's not. So I'm in a bind. *Hinch* isn't my style. Willesee's gone. And I'm not sure about that Jana Wendt. Which leaves me with news. And Channel Eight is supposed to be the best of the lot. I need the job done properly. Is Pratt up to it? If you screw up, I'll lose the business for sure and I don't think my life would be worth much either.'

Kate felt a shiver go up her spine. This was for real. She just knew it.

'Tell me your story. And I'll tell you what we can . . . and can't . . . do.' Kate wanted this desperately. But not so much that she'd risk someone's life and livelihood in the process.

Brothel-keeping was illegal, Irene explained. She'd been paying off the cops for years. But in 1979, the Wran Government had decriminalised prostitution so working girls could ply their trade on the *street* without fear of being arrested.

The legislation was a major blow to the local constabulary. The cops had always made a fortune extorting money from the district's massage parlours. To maintain their cash flow, they needed to get the girls back into the brothels.

They did it by arresting street workers under the Offences in Public Places Act. Arrests had gone up tenfold in the space of just a few years. So the girls had fled to establishments like Irene's, where Morgan and his cronies were waiting with their hands and their dicks out.

Paying bribes had always been an accepted part of doing business in Irene's world. But Morgan was getting too greedy. She was scarcely breaking even. Plus, he'd started roughing up the girls. It was time to take the bastard on.

'Let me speak with Andy and my producers and we'll come up with a plan of attack. Is there a number I can call you on tomorrow?'

Just as Kate was getting ready to leave, a commotion erupted from the next room. For the past few minutes, she'd been aware of hushed murmurs of disagreement coming from somewhere nearby. Without warning, the whispering had become a tornado of raised voices and breaking glass.

A man bellowed above the din. 'Where the fuck is Irene?'

If Kate had any lingering doubts about the brothel-keeper's bona fides, they vanished when the source of all the noise blundered through the door.

Standing, or more accurately, swaying right there in front of her was Mickey Morgan, still enjoying his Saturday-night bender. He was a behemoth of a man, clearly in the habit of using his enormous size to intimidate. His attention was centred squarely on Kate.

'Hello, sweetheart.' Morgan violated her with his eyes. 'My, my. New meat, Irene? You haven't introduced me to this little filly before.'

'This is Katrina. She's too expensive for you, Mickey. On your cop wage and all.' Kate wondered if Morgan could detect the contempt in Irene's voice. Too drunk, probably.

Kate needed to get out and fast. 'Gotta go now, Irene. See you next time.' She bolted from the room as quickly as her high heels would allow. She didn't want Morgan eyeballing her for too long.

A rush of cold air greeted Kate as she stumbled out into the street.

'Oh my God,' she whispered to herself.

Her head was spinning with possibility. Tomorrow, she felt certain, everything would change.

SIX

'Tubby, you hear that? Stop the fucking presses. There are illegal brothels operating in Sydney. That's our gun reporter's news tip for the day.'

Ripley was lounging against the entry to the COS area, holding the butt of a cigarette between his thumb and index finger. He took a final deep drag of his smoke then stubbed it out in a company-issue disposable aluminium ashtray.

Kate stared at the chief of staff with a mixture of horror and bewilderment. She couldn't believe she'd hightailed it to work an hour early for this. Surely Ripley was being deliberately obtuse. She knew she was still a bit wet behind the ears. But this was a story. There was no question about it.

'There's more to it than that. Mickey Morgan is on the take.'

'Fuck me. Let's do a lead story on the bleeding fucking obvious. Katie, tell us something we don't know.'

'But he's—'

'He's a copper who likes a bit on the side. No harm in that. Now, I'm glad you're in early. The RSPCA has twenty abandoned pups that need nice new homes. Santa delivered them to the wrong addresses at Christmas time and the cheer has worn off. We need to do a 'Think before you buy a pup' story. Got it?'

Ripley didn't bother to wait for an answer. He waddled back into the booth and cranked the police radio up to full volume. A cement truck had just collided with a semi on the F3.

Jerk, Kate thought as she trooped back to her desk, a crumpled 'A Puppy is Forever' press release balled in one fist. No matter. She'd just go straight to Andy Pratt. There was no way he'd let Ripley rob him of a big story like this.

Pratt crawled into the office about eleven, wearing sunglasses and the scent of stale beer. It wasn't until the end of the day that Kate judged him in any condition to listen to her pitch.

'Hi, Andy,' she started, pulling nervously at the sleeves of her jacket. 'I went to that brothel last night and met with Irene.'

Pratt flashed a look that was both bored and cross at the same time. 'Mate, save it. Ripley's already briefed me on your earth-shattering revelations.'

'But—'

'Look, sweetheart. I appreciate your enthusiasm. Really I do. But I've been around the block a bit and these stories just don't come off. How were you going to prove it anyway? So the bloke visits the establishment now and again. That doesn't mean he's doing anything wrong. It's just his word against this Irene woman. And he's a cop.'

'I thought I could pose as a prostitute and catch him on tape,' Kate pleaded desperately.

'Now that would be going beyond the call of duty, sweetheart.' He stifled a snigger. 'But I'd sure love to see the tape. Now gotta go. Good on ya for trying though, kid.'

Kate watched helplessly as Pratt waltzed over to the COS area where Ripley and Tubby were packing up for the day. His arrival was followed a few minutes later by great howls of laughter. Pratt had presumably passed on Kate's offer to work undercover. Her face burned as she snatched her briefcase from her desk and marched out the door.

'Wait up,' Gillian called, chasing her friend down the corridor. Kate often wondered how a girl twice her own size could move so quickly and gracefully in such expensive high heels. 'If you really believe in this story then you can't just let them trample right over you. You have to go to Mawson.'

Kate shook her head. 'Mawson made it very clear a long time ago that I wasn't to go running to him every time I wanted something. And even if I did, Ripley would hit the bloody roof.'

'Don't worry about Ripley. He can't treat you any worse than he does already. And I reckon Mawson will go for it. The trick is to approach him like you're asking for his advice. If he thinks you're trying to tiptoe around Ripley, he'll blow you off. But play it right and he'll treat the story like a pet project.'

The next morning Kate arrived at work early again. She checked Mawson's parking spot. Good. He wasn't in yet. Ignoring the curious glances of the women in reception, Kate set herself up in one of the deep and comfortable chairs positioned around the entrance foyer and started scribbling notes.

A half hour later Mawson barrelled through the doors, his shirt already separated from his jeans.

'Kate, how are you going?' Just as she had hoped, Mawson was too good a manager to bowl straight past her without exchanging a few words. 'What are you up to?'

Kate pretended to be flustered, as she collected her notes and stuffed them into her briefcase. 'I've got this story I think is really good. I'm just practising my spiel to Ripley. I tried yesterday but I didn't sell it very well. So I thought I'd have another go.'

'What is it exactly?' Mawson asked, scratching his stubble. 'Why don't you try selling it to me instead?'

Kate wasn't sure whether Mawson had fallen for her ruse or whether he'd just decided to reward her ingenuity. Whatever the case, the next night she found herself on her very first stakeout, much to the annoyance of the newsroom boys' club. Tezza had been assigned to the job. He pointed the car away from the brothel and filmed in the rear-view mirror, rolling on everyone who walked in.

'We could retire right now on the hush money we could earn from this job.' He laughed. 'That last client was a big soapie star.'

Judges. Actors. Corporate high-flyers. As Kate commented between gritted teeth, you never could find a policeman when you wanted one. But then at 1.20 a.m. on the third night, Mickey Morgan finally appeared. Tezza's shot held for twenty-five glorious seconds. Morgan had even been so accommodating as to stand under a street lamp while he lit a cigarette. There was no doubt as to the identity of the hulking figure on Tezza's tape. It wasn't enough for a story on its own. But it was a promising start. Now it was Kate's turn.

From her daily phone calls with Irene, Kate knew that Morgan had been asking about the new girl. Obsessively. The man wanted to screw her every bit as badly as she wanted to screw him.

The plan was simple. Kate would play the role of fresh meat, as Morgan had so charmingly described her. Irene would arrange a rendezvous. And Kate would try to trick the old bastard into incriminating himself on a tape recorder hidden under the side-board table.

The scheme had made perfect sense when she'd outlined it to Mawson two weeks earlier. (Of course he'd presumed that it would be one of Irene's girls who would act as the bait, not his fresh-faced junior reporter.) Now that the big moment had arrived and Kate was standing face to face with a large and very horny policeman, the whole enterprise didn't seem so very smart after all.

'You have beautiful tits, my sweet.' Mickey Morgan's shirt was

87

unbuttoned to the top of his expansive beer belly, revealing tufts of white hair. 'Come and give me a nibble.'

Seemingly that counted for pleasantries in Irene's line of business because Morgan lurched towards her, hands outstretched.

Somehow Kate managed a neat little sidestep that seemed coincidental rather than evasive.

'Let me get to know you a little first, Mr Big Policeman.' To Kate's ears, her reply sounded like something out of a straight-to-video movie. But Morgan didn't seem even slightly suspicious. He was too busy staring at her chest. Not that there was much to see.

Kate was wearing a floor-length red silk dressing-gown. The only visible bits of her body were her toes and her hands. But she still felt exposed. It was the intent of what she was wearing not the volume of material.

She traced a finger along one silk-clad leg. She felt more silly than seductive but the ploy seemed to work. Morgan was virtually salivating.

'What would you like to know about the great Mickey Morgan?' he asked, rubbing himself through his pants.

There was the first tick. She had Morgan identifying himself on tape. So far, so good – as long as the bloody machine was still recording.

Kate kept up the prick tease. This was an area where she did have some experience, as poor Matthew could attest. 'I love a powerful man. And the girls here say you're the best.'

'Well, honey, they ought to know. I've rogered them all. You just get over here and sit on this and I'll show you.'

'Money on the table first, big fella.'

Morgan's face turned from pink to red to a dark purple, with the sudden violence of a tropical storm. Kate thought he was going to explode. Or hit her. Hard.

But the moment passed. Kate let out the breath she hadn't even realised she was holding.

Morgan was smiling again, if his lecherous leer could truly be described as such. 'I'm going to give you a little consideration seeing as you're new, sweetheart. But Big Mickey doesn't pay. It's part of the price of running this joint.'

Jackpot. She had what she needed. Kate doubled over. 'Oh. Oh.' She wailed.

'What the fuck? What's going on?' Morgan demanded.

'I'm so sorry. I had a bout of gastro today. I thought I was over it.'

'Jesus Christ, girl!'

Irene timed her entrance to perfection. She must have had her ear to the door the whole time.

'What's going on, Mickey? You hurting one of my girls again?' she asked sternly.

'I told you don't fuck with me, Irene. I can break you, bitch. Now get me a girl who's not going to crap on me,' he demanded.

'Come this way. You can have the New Orleans suite. Chelsea is free.' Irene hoped he wouldn't be too rough on the girl.

The moment Morgan left the room, Kate scrambled over to the side table where she had hidden her little tape machine. Still recording. Thank God for that. She dared not check the cassette just yet. This wouldn't be over until she was safely home.

She hurriedly discarded the dressing-gown, draping it across the enormous king-sized bed. Underneath, she was wearing a pair of pedal pushers and a Disney singlet top. The outfit was nothing like what Morgan had been imagining.

Kate then quickly stuffed the recorder into her back pocket, grabbed her coat and scampered out the door. All she needed was an interview with Irene tomorrow and she had the story of the year.

She hoped Irene wouldn't be too disappointed when she discovered that it was Kate and not Pratt who was the reporter on the story. But they'd established something approaching a friendship over the past couple of weeks. In fact, Kate suspected the wily old madam would actually approve.

Once the story was committed to tape, everyone in the newsroom conveniently forgot they'd ever questioned Kate's news judgement. Even Ripley seemed excited.

Still, it was a tense three days preparing the story. The station lawyers had insisted on several agonising script changes before they had reluctantly cleared the piece. Then at 4 p.m. on the day of broadcast, just two hours before Kate's big expose was due to go to air, the network was hit with an injunction.

While the entire newsroom sweated, lawyers for the network and for Morgan argued their cases in front of a judge. With just fifteen minutes to air time, the story was still on hold. The entire newsroom was hanging on a single phone call. Carter's hotline rang at 5.54 p.m.

'Carter,' he barked into the receiver. Then his thumb went up.

'You fucking beauty. We're up!' Ripley shouted across the room.

Carter slumped back in his seat, relieved he wouldn't have to fall back on the alternative rundown. On days like this, producers prepared two separate bulletins. The contingency plan needed its own set of scripts. It meant twice the work. It also meant disappointing hundreds of thousands of viewers. The Mickey Morgan story had been promoted all through the previous night and that day both on radio and television. People all around the state were switching on their sets, expecting to see it.

Even Mawson was in the newsroom to watch the story go to air. Kate sat beaming on Carter's right, revelling in the new seating arrangements. The office dynamics had certainly changed. Geoff Jones was now four whole places away. And Kate was delighted to note that Matthew had edged a little closer to the centre of power, sitting alongside Beige.

'Kate Corish Channel Eight News,' came the familiar sign-off and the newsroom erupted in applause. Even Mawson was clapping.

Matthew walked over and gave her shoulder a little squeeze. 'You're a star, Kate, or you will be,' he whispered into her ear. The way he said it, she almost believed it was true.

She looked over at Carter, her eyes asking the question. He gave her an approving half-nod of acknowledgement. And he did it without staring at her chest or scratching his testicles. Kate was almost proud of him.

Soon everyone was crowding around and offering congratulations. Even Ripley joined the chorus.

'Katie, you've humbled me. I'm now your biggest fan. Way to go, kid,' he said within earshot of Mawson, who smiled approvingly.

Wow, Kate thought. I've finally broken through to him. She was surprised to note that it actually felt good to have his approval at last. Maybe they could even put their rocky start behind them.

Ripley plodded back over to the COS booth, and leaned over to a brooding Andy Pratt. 'Should've been your yarn, mate. I'd have made that call. She went over my head to Mawson.'

'Ambitious little slut,' Pratt muttered.

The little police reporter was fuming for two entirely contradictory reasons. Firstly, this was a police story and he was supposed to be the police reporter. So by rights, it was his yarn. And secondly, Corish had made the police look bad. Now, it would be that much harder for him to work his contacts. Stupid bitch.

'She'd sell her grandmother for fame that one. Just watch her.'

Ripley dragged on his cigarette, watching his carefully chosen words torment and darken Andy's features. It wouldn't take much for the guy to blow.

The spark came ten days later. A prime suspect had been arrested over the disappearance and presumed death of a little girl a decade earlier. Ripley needed two packages. One would be a background piece. The other would cover the police operation.

The two reporters would be dancing around each other all day. And if you're out to make a little mischief, who better to assign to the gig than police roundsman Andy Pratt and Channel Eight's new 'it' girl Kate Corish?

The morning passed uneventfully enough but Ripley had conspired to send both reporters to a police press conference that afternoon. The entire Sydney media pack was there, assembled outside the house where the young girl once lived. Radio. Newspapers. All the television networks.

Kate had just emerged from the crew car when she heard Andy Pratt screaming at her from a way down the street. He was bearing down fast.

'What the fuck are you doing here? What the fuck?' Pratt was red in the face and coming at her like a Rottweiler.

'Andy, we work for the same network. Cool down,' Kate said calmly.

The press conference hadn't started yet. So the ruckus was attracting the attention of every journalist in the city. Cameras swung around to commit Andy and Kate's altercation to tape. For the opposition networks, this was gold.

'I don't give a fuck. You get your scrawny arse out of my face. This is my yarn. My yarn. Why don't ya go back and answer my fucking phone and pinch more of my fucking stories, you slut?'

Andy was short and compact, like a bantamweight boxer. And he moved like he was in the ring as well, hopping lightly from one foot to the other. For a moment, Kate thought the little man was actually going to take a swing at her.

'Don't you dare speak to me like that.' Kate was embarrassed by all the attention. But she wasn't going to just stand there and take Pratt's abuse.

'No, you fucking get out of here. I got it covered, all right? And you fuck off too.' With that Pratt gave Kate's cameraman an almighty shove, sending him and tens of thousands of dollars worth of camera equipment lurching into the gutter.

The bloke had lost it. He was mad. Crackers. Absolutely stark bloody bonkers. A gracious withdrawal seemed the only sensible option. The alternative was fisticuffs and a likely trip to casualty. Kate would worry about missing the press conference later.

That night, every television station ran footage of the Channel Eight confrontation. It wasn't exactly a newsworthy event. But the commercial networks never missed an opportunity to present their rivals in a less than favourable light. 'The case sent tempers flaring over at Channel Eight,' reporters stated solemnly. Only their eyes betrayed their mirth.

Kate was just pouring herself a particularly well-earned scotch when the phone rang.

'Oh. Hi, Mum,' she said, dreading the direction she knew the conversation was going to take.

'I just heard my daughter being called a "slut" on national television.' Kate could hear the brittleness in her mother's voice.

'Don't worry about it, Mum. The bloke doesn't like me. What can I say? Anyway, didn't they beep that bit out?'

'It wasn't exactly hard to lip-read, Kate. I warned you the other day that if you dressed like a hooker, you'd be labelled one.'

'Mum, I was working undercover.'

'I don't care what you think you were doing. Appearance is everything. I can't believe I spent all that money sending you to that school.'

'Mum, please. I got the bad guy. That has to count for something. Anyway, I'm a journalist, remember? Not a hooker. Now I've gotta go. Bye.'

And with that Kate hung up, grabbed her bottle of Dimples and switched over to Nine to watch Murphy Brown.

A little after ten the next morning, Mawson stuck his head in the newsroom. 'Pratt,' he boomed. 'My office. Now.'

Mawson was adept at handling his stars. A little massage of the ego here. A firm kick in the pants there. Pratt was in for the latter.

'How's that huge, fragile fucker of an ego of yours, Pratt?' Mawson swung back on his chair and lit a cigarette.

'Oh, mate. She pinched my fucking yarn. My fucking yarn. I've been doing police rounds for twenty years. What right does she have to just take my round?' He was spluttering like a two-year-old.

'And for that you carry on like a complete fuckwit in front of the damned press pack, embarrassing the entire bloody network!'

'She answered my phone. The story was meant for me.' Pratt was pacing the room, clenching and unclenching his fists with fury.

'Andy, it was never your yarn. It could never have been your yarn. You don't have the legs for it. And frankly, I doubt Morgan would want a head job from you, even if it was free. Anyway the hours the kid put in would've interfered with your drinking time. Right?'

Mawson was baiting him. Andy Pratt's temper was becoming a liability. If the prick wanted to resign in a huff, Mawson would accept his resignation and gladly.

'The kid played a blinder. You gotta admit it – talent and ticker.'

'Fuck! There doesn't seem to be much respect for my level of expertise. Maybe I should make some calls to Nine. You know they tried to poach me last year. I've always been loyal to Eight. But here's the question. Who's loyal to me? Twenty years of contacts. Twenty years of hard yards. Twenty years of breaking stories. Twenty fucking years of loyalty.'

Mawson didn't bother to respond. A long and compulsory holiday was in order. But he'd have a little more fun first. He picked a spot in the centre of Pratt's forehead and stared.

'What? What are you looking at?'

'You've got a booger hanging out of your nose.' Mawson said with mock disgust. 'Get outta my office.'

Pratt turned on his heels and left, ego stuffed firmly back in its box.

SEVEN

The step class was well into its warm-up routine when Kate dashed into the studio, her face already shiny and red from running the usually convenient five hundred metres from the office to the gym.

'Sorry,' she mouthed to the instructor for the third time in the space of a week. A flick of Bali-braided hair let Kate know that she was *not* excused.

The woman ran a schedule every bit as tight as her fuchsia-encased buns. The class started right on the dot of 6.30. And if Kate had a late edit, which happened most nights, she ended up arriving well after Young MC had started busting his moves.

Tonight, she'd been delayed by the Royals. Princess Anne and Mark Phillips had announced their separation and although the network's London bureau had provided a perfectly adequate package on the subject, Carter belatedly decided the bulletin needed a local angle. So Kate was sent out to gauge public reaction to the split. Vox pops was the industry term for it.

That was the funny thing about the news business, Kate mused. One minute you were cracking a major police corruption story, the next you were asking women with purple hair what they thought about a marriage bust-up on the other side of the world.

Kate commandeered the last remaining step and skirted around the class, doing her best to dodge the arms and legs now flailing wildly to Janet Jackson. To her great consternation and almost certain humiliation, the very last square metre of floor space available was right up the front. Kate preferred to cower at the back of the room, where her complete lack of coordination and her bum weren't quite as noticeable. She liked to think that her black tights minimised her curves somewhat. Unfortunately, the mirror just a metre from her nose suggested otherwise.

As the music pumped, Kate dragged her hair into a shaving brush of a ponytail and started moving, trying to forget where she was and more particularly where she was supposed to be.

Tonight, most of her colleagues were on their way to the big shindig where the nominations for this year's Walkleys were going to be announced. Next to actually winning an award, there was no greater accolade in Australian journalism.

Kate's name had been mentioned as a possible nominee for her Mickey Morgan piece. She'd stayed on the story like a Rottweiler and even forced a Royal Commission. But she was also twenty-two years old with nothing else of note on her resume. It was a long shot. In fact, Kate judged her chances of receiving a Walkley nomination about as high as getting through this step class as per the intended choreography.

Hopeless. Kate was already a good beat and a half out of step before the first song had even reached its chorus. Flustered, she tried to untangle her legs but ended up stepping on the laces of her high-topped Reeboks instead. The next thing she knew she was sitting on her bum, legs splayed, with the G-string of her electric blue leotard riding much higher than nature intended.

Kate's cheeks (the ones above her neck) were still burning as she stomped up the stairs to her apartment twenty minutes later.

The telephone started ringing just as she negotiated the last couple of steps. She made a desperate lunge for the receiver, tripping over a whining Bernie in the process.

'Hey, Gillian, how are you? Long time no see. What's it been – two hours?' Kate was surprised to hear her friend's voice. Normally only her mother exhibited such exquisitely bad timing.

She tried to concentrate on what Gillian was saying but suspicious noises were issuing from the other side of the couch. Bernie was sharpening his claws on her new kilim. Not that Kate was particularly surprised. She knew from experience that Bernie didn't respond well when she failed to pat and feed him as a homecoming priority. Next time she'd let the answering machine pick up.

Gillian was blissfully unaware of the damage being wrought by idle claws. 'Last chance, Kate. I can't believe you aren't coming tonight. You're a big chance of getting nominated after all.'

'And miss *21 Jump Street*? You can't be serious,' Kate protested. It would take a lot more than wishful thinking to drag her away from Johnny Depp.

'*You* can't be serious. Aren't you a bit too old for that crap? Oh, hang on. You're not that long out of your teens, are you?' Gillian was only five years older than Kate but sometimes it seemed like a generation. 'Well, why don't you come for a drink afterwards? The Taxi Club's just down the road from you.'

'Gillian, I'm sweaty. I'm still in my gym clothes. I'm hanging out for a shower and a scotch. Plus I've got to feed the cat before he tears the place apart. Now if I don't get off the phone, I will miss my date with Officer Tom Hanson.'

Kate hung up and disengaged cat from kilim.

'Okay, Bernie. Let's get you something to eat.' She snipped open a foil pouch of 'kitty gourmet dinner'. The meal that glided out onto the saucer looked surprisingly like the Sunday roast promised on the packet. At a dollar fifty a pop, gourmet cat food was a ridiculous extravagance. But at least someone in the house was eating properly, Kate thought, as she emptied a packet of corn chips into a white plastic bowl. With standard twelve-hour work days and obsessive gym visits, she lacked the energy for most things extracurricular, including cooking.

Right on cue, her mother rang.

'What are you doing about dinner?' Dianne Corish demanded to know. Kate's nutritional and culinary shortcomings had recently become her mother's pet topic.

'I haven't thought about it yet,' Kate lied, guiltily cradling the bowl of corn chips.

'I didn't bring you up healthy and strong only to have you throw it all out the window the moment you left home. You're wasting away.'

'Mum, I'm just under ten stone. That does not constitute wasting away.'

Kate waited. Her conversations with her mother always followed the same script. And about now, Dianne liked to play what she clearly believed was her trump card.

'You might not believe it, Kate, but one day you will have a family. And your husband and children will expect a little more for dinner than microwaved pizza.'

Kate still didn't have a comeback for that one. Instead she promised to make the trek across the Bridge for dinner on the weekend.

She pushed her mother's voice out of her head and another corn chip into her mouth and settled in for a lazy night in front of the television.

The theme music for *Graham Kennedy's Coast to Coast* was just starting to play when the phone rang again. This time she let the machine answer. It would just be Gillian again, probably half tanked by now and missing her preferred drinking partner.

'Kate, it's Matt. You're up! You've done it! You've been nominated for best investigative news feature!' Matthew was shrieking down the phone, trying to hear himself over the din in the background. 'Kate, are you there? Can you hear me?'

Kate dived for the phone. 'You are kidding, aren't you? You'd better not be winding me up, Matthew Keaton.'

'No joke, I swear. Throw some clothes on and get down to the Cauldron. We're kicking on.'

'I don't believe it,' Kate cried. 'I don't bloody believe it.' The word 'nominated' kept repeating itself over and over in her head.

'I can't hear you. But you'd better be there. I'm buying you a drink, or ten. Gillian's on my case too. She says get down here. Now.' With that Matthew hung up.

'Holy shit, Bernie.' Kate lifted the cat to eye level and gave him a big smooch on the nose. 'You're going to have to hold the fort without me. I'm off to celebrate!'

It took ten minutes of determined rummaging through the clothes on her bedroom floor to find her favourite outfit. Jag jeans, sheer floral shirt and maillot style singlet top. Kate wondered about taking her vintage leather jacket but figured she'd be drinking enough scotch to keep herself warm.

Matt was waiting at the club entrance when she arrived, flirting with the emaciated blonde whose job it was to guard the door of the trendiest nightspot in town.

He waved at Kate and leaned a little closer to the woman, favouring her with one of his rakish, and ever so slightly lopsided, smiles. He'd used it on Kate over the years and it had almost worked a couple of times.

'Kate's with us. She's on TV,' Matt confided. Kate started

blushing furiously. 'She's just been nominated for a Walkley, you know. But you've probably seen her reports.'

The woman lent forward with the stamp, pressing it firmly into Kate's inside wrist.

Kate was far from a household name. But people were starting to recognise her, even if only a very few figured out why she looked so familiar. 'I know you from somewhere but I can't put my finger on it' was the usual baffled comment.

Still a vaguely familiar face and a Walkley nomination had just earned Kate entree into the hottest club in town. Being on TV was certainly something special. She hadn't even had to shell out for the cover charge.

Or for any drinks . . . which didn't seem such a great perk a few hours later when she was creeping into the office with a head the size of Jupiter.

'Well done, kid,' Mawson said, breaking from his conversation with Carter and Ripley to shake her hand. Kate wondered for a moment if he was referring to her Walkley nomination or the fact she'd managed to drag herself into work on time.

'Yeah. Way to go, Katie,' Ripley added. 'Getting nominated, mate – it's a bloody marvel. But don't get your hopes up. It's been a big year. Tiananmen Square. Exxon Valdez. Bondy. But well done all the same.'

Kate suspected she'd just been insulted. But she was packing way too many Panadol to attempt a comeback. Strange how the same comment from Mawson would have sounded like kindly advice.

Still, she knew Ripley was right. It had been a monster year for news. And Walkley Awards had eluded the best and brightest in the business. Sandra had never won one. Nor had Jana.

Her Morgan exposé was no Tiananmen Square. And she was no

Jonathan McTavish. Ever the loyal friend, Gillian had tried to talk up her chances. But Kate was happy enough just to be going to the party. By the time the Walkleys rolled around six weeks later, she had almost forgotten she was even up for an award. Almost.

Kate had set aside a half hour to get ready. A late edit combined with a breakdown on the Bridge had robbed her of more than half her allotted time. At least, she'd managed to get to the hairdresser the previous day. So it was just a matter of quickly applying some make-up and pouring herself into her dress.

'Bernie, get off that. Bad, bad cat!' Bernstein had jumped up on the bed and was circling on top of her new frock. She grabbed him just as he shifted into kneading mode. The dress lifted off the bed at the end of a single unfurled claw.

Bernstein was not the kind of cat to meekly accept abandonment. He'd devised all kinds of techniques to get his point across. There had been a particularly ugly period when Kate had woken each morning to find a puddle of urine next to her briefcase. Newspaper shredding was another favourite.

And he was not about to let up on his campaign of sabotage just because Kate had been nominated for a Walkley. As far as Bernstein was concerned, it was just another impediment standing between him and quality time with his care giver.

Kate carefully disengaged cat from fabric and held the strapless chintz gown out in front of her. Strands of grey fur hung off the back bustle. Damn that cat.

The dress was a knock-off of the Catherine Walker number Lady Diana had worn in Melbourne the previous year. This might have been the biggest night of Kate's life but her pay cheque – $30,000 a year – barely covered the rent and petrol for the car. A designer frock was out of the question.

At least she was wearing something new though.

The Princess of Wales had danced with Charles wearing the original. Kate had fared rather better than Diana in the handbag stakes. She was walking out tonight with the handsome Matthew Keaton.

She wriggled into the dress. It was tight. Almost too tight. Thank God she'd had the foresight to put herself on the grapefruit diet at the start of the week. Even so, her curves were spilling out every which way.

She checked herself in the mirror. She could lose a couple of kilos. But besides that, not too bad. Even if the look was less Princess of Hearts and more Kathleen Turner in *Body Heat*.

Outside, a cab beeped its horn. Kate raced around her tiny apartment shoving supplies into her evening bag. Perfume. Cigarettes. Lighter. Lipstick. Panadol. That would have to do she thought as she negotiated the narrow flight of steps down to the street.

'You look great, Kate. Fantastic dress.' Mathew was standing next to the taxi, looking impossibly gorgeous with his trademark grin and dinner suit.

Condoms! That's what she'd forgotten.

No, Kate reminded herself, as she had done on plenty of previous occasions. She was absolutely not going to sleep with Matthew. She wasn't about to trade a great friendship for the sake of wanton curiosity. Anyway, the idea of being just another of Matthew's many conquests rankled.

As the taxi weaved through the city traffic, Kate closed her eyes and reached for Matt's hand. She'd been nominated for a Walkley. And now that the big night was here, she wasn't sure whether she was thrilled or terrified. She certainly felt overwhelmed, and not a little intimidated as she walked through the enormous doors of the five-star hotel.

The auditorium was a who's who of Australian journalism. Paul Barry was there. Chris Masters. The usual king hitters. Channel Nine's star table was dazzling as ever. Jana. Ray. Mike.

She must have looked like a startled rabbit because Matthew leaned down and whispered in her ear, 'Kate, you're not a rookie any more. You belong here. You really belong here.'

The best Kate could manage was a tight, nervous smile.

'Thanks. But right now I'm feeling like a bit of a fraud.' The skin around her neck prickled uncomfortably. She knew the rash would start its assault on her cheeks in a matter of minutes.

'Sorry, Matt. I just have to go to the ladies.' She excused herself. A few moments in the cool of a bathroom, a splash of water and some well-placed concealer would be sufficient to avert the crisis.

As Kate attended to her blotches at one of the marble hand basins, a discussion started up between the occupants of the two farthest cubicles.

'First the host dispensed with his underwear. Now our esteemed executive producer has decided he should free bag as well.'

'Do they wear the same suits again the next day? That's just gross.'

'Well, the Billboard probably doesn't. But I reckon the boss is wearing the same trousers from one day to the next. And they're always just a little too tight.'

'That's disgusting. And I don't even want to know how you came across this information.'

'Relax. He told me himself. Apparently, it's better for his manhood.'

'Oh, please.'

Kate immediately committed the conversation to memory. Gillian would love that titbit of gossip. Not to mention Ben and Al.

The bar proved a similarly rewarding location for a little casual eavesdropping. Although Kate wished Matthew would just hurry back with the drinks. She didn't like being alone in a crowd at the best of times. Standing by herself at the Walkleys like some Neville Nobody was absolutely mortifying. She lit a cigarette to create the illusion she was gainfully occupied.

'He didn't deserve that Walkley last year,' a barrel-chested man snarled an arm's length from where Kate was positioned. His allegiances and prejudices quickly identified him as a print journo. 'Really, he pinched the lot from the newspapers. There wasn't a single fact in his so-called 'investigation' that hadn't already been plastered all over our front pages. Our articles were just fucking research briefs for him.'

'Bloody TV types. Half of them haven't even done a cadetship,' added a thin, bespectacled and much younger man.

'Fucking show ponies the lot of them.' The fat man's voice trailed off as he spotted Kate staring at him.

'Hello, love. You right for a drink?'

'I'm fine, thank you,' Kate said, feeling awkward given the conversation she had just overheard.

'So what's a lovely young lady like you doing at the Walkleys anyway?'

His thin friend peered over the top of his spectacles.

'I've been nominated for best investigative news report,' Kate said, standing up a little straighter.

'Oh yeah? Which paper do you write for, love?'

'Oh, I don't. I'm just a show pony,' Kate said, unable to control her tongue.

'Hey, Kate. Here's your champers,' Matthew called.

'If you'll excuse me.' She grabbed Matthew's arm and steered him away from the line of fire.

'What was that about?'

'Oh, those two were just bitching about TV reporters. Writing us all off as grandstanders.'

'You can hardly blame them. There are plenty of overpaid Jennis in our business. Little wonder they resent us. Maybe now you can see why journalism's night of nights so often ends in fisticuffs. Or so I've been told.' Matt laughed. 'Now let's find our seats before you start the first skirmish of the evening.'

Kate could barely breathe as she sat at the main Channel Eight table and heard her name read out as a Walkley Award nominee.

The presenter was Simon Gilchrist, the executive producer of some serious current affairs offering on the ABC. He was also a man overly fond of the dramatic pause.

Kate waited for what felt like minutes. By the time Gilchrist finally cleared his throat and made the announcement, she was feeling mightily ticked off.

'And the winner for best investigative news story is . . . Kate Corish, for the Mickey Morgan exposé.'

Holy shit, Kate muttered under her breath as she floated up to the podium. It was her last coherent thought of the evening.

She woke up the next morning to a slight hangover and the unfamiliar sensation of another body in the bed with her. The air was heavy with the scent of sex. She turned her head. Matthew Keaton lay beside her still deep in sleep.

So they'd finally done it. Obviously the Walkley had proved quite the aphrodisiac for both of them. Please tell me I used a condom, Kate thought.

Looking around the room, Kate glimpsed the little pyramid-shaped trophy propped up by the clock radio. Bloody hell, she thought. I deserved a little loving for that.

She got out of bed carefully, trying not to wake Matthew, and rummaged through his drawers for a T-shirt and some pants. No way was she catching a cab home in her ball gown.

Wardrobe sorted, she sneaked out the door. She'd have to face Matt at work in a few hours time. But she was happy to delay the inevitable for as long as possible. The whole night was a blur. But Kate had the strong feeling that the reality of their tryst had not lived up to long-held expectations.

Her only consolation was that no one else knew what had happened. She couldn't see any reason why it shouldn't stay that way either. Or at least that's what she told herself as she sneaked into work a few minutes after nine o'clock.

Matt was already there when she walked through the door, a case of beer resting against his desk.

'What did you do?' Kate sniped. 'Call all your mates the moment I left this morning?'

'I didn't tell anyone. I swear.' Matthew looked hurt. 'You don't remember?'

Suddenly Kate had a flashback to the scene at the hotel cab rank earlier that morning. 'I'm taking him home to fuck his brains out,' she had announced to the various media types waiting for a ride home.

'Oh Christ! I completely forgot. What was I thinking?'

'Look, you weren't alone. I was so drunk I was anyone's.'

'Gosh, thanks for that. You sure make a girl feel special.' Kate started laughing.

'Sorry. Want a hair of the dog after work?' Matt said, tapping the case of beer. 'We both earned this after all.'

'What? You want to debrief our new awkward coexistence?'

'Got a better idea?'

'You're on. Might as well keep them talking,' Kate said. 'By the way, it was . . . ' She struggled to find a polite way to finish the sentence.

'Awful. I know. Sometimes fantasies should stay that way.'

Relieved, Kate headed over to her desk to commence her first day's work as a Walkley Award-winning journalist.

Her new status didn't seem to register with any of her colleagues though. At least, not in any positive way. Ripley was even snappier and more dismissive than usual. And Carter yelled at her for being five minutes late with her edit.

'No room for fucking prima donnas here,' he roared as she tried to explain what had happened.

It seemed everyone had made it their personal mission to take her down a peg or two.

Only Gillian congratulated her sincerely.

'I know they're being tough on you. But take it as a compliment,' she went on. 'They actually think they're doing you a favour in their strange and twisted way.'

'How could treating me like dog shit possibly be in my best interests?' Kate hadn't expected a standing ovation. But she did think a few pats on the back were in order.

'It's happened before. Journo wins Walkley. Journo gets a big head. Journo stops being a team player. And journo's ego needs a separate car space.'

'Shit. That's just great. And I thought my career prospects were about to get a whole lot better.'

'Don't worry. Everything's going to change. Maybe not this week or this year. But mark my words. You're going to be a star.'

EIGHT

Mr Beige tilted his face towards the studio lights and closed his eyes. The make-up artist read her cue and dashed over to the news desk to powder the great man's nose. A small steel comb was tucked into her top pocket. She wouldn't need it on this job. It had been years since Beige's thinning locks required any special attention or taming. Nowadays, his hair had the stitched-on look of a Ken doll.

The newsreader checked his watch. Two minutes to go. He adjusted his tie and cleared his throat before embarking on a series of yoga-like moves aimed at exercising his jaw and loosening his facial muscles.

Kate watched from her desk in the newsroom. She had always found Beige's pre-broadcast ritual fascinating. Before the red 'on air' button flashed, Beige would demonstrate a full range of emotions. Smiling. Puckering. Frowning. Surprised. But every second he was on screen, he kept his face absolutely expressionless. It was a mystery.

'In ten, nine, eight, seven, six, five . . . ' The camera operator counted down to the newsflash, using his fingers to signal the last few seconds. Then he pointed to Beige, the studio communication for 'you're on'.

'We interrupt this program to bring you breaking news. Iraq has invaded its oil export neighbour Kuwait today in a swift and decisive military operation. There are fears for the safety of three hundred passengers on board a British Airways flight stranded on the tarmac at Kuwait City airport at the time of the invasion. Early reports say Iraqi soldiers have taken the passengers hostage. We'll bring you more details in updates throughout the day.'

'This will turn into war if Saddam doesn't pull out soon,' Carter commented to Mawson. The two men were leaning against Andy Pratt's old desk, arms folded, soaking up the atmosphere. There was nothing quite like the buzz of a newsroom when a big story broke.

'Let's hope Australia gets involved. It'll be good for ratings,' Carter added.

'Always the company man.' Mawson slapped his news director on the back.

'If you're sending a team, I'd love to go.'

Mawson and Carter swung around to look at Kate. From their doubtful expressions, she knew her suggestion hadn't exactly set their worlds on fire. She hurried on.

'Saddam has a million battle-hardened troops, compliments of the Iran–Iraq war. He has seven hundred combat aircraft, six thousand tanks and the most sophisticated chemical weaponry in the Middle East. And it's tried and tested. Remember Halabja two years ago. Five thousand dead. Ten thousand wounded.'

Kate rattled off the statistics with a fluency that astonished both men. She even surprised herself. She'd only started swotting up on the subject fairly recently. If the world was going to war, she wanted to tag along. And that meant convincing her superiors that she was up to the job.

Carter smiled and shook his head. He'd learned to respect

Kate during her three years in his newsroom. She was smart and hardworking. He enjoyed the kudos associated with having the youngest-ever Walkley winner on his staff. It confirmed him as a first-rate journalistic mentor. But sending a young woman to cover a war? Well, that was altogether different.

'Dream on, Katie,' he replied, one bony paw heading crotchwards. 'How would you go reporting in a top-to-toe tent anyway?'

'I take it you're referring to the hijab, Reg? We're not talking Iran or Saudi Arabia. Iraq's a secular country. The Ba'ath Party are Sunni Muslims. Plenty of Iraqi women don't cover up. Saddam's wife is one of them.'

Kate accompanied her lesson in comparative religion with a dazzling smile. If she was going to contradict a male superior, she knew she had to flirt a little as well. It was all about keeping their egos fed. Although she drew the line at playing up to Ripley.

Mawson laughed as his second-in-command was put in his place. Reg Carter was a bloody good operator. But he'd always been a 'backyard news' man. He believed Australians only wanted to know what was happening in their own little world. Overseas stories generally didn't interest him and occasionally his prejudice showed.

But apathy towards international affairs was not a particular disadvantage in Carter's line of work. He was an iron-fisted manager and a very successful one. He and Mawson actually made a pretty good team with Mawson possessing enough big-picture view for both of them. And right now he was imagining Kate in a flak jacket.

An attractive girl in a war zone, Mawson thought. Part of Jana's early appeal over at *60 Minutes* had been that she was young and pretty. There was something strangely compelling about that combination in a dangerous place.

'Let's see how this develops. Early days yet. Early days.' Mawson walked off, still chuckling.

Kate let out a frustrated sigh. Just over a year had passed since she'd won her Walkley Award. And while her professional life had certainly improved, she wasn't yet the big network star Gillian had predicted.

Nowadays, the lightweight yarns were assigned to other junior reporters. So Kate was able to tackle more substantial issues. But the stories were still strictly local. Nothing in her working life went anywhere close to Jonathan McTavish's heroics at Tiananmen Square or Sandra Cook's Idi Amin interview.

Still, bit by bit, her professional profile was rising.

A couple of months back she'd even been invited to speak at the 'Successful Women in Business' brunch – a bi-annual networking event for women making their way in the corporate world.

'Congratulations on your Walkley, Kate,' Sandra Cook's mellow broadcast voice had purred over the phone. 'Nice work.'

Kate hadn't replied. She was too overwhelmed that her one-time career idol had actually called her. Sandra misread the silence.

'Look, I gave you a hard time when I first met you and I'm sorry. It wasn't one of my better nights. But what I'm ringing about is this. I'd like you to be one of the speakers at the next SWIB brunch.'

Only women would consider holding a networking function outside drinking hours, Kate thought, as she desperately tried to think of a way to politely decline. The prospect of speaking in front of a roomful of brunching women terrified her.

'I'm not sure what I could possibly say, Sandra. I can't even balance my cheque book,' she stalled.

'It doesn't matter. You're a journalist. Tell an interesting story.'

Sandra's move to magazines clearly hadn't blunted her powers of persuasion as three weeks later Kate found herself nervously addressing a few hundred powerfully dressed and mostly older women.

The auditorium was set up like a lecture theatre, with chairs ringed around the speaker's podium twenty deep. There were small writing tables attached to the seats where the women dutifully placed their pagers. Kate was horrified to discover that some of the SWIBs were actually taking notes.

Without any dramatic third-world experiences to draw upon, the only really interesting story Kate had was her encounter with Mickey Morgan. She was surprised to find her audience was fascinated by the story. Their interest took the edge off her nerves and kept her heat rash quarantined to her neck.

'And as I stood in a red satin dressing-gown, looking at this, er, gentleman fondling himself I was wondering whether I could pull it off.'

Laughter rippled through the room.

'Pun very much not intended. Sorry. But I guess the point I'd like to make is that if you really believe in what you are doing, you can't help but succeed.'

Her final words received warm applause. She wasn't absolutely sure whether what she said was true or not. But if it was, she certainly deserved a ticket to the Middle East.

Kate returned her attention to the incoming feed from INN. Jonathan McTavish was already on the ground in Kuwait. She watched his report closely, storing away scraps of information. The Englishman seemed to know his stuff. He was also bloody good looking. Like a roughed-up Pierce Brosnan. And Kate had always been a bit of a Remington Steele fan.

For the next five months, Kate watched as McTavish and the usual band of British and American correspondents crisscrossed the Middle East filing their reports. The United Nations had imposed a trade embargo. A multi-nation task force had assembled in the Persian Gulf. Saddam was holding hundreds of foreigners hostage.

Come the New Year, hostilities seemed inevitable. And barring some uncustomary display of good judgment from the Iraqi leader, Kate was off to cover her first war.

The briefing was held in Mawson's office. Carter was there. So was Geoff Jones. Kate could barely breathe.

'Our man in London will look after events in Kuwait. Jones, I want you in Baghdad. Kate, you'll be covering Tel Aviv. Saddam Hussein will almost certainly attempt a strike on Israel. So we're going to need someone on the ground there. Any questions?'

Kate shook her head.

'Persian pussies, here we come,' Jones announced, pumping his fist by way of emphasis.

'Persians are Iranian, Geoff. Iraqis are Arabs.'

Kate didn't bother to deliver one of her knockout smiles with the correction. She didn't care if Jones thought she was a smartarse. She *knew* he was a twit.

'Persians. Arabs. They're all towelheads to me,' Jones replied, unfazed.

Jesus, Kate thought. The bombs in this conflict were going to be smarter than Channel Eight's man on the ground.

Mawson ignored their sniping. 'I'm sending the London producer with you, Geoff.' Commonsense had prevailed after all. At least Jonesy wouldn't be flying solo. 'He'll meet you both in Amman to hand over flak jackets and gas masks. Kate, you'll catch a connecting flight to Tel Aviv. Geoff, you'll be driving into Baghdad from Jordan.'

The United Nations had given Saddam a 15 January deadline to withdraw from Kuwait. That meant Kate had just three days to get into position and only a couple of hours to pack.

With Bernstein safely billeted downstairs with Ben and Al, Kate did one last whip around the apartment. She was sure to have forgotten something. The phone rang before she could figure out what it was.

Please don't let this be my mother again, Kate entreated silently as she picked up.

'Hi, Kate. It's Sandra. So you're off to Israel I hear. Lucky girl.'

Kate hadn't spoken to Sandra since the SWIB brunch. But she'd placed a call the moment she knew she was being sent to the Gulf. Sandra's advice would be invaluable . . . presuming she chose to share it this time.

'Thanks so much for calling me back,' Kate said as she riffled through her bag, checking for her ticket and passport. 'I was just hoping you might have a few tips for me. I'm new to this. I feel a bit out of my depth.'

'Out of your depth? I doubt that. But look. It's an adventure. Think of it that way. And prepare. Just know everything you can and then some more. The rest comes down to luck, I'm afraid. Sometimes the gods smile on you. And when they don't, you still have a job to do. You'll be fine.'

A horn beeped from the street below. 'Damn, that's my taxi. I was hoping for a bit more time.'

'If it helps, I used to pinch my leg when I had to pull myself together before a live cross. You need to do it hard. It always helped me to concentrate. Other than that, just keep your head down and stay calm.'

Stay calm, Kate thought. What sort of advice was that? She was absolutely terrified. And she was still thirty hours and fourteen thousand kilometres from her destination.

Calm was right out of the question. But she would at least be magnificently well informed.

Reams of A4 paper covered Kate's tray table. It didn't matter. She was too nervous to eat anyway. She'd gathered hundreds of pages of reference material for the trip. Closing her eyes, she did her best to memorise the various names, statistics and other bits of information she'd accumulated.

She needed to be able to rattle it all off under pressure. Kate had never reported live before. She just hoped she measured up. Live television was a tough gig and not for the faint hearted. There was nowhere to hide when the camera started rolling and plenty of ways to look like a fool. Pause a moment too long, struggle even slightly for the right word and millions of viewers around the country would reach for their remote controls.

Kate recited each new fact under her breath like a litany. General Schwarzkopf – US military leader. General Ali Hassan al-Majid – Iraqi military leader and first cousin of Saddam Hussein, now the first 'governor' of Kuwait. Yitzhak Shamir – Israeli prime minister. Born Poland 1915, ex-Mossad security service. She needed plenty of titbits just like that to pepper through her broadcasts. That way people would think she was much older than she looked. And smarter too.

At least, that was the theory.

Her head was starting to ache. This was like cramming for the HSC. But this time she only had a couple of days to absorb it all. On the bright side, at least she knew she would actually be using what she learned.

In the next seat, Geoff Jones was calmly sipping on Piper Heidsieck.

'All work and no play makes Kate a very dull girl.' Geoff grinned. She was a good-looking sheila. But Kate Corish really needed to lighten up and learn to have some fun. He'd never understood how that wimpy Matthew Keaton had prised her away from her desk long enough to get her into the sack. 'Honey, I don't know why you're bothering. All the action will be going down in Baghdad anyway. You'll be sweet, sitting back in your five-star hotel in Tel Aviv. But hey, put that flak jacket on over your pretty blow-waved head and everyone will think you're actually in the thick of it.'

God he was ignorant, Kate thought. Saddam had scud missiles that would easily make the distance to Israel. And a strike on the Jewish state was almost certainly part of his war strategy.

Kate worked for a little longer and finally pushed back her seat. If she grabbed a nap now, she'd be in far better shape in the morning. Her eyes were starting to sting anyway. She stuffed her papers and notebook under the seat in front of her, adjusted her eye mask and willed herself to sleep, the names of prominent Israelis going around in her head.

The plane was already descending when Kate woke five hours later. She pushed up the window shade and squinted against the sun. Below, she could just make out Amman. The city appeared lush. An oasis in the middle of the rugged Jordanian desert.

An enormous grin spread across her face as she thought about what lay ahead. She was in the Middle East. And she was about to start work as a war correspondent. Finally excitement was overtaking the nerves.

She glanced over at Geoff. Quite the opposite seemed to be true for her colleague. The poor bloke was ghostly pale and desperately daubing his face with an aircraft wash cloth. Kate wasn't sure if he was suffering from all the free champagne or if the realities of his assignment had finally registered.

The Queen Alia International Airport was a surprisingly functional and modern building. It was also the strangest and most exotic place Kate had ever been. Women floated past, their kohl-rimmed eyes and ruby-red lips accentuated by brilliantly coloured scarves.

Here and there, she spotted very different women – crow-like figures hurrying along in head-to-toe black. Only their eyes were visible. As an independently minded Western woman, Kate found their presence unsettling.

The London producer met them at the gate as arranged, a flailing bundle of arms and legs and excited energy. Ants in his pants. Kate had never before met anyone who fitted the description so perfectly.

'Hi, Kate. Heard all about you. Here's your flak jacket, gas mask and first-aid kit.' He spoke so quickly, the entire sentence came out as a single word.

'And here's US$20,000 cash. Don't lose it.' He passed over a thick white envelope. 'You're on a connecting flight to Tel Aviv; it leaves in one hour and your cameraman will pick you up at Ben Gurion airport. Break a leg.'

And with that he was gone, a human tornado, dragging an anaemic-looking Geoff Jones along in his wake.

Suddenly she was alone, a tiny figure weighed down by the accoutrements of war and surrounded by luggage. What had seemed so exotic moments earlier now appeared menacing. And she was scared.

Kate took a moment to consider her predicament.

She was carrying a gas mask and a flak jacket with only the vaguest idea of how to use either of them. Stuffed in her jeans pocket was almost as much money as she now earned in a year. She was twenty-four years old and had no previous experience in a war zone. In fact, her entire international travel experience consisted of a two-week whistlestop tour of Europe with her mother at the age of fourteen and a trip to Fiji with her school friends after the HSC.

And yet here she was, standing by herself in a strange airport on the risky side of the East–West divide. This assignment was starting to feel every bit as foolhardy as her scheme to bring down Mickey Morgan. And I won a Walkely for that, she reminded herself.

She quickly found a trolley and set off for the boarding gate. She'd been given the chance of a lifetime and she wasn't about to let a few rookie nerves blow it for her.

NINE

'Tezza. Thank God it's you! Why didn't anyone tell me?' Kate shrieked as she jogged her trolley towards Channel Eight's gun London cameraman.

'And spoil the surprise?' Tezza laughed, dragging Kate off her feet with one of his famous bear hugs.

The flight from Amman had taken just forty-five minutes. But that was more than enough time for Kate's mood to swing wildly from elation to trepidation to doubt to downright fear and back again a dozen times. Now that she knew she was being teamed with Tezza, she was back to being excited again. Mawson's deployment of personnel was starting to make a bit more sense.

'So how's life in London treating you?' Kate asked, surrendering her trolley.

'Bloody cold hole of a joint. Good pubs though.'

'I'll be relying on you big time, you know. Maybe I should start apologising now.'

'I'm just glad I didn't get stuck with Jones. He'll go to water, I reckon. Fancy them giving him Baghdad, geez. But that producer with him is a smart operator. Pretty full on at times but he knows his stuff.' Tezza started heading for the exit. 'Anyway, we have a great hotel, right in the heart of town. It has a fantastic live position on the roof. We'll be up there dodging scuds before you know it.'

At the mention of scuds Kate's internal pendulum swung back towards the nervous end of the scale.

'Don't worry, you'll be great, Kate,' Tezza offered as the colour once again drained from his friend's face. 'Today's the UN deadline so sparks will start flying in the next day or two. We're going to have a ball. That's if we don't end up dead!'

Their accommodation was everything Tezza had promised. Kate dumped her bags on the double bed and pushed open the small window. Immediately, unfamiliar but wonderful smells filled her nostrils. There was the iodine scent of the ocean mixed with traffic fumes and spices. She inhaled deeply, revelling in the strangeness of the place.

'Not a bad pub, eh?' Tezza smiled. He hadn't left her side since collecting her from the airport.

'We're certainly right in the middle of everything.'

Kate looked out over the thousands of simple, pale-coloured buildings that had given Tel Aviv its sobriquet of the 'white city'. In the distance, the sun was setting over the Mediterranean, bathing the world in a glorious rose-coloured glow. It was hard to imagine that war was looming.

'Come and see the live position on the roof. Then I'd better let you get some shut-eye. Given the time difference, most of your live crosses will be in the middle of the night. We can organise our press passes down at the media centre tomorrow. Anyway, you must be exhausted. Twenty-four hours stuck on a plane with Geoff Jones. You deserve a Bex and a good lie down, girl.'

'I managed five hours sleep on the plane. It must have been the company.'

All the same, Kate's body felt cumbersome and heavy as she followed Tezza to the lift and then up a final flight of stairs.

'Mind the airconditioner. You'll have to duck to get under it.'

Tezza held open the door to the roof as she clambered under the unit and up the last three steps. In the day's final light, the view was breathtaking. The Mediterranean to the west. The ancient sea port of Jaffa to the south. The city's residential area to the east. All bases covered. Perfect, in fact.

There were three huge satellite dishes erected. APTN. Reuters. Newsforce. Kate knew the names. These were the companies that followed the world's problems and sold their satellite technology and time to a hungry media. The big networks like CNN and the BBC had their own equipment.

'What's the drill then, sarge?' she asked.

'Well, when Sydney needs a live cross from us, I'll hook you up with an ear piece and plug in my camera. Then, compliments of one of those satellite dishes over there, you'll be beamed live into lounge rooms all around Australia. Simple as that.'

'Simple. That's all very well for you to say on the safe side of the camera.' Kate attempted an unconvincing smile.

'Don't worry. We'll do a couple of dummy runs to get you used to it,' Tezza promised.

But Kate only managed a single day of practice before America and its allies unleashed hell.

'The liberation of Kuwait has begun,' George Bush intoned on CNN. 'We will not fail.'

The aerial bombardment of Iraq began during the early hours of 17 January. Kate was awake when the first bombs dropped. It was bizarre to be watching a war live on television, as if it were a football match or a computer game. She sat in her hotel room spellbound as the TV screen flickered a deadly shade of high-tech green. CNN's Peter Arnett reported live via phone.

'If you're still with us,' the line crackled, 'you can hear the bombs now. They are hitting the centre of the city.'

The night sky over Baghdad lit up like fireworks. Kate thought of Geoff Jones and hoped he was safe.

Arnett's CNN colleague John Holiman joined in. 'Whoa. Holy cow.'

She switched over to INN. She knew she'd be hearing from the Sydney office at any minute. It might have been the wee small hours in Tel Aviv but in Sydney, it was mid-morning. Mawson would probably want to cut into regular programming with a newsflash. Then there was the 11.30 news to worry about. Kate needed as much information as she could get before she made the trek to the rooftop.

The unmistakable voice of Jonathan McTavish filled the room. What was it about that English accent that made the man sound so credible, she wondered, scribbling notes.

'The explosions from America's so-called "smart bombs" are rocking the hotel where we are staying. You might be able to see the rainstorm of Iraqi anti-aircraft bullets. But they're no match for this superpower display.'

The phone in Kate's room rang.

'Ripley here. You ready to go, Kate honey? We'll be crossing to you in half an hour after we take feeds from Geoff.'

Kate and Ripley had reached an uneasy truce over the last six months. She had established herself as a firm favourite with Mawson and Carter, so the chief of staff had no choice but to treat her with a modicum of respect. Sometimes his praise seemed so genuine and generous that Kate wondered if he had mellowed. Or if maybe her recollections of those first months at Channel Eight had become exaggerated over time.

She'd put the proposition to Gillian. But Gill had quickly assured her that Ripley was still the same foul-mouthed bastard he'd always been. 'He's a snake,' she reminded her. 'And snakes are no less venomous for choosing not to bite you.'

'Sure. No problems, Ripper,' Kate said now. She headed upstairs, somehow remembering to dodge the airconditioner. Tezza was at their agreed spot. He was squatting down, camera on one knee, adjusting his settings. He waved her over.

An odd numbness gripped Kate as she walked towards him. It was as if her mind and her body had somehow separated and were operating on different time zones. Her brain was moving quickly, racing through all the possible scenarios for the minutes ahead. But her feet were dragging, as if through quicksand. The sensation lifted as she moved into position, replaced by a vague nausea.

Tel Aviv spread out around her. She strained her eyes east towards Baghdad. There was nothing to see but stars.

As Kate ran through her lines for maybe the tenth time, her knees started to knock together. And it wasn't just the cold desert air. She shifted her weight from one foot to the other. The hopping motion made her look as though she needed to go to the bathroom. But it was bringing the shaking under control. Hopefully, Tezza would think she was just trying to keep warm.

She glanced over at the other two correspondents sharing her roof. They looked much older than her but they too were bouncing from leg to leg, manically rehearsing their lines. It was comforting to realise nerves were a universal condition and not merely a sign of her inexperience.

As Tezza busily established communications with a control room half a world away, Kate ran through what she wanted to say one last time. The cross might have been live but it was still carefully scripted. Ripley had faxed through a list of questions well ahead of time. Hopefully there wouldn't be any nasty surprises.

The director crackled into her earpiece. 'Kate, Dave here, can you hear me?'

'Loud and clear, Dave.' There was silence. She started talking again only to have the director talk over her. Satellite delay. Of course. She'd have to remember that.

'You'll be crossing to Beige in about five.' Beige! What was Beige doing anchoring the program? He was not renowned for his incisive interviewing technique. Kate prayed he'd have the commonsense to follow the script.

'No time for insecurities now,' she whispered to herself as she felt the first telltale prickles of a nerve rash creeping up her neck. 'Remember. You're not a rookie any more.'

Maybe Matthew's words did the job. Or perhaps it was the good hard pinch she administered to her forearm. But by the time Tezza gave the signal, Kate was the embodiment of the cool, self-assured professional.

'We cross now live to Tel Aviv where Kate Corish is our reporter on the ground. Kate, it's very early in the morning there. Has the news hit home yet? Is there any reaction?'

'About one hour after the aerial assault began in Iraq, the Israeli military command issued an order via television and radio for all citizens to stay indoors and prepare their gas mask kits. These kits were handed out in response to recent threats by the Iraqi regime. You may remember just a few weeks ago, Saddam said he would quote "scorch half of Israel" if military offensives began. Well, they have begun and even though it's very dark here, you can see the faces of nervous Israelis peering out their windows watching the night sky and waiting for the sirens to blare.'

'And we know for a fact Iraq has chemical weaponry. Kate?' Good. Beige was sticking to the script.

'That's the fear here. Saddam has a well-documented arsenal of chemical weapons like nerve and mustard gas and he has shown in the past he is prepared to use them. Just over two years ago his attack on the Kurds killed five thousand people. Hence, these kits. I'll just show you. This is the gas mask. And these suits, made of lightweight plastic, have also been issued to every Israeli citizen. When the sirens sound, people here are expected to put on both the mask and the suit.'

'Thanks, Kate. Keep safe. I can't imagine the kind of conditions you must be facing there.' Huh? Kate maintained her best television face, giving the camera a knowing, wordless nod. Beige obviously thought Tel Aviv was some outpost in the middle of the bloody Syrian desert.

She heard him continue. 'We'll come back to you as developments unfold. Now we return to Geoff Jones in Amman, Jordan.'

Amman. What was Geoff doing in Amman? He was supposed to be in Baghdad.

'Well done,' Tezza congratulated her as he carefully unclipped her radio mike. 'No one could tell you were nervous.'

Kate was still buzzing from the adrenaline surge.

'I actually thought I was going to throw up when you cued me in.'

'Now you tell me!' Tezza laughed.

The sat phone rang.

'Yep, I'll just put her on.' Tezza lugged the brick of a thing a little closer to Kate.

'You did good, kid. First time live cross. Nice work.' Mawson didn't often contact reporters when they were out on the road. She must have made a fair fist of things.

'Thanks, chief. But what's Geoff doing in Amman?'

'We told him he could leave Baghdad if he thought it was going to be too dangerous. We didn't need to ask him twice. Actually, almost all the Australians hightailed it out of the city well before the bombing started, just a couple of newspaper hacks hanging in there. But we're getting plenty of good material from CNN and INN. So it's not a critical blow.'

'A safe war zone. I would've thought that was an oxymoron.' Kate couldn't resist the dig.

'Well, things will start hotting up in your neck of the woods soon enough. We'll see if you're so gung ho then.'

Kate reddened. Who was she to judge? So far, the most hazardous event of her tour of duty had been a dodgy eyebrow wax, the result of having forgotten to pack any tweezers.

Mawson went on. 'The good news is we've finally managed to convince his Nibs to cut short his ski holiday in Aspen. So our main man will be back in the chair day after next. And I'm giving your mate Matthew a go tomorrow. Maybe he'll know the difference between Tel Aviv, Tehran and Tanza-fucking-nia. In the meantime, keep your head down and keep up the good work.'

Kate's war started in earnest at three the next morning. The sirens were wailing as she raced up to the roof, her flak jacket digging uncomfortably into her torso. The extra kilos and wider dimensions made the trip that much trickier and she whacked her head on the airconditioning unit. Shit, my gas mask, she thought as she fell up the last couple of steps.

She found Tezza calmly setting up his camera, as relaxed as she was panicked.

'Tezza. Put your bloody flak jacket on. The sirens. Can't you hear the sirens,' Kate yelled as she pulled her gas mask over her head. 'Christ, what am I doing here?' she muttered, scanning the night sky for incoming missiles.

Tezza passed over the microphone. 'You'll have to ditch the gas mask for the live cross, Kate.'

'Fuck. I didn't think that bit through.' She ripped off the mask, wondering what would happen if there really was mustard gas headed in their direction.

'You're on in thirty seconds.' Tezza was as cool as ever. 'What's that mark on your head? Do you have any powder?'

'I hit my head on that fucking airconditioning unit. Shit.' She patted down her body frantically. 'Powder. Powder. It's in my pocket under my fucking flak jacket.'

'Don't worry. No time. Ten seconds and you're up.'

'Concentrate. Concentrate,' she whispered to herself, giving her leg a long, hard pinch. Tezza gave her the thumbs-up.

'Matthew, I'm sure you can hear the sirens. They have been going now for approximately ten minutes. Israel is apparently about to come under attack.' Kate could hear the tremble in her voice. She hoped her mother wasn't watching this.

Halfway through Matthew's next question, the Israeli sky lit up as eight missiles raced towards Tel Aviv. Kate swung around to see what was happening. In a Hollywood-like master stroke, one of the scuds cruised through the night space over her left shoulder, exploding into a ball of flames just a few blocks away. Kate flinched and ducked but remembered to do her job as well.

'Matthew, I'm sure you saw that and wow. Sorry. The building, it felt like it moved then. But I think it was just the air – the shockwaves from that explosion. It looks like at least one of those missiles has landed in a residential area. To the right of me are dozens of apartment buildings. I can't see too much from up here. But I can smell acrid smoke. The air seems dusty too.'

Kate was yelling over the sirens.

'Israel has a patriot defence system in place to intercept these scuds. But they look to have failed. The question now is will the Israelis retaliate?'

It was gripping television. Right time. Right place. A dose of luck. Instant fame.

After several more live crosses, the dawn light finally crept over the horizon and it was over.

Kate collapsed into the shower, twisting the knobs until the temperature was scalding. She pushed her back to the wall and let her legs give way, slowly lowering herself onto the tiled floor. Water streamed over her head and face, mixing with her tears. She cried for a good ten minutes, great heaving sobs of relief. She'd survived. For the first time in her professional life, she really didn't feel like a rookie any more.

Days began to merge into one another, as Kate caught cat naps when and where she could. The 2 a.m. starts were punishing. Her hotel room was more a command post than a bedroom, a place to take calls, make notes and check the latest news on cable television. Sheer adrenaline kept her on her feet night after terrifying night.

'Three people were killed and seventy wounded when the missile landed in a residential neighbourhood.'

'The US is pleading with Israel to exercise restraint and resist retaliation.'

'Israeli defence force spokesman Brigadier General Nachman Shai said two patriot missiles were fired at the scuds but they failed to intercept.'

'The scud missile flattened the apartment building. One infant died of head wounds. A woman died of a heart attack. Of the many civilians wounded, ten were under the age of twelve.'

After a month of relentless bombing, allied ground forces finally moved on Iraqi positions in Kuwait. Two days later Saddam withdrew his troops and Kate was on the line to Bruce Mawson.

'Bruce, I want to go in. I've been watching the pac-man version of this war on TV. But what about the people? I want to get in there and see what happened to the people. No bomb is as smart and as precise as the Americans are claiming. We need to see what really went on during this war. And be there to record what goes on afterwards as well.'

Mawson didn't need any persuading this time. Kate was ratings gold and if she wanted to take a little side trip to Baghdad, he wasn't going to stop her. Hell, he'd fly over and help pack her bags.

Reg Carter took more convincing. The war had screwed the news budget and he wanted his people back at their desks as quickly as possible. 'Betty Blacktown doesn't give a shit what happens to a bunch of filthy Arabs in Baghdad,' he protested.

But Mawson had the last word. 'No. But they do care about what happens to Kate Corish in Baghdad. She's going.'

TEN

Channel Eight's kinetic London producer had somehow managed to locate a car and driver to take Kate and Tezza from Amman to Baghdad. The bloke was an absolute dynamo. Kate suspected he would have supplied her with a colony of penguins and a marching band if she'd asked. She was beginning to suspect he had red cordial coursing through his veins instead of blood.

'Wahlid has done this trip hundreds of times,' he volunteered, bouncing from the street up onto the pavement and back again.

There was no need to check Wahlid's log book to confirm his status as an experienced long-haul driver. One look at his beat-up old troop carrier was enough to verify every dusty kilometre.

Tezza piled their gear into the back of the vehicle. Three silver cases. Lights, batteries, cameras, editing equipment, supplies of water and food. Kate still had twelve grand in her money pouch. The producer pressed the rest of his float into her hands. Another six or so thousand, she guessed.

'You'll be giving it all away in bribes. Nothing surer.' He stepped back from the street as Wahlid urged the car's engine to life. 'I hope you like the place better than Jones did!'

'How long to Baghdad, Wahlid?' Kate asked. A brown and rocky moonscape stretched endlessly ahead of them.

'Oh, about five hours to the border, habibti. Then maybe another five or six hours after that,' he answered in a soothing singsong voice. 'They will like you very much in Iraq. My people love beautiful women.'

Despite her uncomfortable seat and the car's pernicious lack of suspension, Kate slept most of the way. By the time they reached Baghdad, it was ten in the morning and she felt almost rested, although it would take her top couple of vertebrae a little longer to recover.

The city had been scarred by war, there was no doubt about that. But it wasn't any kind of war that Kate recognised. Buildings stood with massive holes punched right through their middle. And yet structures on either side of the target were entirely untouched. The Americans' smart bombs were a whole lot more discriminating than anything they had dropped on Vietnam. Still, Kate found it hard to believe in the Pentagon's high-tech fairytale. Not even America, with all its wealth, power and ingenuity, could take the blood and misery out of war.

They pulled into the car park of the Al-Rashid. The hotel was famous now as Peter Arnett's wartime base. Jonathan McTavish had stayed on too. They were brave men. And because of their courage, they were now international stars as well. Most of the world's media had scarpered within a few days of hostilities breaking out. Not that Geoff Jones had lasted even that long.

The hotel had survived the war unscathed, allowing its staff to maintain the fiction that nothing untoward had been happening beyond its doors over the past few weeks. Kate pressed the button for the elevator. The doors opened to reveal an Iraqi teenager polishing the brass railings that ran along each side of the mirrored walls.

It was an incongruous image. The boy would have to pick his way over rubble to get home at the end of the day. But here in this hotel oasis, guests were able to admire their reflections in the meticulously buffed fixtures.

Just as the lift doors were closing a large and very shiny black boot wedged itself between them. Kate didn't appreciate the hold-up, however brief. After twelve hours hurtling through the desert in a clapped-out troop carrier, she was desperate for a bath. And she was not at all happy with whoever had just come between her and hot, oil-scented water. Ill-mannered bastard, she thought, and arranged her face into a murderous glare.

She quickly revised her opinion when she realised the offending foot was attached to the legendary and, Kate noted, impossibly handsome Jonathan McTavish. At thirty-four, the man was an absolute dish, to borrow her mother's expression. Tall and lean with dark hair, blue eyes and olive skin, he had a dimple in the middle of his chin that had surely broken a hundred female hearts.

Kate rustled up a dazzling smile from her desert-depleted arsenal. Was it possible McTavish was even more gorgeous in real life? The nerve rash was creeping up her neck even faster than the Al-Rashid lift was negotiating the seven floors to her hotel room.

Slow down, she screamed to herself – advice she would have liked to apply to the rash, her pulse and the unnaturally rapid elevator. But Jonathan barely glanced her way. He was too deep in angry conversation with his cameraman.

'The sheer incompetence of that bitch! She must have slept her way to the top. There's no other explanation. I just have no idea who'd want to fuck her with that enormous, desk-bound arse of hers.'

The English accent made McTavish sound as if he'd just said tea and scones. But to Kate it sounded more like 'I'm a misogynist Pommie pig'.

The man she idealised as the exemplar of quality journalism and suave heroic masculinity had morphed into a garden-variety sexist bastard before her very eyes. Her uncharacteristic rush of schoolgirl giddiness gave way to a torrent of contempt.

What made her think he would be any different? He was a man working in the media after all. Jonathan McTavish might look a bit like Pierce Brosnan but he was every bit as ugly as Mike Ripley on the inside.

Maybe McTavish felt the icy glare drilling into his broad swimmer's back. He turned around with a start to see a very pretty girl staring at him. And not with the kind of available, come-hither expression he was used to. Out of long habit, he started to smile.

'Oh. Hello there. Have we met? I don't think I've seen you here before.'

'Kate Corish, Network Eight Australia.' She fixed him with a look of pure disdain. 'Clearly fucked my way here. And you?'

In a magnificent piece of timing, the doors opened at Kate's floor right on cue. She stomped out before McTavish had a chance to reply.

'Lucky bastards,' he whispered to his cameraman as he watched Kate's shapely dust and grease-stained rear storm down the hall.

Kate had no idea that the world of a foreign correspondent was so darned small. All of Baghdad was her stage. And yet she kept running into Jonathan McTavish.

Part of the reason was that they were both reliant on their government-issued guides. And the guide's job was not so much to help reporters find their way around the city as to peddle the regime's campaign of propaganda. Today, they were at a hospital, with every other journalist in town.

'Hi, Kate.' It was McTavish again.

'Hi,' she said shortly.

'Perhaps we should try a proper introduction,' McTavish ventured. 'I'm Jonathan McTavish.'

'I know who you are,' Kate snapped. The guy was obviously used to women falling at his feet. Well, not this time, buster. 'Look, I have to do a stand-up. Would you mind?'

From behind the camera, Tezza raised his hand. 'Katie. My battery's flat. And I'm all out.' He was one of the few people allowed to call her Katie. Even Carter had given in to her scowls. 'I'll have to go back to the hotel to get more.'

Kate wasn't in the mood for delays. Not with McTavish standing nearby. 'Come on, Tezza. You have lots of batteries. You always have lots of batteries.'

'But you've shot four tapes today. I've used them all.'

Jonathan was watching their little spat and sensed an opportunity. Here was a chance to curry some favour with this firebrand Australian reporter.

'We have the same gear. Betacam right? I'm sure we can help.' He brandished a battery over his head as if it were a winning lottery ticket. But in this case, the prize was simply teasing a smile from the deliciously uppity Kate Corish.

No woman had ever spoken to him the way she had in the Al-Rashid lift. And he was surprised to discover he quite liked it. He especially loved the way she said 'fuck'. The memory of it delighted him as he watched Kate prepare for her stand-up.

'Do you mind?' Kate snarled. 'I'd prefer to do this without an audience.'

'Sorry. I'm a bit the same myself.'

Jonathan quickly retreated to admire Kate from a safer distance as she delivered her piece to camera in a single perfect take.

'Geez, Katie, you're being a bit hard on the guy. You do know who he is, don't you?' Tezza asked as they were packing up the gear. He couldn't understand what had got into his usually easygoing colleague.

'Sorry, Tezza. I just need a good night's sleep. It's all starting to catch up with me. I swear I'll be nice from now on. In fact, I'll go over and say thank you now.'

She found Jonathan chatting to a small boy further down the road. In Arabic. Christ all bloody mighty. Who was this bloke? As she moved closer, the kid started polishing his boots.

'But you had your boots polished this morning out the front of the Al-Rashid didn't you?' Kate observed, appalled at the man's vanity.

'Third time today,' McTavish replied. 'It's a dusty place.'

'Well, here's your battery. You saved us time. I appreciate it.' Kate said, starting to leave.

'Before you go . . . .' McTavish switched boots. 'I'd like to apologise for my outburst in the lift the other day. There's a producer back in London who's doing my head in. You know the type. You file a story. But they see something they prefer on CNN and order that up like it's a fucking McDonald's restaurant out here. You do have those desk types back home, don't you?'

'Mmm,' Kate replied thinking of Ripley. 'Well, as I said, thanks for the battery.'

'I'd love to buy you a drink back at the Al-Rashid in the hope of redeeming myself.'

'What's on offer, a Coke? You Englishmen sure know how to turn a girl's head.'

'I'm a Scotsman actually, and I can get my hands on something stronger if that's what you want. You forget. I've been here a while.'

Kate bit hard into her cheek, unsure how to respond. She was being chatted up by one of the world's best reporters. Her hormones and her ambition were voting yes to a drink. Loudly. But the guy was too smooth – clearly a womaniser. So her commonsense was screaming no. She knew where she was getting the best advice.

'No, thanks,' she replied, before she could change her mind.

The shoeshine boy looked up. 'Is good?' he asked, packing away his little wooden box.

'*Shukran gazillan*,' Jonathan said, lightly fluffing the kid's hair as he handed over a couple of hundred dinars.

'Well, I'd like to buy you a Coke, McTav.' Tezza had followed her up the street, presumably to make sure she behaved. He figured he'd arrived in the nick of time. 'Thanks for helping me out. Katie here was about to have my guts for garters.'

'Now that wouldn't be pretty,' McTavish said. His eyes invited Kate to join in the laughter.

Great. Now they were ganging up on her. Kate swung on her heels and stormed off, giving the two men a splendid opportunity to admire her departing bottom.

'You don't want to cross that one,' Tezza observed.

'Unfortunately, I already have.' McTavish gave the cameraman a comradely slap on the back. 'Bugger the Coke, old chap. I have a bottle of scotch stashed away in my room. The INN bureau is on the tenth floor. Come on up when you have time tonight. Kate's welcome too, of course.'

'Thanks, mate. Once I've got this edit done, I might just take you up on that. I reckon I'll need a stiff drink. A man is not a camel, even when he's stuck in the middle of a desert.'

Tezza might not have been a camel. But nor was he a party animal. His little knees-up with the INN boys had completely floored him and by ten the next morning, he still hadn't found the strength to drag himself out of bed.

'Big night, huh?' Kate leaned against his door.

'Too much scotch.' He groaned. 'You should've come.'

'Looking at you I'm glad I didn't. But it's about time we took a day off. I'll think through our next couple of assignments and chat to the desk back home. Sleep all day if you like.'

In the end, Kate decided to spend her downtime wrestling with Iraqi officialdom. She would have preferred to while away a few hours beside the Al-Rashid pool. But the weather still wasn't warm enough. And the red tape had to be tackled at some stage. Today was as good as any, she thought, as she set off for Iraq's famously obstructive International Press Department.

The Ministry of Information building was a nightmare of concrete utilitarianism, monstrous and dusty. The place had been bombed a few weeks earlier but it had quickly sprung back to life. Everywhere Kate looked, labourers were busily laying new bricks. Inside, journalists scurried in and out of makeshift bureaus. The rooms were rented out at an exorbitant price. It was a nice little earner. And it had the added advantage of allowing the regime to monitor every report without having to leave the building.

Dozens of small, grubby rooms honeycombed the Ministry's ground floor. Kate eventually reached the small office designated for media relations and pushed open the door.

The air inside was dense with cigarette smoke, the noxious haze hovering uncomfortably around eye level. On either side of the room, two middle-aged Iraqis sat hunched over a mountain of forms, diligently scribbling and initialling and puffing away. Kate walked over to the nearest desk, smile confidently and firmly in place. Her plan was to bluff her way to the head of the queue. But the official's eyes didn't leave the paperwork in front of him as he impatiently waved her to the back of the room.

Iraqi bureaucracy made Kate's occasional tussles with the NSW

Roads and Traffic Authority seem rational and efficient by comparison. Trying to convince a government official to rubber stamp a trip to Basra was akin to planning a flight to the moon. And almost as expensive.

No one ever actually said no. They just left you hanging. She plonked herself onto a dirty vinyl couch and waited for her turn to be stonewalled.

'Fancy meeting you here.' Jonathan McTavish bounded across the room and sat down next to her. It was a tight squeeze. The couch only just met the basic criteria for a two-seater. 'We missed you last night.'

'Thanks for giving my cameraman a hangover. He's absolutely no bloody use to me today.' Kate stared straight ahead, fixing her focus on the wall opposite. Or at least she presumed it was a wall. She had to take its existence on trust on account of the cigarette haze.

'I'm sorry, Kate.' McTavish didn't sound in the least apologetic. 'But quite frankly, you need to loosen up. A drink would've done you the world of good. '

Fuck you, Kate thought. It wasn't a particularly eloquent response. But it did have the advantage of describing her feelings quite exactly. She turned to confront him, the two words shaping on her lips.

Then she saw his face. He was grinning. Teasing her. And enjoying himself immensely in the process.

In spite of herself, Kate started to laugh. What did it matter? It was way too hard staying cross with someone that gorgeous.

'Finally, a hint of a smile from the beautiful Kate Corish.' McTavish took a giant victory swig from his water bottle. 'What are you trying to get a "Sorry, miss, you cannot film that" for today?'

'I want to get out of Baghdad. Go south. Check out Basra maybe. If that's even possible.'

'We're planning a trip to Basra too. But not through these guys, through a group called Middle East Watch. If we pull it off – and we'll know tonight – you're welcome to come with us.' Jonathan leaned closer and whispered, 'If I were you, I wouldn't even bother asking here. Save your time and energy. I'll be in the Al-Rashid bar at 6 p.m. Come and I'll buy you that Coke and let you know how we went.'

And with that, McTavish waltzed out the door. Broad shoulders, cute arse, mastery of Arabic – he was some package all right.

Kate didn't have to think about it for long before deciding to take Jonathan's advice. There had to be a better way to spend a few free hours in Baghdad than sitting in an office, developing emphysema by proxy.

As she left, Kate spotted McTavish out the front of the building, his boot once again up on a box. A child of about nine was working diligently at the leather. Spit. Polish. Spit. Polish.

'You'll have no boots left by the time you leave this place,' Kate commented.

She jumped into a beaten-up white taxi with garish orange doors. It looked like it was being held together by masking tape.

'Mr Jon always has shiny boots, no?' the cab driver said. Everyone knew McTavish.

'Sure, but who needs their boots cleaned three and four times a day anyway?' Kate shrugged.

'The children follow him. They say he can't say no. And he pays well.' The driver was laughing. 'He is a very kind man with very shiny boots.'

As they drove off Kate saw two more kids hurrying in the direction of the man with the shiny boots, little wooden boxes in tow.

ELEVEN

The hotel bar was almost empty and Kate spotted Jonathan McTavish easily. He was leaning back in a chair, smoking and chatting with his crew. If Pierce Brosnan ever played James Bond, that's exactly what he'd look like, Kate thought

'Kate.' Jonathan jumped up and pulled out a maroon velvet tub chair with a genteel flourish. She sank into it, gratefully accepting his offer of a cigarette.

She'd picked up the habit yet again in Tel Aviv. Most of the journalists she met there were smokers too. War zones and fags went hand in hand it seemed. After all, it was hard to worry about lung cancer when you were dodging scud missiles. She'd wean herself off the things when she got back to Sydney. Bernstein objected to the smell anyway.

Jonathan flipped open a brass zippo. The smell of lighter fluid mixed with his cologne. The scent was intoxicating. In fact, everything about him was intoxicating. Dangerously so.

Kate didn't trust herself to meet his eyes so she lowered her gaze but it wasn't the sexually neutral move she'd hoped. She was now staring at Jonathan McTavish's khaki shirt. The first couple of buttons were undone. She glimpsed a curl of dark chest hair.

Quickly Kate refocused on a pot plant just behind his right shoulder. Safer. Much safer.

'Guys, Pete and Reg. This is Kate, Tezza's journo.'

'Hi, Kate,' the crew chorused in thick Cockney accents.

McTavish signalled the waiter to deliver another Coke. 'We're in luck, Kate. We're hitching a ride to Basra on a Black Hawk with the mob from Middle Eastern Watch. You and Tezza are welcome to tag along, if you're still interested.'

'Wow. That's incredibly generous of you. Not too many reporters would be willing to share that kind of exclusive.' Kate doubted Jonathan's motives were entirely professional. But she wasn't about to knock back the opportunity.

'I'm sure the desk jockeys at INN won't mind if the story gets a run down in the colonies. Truce?'

Kate took his hand and a flutter of little shocks traced the course of his fingers making her stomach lurch. These weren't butterflies. They were pterodactyls.

Settle, Kate, settle, she warned herself. 'How long are you staying here? You must be missing home by now.' Damn it. She was fishing. Judging from the smirks on Pete and Reg's faces, they knew it too.

'I arrived on New Year's Day. So it's been a while. But that's the job.' No mention of a wife or kids. Maybe. Just maybe. Her mind wandered back to that inviting hint of chest hair.

Kate's virtue was only saved by the timely arrival of Peter Arnett. He was an odd-looking specimen. A dead ringer for Friar Tuck. All that was missing was the long brown cassock.

'McTav, how are you, my man?' Peter Arnett enquired at full volume.

'Peter, this is Kate Corish, Australia's finest.' Kate blushed as the world's most famous journalist pulled up a seat next to her.

'Hi, Peter. Nice to meet you.'

Kate couldn't have been more starstruck if she was eighteen years old and meeting Michael Hutchence. Arnett was an absolute legend. And, unbelievably, he was chatting to her as a peer. She was just wondering if it would be too gauche to ask him about the first night of the bombing campaign when Tezza appeared.

'Sorry to interrupt, guys.'

'How's your head?' Jonathan grinned.

'All good now. Bit rough this morning though.' Tezza still looked off colour. 'Kate, the office is demanding a recut of yesterday's story. They want to add some stuff they saw on CNN. So you have to revoice the package.'

McTavish winked and raised his hands in solidarity.

'Damn them,' Kate cursed. 'Sorry to run out on you straightaway. But I have to go. Date with an edit pack. Thanks for the Coke.'

Jonathan stood up as she left. The girl really did have a mighty fine arse.

After a frustrating night reworking a perfectly good story, Kate climbed onto the Red Crescent Black Hawk for the three-hour journey to Basra. Unbelievably, the INN boys had managed to arrange the entire tour without the 'help' or company of their government guides. For once they'd be able to film freely, although the footage would have to stay in their cameras until they were well out of the country. Sending unauthorised material over the satellite could easily invite charges of spying and a stint in Abu Ghurayb prison.

As the helicopter pushed south, Kate peered down at the devastating reality of America's 'bloodless' war. From the air, a clear line was visible where US firepower had punched into the country. Black smoke billowed from dozens of burning oil wells. Immediately below, a column of bombed-out Iraqi tanks appeared petrified in the landscape.

'Can we land here?' Kate shouted to Jonathan over the noise of the chopper blades.

'Yeah. But not for very long. The shells that took out those tanks were coated with depleted uranium. It's not the kind of place you want to linger.'

They set down. The twisted, blackened and melted metal was like a scene from a Salvador Dali painting. Thousands of soldiers must have died in this spot, Kate thought. But there were no signs of what might once have been life. Any bodies had simply been obliterated.

The radioactivity only allowed them a few minutes of filming. But it was enough.

A world exclusive. Kate could scarcely believe it. And to think that lard-arsed Ripley had tried to veto the trip.

'No one cares what happened to a bunch of Iraqis in some fucked-up little corner of the world,' the chief of staff had growled. 'The war's over. You're the only one who doesn't seem to get that.'

Eventually she'd appealed to Mawson (tactfully of course), who had agreed to let her go. Carter had reluctantly fallen into line.

He had made the right call. Kate was even more convinced of that when she arrived in the shattered city of Basra. America's precision bombs hadn't been quite so accurate this far south of Baghdad.

At first the locals were too frightened to speak, scurrying away when Jonathan and Kate approached them. But they finally found an Indian man willing to share his story. He was a plumbing fore-man who had lived and worked in the port city for the past year.

It had been late in January and he was on his way to buy fish for his crew when he saw two missiles cruise overhead. He watched as they crashed into the market about thirty seconds apart.

'I ran to the place and saw many dead. Ten or fifteen. There was a little child. She was sitting next to a dead woman and crying Mummy, Mummy. They were just shopping.'

There was a television tower a three-minute walk from the market. That had probably been the real target. Basra's hospital had also been bombed. So much for the Pentagon's claims of pinpoint accuracy.

By mid-afternoon they had recorded dozens of witness accounts, each more harrowing than the one before.

'Living here during the bombing must have been terrifying. Maybe even worse than Baghdad,' Kate commented to Jonathan as they wandered through the main part of town.

'And it's only going to get worse. The Shiites here folded. Maybe 150,000 of them deserted the army. And as we know, Saddam does a rather neat line in retribution.'

They walked in silence for a while.

'Seen enough?' Jonathan asked.

She nodded. 'For several lifetimes.'

He held her gaze just a little longer than necessary. Kate felt a jolt and hoped he hadn't noticed.

Their helicopter left the ground slowly. Tezza was still filming of course. He treated his camera like a soldier's gun – it was always cocked and ready.

The Black Hawk could only have been a few hundred metres in the air when it started lurching violently from side to side.

'We're under fire,' Jonathan yelled as the chopper began to climb quickly.

The pilots were clearly used to evasive flying but Kate was terrified. Jonathan pulled her down and threw a protective arm over her shoulders. Tezza kept rolling on the action but eventually Kate managed to drag him down too. She could taste the metal of the floor and her own fear rising in her throat.

Then as suddenly as the emergency began, the chopper stopped its violent manoeuvring and all was stable again. The entire episode had lasted no more than a couple of minutes.

'What the hell was that? Who was firing at us?' Kate asked angrily.

'Christ knows. Maybe Saddam's men. Maybe just trigger-happy, war-struck civilians. It happens all the time around here. Anything in the air has to be the enemy, I guess.'

Kate was relieved when they finally reached the relative safety of Baghdad and the outright luxury of the INN bureau at the Al-Rashid. The British network had converted its tenth-floor hotel room into an office and editing suite, complete with kitchen facilities and an impressive array of provisions, much of it contraband.

'Wow, you guys really know how to take care of yourselves,' Kate said, her eyes sweeping the room jealously.

'War is hell, you know. What's your poison?' Jonathan asked.

'Scotch. Neat.'

'I can only offer you Johnny Walker Black, I'm afraid. I keep asking our drivers to include a couple of bottles of Laphroaig with our supplies. But somehow my request gets lost in translation every time. They just keep coming back with JW. At least they got the colour right.'

'Laphroaig. That was my father's favourite – single Highland malt.'

'Only the best. But it's a very subjective field. Anyway, I propose a toast – to our excellent adventure today.' Jonathan grinned and raised his glass. 'When was the last time either of you had that much fun?'

Tezza saluted in agreement. He'd checked his tape as soon as the helicopter had levelled out. It was gold.

'Are you two crazy?' Kate gasped. Although she knew the question was rhetorical. All good foreign correspondents were at least slightly mad.

She felt the scotch burning its way down her throat.

'So how much longer are you two here for?' Jonathan asked.

'I need to speak to the office. But they're getting bored I think. They'll be happy with today's stuff. That will buy us another day. Maybe two. But that's about it, I'm afraid.'

'We'll leave at the end of the week I'd imagine. The show here is pretty much over. But the Ministry of Information is taking us all on another big public-relations jaunt tomorrow. You never know. Maybe they'll come good this time.'

Kate didn't hold out much hope as she waited for her guide in the hotel lobby the next morning. Once again, he'd promised a story exposing the Americans as liars and murderers. But each excursion had started to merge into the next. Kate feared she was becoming jaded, even immune, to what she was reporting.

She'd filmed at hospitals with their wards full of haunted, empty-eyed orphans. She'd interviewed people who'd lost loved ones to the bombs and witnessed their grief, their bitterness and their hostility. She'd sat with wild-eyed fathers in the ruins of their homes. They would hold out empty arms and scoop them in to their hearts, talking through tears of lost children.

But she'd never experienced anything like this.

Kate stood outside the shell of the apartment block, its concrete exterior still intact. Trails of black smoke crept up the walls on either side of the doors. As she stepped over the threshold, she felt the hairs on her arms rise.

The press pack crowded around the sides of a giant round hole where twisted fingers of steel had peeled aside the layers of the apartment block like a banana skin. People had died in this place, lots of people. Every journalist knew that for the truth. The bodies had left their imprints on the concrete floor. And so many tiny silhouettes among them. Children. Dozens upon dozens of children.

No one spoke. The victims of this horror deserved their respect and their silence. Kate looked up to see Jonathan McTavish. She thought she saw tears in his eyes.

Kate imagined the fear on that awful night. The air sirens would have been roaring as the residents of the apartment block congregated downstairs and crowded into their makeshift bomb shelter.

They would have been able to hear the commotion above. Boom. Boom. Boom. The sounds of falling bombs would have penetrated the thick concrete walls. Kate could hear the cries of the children as mothers tried desperately to shield them from the horror all around them. Then a flash of light. Searing heat. Smoke. A missile had found its way into the bomb shelter, its diamond-hard nose punching through four layers of reinforced concrete. Everyone inside was incinerated. There wasn't even enough time to scream.

The US version of events was that its intelligence had identified the bomb shelter as a front for a military command centre. Saddam Hussein using civilians as human shields.

But after what she had seen and heard in Basra, Kate wondered if the US smart bombs weren't just acting on dumb intelligence. Maybe someone at the Pentagon fucked up and killed dozens of people. But even if what the Americans said was true, surely these people were more than just military chess pieces. They were human beings and they had died terrified in a terrible war.

Kate didn't hate America. But she hated its war. Passionately.

'You okay?' A familiar voice jolted her back to the present. She felt Jonathan's hand resting lightly on her shoulder.

'Yes, I think. So many dead. Thank God I'm getting out of here tomorrow. I can't take any more of this.'

'It never gets easier . . . trying to comprehend what human beings are capable of doing to one another,' he said softly.

Kate felt tears running down her face and Jonathan put a comforting arm around her. She turned and buried her head into his chest.

Home. Jonathan loved his job with a passion. But he always looked forward to getting back to London. To his friends and his family. To his quaint little Chelsea terrace. To the local restaurant district, where the food was familiar and the bars actually sold alcohol.

But today as he waited for his bags at the carousel of Heathrow Airport, he felt only numb. Kate had turned his smug little world on its head.

They'd returned to the hotel together after that terrible day at the apartment block. The golden glow of the dusty Baghdad sunset had streamed through his hotel window, bathing her naked body in a luminous light.

'You look like a goddess,' he'd told her.

They'd laughed afterwards about the rumours that the Al-Rashid was bugged. They speculated on what the Iraqi secret police might have learned from their loud lovemaking.

He smiled at the memory. Kate was like no other woman he had ever met. Was it love? He wasn't sure. But he knew he needed to find out.

There was almost an inevitability to what had happened in Baghdad. War. Death. You need to reaffirm life in the most instinctive way. Although Jonathan was keenly aware that he at least should have exercised more restraint.

Memory of their single night together brought feelings of shuddering wonder and intense guilt.

Julia. Dear Julia. They'd been together for five years. He loved her. They were going to marry in the spring, just a few weeks from now. That had been the plan, anyhow. But he knew he would have to break it off with her now. He could not go back, not after this.

Grabbing his bags, Jonathan strode through Customs, a determined set to his jaw.

His resolve crumbled the moment he spotted his fiancée's troubled face in the crowd. She was an ethereal creature. A classic English beauty with dark hair and clear pale skin. But today her complexion seemed almost waxen and there was no joy in her usually warm smile. Maybe she sensed what was coming. Whatever the case, what he had to say could wait until they got home.

'Julia, are you okay?'

Her eyes filled with tears as she fell into his arms. 'Oh, Jonathan. I've got some bad news.'

He wrapped his arms around her and listened.

TWELVE

The dentist's waiting room was suffocatingly hot. Outside, Sydney was experiencing its first truly cold day of winter. And some sadist had decided to mark the occasion by cranking up the heating until it was overcompensating by about five degrees.

Kate had been sitting and stewing in her mohair jumper for almost fifteen minutes. Why couldn't the professional classes stick to a schedule the way a good reporter hit a deadline?

Reading material. That's what she needed. She flipped through the stack of women's magazines piled on the low glass table in front of her. There wasn't a single issue she hadn't already leafed through at some stage during the past month or two. It was a sad indictment of her reading choices. And an unfortunate reflection of her social life since returning from Baghdad.

Kate had spent far too many post-Arabian nights sitting at home in anticipation of an international call. Eventually she had grown tired of waiting and had simply called INN in London. (The gutful of scotch had helped.) But Jonathan hadn't been there. And neither had he returned her call. Now, eight weeks later, she'd given up on the phone ever ringing. But she'd also worked herself into such a funk that she didn't want to leave her apartment anyway.

She tapped her foot impatiently. Forced downtime was like pulling teeth. Which was kind of appropriate under the circumstances.

'It shouldn't be long now,' the receptionist assured her in a singsong voice that made the comment sound more like a platitude than a statement of fact.

It took all Kate's self-control not to snarl. She was in a filthy, nicotine-obsessed mood. She had just given up the cigarettes again after her spectacular fall off the wagon in Tel Aviv. The deployment to Baghdad hadn't helped any of course. Throw in a few hundred hours staring at a stubbornly silent phone and her habit had edged upwards of a pack a day. Now dirty brown streaks stained her teeth. And that wasn't something that could be ignored in the hypercritical world of television. In fact, today's appointment had been a directive from above. But given the context, she was more than happy to comply.

She'd received the summons to Bruce Mawson's office the previous week. Unlike many of her colleagues, Kate looked forward to her occasional trips to the top floor. The news and current affairs chief was someone she liked and respected enormously. He had always been willing to back her. And what wasn't to like and respect about that?

Kate knocked on the door. Mawson was sitting with Charlie Wright, the reclusive executive producer of *Australia Tonight*, Channel Eight's nightly current affairs show. Like Mawson, Charlie favoured the informal look. But on his wiry frame it appeared dishevelled rather than cool and casual. He rarely left his office. That he'd been extracted on this occasion invested the meeting with an unexpected sense of importance.

Australia Tonight was the network's flagship public affairs show. Its smart mix of serious issues and light entertainment was starting to steal viewers from the other two commercial offerings.

In the daily ratings battle, if you won the 6–7 p.m. slot, you usually won the night. And to win the night was to win the week. And to win the week was to win the year. A strong performance in news and current affairs was key to most stations' ratings strategies.

Mawson didn't bother with pleasantries. 'Kate, we think you'd make a valuable addition to Charlie's team.' The news was delivered through the customary haze of cigarette smoke.

'We need a smart female journalist to balance our on air line-up,' Wright explained. Given that Jenni with an 'i' was now reporting for the program, Kate could understand how there was an opening.

'It will be great for your profile and you'll get to stretch yourself a bit,' Mawson added. 'No more minute-thirty stories. You'll get to do five, sometimes even seven-minute pieces. And there'll be lots of travel thrown in as well. So, are you up for it?'

'Of course I'm up for it, Chief.' Kate had been thinking about moving on from the newsroom for a while now. And *Australia Tonight* was the gig she'd been hoping to land. The only downside was that Mike Ripley had made the exact same switch. Still, she wasn't going to let him get in the way of her latest big career break.

'Is there a financial benefit as well?' Kate asked, employing her two most effective negotiating weapons – a friendly smile and a cheeky single raised eyebrow. She probably would have taken a pay cut for the opportunity. But she remembered some advice Sandra had given her during their last phone call.

'That's the difference between men and women in this game. The men expect a pay rise. They think they're worth a hundred times more than they actually are. But women will sit back and wait for their talents and efforts to be rewarded fairly. It doesn't happen. Honey, you've got to ask. But smile when you do it.'

'How does seventy-five thousand suit you? And a three grand clothing allowance.'

'Um, fine. That's fine.' Kate swallowed hard. Her salary had doubled in the space of five minutes. This was madness. Winning a Walkley had only been worth an extra three grand.

'Welcome on board then. We have a promo shoot on Friday. And we'll need you in it,' Charlie said, getting up to leave. The sanctuary of his office beckoned.

'Better book in for a teeth clean, Kate. What were you doing in Baghdad? Sucking on cigars?' Mawson added. 'Get your eyebrows plucked too.'

Kate hadn't ventured into a beautician since the incident at Tel Aviv. But she obediently followed Mawson's orders. Her brows were still red and stinging as she waited for the dentist to round off her misery with a couple of needles and a lecture on the oral health implications of smoking. She suspected none of *Australia Tonight*'s male reporters were being subjected to such treatment.

Kate riffled through the piles of magazines for a second time. Ah. *Tatler*. The English social pages always made for good entertainment in a proper, cucumber sandwich kind of way.

Flicking through the aristocratic and predictably Anglo parade of faces in the magazine, Kate's thoughts naturally turned to that other Englishman. Jonathan McTavish had treated her appallingly, no question. In her rational mind, she considered him the worst kind of bastard. But it didn't seem to matter. She still felt a jolt of longing whenever she thought of him.

She turned the page and the jolt became a lightning strike as the man asserted himself in glorious colour.

Jonathan stared out at her from the *Tatler* social pages, looking more handsome than ever. He'd swapped his correspondent's khaki for a morning suit. Dark tails. Grey pants. Striped vest. Camellia on his lapel. He was standing beside . . . Kate did a horrified double take. Mrs Jonathan McTavish! And the pale, fine-boned brunette in the picture was clearly not his mother.

Then she understood. The woman was wearing a cream wedding sheath. Jonathan had got married and these were the official photographs.

Kate chomped down angrily on her Nicorette as she checked the front of the magazine. April 1991. So the wedding had been five, six weeks ago. Just two weeks after they'd fallen into bed together.

She cursed under her breath. Her instincts had been right all along. The guy was a sleaze and a womaniser. Letting down her guard had been a terrible mistake.

'After a year-long engagement, Julia married her brave INN war correspondent Jonathan McTavish in a lavish Chelsea soiree.' *Tatler* then went on to breathlessly recount every fairytale moment of the couple's big day.

Engaged for a year. Bastard! Bastard!

She heard her name called.

'Fuck,' she muttered a little too loudly, slamming down the magazine and blinking away angry tears.

The dental nurse shot a disapproving look at Kate as she ushered her down the corridor. Plenty of people didn't like going to the dentist but they managed to mind their manners and their language. These television types. They just didn't think the rules applied to them.

'I'd like the gas please,' Kate announced as she stepped into the tiny surgery.

'For a clean?' the dentist asked doubtfully.

'I'm dental phobic.' Her response wasn't altogether a lie. But the pain inflicted by the *Tatler* article was far greater than anything the dentist was likely to administer.

Kate closed her eyes and let the gas take hold, falling with it, away from the present and to that last day in Baghdad. The morning after the night before.

Jonathan had cupped her face in his warm hands.

'That was amazing. *You* are amazing.' His blue eyes bored into her, as if trying to memorise her DNA. 'I have some things I need to sort out back home. But give me some time. And I'll call you. I promise.'

They kissed. The kind of deep, melting kiss that was supposed to mean something. Then he walked away quickly, not looking back.

Stupid, stupid girl. The words swam around her nitric oxide-saturated brain.

There was a tap on her forehead and she opened her watery eyes.

'Are you okay?' the dentist asked. 'We're all finished.'

'Of course I'm not okay,' Kate wailed as she collapsed onto her neighbours' cocoa leather couch. Al was racing around the house making herbal tea infusions and gathering armfuls of self-help books. Ben assumed the unfamiliar role of heterosexual relationship counsellor.

'Was the sex good?' he asked, figuring that was as good a place as any to start.

'Yes. Unbelievably good. The best – unfortunately.'

'Well, there you go, girl. At least you got something out of it, right?'

'No. That just makes it worse. I actually thought it was the real thing. But it was all just bullshit.' Kate launched into another bout of noisy snuffling. Al leafed frantically through *The Road Less Travelled* in search of a few pithy words of comfort.

Kate earned enough nowadays to upgrade from her tiny apartment. But she couldn't imagine ever leaving Ben and Al. She liked the comfort and security of having two men living downstairs. And every Sydney girl needed a couple of gay friends in her life. There was no one else in the world Kate trusted with the sordid details of her love life. Not even Gillian. Not after her one-night stand with Matthew went around the office like a dose of the flu.

'Kate, darling, it was a war zone. People do crazy things. You did a crazy thing,' Ben tried again. 'Now what say we all go and get trashed at DCM's. You can dance away all that unnecessary anguish.'

'You think clubbing is the answer to all life's woes,' Al chastised his lover.

'That and recreational drugs,' Ben corrected. 'Now there's an idea. How about a happy pill, Kate?'

'No way. The last time I fell for that I didn't sleep for thirty-six hours and spent the entire weekend telling all your gay friends I was in love with them. Anyway, I have a promo shoot tomorrow. So I have to get to bed early.' Kate reluctantly forced herself vertical. 'Thanks, guys, you're the best.'

'Try to sleep. And if you can't we're here,' Ben said, pulling her into a fierce hug. 'Don't worry, beautiful. You won't be on the shelf long. You're so gorgeous, I'd almost turn for you. Almost!'

Kate smiled but just for a minute.

'Talking, talking, talking and look to camera – serious expressions now. Good. Okay, let's do it again.'

It was Kate's first real promo shoot. Some of her reports had featured in newsroom promotions of course. But she'd never before been required to dress up and perform under studio lights. She was quickly realising this was not an aspect of the job she liked very much.

She'd been shoehorned into a powder-blue linen pant suit, courtesy of the wardrobe department, and ordered not to sit down to avoid creases. And just to make sure she was wholly unrecognisable to anyone – except maybe her mother – her hair had been sprayed into submission with Doris Day-like flicks at the ends.

Kate didn't feel like herself at all. Worse still, she felt like a fraud next to some of the big-name reporters assembled in the studio. She'd had a pretty good run since joining Channel Eight, what with a Walkley and her recent experiences as a foreign correspondent. But some of the *AT* team were ten, twenty, even thirty years her senior. These were people she'd grown up watching on television. They were her heroes. She was a long way from considering herself their equal.

To compensate, Kate deliberately positioned herself next to Jenni with an 'i'. Admittedly, the girl made her look positively flat chested. But journalistically, at least, she felt she stacked up well.

Jenni's elevation from lowly newsroom production assistant to national current affairs reporter had been the subject of much bitchy speculation. But Kate, at least, was determined not to buy into stereotypes. Jenni was beautiful. And she wasn't particularly bright. But that didn't mean she slept her way to success.

Jenni did love the camera though. She was obviously enjoying the hoopla of the promo shoot. The show's seven reporters were assembled a couple of steps behind the anchor desk. Their role was to talk amongst themselves whilst taking a few steps forward. Meanwhile, the host had to sit at his desk busily reading news copy, apparently unaware he was being stalked by his colleagues. Then all at once, the reporters stopped talking. The host stopped reading. And everyone lifted their heads in unison and stared at the camera as if suddenly witnessing a vision of the Virgin Mary.

'That's great,' the promo producer hollered from the back of the studio. 'And that's a wrap.'

'God, I'm glad that's over,' Kate said, pulling off her wardrobe-issue court shoes and turning to Jenni. But Jenni had already scarpered off to flirt with Mike Ripley at the other end of the studio.

The Gulf War might not have changed a lot in the Middle East but it had redrawn the borders at Channel Eight. While Kate was making a name for herself in Tel Aviv, Mike Ripley had been promoted to editorial supervisor of *Australia Tonight*. He was second in charge to Charlie Wright.

Gillian was now bureau chief of the program's Melbourne office. And Sean Scott was back, headhunted by Wright just as Saddam began amassing troops on the Kuwaiti border. The wily executive producer wanted to recruit the smartest, most experienced people he could find. His tactics had been rewarded with massive ratings.

The main casualty of battle was Geoff Jones. He'd fought his war spooling through CNN footage in Amman. Still, he'd somehow managed to talk up his correspondent's credentials to land a job with a rival current affairs show.

Jenni also owed her dramatic elevation to the Gulf War. But in her case, it was more happenstance. *Australia Tonight* had deployed two of its reporters overseas to cover events in the Middle East, leaving the Sydney office understaffed. Jenni had filled in here and there, filing the occasional colour piece and interviewing visiting celebrities. When Saddam withdrew from Kuwait, Jenni had dug in, stubbornly staying at her new desk until everyone simply assumed she belonged there. She had learned a lot from the newsroom's nightly game of musical chairs.

She'd even crafted a niche for herself as the show's first ever consumer reporter. The arrangement certainly suited Kate. There were only two female reporters on the *Australia Tonight* team and stories tended to be assigned on the basis of gender. So if Jenni hadn't claimed the consumer and celebrity rounds for herself, they would have landed in Kate's lap. So everyone was happy. Jenni was the housewives' friend. And Kate got to chase her share of the more substantial stories.

Not that anyone would have known it from watching the promo. Seeing it on air two weeks later, Kate realised she'd been scuttled. Each reporter had been given a few solo seconds on screen to showcase their work. Despite her efforts in Iraq, Kate's career had been reduced to a lazy stroll along the beach in an oversized sunhat. The breezy jingle chirped, 'You have a date with Kate'.

The vision chosen to accompany the male reporters looked like it had been lifted from an action movie. Testosterone-charged scuffles. Angry confrontations. There was even a car chase. The whole travesty culminated with that improbable studio shot. As the *Australia Tonight* team stared purposefully at the camera, the voiceover proclaimed, '*Australia Tonight* . . . on the pulse.' Kate didn't look like she was on the pulse at all. She looked like she was on a bloody holiday.

Kate suspected this was Ripley's handiwork. He looked after all the show promos, right down to handpicking the vision. There wasn't too much she could do about it now. But she had to let Ripley know she wasn't happy. Staying silent would only encourage him to repeat the insult next time around.

Kate marched into the general production area and up to the main desk. This was where the ruling elite sat and decided what a million plus Australians wanted to watch each night. If they guessed right, they basked in the glory of a ratings victory. If they missed the mark, they hunkered down and blamed whoever wasn't in earshot, usually the host or the viewers themselves. Thursday night shopping was a regular culprit if by chance the ratings dipped on that night.

The main desk was set up in a circular arrangement, with work space for three people. Mike Ripley sat across from the Buddha-like chief of staff. Ripley had somehow managed to install his own man in the COS chair. Tubby didn't really have the creativity or the sharp news sense usually associated with the role. But from Ripley's point of view, the guy had one giant asset. He agreed with everything Ripley said.

The third seat in this axis of power belonged to Charlie Wright. But as the executive producer preferred the refuge of his office, the chair was usually empty. Charlie had an amazing knack of knowing what people wanted to see on television – but that was the only people skill he did have. Staff could go from one week to the next without ever seeing him. Kate glanced over at his office. The door was shut.

'I just saw the show promo.' Kate directed the statement to Ripley.

'Yeah, love it. You look great.'

'I would have expected you to use some vision from Iraq or Tel Aviv.'

'Yeah, I thought about it. But the shot on the beach was so much friendlier. The punters want to see Kate's soft side. Anyway, it balanced out all the other hard stuff.'

'You mean the blokey stuff?' Ripley was refusing to make eye contact. 'Look, I thought that promo was supposed to show off my career highlights. Walkleys. Wars. Scuds. I was one of the first Australian journalists back into Iraq after the war. I do not count swanning along a central coast beach as a career highlight.'

'Yeah, mate. I know, I know. Believe me, I'm your biggest fan. But if you have a problem you'd better take it up with Charlie. He liked the promo just fine.' Kate bit into her cheek. Hard. She'd already allowed her temper to dictate too much of this conversation. 'He's in his office. As you know, his door's always open,' Ripley added sarcastically.

'Don't worry, honey. Everyone knows your work. I told you the bloke was a snake,' Gillian reminded her on the phone a few minutes later. 'Did he blame Charlie?'

'Yeah, and made some snide remark about him being locked away in his office.'

'I've known Ripley a long time. Don't fall for that "I'm on your side" bullshit. The moment you turn your back, he'll have the knives out. He's a master at it. And there doesn't always seem to be a purpose to it either. Sometimes I swear he just does it for the sport. Anyway, just watch your step.

'I don't care about office politics. I just want a decent promo.'

'Look, it could be worse. Jenni's in a bikini'

'I know. But she probably chose that shot herself!'

Gillian was laughing. 'Actually I'm pretty sure she did. She rang me, trying to find the tape.'

'Fuck me. This industry can be absolute crap sometimes. I miss you. I just wish we could go sink a few at the Burdekin tonight. But since you're in Melbourne, I'm going to the gym instead. Try to sweat it out.'

Kate had been spending a lot of time at the gym lately. Five days a week. An hour or more at a time. She looked fabulous. But she felt lousy.

She hadn't been able to outrun her disappointment over her ill-judged fling with Jonathan McTavish. And she wasn't going to transform Ripley into a sensitive new-age guy by raising her pulse rate to 180 bpm. Still, a tough workout might take some of the edge off her frustration.

Kate grabbed a free treadmill and twisted the dial to jogging speed. Looking straight ahead, she started running, willing herself into the zone. She'd barely made it around her first imaginary block when a familiar voice upset her rhythm.

'Hi, Kati,' the woman on the StairMaster next to her puffed. It was Jenni with an 'i'.

'Jenni. I'm so sorry. I didn't notice you there. How are you?' Kate readjusted her settings and reluctantly fell back to a brisk walk.

'Fantastic. How are you finding *AT*?' Jenni's ponytail bounced perkily as she strode up floor after floor. Her breasts, on the other hand, remained curiously static.

'Interesting. Different. Very different to news.'

'The stories are a lot longer,' Jenni agreed sagely.

'Interesting piece you did on washing powder. I've never seen a story quite like it really.'

'Oh, that *Choice* survey? Yeah. I couldn't believe it did so well. Best ratings all year, in fact. I guess everyone washes, huh?' Jenni instinctively understood that in the world of commercial current affairs, ratings were the greatest truth. 'Next week we're putting the actual washing machines through the wringer.' Jenni giggled at her little pun.

'Do you really like all that consumer stuff?' Kate asked. She was suspicious of this new genre of reporting that was fast overshadowing traditional public affairs.

Jenni jumped off the stairmaster, readjusted her sweatband and shrugged. 'It's not up to me to judge, is it? If the viewers want to watch it, then it's relevant.'

As Kate urged her treadmill back to a steady jog, she wondered if she had been underestimating Jenni. She definitely had a point. Their job was to produce television that people wanted to watch. And right now, people wanted to watch washing go round. Just because the subject didn't interest Kate, didn't make it any less legitimate.

Kate watched as Jenni fiddled with the foot straps of a rower a metre or so away, her head bent over in concentration.

That's when she saw it. A familiar looking blotch on the back of her neck, just behind her ear. It was the small anchor-shaped birthmark she'd spotted two and a half years earlier at Sandra Cook's farewell. On the woman servicing Mike Ripley.

From production assistant to weather girl to current affairs reporter. It all made perfect sense now. So much for not buying into stereotypes. Kate cranked the treadmill up another full kilometre an hour. By the time the machine beeped the end of her session, she had sweated herself into a fury.

She was still in a foul temper when she arrived home an hour later. Al's bombshell only worsened her mood.

'Kate. I'm sorry. But I couldn't help myself. I noticed this letter had arrived, postmarked from the UK.'

The mailbox for the old terrace house consisted of a slit in the door at the communal entranceway. Everyone's letters landed in a little heap on the tessellated tiles. Al usually sorted it all when he got home from work, leaving anything for Kate on the stairs to her flat. Today he had decided hand delivery was in order.

Just a few weeks ago, the arrival of this letter would have filled Kate with excitement and longing. But not now. There was nothing Jonathan could say to make everything all right. However he chose to break the news, no matter what excuses, justifications and platitudes, he was a married man.

'Thanks, Al,' Kate said, taking the letter from him.

'We're here if you need a shoulder, Kate.'

She managed a weak smile and trudged up the stairs to her flat. She threw the envelope on the kitchen table and headed straight to the kitchen to slice open a packet of smoked salmon for Bernie. Someone in the house deserved to be happy.

As Bernie chowed down on his owner's unexpected largesse, Kate lit a fire in the old coal grill, located her secret stash of cigarettes and poured herself two fingers of scotch. Then she just sat on the couch and stared at the letter through a haze of smoke and amber liquid.

It took four generous shots and seven cigarettes. But somewhere around midnight, Kate finally decided what to do. She picked up the letter, ripped it in two and threw it into the fire.

Then she watched as the paper burned and curled to ashes.

THIRTEEN

'Fuck-a-duck. Wires say Keating is challenging Hawke for the leadership,' Tubby yelled across the office at everyone and no one in particular.

'Who have we got on the ground?' Ripley bellowed over the ensuing bedlam.

'Work the fucking phones. See if we can get either of them up for a two-way tonight.' Charlie Wright had emerged from his office a few minutes earlier. He always seemed to materialise moments before the big stories broke. It was uncanny.

'Where the fuck is our resident political expert?' Wright was circling the main desk like a shark around a shipwreck. In his present mood, he was just as dangerous. 'We pay him a bloody fortune for his contacts in Canberra. And we find out about a leadership challenge on the bloody wires. Fuck me. Is the fucking host in yet?'

'He hasn't graced us with his presence yet,' Ripley replied, happily seizing the chance to twist the knife a little, as was his habit with anyone who possessed a pulse and had their back to him.

'Half a million bucks a year for what, three hours work, if that. Fuck. Find him, will you?'

'The fucking midget should know where he is,' Ripley replied, unaware the woman in question was standing right behind him.

The host's personal assistant was a diminutive yet highly efficient woman who organised his busy schedule with Teutonic precision.

'I take it you're referring to me?' she said coldly.

'Um, well, shit, Jess, you are, well, you're very petite,' Ripley stammered, shuffling his feet and looking at the floor.

'You were after the host?' Jessica Schmidt managed to keep her voice professional and level but her expression was thunderous.

'Ah, yeah, we may have a two-way soon and we'll need him in the studio. Where is he?'

'He's playing tennis. It's a fund raiser. As you know he won't carry a pager. I'll drive down to the courts and get him.' Jessica turned on her size five heel, and left. She would have stomped out if she had any weight behind her.

'Christ, is that bitch always on the fucking rags or what?' Ripley sneered, emboldened now Jessica had left the room.

'Fucking midget! Good one, you goose.' Doug Spencer, one of the senior producers, called from a nearby work station.

'Come on, Spence. You gotta get the gag,' Tubby leered, opening the lunchbox his mother had packed him that morning.

'I'm on to Keating's press sec. He says we'll get the interview if his man wins the ballot,' a girl fresh out of college yelped across the room.

'Hot stuff! Love ya work,' Tubby shouted back. The researcher beamed with pride. She was new enough to believe his clichéd praise actually meant something.

'Shall I let Kate know we might not need her story tonight?' she asked.

'Nah. Fuck her,' Ripley said.

'Now who's on their rags?' Tubby snickered.

Ripley was indeed in a filthy mood. But it had nothing to do with uppity secretaries and disappearing hosts and everything to do with his rapidly deteriorating home life.

He'd woken that morning to the rumble of garbage trucks and an accusatorial elbow nudging him hard in the ribs.

'Did you take out the garbage last night?' his wife of ten years demanded.

'Oh, fuck. I forgot.' Or at least he presumed he had forgotten. There wasn't too much Ripley remembered from the previous day. A boozy lunch. A couple of beers in the office as the show went to air. All he could be sure of was that he'd woken up in his own bed and that it was his car parked haphazardly across the driveway. Clearly he'd managed to get himself home somehow. But he had zero recollection of the journey.

'What fucking good are you then? It's your only fucking job around the house. Christ, do I have to hire a man to take the fucking garbage out too? Last week I had to pay someone to change a washer. A fucking washer.'

'Shssh, you'll wake the kids.' Ripley cowered. The woman had been sounding more and more like his bitch of a mother ever since the birth of their second child.

'Fuck, I've had it with you,' his wife spat as she stormed off to the bathroom.

Ripley coaxed a jumper over his ample stomach and tiptoed out of the marital home. He was just congratulating himself on his clean getaway when his car phone rang. It was station security.

'Mr Ripley, we are missing one half of our front sign. And according to our closed-circuit vision, it appears it was your car that took it out.'

Yep, the day had started badly all right.

'Ripley, mate. We should let Kate off the hook. She shouldn't rush her yarn if she doesn't need to,' Doug Spencer said from behind the *Illawarra Mercury* form guide.

'Fuck her.' Ripley's head was pounding. 'The bitch can sweat a bit.'

And Kate *was* sweating despite the cool June weather. She was on a stakeout, parked with her crew outside a multi-million dollar mansion in Sydney's east. The owner of the home had fleeced his clients of their life savings in a dodgy foreign-currency scheme. Kate had the rest of the story in the can. She just needed to bounce the bloke. Four hours had passed without any sign of him.

'No bad guy. No story,' Wright had once said to her. Which presented a dilemma because Ripley was insisting he needed the yarn up that night. No excuses.

Even without the extra pressure from the office, her nerves would be jangling. Walk-ins were unpredictable. There was always the chance they might turn violent. Guns were a rare but very real threat. And there was the constant risk of being assaulted by whatever was handy at the time. One reporter from a rival channel had been struck by a watering can of all things.

Then there was the danger of simply getting it wrong. Shoving a camera in someone's face automatically made them look guilty. To then broadcast the scene on national television, a reporter needed to be damned sure of their facts. They could be sued. The station could be sued. Or worse. But Kate had done her homework on this one and she knew her information was good. The guy was crooked. The trick was finding him.

Kate looked at her watch. She could afford to sit for another couple of hours and still get the story to air that night. Happily, she only had to wait a few extra minutes. Kate watched carefully as a new-model luxury car pulled up to the entrance of the house.

She checked the driver against the description she had been given. Mid-thirties. Receding hair. Slight build. Moustache. And the coup de grace, he was driving a Bentley. It was him all right.

The conman got out of the car as Kate knew he would. She had positioned a couple of wheelie bins across his driveway to make sure of it. She wasn't about to let him glide through his remote-controlled gates without stopping for a chat first.

Adrenalin pumping, Kate leapt from the crew car. The camera-man and sound guy followed close behind, tape rolling. It was a copybook current affairs ambush. The guy didn't realise he'd been cornered until he felt a furry microphone tickling the side of his face.

'Sir, we'd like to speak to you about your dubious investment schemes,' Kate fired.

'I don't know what you're talking about.' The little accountant tried to get back into his car but Kate had wedged herself in front of the driver's door. He was trapped. And he was furious. 'Get outta here. Get the fuck outta here!' He gave Kate's cameraman an angry push.

Cut off from his obvious escape route by Kate's skilfully posi-tioned rear, the man started running. She took off after him. Skirt, jacket and Nikes weren't the most attractive fashion combination. But running in high heels looked even more ridiculous. Kate knew better than to wear her best shoes on a stakeout; they were sitting in the car ready for her graceful re-entry into the office once she had her man.

She kept up easily. Those obsessive workouts at the gym had their advantages. 'Nice car. Is it possible you spent all the missing money on yourself?' She was scarcely puffing as she jogged casually alongside her heavily perspiring and now very agitated mark.

In desperation, the man ran up to a nearby house and knocked on the door. He pushed past the astonished woman who answered, slamming the door behind him.

'But this isn't even your house,' Kate shouted deadpan. She had more than enough material.

It wasn't exactly Baghdad but the story was solid enough and it offered some small measure of retribution for the man's many victims. For around the clock adrenalin, Kate would need to join a big overseas news network like CNN. She occasionally hankered for a war zone but she liked living in Australia more.

A week after Paul Keating's failed leadership challenge, Mike Ripley wobbled down the top-floor corridor, nervously tucking his Ralph Lauren shirt into his pants. He knew exactly why he'd been hauled up to Mawson's office. That bitch Jessica Schmidt had opened her mouth. And not for party favours. Sour little slut had no sense of humour.

'G'day, Bruce. How ya doin?' Ripley greeted his boss with a swagger and a handshake. Why should he slink into the lion's den? It wasn't like he'd done anything wrong.

'I was a whole lot better before I got the call from human resources,' Mawson said, swinging back on his chair. 'Mike, we have rules. We have laws that say you can't go round calling people fucking midgets.'

'Shit, Bruce. The broad just walked in at the wrong time.'

'Well, Jessica Schmidt has made an official complaint. So I can't just pretend it didn't happen. I covered for you for the fucking front sign, but this is outside the cone. So you're off to a discrimination seminar and we're throwing in a little one-on-one counselling as well. Maybe next time you'll be a bit more artful and a little less fucking stupid in your discrimination.'

'Oh, fuck, do I have to?'

'Well, I could sack you if you prefer,' Mawson offered. There was silence as the alternative hung in the air. Ripley knew better than to open his mouth. 'Good, that's sorted then. Anyway, how's Kate working out for you down at *AT*?' Mawson asked

'Not too bad. A bit lazy. Resting on her laurels a bit off the back of Iraq.'

'Really? I wouldn't have picked Kate as the lazy type. She's been doing some great yarns though. I loved the walk-in with the bloke who ran into the wrong house.'

'Don't get me wrong. She's great, when she fires. I'm her number one fan. I just have to put a rocket up her sometimes.'

'Well, whatever you're doing, keep it up. It's obviously working. The show looks great and the ratings are even better.'

The two men shook hands.

It had been a good half hour's work, Ripley judged. He'd managed to dodge a bullet from human resources. And he'd taken Kate 'I've got a Walkley' Corish down a peg or two while he was at it. It was worthy of a little celebration. Smiling to himself, Ripley headed off to the pub for a long, liquid lunch on the company card.

Kate sat on a milk crate outside Coluzzi Bar fingering her pristine corporate Amex. She'd been a born-again virgin for most of the year. But with spring in the air and the party season looming, she was just about ready to come out of hibernation. First, though, she needed to update her wardrobe.

'I'm sick of the bloody straight skirt, sensible jacket, pumps and bobbed hair look,' she announced to Ben and Al. 'Every female reporter looks exactly the same. You'd think we all came off a bloody conveyor belt.'

Ben nodded. 'It's so drab. You're famous. You should be wearing clothes that scream "Hey, I'm Kate Fucking Corish. I'm on television and don't you forget it".'

'That's what I reckon,' Kate agreed. 'Although maybe not in those exact words.'

'Well, if you're going to spend some of that three grand clothing allowance, I'd love to help. I'm always up for a little retail therapy, even if the thrill is only vicarious.'

'What say we blow the whole bloody lot along Oxford Street as soon as we finish this latte,' Kate suggested, feeling uncharacteristically reckless.

'Count me out, girls. I've got my Ayurvedic Yoga class. But Ben, please remember. Our Kate still has to look like a reporter.'

'Oh, relax, Al. You are such a worry wart.' Ben clapped his hands. 'This is going to be just like *Pretty Woman*. I'll be Richard Gere.'

The phone rang three nights later as Kate sat in front of the television, nursing her cat, a whiskey and a crush on the cute DJ in *Northern Exposure*.

'Is Janet Jackson there?'

'Pardon. You must have the wrong number.'

'Well, you must have stolen her bloody wardrobe. Kate. It's Sandra here. What the hell was that ensemble you were wearing on television tonight?'

Kate shifted uncomfortably. Ben had assured her she looked absolutely fabulous. But even at the time she suspected his taste wasn't exactly universal.

'I can't believe the wardrobe department stuck you in a black and white checked jacket that strobed across my TV screen. You looked like you had a vibrator up that pert backside of yours. I don't even want to imagine how the outfit affected Channel Eight's loyal epileptic viewers.'

'Actually, it wasn't wardrobe. I chose the outfit myself.'

'First run with a substantial clothing allowance, huh?'

'Yeah, I might have got a bit carried away. I was just trying to break the mould, you know.'

'Please tell me that jacket was a one-off mistake and you still have some allowance left.'

'No on both counts I'm afraid. But I can still take most of the clothes back.'

The following Saturday, Sandra rode shotgun as Kate returned leather pants, multi-zippered jackets and A-line skirts to the cutting edge boutiques from whence they came.

'Now to build you a wardrobe from scratch. We'll be going for classic but chic. Okay?'

'But I hate boring clothes.' Kate didn't want to be mistaken for a houndstooth dildo again but she didn't want to dress like her mother either.

'Honey, trust me. You want people to notice your eyes, your face and your brain. Not your clothes. What you wear has to say 'Trust me. I'm credible'. Next time you want to express your individuality, do it with a scarf. And never, but never wear an A-line skirt. Not even Kylie Minogue would get away with doing that to her thighs.'

By the end of the day, Kate barely recognised herself. Carla Zampatti, Keith Mathieson, Simona and company had transformed her into the cool and glamorous professional she had always aspired to be. Even Ben was impressed.

By year's end, Keating was Prime Minister and Kate had been named one of Australia's most stylish women by *Vogue* (although she suspected the compliment had more to do with Sandra's magazine contacts than her own sartorial endeavours). She had even indulged in a summer fling with a touring American tennis player.

December also brought a ferocious round of downsizing at

Channel Eight. The parent company said it was to 'cut out the dead wood'. But as usual, it was the kindling that got the chop. The great logs of television bureaucracy remained in place. At *Australia Tonight*, three researchers were given notice, along with a camera crew, a part-time receptionist and a production assistant. Jessica Schmidt's name was also on the list.

FOURTEEN

Late June and the western suburbs were about five degrees colder than anywhere else in Sydney. Kate shivered outside the brick-veneer home and took a final deep drag of her cigarette. Four years in the industry and Kate was a death-knock veteran. In fact, she was every bit as skilled in the art as Geoff Jones, although she liked to think she was a good deal more compassionate.

Nowadays, Kate accepted the death knock as part of the job. Grief tended to produce the most compelling television. And that meant ratings. As much as Kate hated walking up that front path, she also liked to win. Her pitch was one of the best in the business. And most days she believed her spiel about making a difference and speaking for the victim. Today that was most certainly the case.

The story was classic current-affairs fodder. A woman had taken out an AVO against her violent former lover before going into hiding. A few days later, she lay dead in the driveway of a women's shelter, hunted down and shot like a dog. STALKED, the headline screamed.

Sitting at her kitchen table at half-past five that morning, Kate had scrutinised the newspaper copy. The victim's nineteen-year-old daughter had apparently begged the police for protection. But they could do nothing until the man broke the AVO. He was arrested when the inevitable happened. But it was too late for Kayleen's mother.

It was the story of the day. Kate was straight on the phone.

'Hi, Tubby. You on your way to the office?'

'Yep. On the Bridge as we speak.' Kate thought she heard the sound of ejecting toast in the background. 'Nice sunrise,' he offered unconvincingly.

'Have you seen the front page of the *Mail*? It's a cracker.'

There was a faint rustling of paper on the other end of the line.

'Oh yeah. Yeah. Good yarn. Great yarn. I've already got a researcher making calls on it,' Tubby lied as he unfolded the high-waisted jeans his mother had so lovingly pressed. 'You interested?'

'I'll get ready now and the crew can swing by and pick me up. We'll head out in the general direction of Penrith. Ring me with the address when we get close.'

Kate stubbed out her cigarette and checked her watch. Quarter to seven. The rest of the media pack wouldn't be too far behind. Finding Kayleen was as easy as opening the UBD. Her address was on the electoral roll microfiche for anyone to access.

Kate took a deep breath and knocked. After a couple of minutes she heard a stir of movement and the door opened a few inches. A plumpish plain girl stared out at her through dull, red-rimmed eyes. She looked a lot younger than nineteen.

Kate smiled gently. 'Hi, Kayleen is it?'

The girl nodded flatly.

'My name is Kate Corish from *Australia Tonight*. I'm so sorry about your mother. I can't imagine how painful it must be for you.'

There was a pause.

'I thought if you wanted to talk to the media, it would be better to see you in person rather than call you on the phone,' Kate pushed on through the silence. 'Perhaps I could come inside for a bit of a chat. No pressure of course. The crew can stay in the car.'

The girl pushed the door open a little wider. In the background, the phone was ringing. It hadn't stopped the whole time Kate had been standing on the porch.

'It's been going since five. I haven't answered it.' Kayleen's voice was leaden as she led Kate through to the sunroom at the back of the house.

'Every media outlet in Sydney wants to speak with you today,' Kate explained as she lifted the phone off the hook.

Kayleen looked confused.

'Your mum's death is on the front page of the *Mail*. More reporters will be here soon. Radio. TV. Newspapers. And they'll all want an interview. I'm just the first. I'm really sorry.'

On the other side of the rickety formica table, Kayleen started sobbing, quietly at first and then in great heaving gulps. 'What am I going to do?'

'You tried to get help and the system let you down. Maybe your mother would want you to speak out. I don't know. But right now you have three choices,' Kate said softly. 'You can do a single interview. And I really hope you do that interview with me. That way you get your point across. You get to tell the world what happened. Then I'll do my bit and pressure politicians and police into strengthening the law to protect women. I know that doesn't bring your mum back, but it's something. All the other journalists will eventually realise they've missed out on the story. They won't bother you again. That's one option.'

Kayleen was still snuffling but she was listening intently. 'Option two. You could hold a press conference. You'd speak to all the journalists at the same time and answer their questions. The pack can be overwhelming. But at least it's over quickly. If public speaking makes you nervous, I wouldn't recommend you go that route.'

Kayleen winced. Kate had calculated the mention of public speaking would rule out a press conference. The last thing she wanted was to be jostling for microphone space with every other journalist in the city. It would be a circus anyway and torture for a grieving teenager.

'Finally, you could tell everyone to piss off, including me. Unfortunately most reporters won't listen and they'll still be camped on your doorstep this time tomorrow. And that's it, I'm afraid.'

The kettle started to whistle and Kayleen busied herself in the kitchen. 'And you'll let me know what questions you're going to ask?'

'Sure,' Kate replied, getting up to signal her crew inside.

As she opened the front door, she noticed two more television cars pulling up. Nine and Seven she guessed. Geoff Jones would be here somewhere for sure.

'Too late, pal,' she thought.

Kate's crew set up as far away from the front of the house as possible. Reporters like Jones employed all kinds of dirty tricks to nobble the competition. He'd been known to holler and knock on the door non-stop just to ruin a rival's interview. Kate made sure that couldn't happen today by pushing a single mattress against the sunroom door. It was a crude method of sound proofing. But it was as effective as installing a mute button.

As the interview progressed, Kayleen's confidence grew. She cried softly as she spoke of her mother's terror. And she was articulate and passionate as she demanded to know why the courts had failed to protect her.

'That was great, Kayleen. After this, the politicians will have to listen. Now do you have any questions?'

'Only one. What do I do about them?' Kayleen gestured towards the front door.

Outside a couple of dozen journalists were milling about on the nature strip, all waiting for Kate and her team to leave so they could claim their pound of flesh.

Geoff Jones was there. But Kate already knew that from the incessant knocking. A little way up the road, a link truck was setting up ready to cross live into a breakfast television show. A senior radio hack was leaning against a telegraph pole, flirting with a cadet from one of the suburban weeklies.

In the driveway, a frighteningly young Eurasian reporter was reapplying her make-up in the side view mirror of her crew car. What was her name? Michelle something or other. Kate had only run into the girl a couple of times but disliked her intensely. There were two types of women in the TV game – the ones who shook their arse to get by and the ones who worked their arses off to be taken seriously.

She'd already pegged Michelle as an arse shaker.

Kate returned to the sunroom where the crew had just finished dismantling their lights. The mattress was back on Kayleen's bed.

'It's the usual crowd. The good, the bad and the vile,' she reported. 'I can get you out of here if you like. Put you up in a hotel?'

'I'd like that.' Kayleen sat hunched over at the table, her head in her hands. She had once again retreated into her grief. The self-possessed young woman Kate had interviewed had vanished.

'Kayleen, go and pack a small overnight bag. Tom, can I borrow your baseball cap? In fact, I'll need your ear phones and the mixer too.' Tom happily obliged.

Kayleen returned with a plastic shopping bag containing some basic clothes and toiletries.

'Kayleen, give the bag to Tom. Put this cap on. Pull your shirt out. You need to look a bit scruffy. We're all going to walk out of here together. You'll carry the boom mike and the sound gear. Keep your head down. Tom, you stay here and call a cab in five minutes. We'll meet you a few blocks away.'

Tom draped the headphones around Kayleen's neck and lifted the mixer onto her shoulder. She looked like any other soundo. Kate was relying on the near invisibility of the audio operator out on the road. Reporters like Jones loved the sound of their own voice but never really noticed or acknowledged the people who committed it to tape.

'Just walk down the path behind Tezza. I'll be right behind you. Okay?' She gave Kayleen a confident wink as they trooped out the door.

The media pack glared as the *Australia Tonight* team trudged towards their car. About bloody time they thought as they checked their watches and considered approaching deadlines.

'Morning all.' Kate adopted her sympathetic 'Here we all are again. Same shit. Different shovel' tone.

Another current affairs crew hurried towards the front door.

'How was she?' the reporter asked.

'Great. But I doubt she's interested in any more interviews today.'

'I suppose ya bought her off,' Geoff Jones shouted as Kate, Kayleen and Tezza quickly loaded their gear into the back of the station wagon.

Kate would have liked to explain the cost benefits of rising early to read the newspapers instead of lazily waking up to breakfast radio. But this wasn't the time. Her priority was finding Kayleen a safe and comfortable hideout for the day.

Five minutes later, a cab pulled up outside the girl's home and tooted its horn. The driver may as well have fired a starter's gun. Cameras were hoisted onto shoulders and white balances hurriedly set. Radio types tapped their microphones and checked recording levels while print journalists fumbled for their tiny tape recorders. Up and down the front path, television reporters staked out their positions. There was an art to picking the spot that would allow them to walk alongside the talent whilst remaining emphatically in camera shot.

They waited hungrily, scores of eyes trained on the front door. The media gauntlet had to be negotiated and the pack did not issue free passes. Not even to a young and frightened girl who'd just lost her mum.

Finally, the door opened and Tom stepped out onto the small cement porch.

'No one home, ladies and gents.' He smiled as he carefully locked up behind him. 'You all might as well go grab a coffee.' And with that he jogged up the path and into the waiting cab.

The mob stood dumb and bewildered, the tools of their trade hanging impotently by their sides.

Then it registered. 'Oh fuck me. She's good. The chick walked straight past us carrying the sound gear,' Geoff Jones' cameraman said, roaring with laughter.

'Shit,' Michelle something or other muttered to herself, almond eyes narrowing with irritation. This was not going to play well back at the office.

Geoff Jones kicked the letterbox hard before exploding at his crew. 'Oh, for Christ's sake. Why didn't you see that? You should know what their bloody soundo looks like. Fuck me.' He fished his car keys out of his pocket. 'You fuckers can stay out here all day and wait for her to come back. I'm going back to the office.'

And with that, he jumped into his calypso red BMW convertible, chubby fingers punching numbers into his car phone as he screeched away. This cock-up was going to take some real fast talking to explain. But he'd already figured out his angle.

'That Corish bitch has been waving the famous Channel Eight chequebook around,' Jonesy told his executive producer angrily. 'She beat us to the punch. Who was on this morning? Why the fuck didn't the researcher tie up the daughter before I got here?'

'Jones, it's only ten. You have all day to get the interview,' the EP said in his 'quiet before the storm' voice.

'I'm fucking telling you there's no one home. Corish has the woman in her car.'

'And that means she must have walked straight past you. Now remind me again why we pay you $100,000 a year?'

'She paid her. She must have paid her,' he bleated.

'Frankly, I don't give a shit. Don't come back without an interview with that daughter. I have plenty of young Turks here who would just love that car space of yours.' The EP hung up.

Fuck. Fuck. Fuck. Fuck. The stalking yarn was gone whatever that fool EP might think. Kate Corish had her scoop. There was no way she was going to let anyone within cooee of the girl now. He was going to have to come up with some exclusives of his own.

The tenth-floor suites of Hamish and Clarke Corporate Psychology Services projected all the warmth and compassion of a successful city accounting firm. But the place did have an excellent reputation for reprogramming and reinvigorating errant executives. Not that Mike Ripley felt his attitude needed adjusting. As far as he was concerned the exercise was a complete waste of time and he was feeling monumentally pissed off. Fucking Jessica Schmidt.

'So tell me about your relationship with your mother,' the counsellor ventured, spectacles perched precariously at the end of her beak.

'She's dead,' Ripley stonewalled.

'Well, tell me about your relationship before she died.'

'About the same.'

'You weren't close then.'

'No, we weren't *close*.'

Ripley had no intention of talking about his mother. He did not want to even think about his mother, and most of the time he was very successful at it.

Celia Ripley had been an aspiring model. But her career (and, she claimed, her life) was ruined when she fell pregnant. Suddenly she found herself married to the wrong man and trapped in the suburbs. She'd resented young Michael from the moment he was born.

'We should send him to boarding school,' he had once overheard her say.

'But he's only seven. And there are plenty of good schools around here.'

'Look, I never wanted a baby. I'm not cut out for this shit. I've had it with his long bloody face, his incessant whining and the continual mess. Either he goes or I do.'

Ripley could just imagine what the counsellor would make of that story. It was the kind of shit psychologists lived for. Well, the woman wasn't going to get her jollies on his account.

'I didn't know her very well. I was at boarding school most of my childhood. She died when I was in Year 11.'

'Did you have any female role models? An aunt perhaps. Or a grandmother.'

'Look, I really don't see the point of this Freudian shit,' Ripley snapped. He checked the clock on the wall. Five to. Close enough. 'I have to go now. I have a real job to worry about.'

His phone rang the moment he started up the car. It was Kate.

'Ripper. We've got the interview. It's brilliant stuff. And it's exclusive. We've got the girl tucked away safely in the Parramatta Travel Lodge. Right now she's watching pay for view.'

'On ya, Kate,' Ripley replied, his mood improving with the promise of a scoop. He'd find some way of sharing in the credit.

'I've been given a contact for the killer's sister,' Kate pressed on. 'Apparently she went to the police as well. She was also begging them to get her brother off the street. And get this. Apparently he had actually told her he was going to kill the woman. It's a perfect follow-up. Get this campaign cranked right up.'

Kate was starting to buzz. Big international stories didn't come around every day. They didn't even come around every hundred days. But there were plenty of local stories worth telling and issues that demanded discussion and action. They were what lifted her job above the banal.

'Look, Kate, you've done well with the story. And good on you for that. But I reckon it's over, honey. Its tomorrow's fish and chip wrapping. It doesn't have any more legs. Let's get this up tonight and we'll move onto the next thing.'

'Stalking is a big deal right now, especially with women. And we could really do some good here.' Kate didn't want to let go, especially when she was convinced Ripley was wrong.

'Okay, okay. I'll talk it over with Charlie. Just get moving, will you?'

Kate had forgotten all about her conversation with Ripley when Charlie Wright bailed her up at the end of the day.

'You scooped them again, kid.' Charlie beamed. 'Good job.'

Kate thought about arguing the case for a follow-up story. But there was little point if Ripley had already done it. When Charlie made a decision he stayed with it.

'Why don't you grab your boyfriend and head up to Noosa for a long weekend? My shout.'

Charlie Wright might not have had particularly strong communication skills but he was still a good boss. You always knew where you stood with him. If you fucked up, you would hear it from him first in a monstrous bellow. But when you did a good job, he let you know that as well. And he always rewarded hard work.

'Thanks, Charlie. A couple of days of warmth sounds perfect. I appreciate it.' Kate didn't mention that she was short the boyfriend half of the equation.

Never mind. She'd find someone to join her for a weekend away. She was an attractive girl after all.

'What would you like to drink, Mum?' Kate asked, staring out at the crystal-clear water of Laguna Bay.

'Just a mineral water for me,' Dianne Corish answered primly.

'I'll have the same, thank you.'

As the waiter hurried off to fill their modest drinks order, Kate's mobile rang. The number on the display confirmed it was the office. For a second she thought about letting the call go through to voicemail but that seemed churlish given that *Australia Tonight* was paying for lunch.

'Kate Corish.'

'Thanks a fucking lot,' Ripley thundered.

'*What?*' The guy's phone manner really needed some work.

'*A Current Affair* had that fucking interview last night.'

'What interview, Ripper? I have no idea what you're talking about.'

'The interview with the killer's sister. And guess what, smartarse? ACA creamed us in the fucking ratings.'

'I don't get what you're saying. You told me you didn't want that interview. And I presumed Charlie didn't want it either.'

'I told you to chase that fucking angle but I guess you were too busy planning your little fuckfest in Noosa.'

Then Kate realised what was happening. Ripley was performing for an audience back at the office. He was trying to cover up his bad call. And he was doing it by blaming her while everyone who mattered was in earshot. No one in Sydney could hear what *she* was saying. All they knew was that Ripley was angry with her for failing to lock down an interview.

Machiavellian prick. There was no point continuing the conversation. She stabbed at the off button on her mobile.

'Cunt.' She spat out the word.

Dianne Corish looked at her appalled. 'I don't know what just happened then, Kate. But I didn't bring you up to speak like that.'

She paused, signalling the approach of an earnest mother–daughter chat.

'Now, I'm glad we're talking openly. And please don't read this as ingratitude. But I am concerned as to why you'd bring your mother away on a trip like this.'

'Why wouldn't I?' Kate countered defensively. This was ridiculous. Her mother played the guilt card whenever Kate found a reason not to visit. Now she was treating her to an entire weekend away, the woman was still complaining.

'I'm thrilled you asked me. Of course I am. But you're twenty-six now. Shouldn't you have a serious boyfriend?' Dianne squirmed uncomfortably. 'Look, I'm just going to ask straight out. Are you gay, Kate? If you are, that's okay. I know you have those gay friends of yours. I'll learn to accept it. But, please, just be honest with me.'

'Oh, Mum. Relax. I'm not gay.'

'Well, that's a relief. Now what happened to that nice Matthew boy? I see he's reading the news now. That's very good, isn't it?'

Kate knew her mum didn't think that was very good at all. Not when the city was full of unattached doctors and lawyers. But at least she was trying.

'Matt's just a mate and he has a serious girlfriend now anyway.'

'Maybe you should read that new book about men coming from Mars and women from Mercury. You're interested in astrology.'

'Venus, Mum. Women are from Venus. But it's just a load of moneymaking psychobabble. It's really not my thing.'

'Well, I'm just saying, a career is not the be all and end all. I just hope you're not going to be one of those career girls who forget to have children?'

'Would you ladies like to order?' the waiter interrupted.

'Yes. Please. And I've had a change of heart. I need a bottle of the Margaret River white. Thank you.'

If Kate was going to endure this line of conversation, she was going to need to get absolutely smashed. It also seemed the only sane response to that phone call from Mike Ripley. There were limits to the recuperative powers of a beachfront lunch after all.

The following Monday morning, Kate strode into the office and plonked a plain brown paper bag on Ripley's desk.

'You'll need these,' she said, shooting him a death stare.

'Oh. Thanks, Kate.' He reached for the package and tried to sweep it into his top drawer.

'She didn't bring *me* anything back from Noosa,' Tubby pouted, ripping the bag from Ripley's grasp.

A box of tampons fell out.

'What the fuck have you done to piss her off?' Charlie asked, walking out of his office with his usual spectacular timing.

Ripley reddened. The box of Carefree sat accusingly in the centre of his desk. None of the men were willing to touch something so conspicuously female.

'I don't get it. What would you need tampons for, Ripper?' Tubby looked confused.

There was a moment's awkward silence before Charlie started laughing. 'She's saying he's a cunt, Tubs.'

'Amen,' a female voice muttered from the other end of the room.

FIFTEEN

The invitation had landed on Kate's desk in March, dumped on top of a jumble of press releases. Its large white envelope had a little gold tassel hanging off the back making it look much fancier than the usual haul of invites to movie premieres, fashion parades and fundraisers.

She turned the envelope over in her hands and worked it open carefully, straining to catch a glimpse of the printed card inside.

The 1994 Logie Awards

Kate giggled, a reaction that sat somewhere between scorn and excitement. She'd always dismissed the Logies as some kind of B-grade version of the Oscars. But that was before she'd scored an invitation. Now she felt the thrill of her career taking off. She immediately rang Gillian.

'I've got an invite to the Logies!'

'Well, aren't you the star then? I hear Jenni's going too. So you'll be sharing the table with her and her breasts – the best and worst of *Australia Tonight*. Oh hang on, Ripley is going too. That makes it the best and the worst and the worst of our fine program.'

'What about Charlie?' Kate asked.

'Honey, he never goes to those things. You know he's agoraphobic, God love him. So instead of Charlie's Angels, it will be Ripley's Angels. It doesn't have quite the same ring, does it?'

'I'm surprised the network's going to the expense of flying us all down to Melbourne,' Kate said, trying to sound nonchalant. 'That's just crazy when there wasn't enough money to send me to Bosnia.'

'Stop being silly. You know quite well we had to either cut the overseas travel budget or shed staff. The Logies operate under a completely different budget. Anyway, news is covering the Balkans for us.'

Kate was beginning to wonder if she'd made a mistake transferring to current affairs. While the newsroom continued to dispatch its correspondents to hotspots around the world, she'd been stuck working the parish pump

'So instead of dodging sniper fire in Sarajevo, I'll be hunting for a Logies frock. That's just great,' Kate grumbled. 'And on that point, what the hell *do* I wear?'

'You're asking me? Look, lighten up and have some fun. Go see the wardrobe girl. Just try not to think where she's had that mouth of hers.' Gillian laughed. 'But seriously she kits out all the network girls. She'll sort you out.'

Kate made her way to the wardrobe department, her imagination dancing with images of beautiful Alexander Perry gowns, sleek Nelson Leong dresses and heavily beaded George Gross numbers.

And for once she was actually going to enjoy preening in front of the mirror. At just 57 kilos, Kate was back to her high-school weight. And it was all thanks to her new gym instructor, who had turned her onto the Fit for Life food combining program. All she had to remember was not to eat meat with bread or potatoes. It didn't even feel like a diet.

Kate knocked loudly. Nowadays she knew better than to bowl through the door without announcing herself.

'Just a moment,' the wardrobe lady spluttered. Today her mouth was full of pins as she adjusted the straps of a magnificent red silk Tea Rose gown across the lovely olive shoulders of the model turned morning show host.

'Jan Logan is going to lend you a stunning diamond choker and a little tennis bracelet to match. But you'll have security people shadowing you all night. It's worth a gazillion.'

Kate could scarcely wait her turn.

'Now, Kate. I have a few dresses over here you might like to look through. Pick one and we'll have it ironed and transported down to Melbourne.' Kate was led past rack after sumptuous rack of billowing silk and taffeta gowns in the most extraordinary array of colours. Unfortunately the back of the bus options were considerably less exotic.

Kate flicked through the dresses. They were all off-the-rack designs. Studebaker Hawk. A few Eileen Kirbys. Even a couple of pink duchess satin Mr K frocks. They were respectable enough, but they weren't in the same league as the haute couture numbers.

'What about the Alex Perry gowns?' Kate asked.

'They're reserved for our network stars I'm afraid,' the wardrobe lady stated firmly. 'The rest of you get to choose from these. We'll deduct the cost from your clothing allowance of course.'

Kate picked a plain black Eileen Kirby strapless gown cut on the bias.

'Now do you have shoes or do I need to find you some?'

'I'm fine, thanks.' There was no way Kate was going to walk down her first red carpet in a pair of Jane Debsters. She'd prefer to go barefoot.

Kate quickly discovered that the celebrity caste system extended way beyond wardrobe. It dictated every aspect of the occasion from seating and scheduling to accommodation and travel.

Reporters didn't merit limousines and business-class air tickets. So Kate flew down to Melbourne squished into an economy seat. Next to her, an elderly woman was craning to see the famous faces sitting at the front of the plane. She was so committed (and so contorted) Kate worried her neck might actually snap free from her body.

'Did you see Ray?' she whispered to Kate excitedly. 'He seems so nice. Do you think his hair is real? It's lush, isn't it?'

'Very lush.' Kate smiled.

'My name's Stella. I voted for Ray for the Gold Logie, did you?'

'I didn't vote,' Kate replied. She didn't need to. The girls from the publicity department had done enough voting for everyone at Channel Eight. Kate had seen them one day, sitting cross-legged on their office floor surrounded by a mountain of *TV Weeks*, snipping, writing and licking envelopes.

But she didn't say anything to her travel companion. It would be like lifting the lid on Santa Claus.

She last sighted Stella standing at the luggage carousel and chatting away happily to Ray Martin. As Kate watched, Mr Australia bent over and presented his scalp for inspection. Stella gave his hair a bit of a tug and collapsed into a fit of schoolgirl giggles.

No wonder all the old dears loved him.

The pecking order asserted itself once again when Kate arrived at the hotel.

'I'm sorry. Your room won't be ready until 2 p.m.,' the receptionist announced, untroubled that less than a metre away her colleague had just issued Gary Sweet with a swipe card and was now rounding up the concierge to help with Ruth Cracknell's luggage.

With an hour and a half to kill, Kate retrieved her bike shorts and Nike runners from her overnight bag and headed up to the health club.

The gym overlooked the Yarra River. But the view was lost in the chronic Melbourne drizzle. Kate heaved herself onto the StairMaster and began her steady ascent, each arm and leg mechanically (and, for the chronically clumsy, mercifully) coordinated. Nowadays, Kate's only permanent relationship seemed to be with hotel gyms. Just four months into the year and she could recall dates with ten different StairMasters in ten different Australian cities. Sailors had a woman in every port. She had a piece of exercise equipment. Clearly, her mother was right and she needed to do something about her love life. An image of Jonathan McTavish flashed into her head. The (married) bastard had set the bar too damned high.

Eighty-seven flights of stairs and three hundred and twenty calories later, Kate decided to head back down to the lobby. Official check-in was still fifteen minutes away but she needed to get moving. The little white itinerary that accompanied her Logies pass had her scheduled for hair and make-up at 3 p.m. in a conference room on the second floor. And she couldn't lob there until she'd scrubbed away her gym session.

The entire timetable seemed unnecessarily rushed, given that the red carpet arrivals didn't start until 7 p.m. Once again the celebrity hierarchy was to blame.

'We work on the big stars last. That way they look fresh for the red carpet,' the make-up artist explained, her breath smelling of tic tacs. 'And before you start pouting, remember most people don't even get an invite.'

Kate hmmmed in response as the girl carefully drew a line around her lips.

'Now, what colour is your dress?' she asked 'I'll match your eye shadow.'

'It's black.'

'Okay, smoky eyes it is,' she declared as she dabbed a brush in the dark grey colours at the end of her giant palette.

Within half an hour, Kate's make-up was in perfect place.

'Now how do I keep it this way for the next three and a half hours?' Kate asked. She was still smarting over the constant reminders of her relative insignificance on the star scale.

'Go watch a movie in your room. They've got *Sleepless in Seattle* on demand.' The make-up girl smiled. 'That's what I plan on doing once I've finished work tonight.'

Next Kate was handed over to a gum-chewing hairdresser who barely spoke, burnt her head with the hairdryer and wielded his brush like an instrument of torture.

'Hey! There's a person under here,' Kate growled as a curling wand seared her right ear.

'Sorry, love. I've got a lot of heads to get through this afternoon.'

Kate thought she'd choke when he firmly and finally sprayed her elegant chignon in place.

With three hours to kill, Kate decided she may as well pick up her frock and jewels.

The wardrobe department had set up shop in a suite on the twentieth floor.

'Hi, Kate,' the wardrobe mistress called as she darted around the room organising what looked like hundreds of frocks and suits. There was a steam machine bubbling away in one corner. Across the room a junior assistant was ironing a white dinner shirt.

'Here's your dress.' She handed Kate a long black suit bag with her name scribbled on a big white sticker. 'Now I've picked some jewellery to go with it.'

Kate waited expectantly. She'd never worn really good jewellery before. And she was looking forward to the girly thrill. Her hopes were dashed when the girl returned a few minutes later proudly holding out a choker of three strings of pearls with a fake tear drop diamond in the middle.

Costume jewellery.

'It looks real, don't you think?' Kate didn't trust herself to answer. As far as she was concerned it just looked cheap.

'These earrings go nicely too.' The wardrobe girl popped the pieces into Kate's hands and darted off, her skin-tight 501s disappearing into the steam.

Kate wandered back to her room, her lowly position on the celebrity food chain brutally underlined yet again. She checked the hotel's selection of movies. As well as *Sleepless in Seattle*, there was *Philadelphia*, *Mrs Doubtfire* and *Indecent Proposal*. It was another sad reflection of her hotel-hopping lifestyle that she'd seen every one of them.

She settled on the bed and picked up her book. Al had insisted she read *The Celestine Prophecy*, confusing a passing interest in her daily horoscope with a search for greater meaning. Kate had pretty quickly pegged the book as a load of new-age crap. But she was determined to finish it, if only to humour Al.

Still, when the Mayans started vibrating their way to another dimension, she was done. She threw the book across the room, grabbed her bag and headed downstairs to the exclusive shops of the Southgate complex. The only insight she was interested in was the kind she'd get from a little idle window shopping.

She was just loitering outside a boutique jewellery store, when she spotted exactly the antidote to her mounting feelings of inferiority. Sitting in the window was an exquisite white-gold choker with two strands of elegantly cascading sapphires. It was the kind of piece she had imagined she would be wearing tonight. More to the point it was the kind of piece she *deserved* to be wearing tonight.

'Oh, stuff it,' she said to herself as she strode into the shop. She'd just been handed a twenty thousand dollar pay rise. What else was she going to do with a six-figure income? She had no one to spend it on and no time to spend it anyway.

Still, her hand trembled as she signed her gold Amex receipt.

The World Congress Centre was only a five-minute walk from the hotel. But that didn't stop the city's various limousine services from doing a brisk trade. Logies guests queued out front, waiting to be ferried across the river and deposited onto the red carpet. Such was the demand on television's night of nights that the limos couldn't circumnavigate the block quickly enough.

Watching the passing parade, Kate wished Jenni and Ripley would hurry up. She was feeling oddly nervous, despite knocking back the contents of a miniature bottle of Chivas Regal on her way out the door. She just wished the night would start. All this lead-up was excruciating.

'There you are.' Kate swung around to see Jenni, a magnificent silver sequinned gown holding up her breasts as if on a platter.

'Alex Perry,' Jenni volunteered. 'And yours looks like a Calvin Klein knock-off. Who did it?'

'I'm not sure,' Kate lied, wondering if there was anyone at all beneath her on the Logies ladder. 'The wardrobe lady picked it out.'

'Well, that was your first mistake . . . although that piece around your neck is pretty good for costume jewellery. I just went to Alex and told him I was presenting an award. It was a little white lie of course. But as long as I get my photo in *WD* or *Who*, he'll be happy.' Jenni smiled triumphantly and gave her breasts an infinitesimal adjustment. 'Oh, look. Here comes Mike now.'

'Well, don't you two look gorgeous?' Ripley gave both girls an appreciative peck on the cheek. 'How does an ugly bloke like me get knockouts like you on each arm?' Kate had to give it to him. Mike Ripley might be a pig of a man, and borderline obese, but he could certainly turn on the charm.

Almost two years had passed since the tampon incident and they'd managed to forge a decent enough working relationship. They didn't particularly like one another. But they rarely allowed their antipathy to break to the surface. And on occasions like this, a ceasefire was called and honoured. In fact given the right set of circumstances (usually involving an amount of alcohol), they behaved as though, and sometimes even believed, they enjoyed each other's company.

'I have to say, you scrub up rather well,' Jenni said, straightening Ripley's bow tie.

'Thank you, RW2.'

'RW2?' Kate asked as she stepped carefully into their limousine.

'Stands for Ripley Wife number 2. I was just saying to young Jenni here if I wasn't married, she'd be in the running.'

'Lucky girl.' Kate didn't even try to sound sincere. 'So what happens now?'

'Well, they drop us at the red carpet. You girls wave and look stunning. Then we all head inside for a well-earned beer.'

Kate experienced a sudden wave of panic. What on earth would she say if someone with a camera asked about her frock? The car stopped before she'd devised a sensible response.

The arrival of each limousine produced a hush of anticipation along the red carpet. Hundreds of young soapie fans crowded twenty deep around the drop-off point. Other luckier teenagers twittered from atop rickety tennis stands brought in especially for the occasion. If the limo contained an acting luminary like Melissa

Tkautz or Bruce Samazan then an almighty commotion ensued. Television cameras swung to attention. Photographers framed their shots. Young girls screamed hysterically.

Unfortunately the emergence of a couple of current affairs reporters produced a more muted response. Bored silence probably best described it. As the *Australia Tonight* team walked anonymously down the red carpet no one stopped to chat to them about their dresses. No one so much as snapped their photograph. What the hell would Jenni tell Alex Perry, Kate wondered.

They were almost inside when an enormous roar of excitement went through the crowd. Melissa George had just arrived, wearing a miniskirt made of feathers.

Kate, Jenni and Ripley each grabbed a drink off the tray as soon as they arrived at the top of the elevator. The lobby outside the auditorium was jam-packed with stars. But not being a fan of local drama Kate was struggling to identify any one of them. The journalists were easier to pick. They looked about as comfortable as she did.

'It kind of feels like we're at a soap convention,' Kate observed to Jenni.

'Great, isn't it?' her colleague enthused.

Ripley obviously thought so. He could scarcely keep his tongue in his head as dozens of nubile young things pranced past wearing next to nothing.

Logies producers had decided to try something a little different for their thirty-sixth awards night. Instead of dining tables and a three-course meal, they'd elected to put on an Oscars-style show. In an industry as thirsty as television, it was an unwelcome innovation.

'Christ, this is going to be fucking boring with no beer or wine to dress up proceedings,' Ripley grumbled as he settled into his tenth-row seat. 'Whose fucking idea was this?'

There were grunts and nods of agreement from all those within earshot.

Kate didn't find the absence of alcohol too distressing. Michael Crawford sang. Bud Tingwell was inducted. The girl in the feather mini was announced as best new talent and proceeded to make an incoherent speech. It was all pleasant enough, even when experienced stone-cold sober. What Kate did need though was a hit of nicotine.

She bolted outside during the next commercial break. Half the auditorium followed her.

As the ad break ran around three minutes and the proper enjoyment of a cigarette required more than five, Kate found herself locked out for the duration of the next segment.

'They can't have people wandering in and out while they're filming live television,' her smoking buddy observed, unconcerned that proceedings were continuing without him. Like Kate, he didn't care too much which channel had excelled in its coverage of sport.

'G'day.' They were joined by a middle-aged man who was already three sheets to the wind. Kate had some idea the guy had been a big star in the eighties. But she couldn't quite place the face.

'It's a fucking tit-fest tonight. Did you get a load of Susie Eleman? Shit, you'd get lost in all that cleavage!'

Kate and her smoker friend exchanged dubious looks.

'No one's tits match up to my niece's though,' the man added proudly.

'If you'll excuse me,' Kate said. 'Nature and good taste call.'

The ladies powder room was an exercise in vanity and indulgence. Hair and make-up attendants were stationed inside the doors like security guards, the tools of their trade spread out over the benchtops, to make sure Logies guests were always camera-ready. Kate nodded hello and hurried through to the toilets. As someone who hadn't merited so much as a single red carpet photo, it would have been churlish to take advantage of their professional services.

She was just about to push open a cubicle door when she noticed a pair of coltish teenaged legs sprawled across the floor a metre away.

'Hello. Are you okay?' Kate called as she bent down to ascertain the condition of the rest of the body. She located a cold, pale hand and gave it a little tug. No response. Trying not to panic, she dragged the unconscious girl out of the cubicle by the legs. She had vomit dribbling from her mouth. Little specks clung to her tiny pink silk dress. She wasn't wearing any underwear.

'Hey! I need some help in here!' Kate yelled.

The hair and make-up ladies rushed through the doors.

'Holy shit. I told you she looked pale when she went in there,' the hair lady said, splashing water on the girl's face. The teenager stirred momentarily.

'One of you, call an ambulance,' Kate ordered as she tried to pull down the girl's dress. It barely covered her thighs.

'Silly kid,' the make-up woman admonished. 'She probably starved herself for a week to fit into that dress. Throw in a few drinks and a dodgy ecstasy tablet and whammo. What on earth did she think was going to happen?"

Before long the ambulance arrived and the girl was carted away. A station publicist issued a press release the next day explaining the starlet had been suffering exhaustion.

Comatose nymphettes aside, the evening was predictable enough. Ray claimed the gold. Gary Sweet took home silver. And *Real Life* upset both *A Current Affair* and *Australia Tonight* by winning best public affairs program.

'These bloody things are so rigged,' Ripley complained. 'You know they probably filled out the forms themselves.'

Despite the publicity department's most diligent efforts,

Channel Eight failed to win a single award. But that didn't stop the station from celebrating. In fact, its party was the most eagerly gatecrashed of all the post-Logies events. No one cared about the quality of its programming. Once the ceremony was over, a network's desirability was judged solely on the calibre of its free booze. The Channel Eight function had Moet on tap.

The bubbles went up Kate's nose and straight to her head. By the time she bounded onto the dance floor with Kerry O'Brien, she was well and truly tanked and at her most perilously clumsy. If she'd had her wits about her she would have warned the guy about her two left feet. Or more accurately her two left *pissed* feet. Instead she attempted an ill-judged Tina Sparkles manoeuvre and head-butted his nose. To his credit, Kerry kept dancing, courageously ignoring the blood dripping down his chin. The fortifying properties of French champagne, she thought, as she slunk out of the party and up to her room.

Kate didn't feel like she'd been in bed more than a few minutes when she heard the newspaper thwack against her hotel door. She glanced at the clock. 5 a.m. There didn't seem much point in trying to go back to sleep. She had to be up in an hour anyway to make her flight back to Sydney. Who decided it would be a good idea to stage the Logies on a Sunday night, she wondered. And in Melbourne at that. Still, all things considered, she didn't feel too bad. Then again, she was probably still a bit tipsy.

Caffeine. That's what she needed. Kate peeled the top off the plunger coffee, only checking the bar menu as an afterthought. Christ all bloody mighty. She was about to make herself a $16 cup of coffee.

'Oh well, a bit late now,' she muttered as she plodded off to fetch *The Age*.

She pushed open the heavy wooden door and poked her head outside. There would still be a few hardcore partygoers roaming the corridors and she hadn't yet got around to putting on any clothes. The coast was clear but the newspaper was just a tad out of reach.

She weighed up her chances and decided to make a run for it. One. Two. Three. As she bent over to grab the paper, she heard the distinct click of the door shutting behind her.

'Oh fuck,' Kate said aloud as she realised what had happened. She clutched the paper to her body and took a step back so she was standing hard against the wall. Her only consolation was that she'd ordered a broadsheet.

There was no cover along the length of the hallway. Not even a pot plant. Kate's only option was to crab walk across to the next room and rely on the mercy and good manners of its occupant.

With both hands engaged protecting her modesty, Kate tapped on the door with her head. There was no answer. She bashed again, this time louder, almost giving herself concussion in the process.

'Hang on. Hang on,' a male voice grumbled from inside. After a few moments, its owner appeared. He was holding a towel around his waist with one hand and straightening his glasses with the other.

'Um, sorry. I know it's early,' Kate said to the floor. 'But I seem to have locked myself out of my room. Can I use your phone to call reception?'

Her request was met with a few seconds of startled silence.

'Haven't I seen you in the news?' The man was now sufficiently awake to enjoy the unexpected appearance of a naked and extremely attractive young woman at his door.

'Very funny. Do you mind? If I stand out here any longer I really will be in the headlines.' Kate finally looked up. Shit. It was Simon

Gilchrist, the ABC current affairs supremo. Despite her predicament Kate registered that he was indeed a rather attractive man, if a little on the short side.

'Well, you certainly put the broad into broadsheet,' he said, admiring the long legs hanging out of the paper as she manoeuvred herself past him.

'I don't know what you're staring at. I'm wearing more than some of those soapie stars last night.'

'I prefer the print on your outfit.'

There was something in the air between them that they both recognised. It made them feel suddenly awkward.

'Um, would you have a robe?' Kate asked.

'Oh yes. Sorry.' Simon reached into the wardrobe and handed her a thick towelling gown.

'I'll just pop it on in here,' Kate said, dashing for the bathroom.

When she re-emerged, Simon was wearing a pair of pants. But he remained shirtless, showing off a slim but firm physique and a smooth hairless chest. He was smiling at her.

'I have to ask you out now simply because I will relish the retelling of this story about how we met.'

Kate smiled. It was indeed a good story and there was nothing like a good story to get two journalists together.

SIXTEEN

Kate was just pulling up outside Simon's house when her phone started ringing from somewhere deep inside her oversized tote bag.

Kate cursed as she blindly dug about in her bag. Her fingers fumbled for and then discarded a dictaphone, her make-up pouch, some loose tampons and a couple of dozen pens. Finally, she pricked herself with an emergency safety pin.

'Ouch. Fuck. Got it. Hello!'

'That pleased to hear from me?' It was Gillian.

'Sorry, mate. You were at the bottom of my bag. And I'm in my usual mad rush. I got held up at the office. I've just negotiated a traffic jam the size of Hong Kong. And I've just discovered a grease stain on my dress. The usual Friday night shit fight. I don't have long. But how are you?'

'I'm actually having a bloody good laugh at your expense. A newspaper mate just called to tip me off. You've made the Sunday gossip pages.'

'Oh no. What are they saying?'

'Let me read it to you. "There's a rumour doing the rounds that a certain tabloid reporter was caught wandering the corridors of her hotel naked after last weekend's Logies. And we hear there's security vision of the incident. Sources tell us that only a copy of *The Age* newspaper saved the young lady from a full-frontal display. This columnist looks forward to confirming the story".'

'Oh shit!'

'Don't worry. I already have the tape in my hot little hands. So you have to be nice to me forever or I'll send it to Ripley. I'm sure he'd love a copy.'

'Don't even think about it. How did you manage to get hold of it?'

'I promised to drop our investigation into illegal workers at their hotel chain. I don't think there was a story there anyway.'

'God, Gill, I owe you one.'

'You sure do. But speaking of Logies' madness, how was your first date with that painfully earnest ABC bloke?'

'It went so well I'm just about to knock on his door for our second date. But it was lovely. Really lovely. We went to some vegetarian place in Balmain.'

'Oh fuck, Kate, I don't trust a man who doesn't eat meat.'

'Gillian, it was a lovely restaurant. And he's got a point. We do eat too much meat in this society. Our bowel cancer rates are out of control.'

'Please don't tell me that was your first date dinner conversation?'

'You're a cynical old cow, Gillian.'

'Then I'm in no fear of being eaten around you two.'

'If you must know, we talked about his travels and time as a foreign correspondent in London. It was fascinating.'

'What is it with you and foreign correspondent types?'

It was a fair call. Simon looked nothing like Jonathan McTavish. But the older, wiser, more experienced journo type did seem to push her buttons.

And how. She didn't usually jump into bed on a first date. But it had been a long time between drinks and Simon hadn't disappointed her.

'So what's on the agenda tonight? Saving a few whales? Couple's macramé?'

'He's cooking me dinner. I've never had a man cook for me before.'

'Ugh. The bloke is way too ABC for me. But whatever floats your boat, sweetheart. Have fun. Although I can't imagine how.'

Kate switched off her mobile and stepped out of the car. She felt a slight April chill on her bare shoulders. She'd worn a black fitted shift dress to work. It was too sexy on its own but looked suitably corporate with the addition of a well-cut jacket. In Kate's line of work, it paid to own an outfit that went from office to evening without the need for a detour home. Still, she would have liked a shower instead of just the two squirts of No. 5 behind her knees.

Kate felt a flutter of nerves as she knocked on the door of the classic Federation worker's cottage. She smiled. It was nice getting reacquainted with her hormones.

'Hello, Kate. You look stunning as ever. Come in.' Simon was dressed in jeans and a long-sleeved white cotton shirt with the top few buttons undone, exposing his smooth chest.

'Gosh that smells good. What are you cooking?' Kate asked as she followed her date down the narrow hall.

'It's a Moroccan vegetable and lentil curry baked in a tangine. I hope you like spicy?'

'Love it.'

Simon guided Kate past two bedrooms, through a cosy lounge and into the kitchen.

'I've chilled some champagne. French, of course. Would you like a glass?'

'Yes, please,' Kate replied. She could get used to this.

Bernstein was screeching dementedly from his travel cage when the phone rang.

'Hi, darling. The removalist just arrived. Do you want me to start unpacking some of your things?' Simon asked.

'No. No. I'm pretty much done here. I should be there in thirty minutes or so.' Kate looked around her now-empty apartment. After six years, leaving was even more of a wrench than she expected.

'Okay then, I'll just get some coffee ready for the much anticipated arrival of my new flatmate.'

'Flatmates.' Kate emphasised the plural 'You're forgetting Bernstein, who as you can probably hear is a bit miffed about travelling cat class.'

'Sure. How could I forget Bernstein?' Her lover responded tonelessly.

Kate really wished Simon could be a *little* more enthusiastic about his new stepcat.

'Okay. See you soon.' She hung up. 'Oh, Bernie. We're moving to the dark side,' she said, pressing her nose up to the wire of Bernstein's cage.

'You sure are,' Ben and Al griped from the doorway. 'I can't believe you're trading us in for some ageing straight bloke on the wrong side of the Bridge. Oh God, we'll miss you so much.' Ben scooped Kate into a ferocious bear hug. Al started to tear up.

'Guys, I'm not leaving the country. I'll be back for your dinner parties. You might even like to come over to my place some time?'

'I rather doubt that, sweetie. They draw and quarter our type over that side you know.'

'Oh rubbish, it's not Queensland. It's Naremburn. And it's only five kilometres away as the crow flies.' Kate said. 'Now, help me with Bernie and I'll be on my way.'

Bernstein's disposition did not improve during the short journey north. He yowled continuously, only drawing breath to urinate as Kate drove her newish Golf Cabriolet through the Harbour Tunnel. She wasn't sure whether he did it out of spite or fear. She suspected a combination of both. Thank God it was summer. She'd be spending the next few weeks driving with the top down.

When they finally pulled up at their new home, Bernstein outdid himself by greeting Simon with an especially malevolent hiss.

'Oh, for God's sake.' Simon growled, screwing up his nose at the smell. 'Give him here.' Simon took the cat and let him out of his cage in the spare bedroom. Chokingly aware that Bernstein's bladder was empty, he shut the door.

'Cats need to get used to one room at a time, right?' he said as he half carried Kate into the bedroom.

'I suppose.' Kate wasn't entirely convinced by Simon's logic. But Bernstein did need some discipline.

'I hope you'll be happy here,' he said, pushing her onto the bed and kissing her deeply. They made love to the doleful mewling of Bernstein in the next room.

Afterwards, they lay on the bed, trying to cool down. It was a typically muggy January day and the strong afternoon breeze made the sheer curtains flap wildly.

'I should get to the hardware store before they close and see if they have any stocks of mission brown for the windowsills.'

'What sort of pillow talk is that? Now I know I'm living on the North Shore.' Kate groaned.

'It's a traditional worker's cottage. Would you prefer I preserved the current dusty pink and white colour scheme?' Simon wheezed.

'You okay?'

'Yeah, it's just Bernie. I told you I was allergic to cats.'

'You'll get used to him. And you never know. He might even get used to you. Okay, handy man. You better go. It's quarter to five.'

Kate rolled over, smiling to herself. She hadn't felt this happy in a long, long time.

SEVENTEEN

'Fuck me swinging!' Tubby exclaimed. 'That piece of crap on the Paxtons rated fucking 43s in Sydney. That's more than the fucking State of Origin and the numbers are like that in every capital fucking city.'

Usually, only big sporting events attracted a national audience of over two million viewers. But the public vilification of Shane and Bindy was as eagerly anticipated as a grand final. Paxton bashing had become an enormously popular national pastime. Hating the family was as much a sport as football, except there were no rules for fair play.

'A great fucking day for our fearless leader to stay at home with the snuffles,' Ripley snarled as he peered over Tubby's shoulder at the computer screen. 'Shit. They creamed us.' He lit another cigarette from the bent and smouldering stub of the one before.

'Perhaps we could get the Paxtons on the show tonight to defend themselves. Maybe sweeten the deal by asking Shane to file a couple of reports on youth affairs or something?' Tubby ventured.

'Tried that yesterday. He's already signed with *Today Tonight*. Seventy fucking thousand dollars I heard. Can you believe that? No we need our own set of Paxtons.'

'How about this lot?' Tubby was reading the phone log from the previous night. The list was compiled by the show's receptionist each evening. Mostly the entries were comments, complaints or requests to speak to the host. But occasionally, they yielded pay dirt.

'The Dobbie family rang in. Not one of them has worked a day in their lives. But they reckon they'll take any job we find them.' The chief of staff stood up, hitching his neatly ironed jeans to within a whisker of his armpits.

Ripley snatched the printout from his hands. 'Denise, Dougie and Ashleigh. I hate the bludging scum already. Let's get it cranked. Just don't assign the yarn to Sean or Kate. They'll turn the thing into some bleeding heart story. Give it to Jenni. She probably thinks generational unemployment is a rock band.' He shook his head. 'I want all of Australia despising these cunts. And make fucking sure you find them jobs they're going to refuse. We're a current affairs show not a fucking employment agency.'

'The Dobbie Debacle,' Simon read out the headline as he and Kate sipped on lattes at their local café in Crows Nest. Denise, Dougie and Ashleigh stared dolefully from page three, their unspectacular welfare-dependent lives in tatters after their brief encounter with tabloid television. *Australia Tonight* had presented them as a family of bludgers who refused to work even when offered perfectly pleasant and acceptable jobs. 'Un-Australian', the host had called them. There was no greater insult in the lexicon of current affairs television.

'Do I really want to hear this?' Kate groaned. She'd been living with Simon quite happily for over a year now. But he had an annoying habit of claiming the journalistic high ground and his holier-than-thou ABC attitude had started to grate.

Ignoring his partner's discomfort, or maybe because of it, Simon read on. 'The Dobbie family's only crime was being naïve and down on their luck.'

Kate cringed. She remembered the story. Mrs Dobbie had refused a factory job because she was unhappy with the wages being offered. Her attitude had outraged Jenni. How could this woman choose to sit at home on the dole rather than go out and earn an honest living?

'It says here the factory was as an illegal sweatshop. It was only offering to pay Denise one dollar thirty an hour. Maybe that's the story you should have been chasing.'

Kate snatched the *Mail* from Simon's hands and scanned the article. Dougie Dobbie had knocked back work at an abattoir. But he was also a committed vegetarian. And while Ashleigh had refused to wear the uniform that went with the hospitality job she'd been offered, she also suffered a skin condition. Her request for a long-sleeved shirt was a medical necessity not a fashion statement.

'What a fuck-up.' Kate tossed the newspaper onto an empty table nearby.

'Sweetheart, how can you work for a program like that? You really should leave. Make a statement.'

'Why should I quit because of the questionable ethics of one of my colleagues? Jenni should be sacked. And Ripley and Tubby for that matter,' Kate stormed. 'Now, if the story had been given to me, I wouldn't have handled it like that. I would have—'

'Come off it, Kate. You'd never have been assigned as the reporter in the first place and you know it. They wanted the story told a certain way. And Jenni delivered. Do you think the Dobbies ended up on her desk by accident? *Australia Tonight* has an agenda. And you're just as complicit as Jenni by the simple fact that you work there.'

'Fine, Simon. So I'm just a big sell-out. It's funny how you didn't complain about my job when you wanted to fly business class to Paris at Christmas time. I wasn't a sell-out then, now was I?'

'Kate, we're talking about journalistic ethics here. You're going off on a tangent.'

Kate bristled. 'Well I'll tell you something. Politicians are watching our show. Not yours. They choose to appear on our show. Not yours. And do you know why? Because everyone is fucking watching our show as opposed to falling asleep and not watching yours.' She slammed her cup into its saucer to emphasise her point. 'I'm going to the gym. See you later.'

Kate had yet to discover a more effective anger-management technique than a tough workout session. And she was in luck. There was a pump class starting just as she walked in the door. She added fifteen kilos of weights to her bar and threw herself diligently into the squat track.

Her hair was soaked by the time she finished although her anger hadn't dampened even slightly. Then she spotted Jenni jogging on a treadmill.

'Did you read the *Mail* this morning?' Kate demanded, arms crossed.

'No, I haven't seen the papers yet. Am I in the social pages?'

'No, Jenni, but *Australia Tonight* is in the shit.'

'Oh, yeah. Ripper rang and told me about that. Bleeding heart lefties. I paid fifty grand in tax last year. Why should my money be used to support no-hopers like that?'

'The jobs were bogus, Jenni. Didn't anyone bother to check? When you put crap like that to air, it makes us all look bad.'

'Have it out with the producers, Kate. The story rated its tits off,' Jenni said, jumping off the treadmill. 'And that's all that really matters.'

Fifty grand tax. Shit. Jenni had to be earning at least a hundred grand. How did that happen, Kate wondered, as she watched her colleague's perfectly shaped rear disappear into the weights room. Of course Kate knew exactly how it happened. And it made her fume all the way to her mother's house.

Dinner at the ancestral home had become a regular Sunday night event. Sometimes Kate felt weighed down by the expectation of her presence at the dinner table week in and week out. But today she was grateful to have somewhere to go.

'Where's Simon?' Dianne Corish had the most disconcerting way of reading her mind sometimes.

'He's busy with work stuff today, Mum. You're just going to have to settle for me on my own.'

Dianne pulled on her mitts and lifted the roast out of the oven.

'I saw the papers today,' she said. 'Horrible business.'

'Not one of our show's proudest moments, that's for sure. But it's a one-off. There's no way the network will chance that kind of bad publicity again.'

'Oh, *why* don't you go and work for the ABC, Kate? Couldn't you get a job on *The 7.30 Report*. I'd be so proud of you then.'

Kate felt her jaw clench. Her mother was a master at serving up backhanded criticism.

'Well, I think it would be difficult working for the same network as Simon,' Kate said evenly as she set the table. 'Plus I'd have to take a big drop in pay.'

'Speaking of Simon, how is that going? Any proposals yet?'

'Mum, marriage is just a piece of paper. It doesn't mean anything to us. We have a perfectly good relationship as it is.' Although 'good' wasn't the adjective she'd use for their partnership today.

'Well, why buy the dairy if the milk is for free?' Dianne sniffed.

'And what about kids? You're thirty next month. What happens if you have children? Surely he'll marry you then?'

'Mum, you're going to have to accept that I'm old enough to make my own choices. Now can we drop this conversation? Please.'

The following night, Kate and Simon relaxed back in their new 'Town & Country' tartan couch. They'd made up in the usual fashion. Simon had cooked Kate breakfast in bed. And Kate had eaten it. It was a system that spared them both from admitting fault or making an apology. Bernstein was curled up on Kate's lap and there was a bowl of microwave popcorn on the floor within easy arm's reach.

The Gilchrist–Corish household never missed an instalment of *Media Watch* although Kate always watched with a sense of dread. Anyone who worked in tabloid current affairs was an obvious target. Though she'd been left pretty much alone so far, she knew that while grubs like Tubby and Ripley worked on the show, it was only a matter of time before she was on the receiving end of a very public roasting.

The opening titles appeared on the screen along with the distinctive *Media Watch* music. Kate was hoping Stuart Littlemore would give *Australia Tonight* a serve for its handling of the Dobbie story. Her only reservation was that it would also probably send Simon off on another rant.

But the program didn't begin with pictures of the luckless Dobbie clan or with Jenni's breathy little-girl voice. Instead grainy black and white vision filled the screen accompanied by some rather disturbing moaning.

'Reporter involvement may be the catchcry of journalism in the nineties but here at *Media Watch* we think tabloid hack Geoff Jones has taken the philosophy a little too far,' Littlemore intoned smugly. 'The promo for the Jones exposé claimed this story would blow viewers away. Well, we saw a little more of the vision than the rest of Australia and, trust us, Mr Jones was the only one who was blown away.

'You see, Jonesy's been doing some undercover investigating into a business owned by one of our elected representatives. But it seems he's been doing more undercover work than his minders realise. Good taste and broadcasting laws don't let us show you any more than this. But rest assured Mr Jones doesn't just pay lip service to the claim the establishment is an illegal brothel. The staff does that for him . . . or should I say to him. We can only wonder how Mr Jones explained this one away on one of his famously imaginative expense forms.'

'Oh my God,' Kate said. 'The bloke has just made Ripley look like a decent and upstanding citizen of the media community. How the hell did *Media Watch* get hold of that vision?'

'It's certainly been a spectacular week in tabloid current affairs,' Simon said smugly.

'Let's not go there again, Simon. What I don't get is why they didn't get stuck into Jenni.'

'Sex wins every time, even on the ABC.' Simon grinned as he nuzzled Kate. 'Speaking of which.' He slid his hands inside Kate's jumper and edged Bernie off her lap. Bernstein growled and slunk off, his tail haughtily perpendicular.

Ripley was feeling pretty pleased with himself when he arrived at the boardroom bar the following Friday. The Dobbie thing had looked like it was going to blow up in his face. But the gods of journalism had been kind.

On the morning after the *Mail* revelations he had received a plain white package in the mail containing a tape marked 'Geoff Jones blows up'.

217

He'd shoved the tape in the nearest VHS machine, expecting to watch one of Geoff's legendary temper tantrums. And there it was. His perfect counteroffensive.

Ripley had quickly run off a copy for his own private use, adding it to the shelf where he kept his compilation of Channel Eight security vision. A decade of Christmas parties had produced some hardcore action. The boardroom table. The helipad. Ripley just about got an erection every time he heard the chopper take off.

Job done, he taxied the original Jones tape to the ABC. Cash, of course.

Sometimes getting ahead in this game really was too damned easy. The bleating of a family of dole-bludging white trash couldn't compare to the spectacle of a national current affairs reporter paying for a blowjob in pursuit of a story.

But Ripley still had some loose ends to tie up. He looked around the boardroom bar. It was a quiet night. A couple of sales guys were huddled by the window, decrying the poor performance of the network's latest foray into drama.

In the far corner, a very ambitious lifestyle presenter was vamping it up with a senior station executive. Her surgically enhanced breasts strained against her tight orange T-shirt. She'd recently announced that orange was her trademark colour. And she'd banned every other woman from wearing it on set. That included people behind the scenes as well.

Ripley spotted Mawson at the bar and walked over.

'Tough week,' he offered, twisting open a beer.

'What the fuck is happening down there?' Mawson demanded through a fog of smoke. He'd already hauled Wright over the coals but he was always keen for a second opinion.

'I dunno. Charlie seems to have gone off the boil. That Dobbie thing was never a good idea.'

'A fucking disaster more like it. I don't care if it rated. It was just plain sloppy.'

'Mate, you know Wright, the bloke never comes out of his office. No one knows what they're doing.'

'Charlie's not known for his social graces. Strange though. It's never mattered before.'

'Maybe he's having problems at home. I don't know. He's been away a bit. But he's the captain and the fucking ship is sinking. I'm taking up the running as much as I can. But it's too hard when so many lousy decisions are being made over my head.'

Mawson nodded. He'd thought Charlie had a few more years in him. But everyone in that job lost the knack eventually. And five years was a solid innings.

Barely a week later, Charlie Wright walked out of his office for the last time. He'd had a gutful of daily current affairs. And today's little piece in Megan Halliday's media column had pushed him over the edge.

Megan described him as the architect of the Dobbie debacle. Then went on to question his future with the show. Stupid bitch. He'd actually been in bed with pneumonia that whole week. But there was no point correcting her. He'd only be shifting the blame onto his staff. And Charlie didn't believe in pointing the finger at the people who worked under him. If you were the boss, you had to cop it square on the chin.

Anyway he seemed to have lost the confidence of the men upstairs. That, more than anything, was the death knell.

Charlie stood next to the main desk and addressed his troops for the last time.

'I'm leaving. Ripley's taking over till they find someone smarter, which shouldn't take long. Some of you are hard workers and have great futures. Thank you for all your good work. The rest of you are crap. Have a nice life, goodbye.' And with that, he walked out.

Kate stared after him, horrified. Not only had she just lost an ally, she had gained a boss whose sole professional mission seemed to be to undermine and humiliate her.

At least it was only a temporary appointment. A few months tops. Surely he couldn't do *that* much damage.

EIGHTEEN

Kate dug around in the bottom of her leather tote fumbling for the door key.

'Shit, Simon. You could've left the porch light on,' she grumbled.

It was odd he wasn't home. He rarely went out on Saturday nights. And he almost never worked on weekends. Kate's job was nowhere near so accommodating and Simon never stopped complaining about it.

He'd had an opportunity for another whinge that morning, when their Saturday sleep-in had been scuttled by a cracker story on the front page of the *Mail*. The parents of a thirteen-year-old Downs Syndrome girl were petitioning to have their daughter's tubes tied. She was sexually active. And as they hadn't been able to stop her various liaisons, they at least wanted to avoid a pregnancy.

'Can't someone else cover the story for once?' Simon had mumbled from somewhere underneath their blue and white striped doona.

'Unfortunately I don't have a nice cushy ABC job like you.'

'But I like to fuck on Saturday mornings,' Simon sulked.

'You like it every morning, Simon. Who are you kidding?' Kate laughed, leaning over and pecking him on the cheek.

Simon grabbed her by the arm and dragged her back onto the bed. But rather than rousing his partner's passion, the manoeuvre only created an angry cat sandwich. The moment was lost in a flurry of claws and fur.

'What's the bloody cat doing on the bed?' Simon snapped. 'You know I'm allergic.'

Kate wasn't about to admit that Bernstein crept into bed with them most nights. He just wasn't the sort of cat to meekly accept a leopard-print igloo in the laundry as his permanent sleeping quarters. She picked him up and scratched him under the ear.

'Come on, Bernie. Let's leave old grumble-guts to himself,' she said as Simon fell into a fit of sneezing.

Filming took far longer than Kate had expected, mainly because the girl in question had taken off during the afternoon. She was finally located three hours later, playing with some teenaged boys in a makeshift cubby house a few blocks away. The episode underscored her parent's fears exactly.

'It's like this every day,' they cried. It was a strong current affairs story and one well worth sacrificing a day out of her weekend for, Kate decided.

She called Ripley on her way home. More than two months had passed since Charlie left the show and Kate was still waiting for someone smarter to take the reins. She couldn't believe it was that difficult.

'Hello?' Ripley's daughter picked up the phone.

'Hi there, it's Kate.' She guessed the girl at about six. 'Can I talk to your father please?'

'Daddy, Daddy. It's Kate on the phone.' There was a moment's silence. 'Daddy, why are you rolling your eyes?'

'Give me the phone. Hiya, Kate. How'd ya go?'

'Great. The young Downs girl even gave us a demonstration. She disappeared. The police were called. There was a frantic search. And she was eventually found playing doctors and nurses with a couple of teenaged boys down the street.'

'Goodo. Can you drop the tapes in to the station tomorrow? I might stick the yarn on the end of the weekend promo. That way Sunday night viewers can get a taste of it. Good on ya.'

It had been a long day and *Hey, hey, it's Saturday* beckoned. Kate pushed open the door and went to switch on the light. Damn, the bulb had blown. And the one in the bedroom too. Maybe it was a fuse. She walked blindly down the hallway, her shoes clacking loudly on the freshly polished kauri floorboards.

As she reached the lounge, the lights flicked on.

'Surprise!'

'Shit!' Kate exhaled, adrenalin surging.

Thirty or so pairs of eyes smiled back at her. A 'Happy 30th birthday' banner stretched over the open fireplace. Above her, a dozen helium balloons gathered around the ornate ceiling rose.

'Happy birthday for Monday, darling.' Simon wrapped his arms around her waist and kissed her neck.

'You bugger. For the life of me I didn't see this coming.'

'I took a punt you'd be called in to work today. But whatever happened we were always going to celebrate. Thirty is an important milestone. Or at least that's how I remember it.'

'Champagne?' Gillian said emerging from the crowd and handing Kate a glass of Chandon.

'Gillian. Oh my God. You came all the way from Melbourne for this?' Kate took a step back. Tonight Gillian was resplendent in a Swiss-inspired lamb's wool vest and crimson sateen slacks. She'd teamed it all with a spectacular pair of Prada wedges.

'I would have flown up here especially for your birthday of

course. But I've been holding out on you.' Gillian paused. 'I've moved back to Sydney.'

'Oh my God. This is brilliant.' Kate shouted over a drunken chorus of 'Wonderwall'. 'I've missed our sessions at the Dug Out bar. Are you coming back to the office?'

'No. I start with the opposition on Monday.'

'You're kidding me. I can't believe you're leaving Channel Eight. How many years has it been?'

'Well I started in the newsroom in 1983. So let's just say quite a while. But it was time to move on. I've been out in the cold since Charlie left. Ripley stopped returning my calls. And you can hardly run a bureau if the boss isn't talking to you.'

'The stupid, fat bastard! You're the best we've got. We shouldn't be letting you go,' Kate said angrily.

'Hey, I sort of understand it. Ripley thinks I'm too close to Charlie. And every new boss likes to surround himself with his own people. Charlie did the same. Anyway I got a sixty grand pay rise. So the guy's actually done me a favour.'

'I guess he's good for something then. God knows it's not journalism.' Kate smiled. She was going to enjoy having Gillian back in town. 'Oh well, I guess I should mingle and see which of my so-called friends were in on the big secret.'

The little cottage felt tiny with so many people crowded into every cranny. Kate spotted Simon in one corner, looking through the CD tower. She figured he was lining up Neil Young or the Eagles. The twelve-year age gap was nothing socially or professionally. But musically it was a yawning chasm.

Kate moved out of the lounge and into the dining area with its floor to ceiling bookcase, jammed with Simon's impressive book collection. Matthew was checking the titles on the spines and looking a little intimidated. Kate suspected that was the point.

'Here's the birthday girl,' he said. 'Can you believe we're getting so old?'

'Speak for yourself, Matt. Thanks for coming. We never see each other any more. It's ridiculous given our offices are only one floor apart.' She turned to Matthew's girlfriend. 'Anthea, nice to see you again.'

They were the power couple of the newsroom. He was the heir apparent – the man being groomed to take over the 6 p.m. news spot. And she was the young gun reporter tipped to be the next Kate Corish. She even looked a little like Kate with her blonde hair cut in the popular elfin style.

The bush fires of 1994 had provided Anthea with her first big break as a reporter. She had strayed a little too close to the action in Bundeena and ended up stranded in the national park overnight as the fire raged around her. Somehow she'd kept her nerve and filed a heart-stopping report. The result had been a permanent reporting gig and an overnight stay in hospital for smoke inhalation.

Taming Matthew was just one of her many achievements. He was definitely a one-woman man nowadays. And he seemed pretty happy about it.

'We have news. Anthea and I are engaged!'

'Oh my God. Congratulations. Shit. Matt, that's great. I'm so happy for you both.' Kate felt a strange stab. They really were getting old. 'When's the wedding?'

'We thought January would be nice. Gives us six months to plan.'

'It's a good time for a honeymoon too,' Anthea added. 'Out of ratings.'

In the background, Oasis suddenly fell silent, replaced by the tinkling of glass. Kate drifted back to the lounge.

'Hi, everyone. Can I have your attention please?'

Simon was standing on the ottoman.

'Thank you all for coming tonight. Well, there hasn't been much to celebrate so far in 1996. Paul Keating lost the election and little Johnny is now our Prime Minister.'

The crowd groaned.

'We've got a fish and chip woman setting the political agenda. And may we thank our tabloid friends here tonight for Ms Hanson's undeserved rise to fame.'

'Hear, hear,' murmured a portion of the crowd. But Kate heard a 'piss off wanker' in there as well. The voice sounded suspiciously like Gillian's.

'Come in, spinner.' Simon smirked. 'Some madman shot up Port Arthur and there's no understanding what is happening in Rwanda right now. God, even Crowded House is breaking up. So what is there to celebrate you ask? Well, a beautiful lady, a talented journalist and my wonderful partner is turning thirty. So please, all charge your glasses . . . To Kate!'

'To Kate!' everyone responded.

Simon jumped down from his perch and strolled over to where Kate was standing.

'Thanks for my party Simon and for the lovely speech.' She kissed him.

'I'm glad you're happy. Now can I get you another drink?'

'No, I'm fine for the moment thanks. I think I'll just step out the back for a few minutes peace. See who else is here.'

Kate grabbed her smokes from their hiding place in the kitchen and stepped through the glass double doors to the tiny back patio.

'Kate, darling!' Ben and Al immediately swooped on her.

'I was hoping I'd find you two out here,' Kate said, breathing in their exotic colognes.

'We had to come outside to escape that dreadful music. What on earth is that noise?' Al asked.

'Ah, that would be Steely Dan. I swear I'll have to accidentally lose that CD. It's Simon's favourite.'

'Poor darling. Come back and live with us. It really is just awful over here.'

'Don't say that, Ben. It's rude,' Al scolded.

'But it *is* awful.'

'Guys, I'm happy. Very happy. Despite the music.'

'Truly, Kate sweetie, it's too suburban,' Ben said. 'Next thing you know you'll be up the duff.'

'I've spent the best part of the last fourteen years successfully avoiding that. So I think I'll be right,' Kate promised. 'Anyway, I have heaps of time. I'm turning thirty on Monday, not forty remember.'

'Well, the clock starts ticking around now, doesn't it?' Al speculated.

'I'll let you know.'

Kate had actually tried to draw Simon on the subject a few weeks earlier.

'What do you think about kids?' she'd asked one Sunday morning as they were reading the papers in bed. They'd been together three years and hadn't ever discussed the subject. It seemed like a pretty big oversight.

'I'm not that keen. Not keen at all, actually. How about you? I kind of figured you for a career girl,' Simon replied.

'Well, women have been known to have both,' Kate said, a little too sharply.

'I guess I just don't particularly like children. That kind of rules me out.'

'I'm the opposite. I always presumed I'd be a mum. Not right now. But one of these days.'

Kate waited for Simon's response. But it seemed the conversation was over as he quickly found an article that demanded his immediate attention.

Ben broke into her thoughts. 'Look over in the kitchen. I don't think your best friend and your lover are getting along very well.'

Gillian had Simon bailed up against the Miele dishwasher and was haranguing him over his birthday speech. She didn't like people casting slurs on tabloid television. That was her prerogative.

'How on earth do you argue that we created her? The media didn't create Pauline.'

'You give her airtime.' Simon was as cool as Gillian was hot-headed.

'We have no choice. She's a newly elected politician with controversial views. I don't agree with them. But who are we to censor her just because she's not politically correct?'

'My point is she would just go away if you didn't keep putting her face on the box. Your lot just give her oxygen.'

'That's bullshit. She was a nobody liberal until John Howard chucked her out. So you could say *he* created her.' Gillian's arguments were becoming more imaginative with every swig of champagne.

'Yeah, and you guys turn her anti-aboriginal views into tabloid headlines. Next thing you know the voters hand her Oxley with the biggest swing in the country. If you'd just ignored her, it wouldn't have happened,' Simon reasoned. 'We all have a heart of darkness, Gillian, and the masses need to be protected from theirs.'

'Oh, don't be so fucking patronising,' Gillian snapped.

'Sounds like you two are getting along as famously as ever,' Kate said, sliding in between them. She would save them from each other, she thought. If indeed either wanted saving.

'Hi, Kate' Simon slipped his arm around her waist. 'I was just lamenting the fact that Mr and Mrs Average are led astray, some would say *seriously* astray, by programs such as the one you work for.'

'Simon, it's my birthday. I really don't want to get into this now,' Kate said, abruptly disentangling herself. The two of them could come to blows for all she cared. It was time for that drink.

Pauline Hanson raised her reactionary red head again on Monday. And ruined Kate's birthday in the process. She'd spent the day carefully scripting and editing her story on the Downs Syndrome teenager. It was a complex issue and needed every second of the six minutes allotted to it in the rundown.

But that was before an aboriginal boy called the member for Oxley a cunt on camera.

'Kate, you're going to have to cut back that nuff-nuff story to three minutes,' Ripley ordered, sticking his head into her office. 'That gear from Brisbane is fucking gold.'

'Surely we shouldn't be giving the woman any more publicity. We're creating a monster,' Kate argued. Christ she thought. I'm channelling bloody Simon.

'Nothing I can do about it. The punters want to fuck her. And I want the show to fucking rate.' Kate stared at him, appalled. 'Anyway, she's got good legs,' he added, as if that somehow justified his earlier observation.

'Can't we just hold my story over for tomorrow night? Do it justice.'

'Nah, *ACA* has interviewed the family as well apparently. So we run it tonight or not at all.'

'Surely we can drop something else? The diet story perhaps?' Kate begged.

'We need the diet thing at the back end to keep the punters with us.' His mind was set. 'You're just going to have to bend over and show the pink on this one. Now I'm over this. You're not the only reporter on this show, you know.'

Kate dropped her head into her hands and massaged her temples with her thumbs. Sometimes the job was simply not worth the angst.

Her phone rang and after a moment's hesitation she picked up.

'Happy birthday,' Gillian chirped.

'Oh hi,' Kate said flatly.

'That doesn't sound good.'

'Everything was just fine until a moment ago when Ripley decided to give my story a major chop. And get this. He told me to 'bend over and show the pink'. Can you believe that?'

'Sadly, I can believe that. But you don't have to put up with that crap you know. We have a great bloke over here. And I know he'd love to poach you. So maybe you should talk to him.'

'Maybe I should. My contract is up at the end of the year.'

'Food for thought, sweetie,' Gillian cooed. 'Food for thought.'

'More champagne, miss?' The waiter asked as he slid the twice-cooked duck in front of her.

Kate lifted her glass in assent. She liked being courted by the opposition. And she particularly liked their taste in fine dining. She'd always fancied eating a meal at Level 41.

'We'd love to have a journalist of your calibre and experience on our show.' The youngish executive producer came straight to the point. 'So what can I offer you to make that happen?'

'Well, the reason I'm thinking about jumping ship is because *Australia Tonight* is becoming too tabloid. There's scarcely any over-seas coverage any more. And that more than anything is what I'm looking for.'

'Well, we cover most of the big international stories when they happen. We had a reporter in Bosnia. We covered Mogadishu from our London bureau. You would certainly have opportunities to report on major world events if you decided to join us.'

'Say I do sign with you. How do I know I won't just get lumped with the consumer rounds?' Kate asked.

'You'll just have to take my word for it. Of course we'd be happy to double your current wage if that would help us overcome any trust issues.' He smiled.

Kate choked on her champagne.

A quarter of a million dollars! The figure danced around in her head, more intoxicating than the champagne.

'I'll have to think about it.' And she surprised herself by actually meaning it. She had accepted the lunch invitation more out of curiosity than with any real intention of switching camps. But suddenly the grass was looking awfully green.

As she jumped in a cab to head back to the office, her mobile rang.

'Enjoy your lunch, Kate?' Fuck. It was Mawson.

She should have known she'd never get away with her covert tête-à-tête. Sydney was a small town and Mawson had a formidable network of spies across the various networks.

Ambitious types would call him with any snippets of gossip. What they didn't realise was that Mawson prized loyalty above all. Their subterfuge only meant they would never get a job at Channel Eight.

'You'd better come and see me when you get back,' he said gruffly and hung up.

Fifteen minutes later, Kate walked sheepishly into the news and current affairs chief's office.

'Why would you be having lunch with the EP of the opposition,

231

Kate? If there's a problem I expect you to come to me first.' Mawson was squeezing a stress ball. Hard.

'I'm just sick of all the small fry crap stories we've been peddling. There are plenty of bigger and more important issues we could be covering. Why aren't we looking at Wik for instance? Every time I mention it, Ripley groans.'

'Kate, that sounds like you want to work for the ABC. You know quite well that *Australia Tonight* or any other commercial current affairs show are not going to suddenly start running stories on blackfellas just because you say so.'

Mawson was right of course.

'How much did he offer you?'

'It's not about the money, Bruce,' Kate said, and then realising that wasn't entirely true added, 'Two hundred and fifty thousand.'

'Okay, done,' he said, abandoning the stress ball and reaching for a cigarette. 'And I promise the next big international story is yours. But what you have to believe is that I have big plans for your future, Kate. I've invested in you and I expect some loyalty back.' Mawson did not take his eyes off her throughout his little speech. 'Do we understand one another?'

What Kate understood was that she was going to have to learn to deal with Ripley if she wanted the prize at the other end.

NINETEEN

'Germs,' Ripley announced at the weekly planning meeting. 'The cunts fucking love germs.'

Kate winced. She would never get used to the way *Australia Tonight*'s executive producer described the show's audience. Two and a half years had passed since Ripley was handed temporary stewardship of the show. It was now clear the appointment was permanent. Kate simply had to accept she was stuck with the bloke.

'Come on. Germs are rating their tits off. Surely one of you arseholes has an idea.'

The assembled arseholes stared back at him blankly.

A Current Affair had pioneered the tabloid obsession with germ detection by testing television remote controls in hotels around the country. Poo. Semen. All kinds of nasties were found lurking on the devices' seemingly innocuous black plastic surfaces. *Today Tonight* had gone even further, swabbing toilet lids, escalator handrails, playground equipment and kitchen dishcloths. They too found germs. *A Current Affair* hit back with a report on disease-laden shopping trolleys. The horror!

The fact that bacteria is found everywhere outside a properly sterilised hospital operating theatre didn't bother the geniuses of current affairs television. If viewers were prepared to tune in to be apprised of a long-established scientific truth then so be it. Germs rated. And now *Australia Tonight* wanted to catch the bug.

'There must be something left to test,' Ripley demanded, lighting another cigarette. His office was a pea soup of tobacco haze despite Channel Eight's decade-old smoking ban.

'How about we germ test hands?' Tubby piped up, his usually foggy expression clearing momentarily. 'Everyone has hands and they touch lots of stuff!'

'Hey, liking that.'

'Not liking that one little bit,' Kate jumped in. Maybe they should germ test Ripley's mouth, she thought. Plenty of shit came out of that.

It was clearly time to inject a little commonsense into proceedings. It was mind boggling the half-baked ideas that crept out of these meetings and into lounge rooms around the country. Kate wasn't sure what surprised her more – the dross that passed for current affairs nowadays or the fact that people actually sat down to watch it.

'You guys do realise that exposure to bacteria is what keeps us all healthy?'

'Mate, the punters love this shit. Can't get enough of it,' Tubby and Ripley replied in unison. The only other attendee at the meeting was the man Kate still thought of as the Urinator. There was no need for a new moniker. She'd seen him douse plenty of pot plants in the years since that first boardroom party. He nodded in sage agreement.

Despite the often-cited fact that women held the remote control during prime time, the *Australia Tonight* agenda was set almost exclusively by men. And they were men uniquely ill-equipped to represent female interests.

Ripley hated women. Although given the amount of airtime Jenni had been getting recently, he obviously still had a soft (hard) spot for his consumer reporter. As for Tubby, he had very little contact with the opposite gender at all, his sexual preference being the subject of much office conjecture. At the very least, his weekly lessons in Ceroc dancing, expansive collection of Lladro figurines and swanky eastern suburbs address suggested he had a different set of interests from the majority of the viewing audience.

Together, Ripley and Tubby came up with all kinds of stories designed to tempt women into watching the show. They road tested diets. They compared various household products. They told their audience where to pick up a bargain. And they did it over and over and over again. Women got fat. Women used stuff. Women liked to shop. What more could a woman possibly be interested in?

Kate had recently made it her mission to give them a few suggestions.

She'd been sinking a few too many beverages at the Venus Trap when Gillian came up with the bright idea of Kate gatecrashing the boys' weekly programming meetings.

'Well, Kate, if you don't like the crap they're pushing, you need to do something about it. The journos are not just welcome they're *expected* at our story meetings. But of course our show offers a far saner working environment. Something you would know if you'd chosen to join us,' she said, draining her overpriced European beer. 'But far be it from me to rub it in. Get in there and give them the benefit of your experience and gender. And if you can't do that, just get in there and piss them off.'

Of course, Kate only ended up pissing them off. Ripley and Tubby resented her input. But they weren't entirely sure how to get rid of her. So they did their best to ignore her instead.

'How about we leave bags and cameras and stuff in parks near crappy housing-commission flats. And film the blackfellas stealing them?' The suggestion came from Tubby.

Kate rolled her eyes. 'We did that story last month. And it was entrapment then too.'

'Kate, we all know the difference between right and wrong. They're scum. And they're still fucking doing it!' the Urinator chimed in. He had no discernible journalistic background and a questionable moral compass 'Anyway it rated.'

'So the ratings justify the means. That's bullshit.'

Ripley ignored her. 'Yeah, let's take it round the block one more time,' he decided. 'The punters will have forgotten they ever saw the story by now anyway. Four weeks is a long time in television. Jonesy can look after it.'

Kate couldn't believe it when Geoff Jones turned up for work at *Australia Tonight* only a few months after his infamous appearance on *Media Watch*. It seemed men could survive any amount of scandal. A forged legal document. A staged car chase. What was a teensy blowjob in the scheme of things? In fact, the incident seemed to have enhanced Geoff's status around the office, at least among the blokes. They all now owned signed copies of the unedited tape.

Tubby moved onto the next item in his fastidiously neat and organised notebook. 'How about we road test which razors work best? You know, for women shaving their legs.'

Kate only just stopped herself from moaning. Save a buck. Find a bargain. Scare people silly. *Australia Tonight* was looking more and more like one of those new breed of infotainment shows. In fact, some nights the viewer may as well have been watching *Good Medicine* or *Money*.

'Didn't *A Current Affair* test razors a few weeks ago?'

'Good thinking, Kate,' Ripley said. 'Tubby, print out the story brief from their website. They've already done the research for us. That will save us some time.'

There seemed no end to it. Road testing razors was the perfect companion piece to the previous week's journalistic triumph – Jenni undertaking an in-depth investigation into the durability of leading brands of pantyhose. The story gave Jenni an excuse to wear an extremely short skirt. She'd even roped in a bunch of air hostesses to help with the survey, an innovation that delighted the sales department.

Sales liked to know in advance if *Australia Tonight* was planning to run a consumer yarn because then they could convince the appropriate clients to pay for a slot in the ad break straight after the story. The tactic backfired sometimes. There had been a nasty incident when Kate investigated the safety features of various four-wheel drives. One model proved to be a complete lemon. The makers of the lemon immediately withdrew their highly lucrative sponsorship of the program.

'Hey, I heard of a good product,' Kate offered in what she considered an unmistakably sarcastic tone. 'It's these amazing swimsuits. When you pull them off, they wax your bikini line.'

'Fuck. That sounds great. Waddaya reckon, Ripley?' Tubby was bouncing about in his chair like a preschooler anticipating a trip to the bathroom.

Kate sighed in disbelief. 'Guys, I was joking'

'Pity.' Tubby sounded deflated. 'It would have worked for us.'

'Let's get Jenni onto the razor yarn. She can do her piece to camera in the bath. That should spike the ratings.'

'I'd love to be doing sound that day,' Tubby snickered, although no one believed him.

'Let's stick germ-infested hands into the weekend promo,' Ripley continued. 'What else have we got?'

The question hung heavy in the smoky air. Mondays and

Tuesdays were the biggest viewing nights in television current affairs. So stories promoted over the weekend had the potential to deliver huge ratings. And if a show drew a good-sized audience on the Monday, the chances improved that those same viewers would tune in again the next day. And the day after that. The most important decision an executive producer ever made was not what questions to ask the prime minister or whether to chance a lawsuit. It was what stories to put in the weekend promo.

'How about that African junket with the soapie chick? I think she was feeding the world's starving. She's pretty popular right now,' Tubby offered.

'No one wants to watch a bunch of whinging starving black people. Certainly not at dinner time anyway,' the Urinator countered.

'You like black people just fine when they're caught thieving,' Kate fired.

'That's different. That's interesting.'

Ripley lit another cigarette. 'I reckon we can edit the promo so there aren't any black people in it. The voiceover can say something like the secret agony of television's brightest star. That will get them in.'

So *Australia Tonight* planned to broadcast a story about a celebrity's life-changing journey to Africa that ignored the inconvenient presence of a few thousand hungry Africans. Kate felt like her head was going to explode.

Ripley continued. 'Or we can knock together a bargain shopping guide. The mums love that shit.'

'Surely you're not going to stick Jenni on that pink bus again? She must have a reserved seat by now.' Kate was losing her cool. 'There's a fucking war on by the way.'

'For Christ's sake, Corish. Don't start on that Balkans shit. No one here gives a flying fuck about Kosovo.'

'Well, a looming humanitarian crisis then, with half the population spilling over into Albania,' Kate tried again.

'Forget it. Until they start turning up here in boats, I don't give a fuck.'

Ripley had no intention of covering some ethnic skirmish half a world away. He'd just been offered a ratings bonus. If he lifted audience numbers by five per cent, he would line his pockets nicely. He wasn't about to send the figures into free-fall by covering events in Kosovo. Real news just didn't rate as well as the consumer stuff. And when the choice was between responsible, informative journalism and thirty pieces of silver, Ripley would go the Judas Iscariot route every time.

Kate got up and left, once again feeling like she had wasted an hour.

'Fuck worthy reporters. They fucking bore me fucking senseless,' Ripley complained, feeling considerably more relaxed now that his office was double X chromosome free. 'Is there some way we can make sure that bitch doesn't join these meetings from now on?'

If she wasn't such a favourite with the chief he'd have rid himself of the woman a long time ago.

Kate was fuming as she stormed up the stairs to Mawson's office. She was two years into the lucrative three-year contract she had signed at the end of 1996. And nothing had changed. If anything standards were getting worse. She didn't think it was a coincidence that ratings were also falling.

Mawson's promise to let Kate tackle some meatier issues had fallen well short of her expectations, having manifested as a three-day trip to Hong Kong to cover the handover. It was a splendid thirty-first birthday present but that was about it. There had been a few other stories that had piqued her interest. The Thredbo landslide. The Republican convention. The waterfront dispute. But it was hardly enough to sate her over two years.

'I want to move back to the newsroom, Bruce,' Kate announced, her jaw set firm with determination.

'Kate, you're the star reporter at *AT*. The show needs you.' And the public love you he could have added.

'You don't need a so-called 'star' reporter to cover the crap I've been dishing up lately.'

'You've signed a three-year contract with *AT*, Kate,' Mawson reminded her, leaning forward on his desk.

'I signed a three-year contract with you, Bruce,' she responded evenly. 'We had a deal. I'm supposed to be first in line for any over-seas assignments. But we're ignoring Kosovo, just like we did with Sarajevo, Mogadishu and even Indonesia last year. If we do touch on any international stories, we cross to the news guys to save on the budget. Kosovo is going to blow up in March. And I want to cover it for news. And if *AT* wants I can file for them too.'

'Okay, okay. I hear you. But you're staying with *AT*. Do you understand?'

Kate smiled. She couldn't wait to tell Simon. Maybe now he'd let up on those interminable lectures about the shallowness of tabloid television.

The phone was answered on the first ring.

'Good morning. Simon Gilchrist's office. Denise speaking.'

'Oh. Hi, Denise. It's Kate.'

There was a pause that Denise clearly did not feel obliged to fill.

'Is Simon about?'

Another pause.

'I'll see if he's free.'

Officious old biddy, Kate thought. How dare the woman treat her like some pesky college kid. She was Simon's girlfriend!

She had never met Denise. But Kate imagined she looked a bit like a post-menopausal librarian clad entirely in tweed. She had suggested as much to Simon once but he'd cut her off angrily, accusing her of being a bitch. Still, he wasn't the one who spent ten minutes at a time on hold.

By the time Denise returned to the phone, Kate had identified more than a dozen words in that day's Target quiz.

'I'm afraid he's tied up right now, Kate.' Denise spat out her name as though it was poison. Kate wondered what she objected to exactly. The fact she worked in commercial television or that she wasn't at home tending to the great Simon Gilchrist's domestic needs? 'Can I take a message?'

Kate pushed the newspaper aside angrily. 'Tell him I'm going to Kosovo. I might be tied up for a while.'

That afternoon Mawson called Ripley into his office.

'What are you doing about Kosovo?' he barked. He had assumed his preferred interrogative position, feet up on his desk and hands behind his head.

'Yeah, we've had a couple of meetings on that one, mate.' Ripley was pacing. Just what he needed. Another cunt who didn't give a toss about his bonus. 'I'm thinking we'll just piggyback off news. Save some outlay. Waddaya reckon?'

'I've decided to send Kate. She can file for news and *AT*. She's getting antsy. And we need to keep her happy if we want her to re-sign at the end of the year.'

So the bitch had been in here complaining about him, Ripley thought. He just knew it.

'Staying in a tent in a refugee camp might not be her style

though. I don't know how she'll manage if there's nowhere to plug in her hairdryer.'

'That's bullshit and you know it,' Mawson grunted as he nodded Ripley towards the door.

He was starting to lose patience with his henchman.

Ratings were soft and the bloke had been ducking and weaving, trying to explain the trend. The network was on the nose. The host was on the nose. Viewers preferred watching Ray. Viewers preferred watching Stan. The show's biggest billboard had been pulled down. It was daylight savings. It was late-night shopping. Audience share was down in general. The internet was dragging viewers away. The opposition was playing cheap tricks. The latest budget cuts were misguided. They weren't getting enough promos. And on it went.

Still Mawson reminded himself, this was television. And Ripley did a better line in spin than Shane Warne.

TWENTY

Milosovich, Mladic, Karadzic. Kate had spent hours on the plane practising the tongue-twisting Slavic names, poring over maps and memorising the intricate satellite schedules. It had all seemed so vital thirty thousand odd feet up in the air. But a business-class seat to Europe was a world away from the misery of Kukes. On the muddy and desperate Albanian border, her careful preparation counted for nothing.

The refugee camp was a teeming tent city built on a million tales of misery and pain. Up to four thousand people a day had been streaming across the border from Kosovo. They were homeless. Stateless. The Yugoslav army had confiscated their papers as they fled across the border. They had been left with nothing. Even their identities had been stolen.

'Our village was razed,' the old lady sobbed. 'They burnt everything. Our homes. Our farm animals. Only the church was left untouched. The Serbian Orthodox church. Our cattle were cut up and thrown in the well. They took our men. Our boys.'

Kate's interpreter had tears rolling down his young face as he recounted the old woman's story.

She rocked back and forth on arthritic haunches, fist to her heart. 'My son. My son. They took my only son,' she moaned again and again. The cameras kept rolling as Kate moved from one tragic story to the next.

It was a disaster on a scale Kate could scarcely comprehend. For two nights she had slept in the back of the crew's hired Land rover. She had witnessed and painstakingly recorded as much of the human drama as she could manage. It was almost time to move on.

As she waited for Tezza's cue, Kate took a couple of deep breaths and pinched herself hard on the thigh. She did it more out of habit nowadays. Nerves had stopped being a problem since the near-miss over Basra.

'There are already one hundred thousand people living in this camp. And the aid agencies are predicting the population will jump by half as many again over the next few weeks. The next front-line, of course, is disease. Back to you.'

'And we so we say goodbye to the delights of Kukes,' Tezza said, unclipping Kate's radio mike.

'Don't look so pleased. Our next stop is Belgrade. And we're only going there because NATO is bombing the shit out of the place.'

'The life of a foreign correspondent is *so* glamorous.' Tezza winked as he packed away the gear.

They grinned at each other. Who were they kidding? They loved every dirty and dangerous second.

'Sorry, no rooms. All full.' Kate had lost count of the times she'd heard those words over the past few hours.

With flights into Belgrade grounded, she'd thought getting to the Serb capital was going to be her biggest challenge. But she'd lucked into a United Nations convoy heading out of Kukes that fitted her timeframe nicely. She and Tezza had ended up making the

244

cross-country trip in relative safety. It was only now they'd reached their destination that their luck had run out.

The world's media had descended on Belgrade and the big hotels, like the Hyatt Regency, were fully booked. Journalists from smaller countries always had to scramble for a bed. They were the last to reach a trouble spot. And with the bigger networks booking out entire floors, they were also the last to secure a room.

Finally, as they were making yet another fruitless sweep of the downtown area, Kate spotted a sign advertising the Hotel Jugoslavija. It was located in the embassy district, an unlikely target for NATO's bombs. Admittedly, it was some distance away from the media action. But it sounded reasonably safe. She figured it was worth a try.

The hotel must have been a local wonder back in the communist seventies, with its marble foyer, shimmering metallic ceiling and sweeping entrance staircase. Queen Elizabeth, Richard Nixon and Neil Armstrong had all stayed there. So had Tina Turner. But the Jugoslavija's glory days were well behind it. Now it was snubbed even by that ragtag bunch of foreign correspondents and misadventurers who chased trouble around the globe. But it did offer the one feature Kate had been searching for all day. It had two available rooms and they were going for the relative bargain price of US$100 a day.

Kate dropped her tiny bag on the mustard and cream brocade bedspread and started to unpack. First out were two pairs of khaki trekking pants. They weren't the most flattering trousers she owned but they did have the advantage of never needing ironing. Plus they dried in half an hour flat. Next came two cotton button-down shirts, two white T-shirts, a few pairs of undies and some cosmetics. Those few items and the Levi jeans and leather anorak jacket she was standing in accounted for her entire working wardrobe.

She grabbed the small, stiff towel folded at the end of the bed and headed for the shower. Even with the cold tap twisted tightly closed, the water was lukewarm. But after Kukes, it was luxury.

As the air-raid sirens wailed, signalling another round of NATO strikes, Kate fell into a heavy, exhausted sleep.

She woke the next morning, revitalised and impatient to get to work. There was a big story breaking. Reverend Jesse Jackson and his posse of preachers had lobbed into town a few days earlier as loudly and as forcefully as an Allied bombing raid. The Serbs had captured three American soldiers. Jackson wanted President Slobodan Milosevic to release them. It was an improbable mission. It was also a great story.

'We're off to the Hyatt Regency, Tezza. 10.30 a.m. press conference,' Kate chirped.

'Any idea how to get there?' Tezza asked.

'The man on the desk said to turn right towards the Sava Centre. It's on the corner of Milentija Popovica Street and Vladimira Popovica Street. And don't ask me to spell it. I can't believe I just pronounced it.'

'I'll just follow the river and see if we bump into it.'

'That works for me. I can't read the frigging map anyway."

'What woman can?' Tezza teased.

'You'll keep, mate,' Kate said, for once stuck for a smartarse comeback.

The conference hall of the Hyatt was abuzz when Kate and Tezza arrived. There was a whisper that Jesse Jackson had actually pulled it off and that the three American prisoners were about to be released.

Kate loved the rush that came when big news broke. And right now the attention of the world's media was focused on this one hotel in Belgrade and Kate Corish was there in the thick of it. For a few moments, she was conscious of being perfectly happy.

Then Jonathan McTavish entered the room.

Kate watched as he commandeered a seat in the front row. She had scarcely given him a thought in years. But that didn't stop her heart from skipping a beat.

Why do men get better looking with age, she wondered? The INN reporter would have to be at least forty now. Maybe forty-three. The silver hairs at his temples just made him look more credible. More distinguished. He had the kind of skin that didn't accumulate wrinkles. Just smile lines around the eyes. They were kind eyes. Or they appeared to be. Kate knew better. Two-timing bastard, she reminded herself.

He caught her staring at him and smiled. The mature response would have been to acknowledge his presence with a slight nod. But Kate was paralysed. Happily for her dignity, the conference started, sparing her the need to produce any reaction at all.

As rumoured, Jackson announced the imminent release of the three American soldiers. Members of his delegation wept and exchanged hugs.

The spirit of joy and self-congratulation didn't last long. McTavish fired his first question.

'Don't you find it ironic that so much effort has been put into three American lives when NATO 'accidentally' bombed a bus killing forty-seven civilians?'

Jesse Jackson stood silent. He had only the sketchiest understanding of this war. The body count. Balkan history. The role of NATO. None of that interested him. It was why his mission was so effective. He was persuasive because he was not judgmental. How could he be? He was too naïve.

'Are you going to meet with Rugova?' another journalist asked.

Again Jackson's expression was blank.

'Ibrahim Rugova,' the journalist prompted. But the American politician had never heard of the leader of the Kosovar Albanian political movement.

'This is a moral appeal that will have consequences.' Jackson kept to the script. 'The powers that be will look kindly upon the generosity of human spirit we have seen today.'

At the end of the conference Kate slid out a side door. She didn't need to be reminded how naïve and how foolish she'd been all those years ago. Her face burned just thinking about it.

The manoeuvre worked. She gave McTavish the slip, which was a huge relief. Unfortunately, her exit was so stealthy that she also managed to outwit her own cameraman.

Where the fuck was Tezza?

Kate stood in the lobby, smoking a Marlboro light and trying not to look like she was hiding behind a giant marble column. Her eyes darted around the vast entry foyer.

At last she spotted Tezza, talking enthusiastically to McTavish and his crew. Fuck. A quarter of an hour must have passed before Tezza finally appeared in front of her. He was bouncing around like a puppy, all keyed up after his little reunion with the INN crowd. God save me from cultural cringe, she thought.

'Hey, I just ran into the legendary Jonathan McTavish. You remember him from Baghdad, don't you? Lent us his gear for your stand-up that day.'

'What did he want?' she snapped.

'Geez, girl, I thought you two got on well. He just asked where we were staying. I told him that bum-fuck Hotel Jugoslavija. And I gave him our sat phone number. The bloke is wired. He said he'd let us know if his sources had anything interesting. What's wrong with you anyway, periods due?' Tezza didn't sound like he was joking.

'Fifteen minutes talking to the big boys and you turn into a sexist arsehole. But if you must know, they're due tomorrow, so don't fuck with me!' With a lifetime's experience living with three sisters and now a wife, Tezza knew not to push the conversation any further.

The release of the American prisoners did nothing to soften NATO's resolve. Every night Belgrade was pounded. And Kate was supplying material for all of Channel Eight's news and current affairs programs. She wondered how she could feel so exhausted and so totally exhilarated at the same time.

She wished she could get a bit of shut-eye. But since that first night in the capital, she'd slept only fitfully. Sometimes the explosions seemed so close. Tonight would be the forty-fifth consecutive night of bombing and there was no reason to hope there'd be any let up in the Allied campaign.

It was 9 p.m. and Kate and Tezza were hunched over an edit pack putting the finishing touches on their latest story when the sat phone rang. Kate answered, surprised to be hearing from the office so early in her evening.

'Kate. It's Jonathan McTavish.'

For the first time in her life, Kate was grateful for the satellite delay. It allowed her a couple of desperately needed seconds to collect her thoughts.

'Kate, you must get out of the Hotel Jugoslavija,' Jonathan said urgently. 'My sources say it's housing an underground bunker used by paramilitary leader Arkan Raznatovic.'

'How do you know that?' Kate shot back.

'You're near the Chinese embassy as well. And if my sources are correct, that building is also a target tonight. Get yourselves out of that hotel now. If you won't do it for your own safety, do it as a journalist. Get out on the ground. Point your camera in the direction of your hotel and the embassy. You've only got minutes. Please, Kate. Get out now.'

'Okay, okay. We're gone.' Kate's gut instinct kicked in. She believed McTavish. He may have played her for a fool in Baghdad but a hoax like this wasn't his style. Plus she'd been feeling weird about the hotel for a while. The strangest looking men were always shuffling in and out its doors. She had suspected they were gangsters. If they were Arkan's men, it made sense. His Serb Volunteer Guard was no more than a vicious pack of profiteers, sadists and thugs.

'Tezza. Grab the edit pack and the camera. I'll grab the lights. We've gotta go.'

'Hang on. Just one more shot and I'm done.'

'We don't have time,' Kate barked. 'That was McTavish. He says this hotel has a bunker under it. We're a target. You're the one who keeps saying he's wired. Do you still want to lay down that last shot?'

'Let's go.' Tezza was grabbing bits of equipment and throwing them onto the hotel trolley. By a stroke of luck, he'd kept forgetting to return the thing to the foyer. 'Get your stuff and I'll meet you outside.'

In two minutes flat, they were out the door and wheeling their gear up the road. As they reached the end of the block, the lights of the city went out and the air-raid sirens started blaring.

'Kate! Kate!' Jonathan yelled from a hired Land rover as it screeched to a stop next to them.

He jumped out of the car and bounded over. 'Thank God you got out of—' He didn't finish his sentence as the first deafening bomb hit its target. Three more blasts followed in quick succession.

Jonathan instinctively threw himself across Kate as they all fell back from the impact.

Kate wasn't sure how much time passed before she opened her eyes. She was dazed. Perhaps she'd even been knocked out for a minute or two. McTavish was still on top of her. A heavy weight. Too heavy. She wiggled out from under him. There was a deep cut on his forehead.

'Shit. Shit. Don't be dead,' she yelled. 'Don't be dead.'

Tezza had propped himself up against Jonathan's car, still stunned and trying to make sense of what was happening. He saw Kate hunched over McTavish.

'Fuck, is he all right?' He stumbled the few metres to where the INN reporter was sprawled and felt for a pulse. It was beating strongly.

'He's fine, Kate. He's just unconscious. Must have hit his head on the road as we fell.' An enormous sense of relief swept over her. Safe. They were all safe.

Tezza straightened slowly. He was sore but he'd worry about that later. 'You look after the big bloke. I'd better get moving. There's work to do.' Within minutes he was up and rolling tape.

Most of NATO's firepower had been aimed at the Chinese embassy but one bomb had scored a direct hit on the hotel Kate had called home for the past several days.

Further up the street, civilians were pouring out of the Chinese embassy. Some hadn't even had time to find their shoes.

'How could they bomb civilians?' she asked the dark and the dust.

'Kate. Kate. Get out,' Jonathan was mumbling. He opened his eyes to find Kate looking down at him, his head cushioned in her lap.

'Kate. You're okay. Thank God.'

'How are you feeling? You've cut your head.' She touched the area carefully.

'I'll be fine.' Jonathan sat up slowly, still dazed, and looked over at what was left of Kate's hotel. A large section of the building had collapsed, dumping tonnes of metal, concrete and glass into the car park below. There would be fatalities tonight. He was sure of it.

'Thank God you got out. Are you okay?'

'Yeah, I'm fine. Here. Hold this to your head,' Kate said, pressing a wad of tissues against his wound. 'How did you know?'

'I have a contact in intelligence. I don't even know his name. He called and said there was going to be a raid and that the Chinese embassy was being used to transmit Yugoslav army communications. The embassy was removed from the prohibited target list yesterday. And he mentioned your hotel was a headquarters for Arkan. I knew you were staying there. Oh God. I'm so glad you listened to me.'

'I'll say. Look, I have to go to work now. But I can give you a lift to the hospital if you like.'

'No, I'll be fine.' His expression became serious. 'You know you haven't changed a bit.'

Kate stared at him, tongue-tied all of a sudden.

'Sure, um, gotta go,' she said finally as she backed away and turned to join her cameraman. She had to interview survivors. Determine casualties. Verify the target. File a story. Forget about Jonathan McTavish.

She checked the watch on her right wrist. When she was away on assignment, Kate always wore two watches, one for local time and one for Sydney time. It was now 11 a.m. in Sydney. The news went to air at 6 p.m. The bombing of the Chinese embassy and her own close shave would lead the bulletin. She had a busy seven hours ahead.

Not long after Kate's story went to air in Australia, the international media gathered in the Hyatt Tea House to watch the BBC transmission of NATO's Brussels press conference.

'We attacked what we thought was the Federal Directorate for Supply and Procurement,' Major General Jertz announced.

'What do you say to reports that the embassy was being used as a rebroadcasting station for military transmissions? And why was it removed from the prohibited targets list a few days ago,' a BBC journalist asked.

'We have no information on that,' said the Major General.

Kate sat at a small glass table taking notes. Her body ached to sink into one of the Tea House's many and stately lounge chairs. But she feared any deviation from the ninety-degree upright position would tempt her into sleep. She'd been awake now for well over twenty-four hours and getting by on massive doses of coffee and adrenalin. Just one more on-air commitment to go and she could finally get some rest.

And to get past that last hurdle, she needed to hear and evaluate NATO's response to the embassy bombing. The information would provide the centrepiece for her cross into Channel Eight's late-night news bulletin. But as the press conference droned on, her head started feeling impossibly heavy and her mind drifted. If she just shut her eyes for a few moments. Surely, there would be no harm.

'Kate, if you need to lie down for a bit, you're welcome to use INN's suite.' It was Jonathan McTavish. They were the only two left in the room. She must have fallen asleep. 'We'll be editing. But there is a comfy couch.'

'Coming to my rescue again?' Kate struck a deliberately light note as she tried to kick her brain back into gear. 'Thank you, I have one more deadline to meet first. But I'd love to take you up on the offer after that. As long as Tezza can crash there too.'

'That's a given. I'll expect you in a few hours. You two can get some rest on the INN tab. But after that I'd really like to talk to you, Kate. I think you owe me that.'

'Sure.' She really didn't feel like having a drawn-out conversation about that night in Baghdad. The guy just wanted to appease his guilt. And that was fine. Noble almost. But it was a high price to pay for a few hours sleep. Still, she felt some obligation now. It was hard to trump the 'I saved your life' card.

'Kate, they want that sim sat.' Tezza burst into the room, saving her from any further conversation. 'They've booked the bird. It's only up for thirty minutes. We better get to the live site now before we lose it. Let's go.'

Kate was grateful the office had opted to go with a simulated interview, mostly because it would shorten her day by three or four hours. But she also realised she was sleep deprived and not in any condition to handle the stress of a live cross.

Of course, the Sydney office hadn't given Kate's physical well-being the slightest consideration when making the decision. The sim sat was simply the most convenient and practical option available. Where possible, it made sense to pre-record satellite interviews because editors could then cut out the awkward three-second gap between questions and answers. A pre-record also gave producers some control over the length of an interview. In a live situation, presenters would often ignore the most frantic wind-up signals from the floor. Short of pulling out a Vaudevillian hook and dragging the anchor off set, producers could only curse in the control room and sweat on the clock.

Kate was delighted to hear Matthew's voice on the other end of the satellite.

'I'm anchoring the half-hour late news now.'

'Congratulations, Matthew. That's terrific.'

'And congratulations to you too. You've been doing a brilliant job. But I'm afraid I'm the one who has to break the bad news. They've decided to pull you out.'

'No!'

'Too dangerous. The hotel bombing really spooked them. That was close, Kate. I have to say I'm on their side for once.'

'I survived, didn't I? I would've thought that proved I can look after myself. And let's face it. They wouldn't be getting all wobbly right now if I was a bloke. It's not fair.'

'It might not be fair, Kate. But that's the decision. It has nothing to do with gender and everything to do with the insurance company pulling your cover. Management is ordering you out. Right after this interview, you're to start making your way home.'

As Kate bumped out of Belgrade in the back of an aid truck, she almost felt relieved. Professionally, she was disappointed of course. But personally, she was happy to be avoiding an earnest discussion about relationships with Jonathan McTavish. After a brush with death, and a few weeks in squalor, she needed what all jaded correspondents needed – a long, hot bath, a stiff scotch and a hug from a loved one.

TWENTY-ONE

'Fancy a walk along the lake before dinner?' Tezza asked as they checked into their functional, clean and ever so Swiss hotel.

'Just let me wash off the war zone. But yes. I love the idea of taking an early evening stroll without fear of getting bombed.' Kate couldn't wait to peel off her jeans and no longer white T-shirt.

The fastest route back to Australia had been via an overnight stopover in Zurich. Normally Kate considered Switzerland a little on the dull side. But after a month traipsing through filth and dodging flying shrapnel, it seemed a splendid destination. And best of all, her room included her very favourite luxury hotel feature – a phone within arm's reach of the bath.

Heaven.

As she soaked away her exhaustion, Kate dialled home. The phone rang out. Next she tried Simon's mobile but he didn't answer that either. It didn't even go to voicemail.

Well, if I can't get through, I'll just surprise him tomorrow instead, she thought as she hurried into the foyer to meet Tezza.

Lake Zurich was just a block from the hotel.

'God, Tezza. Look at this place. Blue water, swans, snow-capped mountains in the distance. I feel like I've wandered onto the set of *The Sound of Music*.

'It's nice. But I just want to get home to the wife and kids. Geez. I'm getting too old for this crap.'

'Oh, shut up. I'm only a couple of years behind you.'

'Exactly. Don't you want a family some day?'

'One day maybe. But Simon's not that keen. So who knows?'

'Katie, I can't tell you what it means to leave work behind and get home to my kids. Don't miss out on that. It's real. I know being on the road is exciting. And it's dangerous and scary and fun. But don't miss out on the real stuff.'

'I'll try not to. But you never know what life has in store. I mean, if you hadn't told Jonathan where we were staying . . . if he hadn't called . . . we wouldn't even be here. So yeah. Who knows?'

But Kate did know. She was just a few months shy of thirty-three. And while she didn't like to admit it, that clock Al had been prattling on about was definitely ticking. It was well and truly time she had a proper talk with Simon.

When the cab pulled up in front of the cottage, Bernie was sitting on the veranda waiting for her. Kate hoped he hadn't been stationed there for the whole four weeks.

'Bernstein. It's winter, you duffer. What are you doing out here?' She picked him up. He was at least a kilo lighter. 'Have you been pining for me, sweetheart?'

Then she noticed his igloo and empty food bowl sitting out on the porch. No wonder he was so happy to see her, she thought crossly. Simon was going to have a hard time explaining his way out of this one.

Kate tucked Bernstein under one arm and let herself into the house. The lights were off but there was a dim glow issuing from

257

the kitchen. Supertramp was playing on the stereo. The soundtrack of home, she thought.

'Hello. Hello,' Kate called as she clomped down the hall. It was after eight o'clock and she wondered what Simon was serving up for dinner.

The answer was lying naked and spreadeagled on the benchtop.

'You bastard,' Kate heard herself say even before she fully registered what she was seeing. The chubby brunette on the kitchen counter yelped and tried to cover herself with a Ken Done tea towel.

'Kate, Kate! I can explain,' Simon shouted after her as she marched back down the hall juggling Bernie and her already packed travel bag.

'No need to explain, Simon,' she yelled, slamming the front door and jumping into her recently purchased VW Beetle.

Kate would have liked to make a quick and dramatic exit. But she had to turn the engine over three times before it started. Not even a car liked being neglected for weeks on end. Bernstein sat tall in the passenger seat, purring happily.

'Kate, Kate, I can explain. That's what he said,' Kate spat as she downed a double scotch at the Burdekin.

'It's a pity you didn't hang around to hear what he had to say. I'd love to know what innocent explanation he had for rooting some woman senseless on your kitchen counter.'

'Thanks for the visual, Gillian,' Kate frowned. 'How could I be so naïve? Now I think back on all those times I wasn't able to contact him and it's driving me nuts. How long had he been cheating on me?'

'It doesn't matter, honey. The bloke was a pain in the arse,' Gillian said.

'That doesn't make me feel any better, you know. The fact you didn't like him.'

'But it makes me feel better, that you're not with him any more.' Kate looked on the verge of tears yet again. 'Oh, come on. You're a young, glamorous reporter. He's forty-five and having a mid-life crisis. I mean, an affair with his personal assistant? That's so passé.'

Kate had discovered the identity of the kitchen whore (as Ben and Al liked to describe her) from the *Mail*'s gossip column.

Which ABC current affairs titan has finally been caught out in his long-running affair with his PA? Word has it they're going to make it official.

'I can't believe I thought Denise was a hundred years old,' Kate whimpered. 'And why would he marry that cow and not me?'

'Maybe you overshadowed him. He's not a big man. And I suspect you made him feel even smaller. If he married you he'd be Simon Corish. And I bet it pissed him right off that you earned more than him too. Honey, you had his balls in your hands.'

'But I was a young woman when I met him. Now I'm thirty-three. Christ, at my age, I'll scare men off. They'll think I'm desperate,' Kate moaned.

'Stop it, Kate. Cut the crap. You're an exciting, fabulous woman. And men will walk over hot coals for you.' Gillian decided it was time for a bit of tough love. There were a truckload of practical considerations to address. 'Now, we need to get you sorted. Where do you want to live?'

'Oh, God. I have to get out of Mum's place, that's for sure. My room's a time warp. There are still INXS posters on the wall. Plus the woman keeps trying to feed me bloody carbohydrates. And the chicken soup sympathy is driving me mad. I came home from work last night and she'd left the Dalai Lama's *Art of Happiness* on my pillow!'

'Let's go house hunting then. It's time you got a foot in the property market anyway. I know they pay you enough.'

Kate thought about protesting. But the fact was it was actually a pretty good idea. She'd managed to save quite a nest egg over the years, mostly because she never had any time to shop. Gillian was right. It was time to get a place of her own. She couldn't live with her mother forever . . . although it was surprisingly tempting.

Kate wasn't about to spoil Gillian's long-held image of her tennis-playing, interfering, socialite mother. But the truth was Dianne Corish had been magnificent during the entire crisis. Kate expected plenty of 'I told you so's and she probably deserved a couple too. But they didn't come.

'I wasted the best years of my life with that man,' Kate had blubbered during one drunken and lengthy crying jag. 'I wanted to have his children. But he didn't want any. And I pretended it didn't matter. And now it's too late. Oh fuck, Mum. I really fucked up this time. Oh fuck. I just said fuck in front of my mother.'

'He's the one who fucked up, Kate.'

Hearing Dianne Corish say the 'f' word worked like a slap in the face. Kate stopped howling immediately.

'We all make mistakes, sweetheart.' Dianne grabbed her stunned daughter and hugged her. 'But trust me. The best years of your life are still ahead of you. You need to pick yourself up, dust yourself off and move on.'

And that's what Kate decided to do. She was going to buy a place of her own. Now that would be a spectacular piece of retail therapy.

The view from the apartment was breathtaking. Kate leaned over the balcony and gazed at the Sydney of glossy tourist brochures.

The Bridge. The Opera House. The harbour. She could just imagine herself sitting here with a coffee and a cigarette reading her newspapers and staring at the view.

The interior of the flat appealed to her too with its cool sleek lines, white walls, white kitchen and beige carpet. It was the absolute antithesis of Simon's cluttered and comfortable Federation cottage. And for Kate, that was a big selling point.

'There's even a media room here,' she heard the agent enthuse to Gillian inside.

'Please don't tell me you're talking about that alcove thing? Come off it. You can't call that a room.' Gillian played bad cop very well.

'$500,000 is my limit,' Kate said, walking back inside. She could easily afford the asking price and she'd pay it too if necessary. But haggling was all part of the rich property-buying experience.

'They want 560,' the agent replied doubtfully.

'Yeah, we already know that,' Gillian added. 'But you can knock sixty grand off just for trying to get away with calling the place a two-bedder with a media room. That's a cupboard, pal.'

The agent looked beaten. He hated dealing with lesbians. Although the lipstick one seemed nice enough. Where had he seen her before anyway? It was the one in crushed velvet dungarees that scared him.

Six weeks and three days later, Kate woke up in her new apartment with a crashing hangover and a distinct sense of dread. She lay staring at the ceiling as Bernstein made himself comfortable on her pillows, trying to piece together the previous night's dinner with Ben and Al at Chicane. There were some disturbing blank spots . . . most particularly, how she got herself home and into bed.

As she was pondering the mystery, the phone rang.

'Hi, sweets. Just checking up on you. How are you feeling?'

'Like I've been flattened by a Mack truck. What the heck did you and Al do to me last night?'

'It was all your own work, my love. You should be thanking us for pouring you safely into a cab.'

The mention of the cab triggered a hazy memory.

'Oh shit.'

'What?'

'Let me check my mobile.' Sure enough Simon's number was listed as the last call she'd made. The time was 3.17 a.m.

'I called Simon.'

Ben groaned. 'I knew I should have confiscated your mobile along with your car keys. Do you know if you spoke to him? Maybe you just hung up?'

'Maybe,' Kate responded doubtfully.

Three hours later the answering machine intercepted a call from Simon.

'Kate. I really think you need to see someone,' her former lover coaxed in his most sympathetic voice. 'You seem to be holding on to a lot of anger and resentment.'

And I wonder why that might be, she thought. Fucking men. They were all the bloody same.

'You did great, Kate. But the punters didn't like it much. The ratings are down.'

Kate had been back from Yugoslavia for two whole months but she was only now sitting down with Ripley for the debrief. She wasn't sure who'd been avoiding who.

'You know that sort of stuff doesn't work for us,' he continued.

'What doesn't work? Journalism?'

Ripley ignored the barb and reached for another Tim Tam. 'I think the punters are starting to turn on our host too. He's been looking too smug for too long. They don't like him.'

'Really, the host? He's worked for a long time. How do people just decide they don't like him?'

'Upstairs commissioned the research. Viewers reckon he isn't credible any more.' Ripley was shuffling his feet under the desk and avoiding Kate's gaze. It must have been so easy to tell when he was lying as a kid. It amazed her no one picked it now that he was an adult.

'How does that happen to someone after thirty years in the industry? You don't think it might have something to do with the kinds of stories he has to present? No one can retain their credibility when they're spruiking miracle arthritis cures and cellulite treatments.'

'What would you have us do? Political interviews? The last time we had the Prime Minister on we lost three hundred and fifty thousand viewers in the space of one minute. And do you know where they went? To the neighbourhood cat fight on *Today Tonight*. Our audience wants crap,' Ripley concluded. 'And as much as I hate to say it, that's what I intend to give them.'

Kate had heard enough. She was just planning her escape when the phone rang. Ripley peered over and checked the caller ID.

'Sorry, Kate, I've got to take this one.'

As she left, she heard him chuckling into the phone. 'Megan. Thanks for getting back to me. How are you? We really must catch up for lunch soon.' He sounded like he was flirting.

The next morning's *Mail* led with a Megan Halliday exclusive: 'Smug host faces axe'. It was news to *Australia Tonight*'s genial presenter, who was holidaying with his family in Far North Queensland. The article quoted him as saying the report was nonsense. In fact, he'd had an extremely positive lunch with the network CEO just the day before he'd left town. Beige was being touted as the likely replacement. He denied having been approached. But he said he would be very flattered if he was ever considered for such a prestigious position.

Kate desperately hoped it was all just a case of the press or some rival station making mischief. She'd find out soon enough she supposed. Mawson had called soon after she'd arrived at work, asking to see her. Surely, he'd let her know what the hell was going on.

She found him in his office, packing away his photographs into a cardboard box.

He turned as she entered the room. 'I never did get around to getting a photo with you, Kate.'

'Bruce? What's happening? I don't understand.' She stood, anchored to the spot, trying to find an acceptable explanation for the scene playing out in front of her.

'I just handed in my resignation. Told them exactly where they could shove their bloody job. You read the Halliday piece this morning I take it?'

Kate nodded.

'She knew my number one presenter was for the chop before I did.'

'It's true then?'

'Every word. I can only hope Simpson has finally had the courtesy to call the guy and let him know.'

'And he's being replaced by Beige? I can't believe this.'

'Believe it. And I'm going on a very long sailing holiday. I'm too old for this crap.'

Mawson picked up the oversized photograph of his younger self and ran his thumb over the glass.

'You know. I understood the news game back then. You went

out. You told a story. Simple. Sometimes sitting up here in an air-conditioned office and dealing with all the petty politics, you forget that. This photo could have been taken any day . . . on any story. I've kept it around to remind me what the job is supposed to be about.'

He gently placed it in the box. Catching a glimpse of Kate's downcast expression, he continued.

'Don't worry, Kate. You'll be fine. You're smart. And the industry hasn't changed that much that they can manage without good journalists.

Kate wanted to cry. 'I'm so sorry.'

'No need to be sorry. I'm being warehoused. I get a year's pay as long as I stay away from the opposition. There are worse ways of bowing out.'

'Ripley knew,' Kate blurted.

'Of course he did, kiddo. He didn't just know. He orchestrated it. He's not a great journo. But he's a hell of a smart politician. He'll probably end up sitting in this office one day.'

Kate hoped she wouldn't be around when that day came.

'10, 9, 8, 7 . . .' The crowd chanted, counting down to the new millennium, and crossing their collective fingers that the world wouldn't stop turning when they reached zero. '. . . 3, 2, 1 – Happy New Year!'

Everyone went wild as fireworks lit up the sky over Fort Denison.

As favoured Channel Eight clients, celebrities and executives settled in for a night of serious partying, Kate bid good riddance to a very bad year. An absolute shocker, in fact. Her former partner was now married and expecting a child with the kitchen whore. Her mentor was paddling around somewhere in the south Pacific. And

Mike Ripley was steering *Australia Tonight* into ratings oblivion. But at least she owned a harbour-view apartment and had somewhere to go on New Year's Eve, she reminded herself. After what she'd witnessed in Kukes, she knew she really didn't have that much to complain about.

'Happy New Year, Kate.' The new head of news and current affairs sidled up next to her, the exact position of his right hand obscured by shadows.

'You too, Reg.'

'Look, I know you probably don't want to talk shop tonight. But I really need to get your signature on that new contract. I'll do whatever it takes to keep you happy.'

Kate wanted to tell Reg Carter that she hadn't been happy professionally or personally in a very long while but she was a few glasses of Moet short of full disclosure.

'My concerns are well known, Reg,' she replied.

'Well, we have the Olympics here in Sydney this year. We don't have the rights. But there should still be some fun in that for you. But more importantly, I can tell you now I have you in mind as the eventual host of *Australia Tonight*. It might take a few years. But you have my word.'

Kate had been around the block enough times to know someone's word in television wasn't worth very much. But she was tempted. Hosting a nightly current affairs show was the stuff of billboards and magazine covers. She'd be famous. Dianne Corish would love that. And so (secretly) would she. Plus, she reasoned, as the face of the show, surely she'd have some control over the stories that went to air.

As if divining her thoughts, Carter continued. 'We're planning to take the show upmarket, you know. We just need the right person in the chair to do it.'

The Faustian bargain of course was that she was going to have to put up with a lot more of Ripley.

Oh well, Kate thought. What else is there in my life anyway?

She looked at the people partying around her and spotted happy couples everywhere. Matthew was there with his two-year-old son on his shoulders. Anthea was pregnant with their second child. She thought of Tezza and how much he loved his wife and kids.

Even Ripley had a family.

And that really did hurt.

TWENTY-TWO

Mullah Mohammed Omar. Jalalabad. Hamid Karzai. Burhanuddin Rabbani. General Pervez Musharraf. Once again, the world had surrendered to madness. And once again, Kate was forty thousand feet in the air introducing her tongue to a brand-new set of sounds and educating herself in another nation's bloody history and cultural imperatives.

Islamabad was thirty-six hours from Sydney, with more than half that time squandered in airport hotels and transit lounges. Her final destination lay many more bumpy hours to the west. There was plenty of time to read and to study before she reached Afghanistan. But Kate could circumnavigate the globe one hundred times and still be no closer to understanding what was about to happen to this wretched and misgoverned country.

The history of Afghanistan was as tangled and complex as the country was backwards and remote. Alexander the Great, Genghis Khan, the Persian, British and Soviet empires . . . They had all forced their way into this inhospitable land and tried to impose their will. And every event, every new atrocity had been a domino. Each one triggered the next until at 8.49 a.m. on September 11, 2001, a commuter jet crashed into the World Trade Center in New

York, changing the world forever. Now the most powerful nation on earth was demanding vengeance.

For Kate, the road to Afghanistan had been a far speedier and more straightforward affair, beginning just three weeks earlier at the arse end of yet another dud date.

She'd been treated to dinner and a movie by a particularly persistent and unimaginative lawyer type. They'd met during the Sydney Olympics. He'd called a few times after that pestering her for a date. But she'd managed to fob him off. There wasn't anything especially wrong with him. In fact, he seemed a decent enough bloke. But he really wasn't her type. Men, generally, hadn't been her type since Simon's betrayal. Not that she'd swapped teams. It was just that, a year on, she still didn't feel ready for a relationship.

Then the guy had resurfaced at an Opera Australia function. Several months had passed since their first meeting and this time Kate had her mother at her side.

'You ducked me last year but tonight I simply will not accept no for an answer.' The lawyer winked at Dianne as he spoke. 'I insist on taking you to dinner.'

'Kate, how lovely. You need a nice night out,' Dianne chirped.

Oh, good on you, Mum. *Not*, Kate thought irritably.

Dianne Corish was becoming increasingly stressed that her daughter was still single at thirty-four. To turn down a bloke – worse still, to turn down a *lawyer* – in front of her was simply begging for a lecture. With pressure coming from both sides, Kate gave in. It had not been one of her better decisions.

For a start, her date had chosen to take her to *Bridget Jones's Diary*, presumably expecting Kate to enjoy his little attempt at irony. Unfortunately, Bridget just annoyed the crap out of her. The main character was a pathetic thirty-something single with a nasty habit of dumbing down television reporting whilst smoking and drinking to excess. Carl Jung's shadow, Kate noted wryly. Hate the very things that bother you about yourself. Quite apart from that, Hugh Grant wasn't her type. She preferred her Englishmen a little more rugged.

The film left her in a crabby mood. But she was too polite just to blow the guy off outside the cinema. They'd finished up at a pleasant enough bar with Kate wondering how soon she could extract herself, and her date plotting ways to extend the evening into the following morning.

Kate was looking everywhere except directly at her overly solicitous companion when her eyes strayed to the television for the umpteenth time.

'Holy shit!' she exclaimed. On the screen at the other end of the room a plane had just slammed into one of New York's famous twin towers. She shook her head, trying to dislodge the impossible from her mind. Special effects. It had to be. A preview of some new Tom Cruise movie or something. But as the vision was repeated over and over, from one angle and then another, she noticed the tickertape running below. This was American breakfast television. And something truly awful was happening.

'How do we get the sound up on that thing?' Kate was out of her seat and screaming at the barman, ignoring his backed-up orders and the dagger glares of other customers.

As she continued to point and shout, attention shifted from the lunatic at the bar to the hellish images filling the screen. Soon everyone was staring at the television in disbelief. The silence was only broken when the barman finally found the remote control and pumped up the volume.

In what appears to be a terrorist attack, a plane has flown into New York's World Trade Center.

270

Kate stood a metre from the television, her head tilted back, one hand covering her open mouth. She stared at the pictures, frozen. Then another plane crashed into the second tower. What she was seeing made her head spin.

The scene was unthinkable and frightening beyond belief. And she was watching it live. Who knew what horrors were still to come?

With the same appalling lack of judgment that had guided his choice of movie for the evening, Kate's date sensed an opportunity and appeared by her side.

'My place is just around the corner. We can watch this over a glass of port if you like. I have a bottle of Grandfather's I bring out for special occasions.'

Special occasions? The world was hurtling towards a confrontation of biblical proportions and this guy thought the moment called for a tipple of his best port. She sure knew how to pick them.

'I'm sorry but you're going to have to toast Armageddon on your own. I need to get to work.'

Kate had headed straight into the office and scarcely returned home since. And now she was on a plane to Pakistan. So the world was going to hell in a hand basket. But damn she loved her job sometimes.

Kate's tray table was piled high with the latest issues of every credible international newspaper and magazine she'd been able to find. She needed a broader, more thoughtful perspective on the pending conflict than she'd been able to glean from the local press. Newspaper coverage had been little short of hysterical. It had printed rumours that Al-Qaeda was setting up training camps in the Australian bush. Another report expressed fears that the hijab could be used to conceal suicide bombs. It was all plain silly.

Not that *Australia Tonight* was in a position to claim the moral high ground. Far from it. Ever since 9/11, it had pursued a simplistic agenda of jingoism, fear and bigotry, recklessly blurring the distinction between refugees and terrorists.

And during the show's one opportunity to grill the Prime Minister, there were no tough questions about the government's hardline approach on boat people or on the increasingly doubtful claims in the children overboard affair. Instead, Beige had taken a consumer approach to the terrorist threat, divining how average citizens could protect themselves and their families in these uncertain times. And helping people distinguish whether that quiet Muslim family next door was planning a fiendish attack on Australia's democratic values.

The Prime Minister's office carefully handpicked the reporters and presenters and women deemed suitable to interview their man. Beige was among the anointed. The rest of the media could only observe the journalistic equivalent of a relaxed and comfortable aromatherapy massage.

Kate wondered if Beige's questions had been faxed direct from Kirribilli House. She wasn't sure how she felt about the 'terrorist menace' locally. But the growing politics of prejudice and the media's eager acquiescence to the nation's mood did have her both alert and very alarmed.

Beige ended the 'exclusive interview' with an effusive thank you to the Prime Minister. He then turned thoughtfully towards the second camera and announced with his most earnest expression, 'And after the break, the new wonder bra to beat them all.'

It was a surreal segue. From Howard to hooters. Although Kate had to admit it was a smart editorial decision, if the goal was ratings rather than reputation or respect. The wonder bra story had been promoted all day and at the top of the show. Viewers knew to look out for it.

Television execs were able to track exactly what people watched from one moment to the next using people meters. Every minute of every day, these units recorded what station a few thousand sample televisions were tuned into.

For the senior staff at *Australia Tonight*, the figures arrived in graph form the next morning, the seismic pattern of peaks and troughs alerting them to the viewing preferences of a nation. Numbers climbed when a popular story was running and plummeted during commercial breaks. They also nosedived when the show carried a political interview.

The next day, Kate checked the minute-by-minute figures for the Prime Minister's appearance. Sure enough a couple of hundred thousand people reached for their remotes the moment the PM started talking. And they all switched back nine minutes later to watch the spectacle of already ample breasts jiggling about in the latest miracle bra.

It was a wonder Ripley had agreed to send her to Afghanistan at all. International politics held even less appeal than the local variety. But this time, unlike in Kosovo, Australian troops were being sent into battle. That had tipped the balance. Our brave boys fighting and maybe even dying on foreign soil was definitely a tabloid-worthy event.

Kate's eyes were beginning to tire from the dry plane air so she decided to wind down with a quick flick through the *Times* glossy magazine. As she admired the cream on cream décor in a very English country manor, she did a sudden double take. Sitting on the couch in that lovely room were Jonathan McTavish and his doe-eyed wife.

Jonathan and Julia, courageous as ever, at home in their week-end country manor.

Curious, Kate read the piece.

INN war correspondent Jonathan McTavish is famous for his fearless pursuit of the truth in the world's trouble spots. But he says it is his wife Julia who is the brave one. Her battle with breast cancer began the very year they married.

'I remember when Jonathan first got off the plane from Baghdad,' Julia says. 'It was two weeks before our wedding and I dropped the cancer bomb on him. He just said, 'We'll face this together.' I'll never forget the look on his face.'

Julia's fight is ongoing. Last year the cancer returned for a third time and she needed another round of chemotherapy. Still she remains positive. 'I accept the diagnosis, but not the prognosis,' she says.

'Holy shit!' Kate whispered. She read the article again, trying to arrange the jigsaw pieces of their time together.

The letter she had burnt. She wondered if Jonathan had tried to explain.

At the very least, he was not the selfish cad she had supposed. Even if he had two-timed his wife to be, his decision to marry her now seemed noble. Life had not been as easy for him as she'd imagined.

Kate reached down into her handbag and found the tiny sleeping tablet her mother had foisted on her the day before she left.

'Take this. You'll need it if you end up sleeping in a tent.' Dianne Corish had pressed the little orange capsule into her daughter's palm.

'I'm going to a war zone, Mum, not an Outward Bound camp,' Kate had replied, enjoying watching her mother flinch. Dianne didn't like being confronted by the more dangerous aspects of her daughter's job.

'Just take it, Kate. You never know.'

Now on an aeroplane thousands of kilometres away, Kate muttered a thank you to her mother as she knocked down the tablet with a gulp of water. It did the trick. She slept the rest of the way to Islamabad.

Like so many of the world's capitals, Islamabad was wholly unrepresentative of the country it governed. If it wasn't for the erratic driving of its inhabitants, Kate would scarcely have believed herself in Asia. The city was green, clean and unexpectedly modern. But after the usual rounds of interviews with politicians, academics, newspaper editors and diplomats, she realised it was also a waste of her time.

'Tezza, I think we should bite the bullet and head into Afghanistan before the Americans start flexing their muscles. Waddaya say?' Kate sat on the edge of her bed, clasping a Murree's Classic Lager.

Surprisingly, Pakistan had its own brewery. Although Kate wondered how the business survived if every thirsty tourist had to provide room service with details of their religion and father's name.

'I figured you'd be getting itchy feet pretty soon.' Tezza laughed. 'We just need to work out how we get in there.'

'I heard the best way is to head in from the north, through Tajikistan and then hook up with the Northern Alliance. ABC America left this morning and the Canadian lot are going tomorrow. Maybe we should tag team with them? Travel in numbers.'

'I'll ask around,' Tezza said, knocking back the last of his beer and heading for the door. There were plenty of brains to pick downstairs. The Marriott was teeming with the world's media, all waiting for the bombs to drop.

Kate turned up the television and switched on her laptop. As she was scrolling through the *New York Times* site, the INN theme music filled the room followed by a familiar voice. Kate looked up. It was Jonathan McTavish, already in Afghanistan, filing a report from the rocky north. Still drop-dead gorgeous, she noted. And for once she didn't mind.

Her thoughts were interrupted by a knock at the door.

'Hi, Tezza. That was quick. Come in.'

'Your wish is my command. *Médecins Sans Frontières* is going in tomorrow. I just spoke to their PR lady and she's happy for us to hitch a ride in their convoy. And better still there's an Australian doctor onboard. We just need to get ourselves to Takik to meet the convoy. But it sounds pretty good. Best get packing, old girl.'

'A way into Afghanistan plus a story on a courageous Aussie doctor heading into a war zone as well. God I love you, Tezza. Where would I be without you?' She planted a light kiss on her cameraman's forehead.

He reddened. He'd known Kate Corish for well over a decade but she could still make him blush.

TWENTY-THREE

Dushanbe was a charmless and austere city. But it proved to be an adequate enough staging post to gather the supplies they needed for their journey. A couple of tents, food, water purification tablets and plenty of rugs. It wasn't quite winter yet in Afghanistan but the nights would be cold.

Kate and Tezza always travelled as lightly as modern news gathering allowed. But with a payload of satellite phones, edit packs and camera gear, there was no hope of hitching a lift. Ever the magician, Tezza had somehow managed to lay his hands on a beaten-up old jeep.

Kate peered suspiciously at the jumble of rusty and battered metal panels that had rattled to a stop in front of her. 'What if it breaks down?'

'Anything more upmarket and we'd be kidnap material. Anyway, you saw what happened to our hire car in Belgrade. I'm not sure we deserve luxury transportation.'

'Fair enough.' Kate tried to sound upbeat. The jeep looked desperately uncomfortable and northern Afghanistan was not famed for the quality of its road system. 'But trust me. We're not going to be kidnapped. I'm planning to stick with the convoy.'

Staying close to the folk from *Médecins sans Frontières* became an even more attractive proposition when she met up with the young Australian doctor the next day. His name was George Ross. Which was appropriate, because he not only looked like a young version of Dr Ross on television's *ER* he was also a natural in front of the camera. Kate figured he was in his mid-twenties – twenty-eight tops.

'Have you given much thought to what you'll be confronting in the days ahead?' Kate asked as she settled into the interview.

'Well, I've never been to a war zone before. And I'm pretty sure the reality is going to be far worse than anything I've imagined. The trick will be to keep my composure. I just hope I'm up to it. A lot of people will be depending on me.'

'What about concerns for your own life? I'm sure your mum isn't too happy about what you're doing?'

'Well, you're right about that.' George Ross laughed, dimples appearing above his day-old stubble. 'But my mum also taught me to do what's right. I have a useful and desperately needed skill and I should share it. Sydney won't miss my services for a few months. You know, we're so lucky in Australia. We don't ever have to deal with this kind of stuff. This is my way of giving back.'

Good looking. Smart. Compassionate. Way too young. The guy was getting more attractive by the minute. He ran a hand through his thick dark hair. He held Kate's gaze, his head cocked slightly to one side. Arched eyebrows asked the question and let her know he was available.

Kate felt the unmistakable stirrings of sexual interest. It was a novel sensation. But lust had no place on the job and especially not in a war zone. Kate had learned that lesson the hard way.

She looked down and pretended to read her notes, hoping George Ross hadn't noticed her momentary lapse in concentration. Damn, he was cute.

Kate straightened, steered her thoughts firmly back on track and wound up the interview. *Australia Tonight*'s audience was going to love this guy.

The convoy reached its destination right on sunset. The camp had been set up in advance. The Red Cross was there, along with some media. Shades of pink and orange bounced off the mountains transforming the harsh, rocky landscape into something quite beautiful.

Kate and Tezza staked out their tent. Kate happily indulging her Dr Ross fantasies as she banged the pegs a little too firmly into the ground.

Eventually they cobbled something together that resembled sleeping quarters and started work on their story.

'How's it looking?' George Ross asked as he wandered past. His chocolate eyes glinted with possibility and mischief.

'Your mum will love it,' Kate said carefully.

'Good to know,' he said as he sauntered off, whistling.

'I think the guy likes you,' Tezza commented. His head was still bent over the edit pack he'd set up on the tailgate of their four-wheel drive.

'And I think the guy was still in kindergarten when I was looking for a date for my formal. How much longer on this edit do you think?'

'An hour or two. You can head to bed once we get the guts down. I'll look after the rest.'

'Have I mentioned lately that I love you, Tezza?'

Kate woke early the next morning to the sound of artillery fire off in the distance. Tezza was still softly snoring away, untroubled by the noise. He was a heavy sleeper, which was an asset in his line of work. Not even the bombs and air-raid sirens of Belgrade had bothered him.

Kate crept out of the tent and fixed herself a cup of tea. She'd let him sleep. There was no knowing when he'd next get the opportunity.

When Tezza finally poked his head out of the tent an hour later, she had a map of Northern Afghanistan flattened out on the hood of the jeep.

'Planning already underway?'

'Good morning, yeah, we need to hook up with the Northern Alliance. Follow them as they advance on Taliban positions. I don't suppose you heard all the noise this morning.'

'What noise?'

'Rocket launchers mostly. We can't be that far away. No point in us staying here just doing the aid stuff. The network will want to see some action. Real action. Otherwise they'll be ordering us back before we know it.'

Tezza nodded. He wasn't ready to go home yet either. 'The Canadian TV crew is heading to the front-line this morning. We could team up with them.'

'Or we could get our own guide.'

Kate was hardly an expert on Afghanistan but she did know that ambush was a way of life in this part of the world. Their best chance of making it to their next destination in one piece was to hire someone who knew the lay of the land.

The camp had attracted dozens of locals in need of work including a young ethnic Hazara man. Abdul had been just thirteen when the Taliban captured his home town of Mazari Sharif in 1998. Four thousand were killed, including all of his immediate family. Abdul was lucky to escape the slaughter. He'd been helping out a sick uncle on the other side of the Balkh River.

For thirty American dollars, he led them along rocky Third World roads, skirting landmines and bandits until they reached the Northern Alliance stronghold a terrifying two hours later.

'You must meet Commander Hafiz,' Abdul announced as their jeep bumped into camp. The young guide's English was far better than Kate had realised. 'He has fought many battles. A very brave man. I am honoured to meet him again. Let me find him for you.'

Kate jumped gladly out of the jeep and followed Abdul past rows of tents. As they got closer to the main headquarters, she stopped, eyes squinting into the setting sun. Ahead of her was the unmistakable figure of Jonathan McTavish. He was talking to a military commander, camera rolling.

'Hah, we are in luck. Commander Hafiz is here,' Abdul announced, his pace quickening.

She held the teenager back. 'We must wait for the interview to finish,' she said, adjusting her flak jacket and fixing her hair. It was a pointless vanity. Like the rest of her, Kate's hair hadn't been washed for four days.

Jonathan looked up, sensing her presence.

'Kate. What a wonderful surprise. You're here.' He signalled to his cameraman that the interview was over.

Kate smiled nervously as she walked towards the men.

'Commander Hafiz. This is Kate Corish, Australian television.'

The commander gave Jonathan a comradely slap on the back. 'Ah, she is much prettier than you, McTav.' His English was broken but his meaning was clear as his gaze lingered on the camp's newest guest.

Jonathan grinned. 'We keep running into each other all over the world.'

God, he was so damned handsome!

'You are welcome tonight as well,' the Commander said.

'Commander Hafiz is taking a few of us out on a mission,' Jonathan explained.

'You excuse me now. We see you tonight.'

As the Commander made his exit, Jonathan turned towards Kate, moving so close to her that their bodies almost touched.

'How are you?'

'Fine. I'm fine. Sorry for running out on you in Kosovo by the way. I was pulled out that day. I guess the story I filed on the embassy bombing spooked the suits back home. Insurance doesn't come cheap.'

'I wondered what happened to you. You just disappeared. But look, about tonight's mission.' Jonathan's expression became suddenly serious. 'Hafiz is going to advance on a Taliban front-line. It may get a little hairy. If you like I can give you our camera tapes for some action vision . . .' He trailed off as he caught sight of the thunderous look on Kate's face.

He shrugged. He should have known Kate wouldn't take the safe, easy option.

'I'll see you there,' she stated firmly.

Sometimes dealing with the woman was like trying to pat a snake, he thought, as Kate flounced off to find her cameraman.

Despite her bravado, Kate was terrified as she took her place next to Jonathan aboard the Alliance carrier. Colonel Hafiz was standing at the wheel, immediately in front of them.

'Hold on,' Jonathan whispered as the engine started to rumble.

Soon they were hurtling through the darkness at top speed. Poor Tezza was hanging on to his camera with one hand and for dear life with the other. Two other journalists had also come along for the ride.

'1500 metres to the front-line,' Jonathan yelled over the roar of the machine.

As the truck vaulted over the crest, there was a burst of automatic gunfire. It seemed to be coming from every direction. The

Taliban had been watching and waiting and expecting them. They were surrounded on three sides.

'Fucking ambush,' Jonathan shouted, throwing an arm over Kate. 'Stay down!'

'The others are getting off,' Kate screamed, straining against him. Every instinct was telling her to run as bullets clattered against the metal around her.

Jonathan was pushing Kate's body hard into the floor. Tezza was beside her.

'Fuck. Oh fuck,' he was yelling, but he was also filming it all.

Jonathan looked up at Commander Hafiz. The man was still standing. He'd turned the carrier around and was driving like a mad man.

'If he jumps, we jump,' he yelled into Kate's ear.

'Tezza. Stay down. Don't go anywhere.' Kate grabbed him by the arm before he could jump.

Pounded by round upon round of gunfire, Hafiz urged the vehicle back up the steep hill. They were sitting ducks, their bodies facing the direction of the gunfire. Whoosh. Clank. Kate knew what she was hearing were near-misses.

The carrier lurched, and Kate nearly lost her grip as it swayed dangerously. But Jonathan pulled her back.

'Hang on, Kate. *Hang on.*'

Her helmet banged violently against the armoured plates of the carrier. But Kate didn't feel anything. Fear and adrenalin coursed through her, numbing the pain.

As they limped back to camp, they could scarcely comprehend what had happened. Two journalists were missing, probably dead. If Kate and Tezza had surrendered to instinct and jumped, they would have been among the casualties.

Kate sat by the fire shaking violently, knees pushed up under her chin. Jonathan brought over a blanket. She cried as he put his arm around her.

They were alone. Tezza was marching around the camp, trying to walk off the adrenalin still surging through his body.

'I'm so sorry. We should never have gone.'

'Don't be crazy. It's not your fault. God, how did you know not to jump?'

'Christ knows. I just saw Hafiz. He wasn't leaving his post. He wasn't even ducking. I figured we should do the same. He's an experienced soldier. The rest of us are rookies. I try never to forget that. We're just rookies.'

'I think I've been cured of war zones,' Kate said, staring into the fire. She'd had a few close calls over the years. But knowing there were journalists . . . her own kind . . . out there in the dark, possibly bleeding and dying, maybe already dead. It scared the hell out of her. She knew Jonathan was thinking about them too.

'How can we just leave them?' she asked.

'How can we rescue them without getting killed?' he replied.

They fell silent as they gazed into the fire, wondering why fate had allowed them to survive.

After a while Kate turned to face him. 'I'm really sorry about your wife. I didn't know until a couple of weeks ago.'

'But . . . my letter? I told you everything.'

'I never read it, Jonathan. I just thought . . . I thought . . . oh, it doesn't matter what I thought. Anyway, I'm sorry. It must be so hard.'

'I was going to call off the wedding, you know, Kate. After meeting you, I knew that's what I had to do. But then Julia told me she had breast cancer. I couldn't leave her then. In the end, I did what I thought was best. I figured you'd manage fine without me. I'm not sure Julia could have.'

'You made the right decision,' Kate said quietly.

'I don't know whether there was a right decision. Julia needed me. I couldn't abandon her because I was falling for another woman. But how could I stay with her knowing that? Which is the bigger betrayal? I'm not sure what the answer is.'

Falling for another woman? The words pounded at Kate's head. 'Is she going to be okay?'

'She's in remission from a secondary cancer. That's positive. But it's not something that will ever go away for good.' He sighed.

'So she's fighting for her life and here you are risking yours. We're selfish creatures, aren't we?'

Kate had never prayed before. But she did now and for once she thought of her mother. Dianne Corish had already lost a husband. Should she have to lose a daughter too? For the first time in Kate's professional life she actually looked forward to reporting on the mundane.

The bodies of their colleagues were rescued the following day. The ambush had been reported and the Taliban had been forced to retreat under relentless air fire. Kate had decided it was time she withdrew as well.

'Good luck, Jonathan,' she said. 'I can't believe you're staying on.'

He shrugged. 'Well, that's my job. They expect Kabul to fall in the next day or two.' It was as if the ambush had never happened.

'You're mad, you know,' Kate said, shaking her head.

'Takes one to know one.'

'Not any more. I'm all for the quiet life.' Kate tossed her dusty canvas bag into the back of the jeep. 'Right. Time to blow this town.'

'Kate . . .'

She turned around. 'Yes?'

'Look after yourself.'

Jonathan stood and watched as their four-wheel drive bumped across the rocky landscape and out of sight.

TWENTY-FOUR

'Nice house, Matt,' Kate called out as she strolled up the path of her friend's new and very expensive purchase on Sydney's lower north shore.

'Well, it will be a nice house when we've finished renovating.' Matthew was sitting back in an old wicker chair on the cool and spacious verandah. 'Right now, she's classic Fediterranean. Why do people take perfectly good Federation homes and turn them into rendered Tuscan yellow nightmares anyway?'

He got up and gave Kate a peck on the cheek.

'Josh. Josh. Come here and say hello to Aunty Kate.' Matthew grabbed his son and hoisted him onto his shoulders.

'Hello,' the little boy said shyly. He had been blessed with his father's cobalt eyes and thick blond hair.

'Hi, Josh. I hear your little sister's having a birthday today.'

'She's one. But she can't get all the presents. She has to share.'

'Fair enough.' Kate laughed, pulling a brightly wrapped gift out of her environmentally aware hessian shopping bag. 'Just as well I came prepared.'

Josh scrambled down from his father's shoulders and began tearing at the paper.

'I just hope this present is a little quieter than the toy guitar you gave him for Christmas.' Matt laughed. 'One of these days I'm going to pay you back.'

Kate felt a familiar stab of pain. She knew her friend would probably never get the opportunity to make good on his threat.

Realising his mistake, Matt hurried on. 'Anyway, come on in, Kate. What can I get you to drink? A nice sav blanc? I've made sure the Margaret River is amply represented this afternoon.'

She checked her watch. 'It's past midday. The sun is over the yardarm. Works for me.'

As Kate followed her host down the wide hallway, she understood what had driven Matthew to bid well beyond his self-imposed limit. The previous owners had taken outrageous liberties with the house's exterior. But inside, the place retained all its original charm.

The place would have been quite grand in its day with its polished floors and ornate ceilings. But now, nearly a century later, it was unmistakably a family home. Somehow, Matthew's domestic goddess of a wife had managed to furnish the old house so that it was both authentic and inviting all at the same time.

Kate thought of her own home. Modern furniture. Sleek lines. And hideously child unfriendly. An inquisitive toddler would be lucky to survive a day there.

Matthew ushered Kate through to the back of the house where an open-plan kitchen and living area flowed seamlessly onto a rear porch and garden.

Anthea was gliding around the kitchen with the ease of the natural hostess. It was quite a talent with two young children and a labradoodle constantly underfoot.

'Kate!' she exclaimed, untying her apron. 'How wonderful to see you again.' She lifted baby Alice up onto her hip and passed over a glass of wine with her free hand.

Anthea's stellar career had stalled with the birth of her first child. Some women lucked into presenting positions. But for most, television and motherhood were not even slightly compatible. The hours were a jumble and constant travelling was a basic job requirement. Anthea had tried to return to work when Josh was six months old but she hadn't lasted long. There were more important things in her world for the time being. Chasing fire engines just didn't rate.

And the Keatons were in the fortunate position of not needing the second income. Matt's career was on a fast track. Word had it he would be taking over the main evening bulletin in a year or two.

'Happy birthday, Alice,' Kate cooed as she fished about in her shopping bag. 'I have something for you, sweetheart.'

Kate hadn't bothered to wrap this present. What would a one-year-old want with wrapping paper anyway? 'Apparently this is the very latest in Swedish toy technology, Anthea. It lets babies explore different textures.'

Anthea gave the instructive, bite-sized building blocks a suspicious look before swooping on them.

'Brilliant job in Afghanistan last year,' she said, depositing Kate's present on a shelf well out of Alice's reach. 'And congrats on the latest Walkley. Needless to say, well deserved.'

'Walkleys are easy to win, Anthea. For the last two, all I had to do was almost get killed.' Kate smiled, raising her glass and one eyebrow to her war experiences.

Outside, Matthew was piggybacking his son around the backyard. The little scene made her smile. Mathew had everything he had ever wanted. A gorgeous wife. A beautiful family. The lovely home. The big media career.

For Kate, it was like watching an alternate version of her own life. Could this have been her house? Her perfect family playing in the backyard? She was genuinely happy for Matt. But that didn't stop her feeling a bit sorry for herself as well.

Maybe love and family had passed her by. The first man she really fell for turned out to be engaged. The second cheated on her. In between, there had been a lot of mediocre sex with forgettable men.

'Refill?' Anthea asked as she deposited Alice in her playpen. Kate had downed her first glass of wine in double quick time and was looking thirsty.

'Oh, why not? Thank you. I've been drinking way too fast since giving up the fags.' It was Kate's eighteenth attempt to quit. Not that she was counting. This time, three months down the track, she was starting to think she'd finally beaten the habit.

'Do you ever miss it?' Kate asked as Anthea topped up her glass. 'The thrill. The chase. The deadlines.'

'Sure I miss it. Sometimes. And when something big happens, like September 11 or Afghanistan, I do get incredibly restless.' Anthea looked out over the garden where Matthew and Josh were now putting the kiddy swing set through its paces. 'But I'm okay with my choices.' She grinned. 'For now, anyway.'

'Well, you're a big loss. I'd way prefer to be working alongside you than this new breed of upstarts. God save me from Generation Y. Now it seems the more ambitious and poisonous you are, the further you go.'

'Come on. There's always been an element of that in our industry. But I take it you're referring to young Patrick Riley.' Anthea laughed. 'I worked with him in news. Smart kid. I'll give him that. But ambitious beyond all reason.'

'The bosses love him. Almost as much as he loves himself. But I suspect he's the architect of much of his own publicity.'

'Meaning? Come on, Kate. Out with it.'

'Well, every time one of his stories goes to air, the phones go crazy. All I ever get is complaints of bias or comments about what I'm wearing or how I've done my hair. But when Patrick has a story up – and let's not pretend any of his work is earth-shatteringly good – we get this amazing response. You should read the phone logs the next morning.'

'That Patrick is the best reporter you guys have.'

'Can we see more of Patrick?'

'When will Patrick host the show?'

'Patrick is the new Mr Beige.'

'Patrick is hot!'

'His friends are very busy then.' Anthea grinned. 'The same thing went on in news when we were cadets. The guy should have gone into PR instead of journalism. And what's more, I bet he goes all the way. Refill?'

'Oh, what the hell.' Kate held out her glass again. 'His move to *Australia Tonight* was amusing on one level. Geoff Jones spat the dummy and went on a week's stress leave. Apparently he's never got over losing his parking spot to Patrick back when he worked for the opposition. Too funny.'

'That ego could do with a little deflating. So could his waist-line for that matter. It's all right for Laurie Oakes. He's actually smart.'

'Touché.' Kate took another swig from her glass. 'Where's every-one else?' The only other guests appeared to be a young couple chatting on the back porch.

'Oh, we had the tragic family, million-kid thing yesterday. We know better than to subject any of our child-free friends to that kind of agony.'

The kid thing again. At thirty-six, with no man and no child, Kate was unremarkable in her working life. But out here in the real world, the issue kept coming up. Inadvertently today. But often quite pointedly.

Just the previous night, Kate had been harangued yet again by her increasingly desperate mother.

'You don't want to go through life without experiencing motherhood. I'd be very sad for you. And your late father would be very sad too.'

Kate wondered if she would get away with switching off her phone and claiming a dead battery.

'Mum, please. Leave Dad out of it. I'd love to marry and have kids, you know that. But I haven't met the right person. And that's just the way it is. If it happens, it happens.'

'Beggars can't be choosers, you know. Not at your age.'

'Mum!'

Dianne Corish hurried on. 'Remember Annette, my bridge partner, well her son is a fertility doctor and Annette says many of his patients are women just like you, freezing their eggs.'

'Mum, I really wish you wouldn't go round discussing my fertility with your friends. You hear me?'

'Well, it's something you might like to think about, that's all.'

'Mum, I'm going now. Bye. Love you.' She'd quickly hung up. It was that or end up saying something she would most certainly regret.

Kate told Ben and Al the story at dinner that night. She'd organised to meet up with them after leaving Matt's place. It seemed the perfect antidote to an afternoon of happy families on the upper north shore.

The boys howled with laughter.

'You know Ben and I would be happy to donate sperm if you ever wanted to go that way.' Al was still chuckling but Kate could tell from his eyes that he was completely serious.

'Bloody hell, do I have a sign saying "pathetic childless career girl" stuck on my head?'

'Offer's there, Katie darling. As you can see, we've got gorgeous genes.' Al threw a companionable arm around his long-term partner.

'And we're thinking about becoming parents ourselves. So it could work out for everyone,' Ben added.

This was too much. The entire world was pairing up and propagating. Kate decided her best course of action was to keep drinking. Heavily.

Kate's head was pounding the next morning as she reached into the top drawer of her desk. Somewhere amid the tea bags, pens, cigarette lighters, paper clips and sugar-free chewing gum was an envelope of tablets her mother had given her 'in case of emergencies'. This counted as an emergency for sure.

And she suspected her day was about to get a whole lot worse as she watched Ripley waddling down the corridor, making a beeline for her corner.

Kate's job was safe under Reg Carter's stewardship. But that didn't stop her immediate boss from needling her at every opportunity. Maybe he thought she'd up and leave. If that was his intention, his latest salvo was a masterstroke.

Ripley stopped outside her door, a malevolent smile forming on his oversized potato face. 'Kate, have you met Michelle?' A girl with familiar almond-shaped eyes materialised beside him. 'She'll be sharing your office.'

An empty desk had been Kate's only company for the last year. She liked it that way and Ripley knew it.

He brought a protective hand to the base of Michelle's back, almost but not quite touching her. He was displaying his new reporter like a trophy wife.

'Yes. I know Michelle,' Kate replied. Michelle's profile was almost as high as Kate's own – although her celebrity was based more on her social life than her journalistic credentials. And Kate polled far better with female viewers.

Kate and Michelle had had their share of on-the-road stoushes over the years. It was a question of ethics. Kate just didn't like Michelle's approach or her attitude. And she'd let her know about it. Bluntly. And often.

She couldn't imagine how they were going to get along, trapped together in a confined space like this.

'Welcome aboard.' Kate somehow managed to force a smile. There was no point causing a scene.

'Thanks. I'm looking forward to it.'

Michelle strolled over to the empty desk, swinging her hips a little more provocatively than the journey or the occasion required. Ripley lingered at the doorway just long enough to enjoy the show.

'You two alpha girls have fun,' the old lecher offered as he wandered off, cheerfully imagining what he would like to do to Michelle's tight little arse.

'I've got to go.' Kate grabbed her bag and a couple of magazines. She wasn't in the mood for faux sisterly chit chat. And she was supposed to be on a stake-out anyway.

It might have been a stinking hot February day but heatstroke and a hangover seemed quite appealing when the alternative was an afternoon in close quarters with Michelle Arse-Shaker.

The hired Nissan van was well disguised with the logo 'All Good Plumbing' running along both sides. Like giant fridge magnets, the signs could be attached to any surveillance van. They provided the perfect cover. If they hadn't already been spotted. She was starting to wonder.

'When is this guy ever going to come out of his bloody house?'

Kate's head was pounding again. Her mother's tablets had kept the aching at bay for four hours but the pain was starting to push through again. She didn't dare swallow a second pill. The first had made her feel drowsy enough. Commit the crime, do the time, she reminded herself.

'Why can't we just knock on the bloody door, ambush the bloke and head down to the pub for a beer?' The cameraman was getting cranky. A couple of hours sitting and sweating in a furnace tended to have that effect. 'It's not like we haven't done it before.'

'Yeah, and if we do it again, we'll be in big trouble. *A Current Affair* just got busted for doing exactly that. The judge decided that knocking on someone's door with a camera rolling is trespassing. So we've got to wait for the guy to leave his house and set foot on public property. From now on, there's going to be a whole lot more time spent in the back of vans. I can't say I'm too thrilled at the prospect either.'

Kate's phone rang. 'Hiya, Katie.'

'Ripper, what can I do for you?' But Kate already knew what he wanted.

'Mate, we don't have an overnight promo. We'll be using your Nigerian scam story.'

'But I haven't finished filming it. We have no vision of the guy. I'm sitting in the back of a hot van right now, waiting for him to come out of the house. He hasn't sent me his schedule so I don't know when that's going to be. The way it's going, I might still be here this time next week.'

'You better fucking not be. I want you to get the bloke. And get back here. We need the confrontation for the promo.' Ripley wasn't budging.

'But what if I don't get him?' Kate pleaded.

'You'll fucking get him. This is not open for debate. The story is locked in. So bleat elsewhere. Just come back with the yarn.' And with that Ripley hung up.

Kate knew she should have told Ripley to shove it. But the truth of the matter was that she wanted to get her hangover home and to bed almost as much as her boss wanted a story to promote. Unfortunately, the only way to make any of that happen was to break a few rules.

What the hell, she thought. With a brief guilty flashback to the ethics lectures she'd given Michelle over the years, she jumped out of the van and walked up the path to the con man's front door.

She buzzed the intercom.

'Hello.' Good. He was home.

'Hi. Look, I'm sorry to bother you. I'm a neighbour and my garage door is stuck. I need someone to give me a hand. I don't suppose you could help me out?' It was a flagrant breach of the journalists' code of ethics. And from a Walkley Award-winner at that. Kate hadn't properly identified herself and she was hardly employing fair and honest means to obtain information. But she had a deadline to meet and a very sore head. Surely she could be forgiven. Just this once.

The man thought the pretty blonde looked familiar. But he didn't make the connection with the girl who had been ringing him incessantly all week, demanding an interview.

'Sure, I'll be down in a minute.'

Kate led the man off his property and onto the footpath where her crew was waiting to pounce.

'Actually we'd like to ask you a few questions about your role in this grubby little Nigerian scam.'

'Oh, fuck off,' the man snapped, pushing the camera out of the way and hotfooting it back into the house.

Kate had her man and her footage. She also had that same queasy feeling she got after eating fast food. She recognised it as guilt.

TWENTY-FIVE

Kate opened the beautifully packaged parcel delivered via courier right to her desk. Inside was a pot of gold. Or at least that's what the accompanying PR blurb claimed.

Fifty years of research into the secrets of beauty and longevity enjoyed by the inhabitants of a remote Japanese fishing village has resulted in the creation of La Shisoko, the most potent anti-ageing cream on the market.

At $300 for a small jar, it would want to work, she thought. The company was obviously hoping for a free plug on prime-time television. Kate was inclined to do the opposite and expose the product as nothing more than an empty and very expensive promise in a jar. But the truth didn't rate. If *Today Tonight* ran a story on the cream's amazing anti-ageing properties the same night, viewers would tune into that instead. Everyone wanted to believe in miracles.

'I hope that's not payola, Kate. We have standards to uphold here, you know.'

'Just another miracle cream, Michelle. No need to worry.'

Kate had been surprised to find she actually enjoyed sharing an office with Michelle. The girl had a vicious wit. And while it was directed towards the likes of Ripley and Tubby, Kate was happy enough to laugh along.

But as much as Kate appreciated Michelle's sense of humour, she despised her tactics. Here was a girl who was bright, talented and climbing the ladder two rungs at a time. But she'd long ago discovered that flirting was the quickest way ahead. And she could shake her arse with the mastery of a professional pole dancer. She was even giving Jenni a run for her money.

Every Tuesday night before Michelle popped off to the gym, she would change into her teensiest shorts and midriff-baring crop top. Then she'd bound down the hall to Ripley's office to say goodnight. The girl had absolutely no shame. She sure as hell got assigned some terrific stories though.

'They're talking about war in Iraq.'

'Mmm.' Kate was rubbing some of the miracle cream into her hands.

'If that happens do you want to go? Because, well, I'm really keen to do my first war zone. And I'm letting you know I've already put up my hand.'

Michelle had her sights firmly set on Kate's mantle. Senior reporter. War correspondent. Eventual host of the show. Kate didn't know whether to admire the girl's honesty or slap her for her gall. She screwed the lid back on the jar to concentrate on this unexpected assault on her career. At least her colleague wasn't a backstabber. With Michelle, you always saw the knife coming.

'Iraq is my old stomping ground, remember? I know more about the place and the issues than anyone else at this network.'

'Well, getting a gig like that opens doors. How many Walkleys do you want anyway? Shouldn't the younger ones get a go? Ripley certainly thinks so.'

'I'm sure he does. Let's just see what happens. It's not up to you and me anyway.'

That was true enough. But Kate still figured she should make sure Ripley was in absolutely no doubt about her feelings on the matter. She left the office and marched up the hall.

Ripley was on the phone as usual. Sometimes Kate wondered if the thing was surgically attached to his ear. She stood outside his office door, waiting for him to hang up. Smoke swathed his upper body. But strangely enough, its source was nowhere to be seen.

Recently, HR had ordered him, yet again, to stop fagging in his office. They'd come down so hard even Ripley realised he finally had to modify his behaviour. His solution was to place his ashtray on the ground and simply bend down to pick up his cigarette. It looked like he had smoke coming out of his arse all day long.

And it was quite an arse. The years hadn't been kind to Michael Ripley. Ripley's ginger freckles were starting to morph into liver spots and his hair was now reduced to a few oily strands that formed a sparse comb over.

He was a singularly unattractive man. A face only a mother could love. Of course Kate had heard the stories that even that wasn't the case.

'Look, I can't be responsible for the brains or lack thereof of every cameraman on station. The bloke thought he was doing the right thing. But frankly, he's not the brightest peg in the bucket. And he made his decision, as ill-conceived as it was, on his own.'

Kate didn't know exactly who was on the other end of the phone but it had to be *Media Watch* or one of the TV writers. And Ripley was hanging someone out to dry.

Ripley had become meaner over the years. Kate guessed it was the only way he was able to survive. Downsizing, management changes and network takeovers made holding down a job in the industry a tricky task. Divide. Conquer. Undermine. Lie. That was his management style. And right now he was practising his art to perfection.

'Look, it was a dumbshit decision. He should have checked with us. But frankly, we all need to move on. Now I have a show to run. So if you have any more questions, you'll have to email me. Goodbye.' Ripley slammed the phone down. 'Fuck me. Bloody armchair critics.'

'So much for sticking up for your troops,' Kate grumbled to herself as she turned and walked away.

Now was not the time to discuss reporter options in Iraq. Best to cool down over the weekend and tackle the matter on Monday.

She didn't get the chance.

It was late on Sunday morning and Kate was driving home from the gym. She had opted for a body combat class, imagining Ripley's head as she kicked and punched at the air. The strategy worked. She was feeling considerably less tense, at least until she switched on the car radio to hear that the war on terror had arrived on Australia's doorstep. Two Bali nightclubs had been bombed. Dozens, perhaps hundreds of tourists and locals had been killed.

She swerved into a parking spot across three lanes of traffic, fished out her mobile from the bottom of her gym bag and rang Ripley.

'Should I pack a bag for Bali?' Kate asked when he answered the phone.

'I'm afraid you've been beaten to the punch, Katie. Michelle called half an hour ago. She's on her way to the airport now.'

Kate knew Ripley relished passing on that bit of news. Don't take the bait, she counselled herself.

'Okay. But surely we still need someone in Jakarta to chase up the whodunnit angle?'

'Mate, we're covered. You're just going to have to let others have a go. It's not the fucking Kate Corish show, you know. Now go and enjoy the rest of your Sunday and let me enjoy mine. Goodbye.'

'Stupid bastard,' Kate muttered.

The next day she stomped into the morning meeting, ignoring Ripley's closed door.

'Abu Bakr Bashir. That's who we should be chasing. He's the spiritual head of Jemaah Islamiyah. This is their handiwork,' Kate announced. She'd spent most of Sunday on the internet, swotting up on Indonesian politics.

'I can get on a plane to Jogjakarta and track him down for an interview if you like.'

Ripley was fuming. He'd shut his office door for a reason. And that reason was to keep Kate bloody Corish out.

'I don't know how many times I have to tell you this, Kate. But we're covered. How about you write up a brief for Michelle? She may be able to add some of your material into her report.'

That night all the current affairs programs devoted their shows to the carnage in Bali. The next night all but one featured an interview with Abu Bakr Bashir. He was now the number-one suspect as the man most likely to have masterminded the horror. And he'd opened his doors to anyone who'd come knocking. Unfortunately for *Australia Tonight*'s flagging ratings, no one from that show had thought to knock.

Ripley didn't speak to Kate the next day. Or the day after. In fact, he avoided her for a whole week. She didn't even have to say 'I told you so'. It hung in the air like a bad smell.

'Surely management has to notice this,' Kate commented on the phone to Gillian.

'The bloke manages upwards. He shitcans his entire staff to cover his own arse. Someone else will cop the blame. You just watch,' Gillian predicted. 'I've seen it all before. And it's why I don't work there.'

'Well, my contract is up soon. So maybe I won't either.'

'We can't afford to miss stuff like Abu Bakr Bashir,' Carter pointed out as he shovelled an enormous fork load of fettuccini boscaiola into his mouth. Ripley shuffled his feet nervously under the table.

'Well, you know, you've got to trust your people on the ground. And they just missed it. As simple as that.' Ripley watched Carter's expression carefully. He seemed to be buying it. 'And that Perth producer hasn't really worked out. No bloody news sense.'

'Well, our ratings are down. And it's not just a blip either. We're losing consistently.' Carter gestured to the empty basket in the middle of the table. 'More garlic bread?'

'Yeah, thanks. I think they've gone off Beige. He worked for a while. But not any more. We need someone fresh. Someone new. I've also had a lot of staff complaining about his abusive behaviour.' That wasn't entirely true. There had been a single complaint from a part-time researcher. And from all accounts she had deserved a good bollocking. But what the hell, Ripley thought, it sounded good. 'The set's looking a bit tired too. We may have to revamp it for 2003.'

'What do you think of Corish as host?' Carter asked.

'She'll be good. One day. She's not ready yet in my opinion. Why don't we poach someone from the ABC? That way we get instant credibility.'

'Nah. Those ABC types go all fucking wobbly in the commercial world. I really reckon Corish might be the go. She has way more journalistic cred than Naomi. And she'd offer a nice alternative to that bovver boy over at *ACA*. Although I hear he's up for the chop. Ray's back in the frame apparently.'

'Fuck. Ray will be hard to beat. Maybe we should think about poaching Munro?'

'He's still contracted to Nine for another year. And I'm not up for that battle.' Carter grabbed a passing waitress. 'Some more garlic bread and another VB, please, love.'

'How's the veal?'

'Yeah, good, mate. Tender.'

'What say we commission some viewer research on Beige? Kate's contract is up soon. And I sure as hell need some sweeteners. She's pretty pissed off about not covering Bali. Why is that by the way?'

'She was at the gym or sipping a latte somewhere when the shit hit the fan. Michelle jumped on the plane first,' Ripley lied smoothly. The bitch had obviously been complaining about him. He'd better step more carefully in the future. 'Gotta train up new Kates, right?'

'Look, I think we should consider Kate as host if the ratings don't pick up in the New Year. She can cover Gulf War Two, which is looking more and more likely. And we can remind everyone she was there during the first Gulf War. That will give her all the cred we need.'

Carter paused to wipe a large dollop of cream from his chin. 'By the way, has Corish got a bloke? I mean is she likely to get up the duff anytime soon? That would throw a spanner in the bloody works.'

'Still single. She scares the fucking pants off most blokes. Eats 'em alive,' Ripley said, laughing.

'Still a bloody good sort. Wouldn't mind her scaring *my* pants off,' Carter snickered.

The two men swigged on their beers, both imagining a pants-off with Kate Corish. Carter's hand journeyed under the table.

TWENTY-SIX

'Kate. You promised me you wouldn't be going to any more war zones.' Dianne Corish was standing in the kitchen, hands on hips. At her feet, Bernstein was tucking into a dinner of roast lamb and vegetables. The meal had been thoroughly mushed in the food processor beforehand for the sake of Bernie's old teeth.

It was no wonder he liked staying here.

'I know what I said, Mum. But this is different. I've been to Baghdad before. I know the lay of the land. And we're planning to get out well before the bombs start dropping anyway. It's no more dangerous than reporting from Washington.'

Kate really did intend to leave Iraq well before war broke out. Afghanistan had taught her to be a lot more cautious. But it hadn't taken away her passion for life as a foreign correspondent. And there was her career to consider as well. Her deployment to the Gulf was supposed to launch Kate as the new, credible host of *Australia Tonight*. It had been the carrot that had convinced her to sign with Channel Eight for another two years. That and the promise that the show would be tackling more serious issues. The Baghdad assignment was a good start.

Kate felt a little sorry for Beige. But he knew he was for the high jump. She just wished someone would tell him outright. It couldn't be much fun reading about it in the television gossip columns. The same words kept appearing. He was 'arrogant', 'tired' and 'overexposed'. But in reality, he was just out of favour with management.

'Can you at least promise me you won't be hitching any more rides on personnel carriers?' Dianne was treading lightly but there was fear in her eyes.

'I'll be fine, Mum. I promise,' Kate assured her as she gave Bernie a final stroke and headed out the door.

'This sure ain't the Al-Rashid,' Tezza grumbled as he set up his edit equipment inside the cramped room. 'What a bloody dump. Wasn't there a YMCA somewhere they could book us into?'

'Yeah, I know. But at least the place isn't on any American hit list. And that has to be a feature.' Kate tapped a cigarette out of its reassuring soft gold packet. 'Surely you haven't forgotten Belgrade already?'

Safe or not, Kate had to admit the rooms of the Hotel Palestine were uninspiring. A grubby combination of dirty orange walls and tattered carpets. Concrete awnings like spider webs impeded the view and prevented the entry of any natural light.

She edged out onto the tiny balcony and lit up. War zones and Marlboro Golds went hand in hand she thought. That was how she justified her most recent lapse anyway. The nicotine hit gave her a little head rush as she looked out over the city.

Her mind strayed to Jonathan McTavish. Although it had been twelve years, with the familiar smells and dusty golden hue of the city polishing her memory, it seemed like yesterday. She was surprised to discover she was actually feeling a little anxious about seeing him again. Or maybe she was excited. She couldn't tell.

There was a knock at the door. Kate took a last hungry drag on her cigarette and hurried back inside.

'Al salaam a'alaykum habibti,' the young Iraqi man said as she opened the door. He was holding a bunch of pink and white carnations. 'Flowers for Miss Cor–ish.'

'Flowers?' Kate said doubtfully, handing the delivery man a 10,000 dinah note as a tip.

'Happy Valentine's Day, Miss Kate Corish,' Kate read aloud. 'Welcome to Iraq. From Uday Saddam Hussein.' Saddam's murderous son had tracked down every female reporter working in Baghdad and sent them Valentine's Day flowers.

'No wonder you're still single, Kate. You attract the wrong types,' Tezza said, laughing.

'Yeah, right.' Kate fingered her cigarette packet, wondering if it was too soon to light up again. 'This isn't a gesture of welcome you know, Tezza. They're just letting us know they're watching. Anyway, I'm heading downstairs to look around. Check out who's here.'

Kate spotted plenty of familiar faces in the lobby as she wandered over to the reception desk. She exchanged a few nods and smiles of recognition. She didn't always know their names. She didn't even speak their language a lot of the time. But she'd crisscrossed the world with these people now for more than a decade.

'Are there any rooms booked under INN?' Kate asked the young man behind the counter.

'Yes, miss. They have three rooms on the seventh floor.'

'Thank you.' She smiled as she headed towards the lift.

INN's makeshift offices weren't hard to find. A piece of A4 paper had been stuck to the door with two rows of gaffer tape. 'INN Baghdad Bureau' it announced in emphatic capital letters.

The door was ajar and Kate poked her head inside, scanning the busy room looking for Jonathan.

'Can I help you?' a balding middle-aged man asked pleasantly. Kate recognised him as INN's Middle East correspondent Max Rogers.

'I'm an old friend of Jonathan McTavish. Is he here?'

'No. He's back in London. On leave,' Rogers said.

'Not like him to miss a war.' She laughed. But then she caught something in Rogers' expression that made her pause. 'Oh, it's Julia. Has the cancer returned?'

'I'm afraid so. It's not looking good. I don't expect to see him this time around. But I can pass on a message if you like,' Rogers said.

'Oh. Just tell him I'm thinking of him,' Kate said as she backed out the door.

For the next month, Kate and Tezza filed their reports and held their breath as war loomed. Plenty of correspondents came, succumbed to the jitters and turned tail. But they considered themselves old hands. They'd pull out at the very last minute. What they didn't count on was the vagaries of Iraqi bureaucracy.

'Where the hell is everyone?' Kate asked as she stared at the locked doors of the Ministry of Information building.

With twenty-four hours to go before the US deadline expired, Kate and Tezza had finally decided it was time to organise their exit papers.

But on the day when its services were most in demand, the Ministry of Information had decided to shut up shop.

'We need to pay our taxes,' Kate explained to the soldier standing out the front of the building. Foxholes had sprung up everywhere almost overnight.

'If you haven't paid your taxes, you will not be able to leave our country.'

'We know that. That's why we are here. To pay our taxes.'

'You are too late. The office is closed.'

Closed! Kate felt a surge of terror rush through her body. In the next twenty-four hours bombs would start dropping. Next door. Across the road. Up the street. The image of those two dead reporters in Afghanistan kept playing in her head.

'Christ, Tezza, what are we going to do?' she cried. 'Bush's deadline is up tonight. We can't even risk driving to the border now. If we get turned around, we'll be driving back in as the war starts. I don't want to be out on the road when that happens.' Kate recognised an edge of hysteria to her voice.

'Come on, girl, don't go to water on me now. Let's think this through. So, we're stuck here. At least the US knows where the media is staying. Given the choices, it's probably the safest place to be right now. And as we learned in Afghanistan, sometimes it's better not to jump.'

They spent the rest of the day squirreling away supplies. They sourced a good generator and lugged box upon box of food and water up to their ninth-floor bolthole. Tezza taped up all the windows. Bombs would definitely drop but they were far more likely to be injured by flying glass than by a misguided missile.

Twelve hours before the deadline, the Channel Eight team was ready for anything.

'I guess it's not the end of the world, Tezza. Although my mum's going to think it is,' Kate said reaching into her bag. 'Care for a scotch?'

They'd managed to smuggle three bottles of Johnny Walker Black amongst all their various camera equipment. She hadn't expected to need it.

She raised her glass. 'Well, if we're stuck here, we might as well enjoy the ride.'

The war started punctually, with the Coalition launching its first probing strikes just ninety minutes after the deadline lapsed. Kate was off and running, her terror of the previous day forgotten in a whirl of deadlines and disinformation.

'We begin our show tonight with the war in Iraq. Our correspondent, Kate Corish joins us now via satellite phone. Well, Kate, it seems we're finally at war. Can you tell us what it's like on the ground in Baghdad?'

'Well, it was quite an early wake-up call. At 5.20 this morning, a single enormous explosion rocked us out of our beds. This was not the promised shock and awe we've all heard about, but a so-called precision 'decapitation attempt' on Saddam Hussein. Our sources say the US had strong intelligence that the Iraqi leader and several of his ministers were together in a bunker at the Al-Rashid military complex. For a while, it was rumoured that Saddam had been killed. But a few hours ago he appeared on Iraqi TV, looking rattled but very much alive. Here's the report I filed earlier.'

Channel Eight was the only Australian network with a reporter in Baghdad and it was hammering home its advantage. Kate was getting precious little sleep. She filmed all day. Bombs kept her awake all night.

Baghdad was copping a pounding. And, according to the Sydney office, so was the rest of the country. Saddam had to surrender soon. Indeed, the only person who didn't seem to fully grasp the situation was Iraq's Information Minister – the man dubbed Comical Ali.

'I can say, and I am responsible for what I am saying, that they have started to commit suicide under the walls of Baghdad. We will encourage them to commit more suicides quickly.'

It was day twenty and Comical Ali seemed oblivious to the sounds of coalition tanks rolling into his city.

The satellite phone rang as Kate was standing out on her little balcony, smoking and nervously watching the steady progress of American tanks. For once, the Hotel Palestine was the place to be, even with its obstructed view.

'Hi, Kate. It's Jim. We've had a shocking time getting through to you. I must've tried about twenty times. The powers that be reckon we should go for a pre-recorded interview to make sure we've got something in the can for news.'

'Makes sense. The satellites are being jammed because the US military is closing in on central Baghdad. So, yeah. We better get this done while we can. I can see the tanks from here and God knows what will happen.'

Twenty minutes later, Kate was in position, her ear piece connected to the sat phone. The countdown sounded like someone was shouting at her from down a tunnel. Then she heard Matthew's voice reading the introduction to her piece.

'Coalition forces have pushed deep into Iraq and are now within sight of our correspondent in Baghdad. Kate, can you tell us what you see?'

'Yes, Matthew. It's been twenty long days of shock and awe but Coalition forces are now in the centre of Baghdad. From where I stand on my balcony, I can see a US tank on the western side of Jumhuriyah Bridge, directly across the Tigris from where we are now.'

As Kate talked into the sat phone, images of the tank were beamed back to the Channel Eight newsroom. Deskbound journalists watched as the turret swung to one side and aimed at a building to its left. The feed from Al Jazeera showed a direct hit on their bureau . . . and their correspondent.

The tank then swung back and pointed at Kate's hotel. The entire office held its breath as it paused for a moment then fired.

Kate was knocked to the floor by the impact. The windows

shattered. Large shards of glass hung like a sheet from the gaffer tape. Thank God Tezza had thought to strengthen the windows.

As Kate scrambled to her feet she saw that Tezza was still filming. The bloke was a trooper.

'Kate, Kate, are you there, Kate?' Matthew's voice was loud and urgent. She struggled to her feet, plugged her ear piece back in and started talking.

'Yes, I can't believe what just happened. It appears our hotel was fired on by an American tank. I'd say the shell hit one of the floors above us. We're fine. But I'm guessing there will be some casualties. This hotel is packed with international media.'

Kate ended the interview quickly. They needed to get moving. There was a big news story to report. And they were right in the thick of it.

'You okay, Tez?' Kate asked, picking a piece of glass out of the palm of her hand.

'Yeah. Bloody pissed off. But fine.' Tezza's camera was resting at his feet and he was glaring at the tank. 'Fucking amateurs,' he shouted.

'Come on, let's get down to the lobby. Find out what the hell just happened.'

Downstairs, the international media was milling around. A few had makeshift bandages around their arms and heads. Most were in shock. There was yelling and screaming as two seriously injured cameramen were brought down in bloodied sheets. Dozens of cameras filmed them as they were bundled into a car. Today they were on the other side of the lens.

Kate picked up what little information she could. The tank had fired a single round, its shell slamming into a corner room on the fourteenth or fifteenth floor of the hotel. Five people had been injured. The cameramen weren't expected to survive the day.

The speculation was that the tank had mistaken a camera lens for a rocket launcher. A glint of metal against the desert sun. The difference between life and death.

Kate scanned the lobby looking for Max Rogers. She wanted to make sure the INN correspondent was safe. She spotted him on the other side of the room, moving from group to group, jotting down information in a dog-eared notebook.

'Am I glad to see you,' Kate greeted him.

'Can you believe it? There's enough to worry about here without your own bloody side taking potshots. You okay?'

'Sure, just a little rattled.'

'McTavish watched the whole thing live and immediately called to see if you were okay. So I'll pass on that I've seen you and that you're still in one delightful piece.'

'How's he going anyway? Is everything all right?' Kate asked.

Max looked at her, his expression suddenly serious. 'You don't know. Of course, you don't know.'

There was a pause.

'Julia died two days ago.'

Julia's death had been inevitable. But that didn't diminish the shock. Kate had wondered how she would react when it finally happened. And now she knew. All she felt was sadness. A deep and terrible sadness.

TWENTY-SEVEN

'And after the break, butter versus margarine. What's best for you and your family.'

Kate smiled into the camera, feigning enthusiasm for a topic that had already been more than adequately dealt with on three other occasions during the year.

The monitor dipped to black. 'I thought we were running that reheated trash tomorrow night,' she groaned. Her microphone was still switched on so her voice boomed into the control room.

Tubby responded through her ear piece. 'We are. We're just letting people know to watch out for it then.'

Kate rolled her eyes. 'So let me get this straight. We are teasing to an item after the commercial break which in turn is teasing to a story we're running tomorrow night. That's ridiculous.'

She would have liked to swear. But many a television career had faltered simply because someone had flicked the wrong switch at the worst possible time. Or in Naomi's case, pressed the red record button right on cue. The *Today Tonight* host's colourful tirade had ended up on the internet, which in turn had led to an awkward on-air apology. No way was Kate going to let something like that happen to her.

It had been just over a year since Kate replaced Beige at the helm of *Australia Tonight*. Host of a nightly prime-time current affairs show. It should have been the pinnacle of her career. But Kate missed being out on the road, especially when the alternative was encouraging people to angst over sandwich ingredients.

Oh well. It wasn't like she hadn't been warned. Matthew had certainly tried to dissuade her.

'Are you sure you're not going to find hosting a bit sedate after all your adventures?' They were huddled together at the far end of the boardroom. Channel Eight was hosting a little party to celebrate Kate's appointment.

'Reading an autocue isn't exactly stimulating work, especially when you're used to dodging bullets.' Matt grabbed a beer from the tray of a passing waiter. 'I mean, where's the challenge? I've been able to read aloud since I was six.'

'Well, I'll be doing plenty of studio interviews and if something big happens, I'll be presenting the show on location. There will be loads more live broadcasts as well,' Kate argued, channelling Ripley's assurances as if his word could be trusted. She wanted the job. And she wanted to believe it would be as fabulous and rewarding as senior management kept promising her.

'Anyway, maybe I *need* boring for a while. I've had more than my share of near-misses in the last few years. I don't think I should be pushing my luck.'

Jenni was clearly not concerned about pushing hers as she flopped uninvited into the tub chair beside them.

'Hey. Congratulations, Kati,' she said with a smile that hinted at a million thoughts, none of them particularly friendly. 'All I can say is it's about time you got off the road. Now the rest of us will get a crack at the big stories. I've always fancied a Logie on my mantelpiece.'

Jenni leaned forward, offering Matthew an unencumbered view of her most valuable journalistic assets.

'Now that's something I've never won,' Kate replied, baffled by the direction the conversation was taking.

'Then why are you always referred to as an award-winning journalist?'

Kate stared at her colleague in disbelief. Entertainment. Journalism. Did she not know there was supposed to be a difference?

'You might be in the running for a Logie now you've got your own show, hey, Kate. If Ray can do it . . . ' Matt teased. 'You won't have to settle for any of those second-rate Walkleys any more.'

He winked at his friend.

'By the way, Ripley said I can host over summer,' Jenni announced smugly as she pulled herself out of the chair. 'He's really been a wonderful mentor to me, you know.'

'Believe me I know,' Kate agreed as Jenni sauntered off, presumably in search of the man who had been so dedicated in fostering her various talents.

'Is she for real?' Matt asked.

'Every bit of her,' Kate said. 'Except maybe the boobs.'

Matt had been right about hosting of course. She was going stir bloody crazy. All those promises about taking the show upmarket had been forgotten. Over the last year, *Australia Tonight* had only ventured out of the studio once. That was to cover the tsunami. And even then Ripley hadn't budged until he saw Ray reporting out of Aceh.

Kate had dreamed of hosting a show like *AT* for as long as she could remember. But the reality didn't match her teenage fantasies.

Kate didn't particularly enjoy sitting behind a desk night after night, always perfectly groomed by a team of hair and make-up professionals. She missed being at the mercy of an ill wind, torrential rain and swirling dirt. The greatest hazard Kate faced nowadays was Tubby's excruciatingly bad copy. As a line-up producer, the bloke had made a terrific chief of staff.

She watched the preview of the butter versus margarine report. Same set of interviews. Same information. Same reporter. Exactly the same shit as last time around.

And Kate had to deliver the same tired old line that was supposed to make women in the target demographic desperate to watch the show again the next night.

'A story no family can afford to miss. That's tomorrow. Good night.'

Kate signed off staring straight down the barrel of the camera, then glanced down to the laptop she kept on her desk in the studio. The news wires were going crazy, something about an explosion in the London Underground.

Holy shit, Kate thought. She stayed seated at the host's desk, reading the wire services as details started filtering though.

AAP was sending updates every thirty seconds. There was speculation that a bomb had gone off. Definitely a bomb. One bomb. Two bombs. Another. On a train. A city bus. Christ Almighty. And this was all happening during London's Thursday morning peak hour. It had to be absolute mayhem over there. Kate picked up the studio phone.

'Ripper, have you seen the wires? Looks like there's a terrorist attack underway in London. Whatever is going on, it's big. We need to change the show for Perth. I'm still here in the studio. I'm happy to wait around and go live.'

Perth was two hours behind the east coast so by the time *Australia Tonight* reached Western Australian lounge rooms, some of the material looked a bit mouldy, especially when there was a big story breaking.

317

'Ahhh, fuck 'em! Forget it, Corish. Who gives a shit about Perth? No one there fucking watches us anyway,' Ripley grumbled.

I wonder why that is, Kate thought, as she watched the story get bigger and bigger with each incoming wire. Surely, they'd let her out of the studio now.

'The death toll is now over fifty. There's a Melbourne man who's in a critical condition and a girl who's had her legs amputated.' Doug Spencer was reading from his notebook in the back of a traditional black London cab. 'Sydney's already lined up interviews with some of the Aussie survivors. So we can hit the ground running first thing tomorrow.'

Kate had jumped on a plane straight after Friday night's show, giving her the weekend to get to London and start filming. Just forty hours after touching down at Heathrow she would be hosting *Australia Tonight*. With such a tight timeframe, she was grateful Doug had been assigned as her producer. For once the gig had been allocated on the basis of talent and seniority rather than mateship and sexual favours. Doug Spencer was smart, efficient and old school. Just what was needed.

Kate could never figure out how or why Doug tolerated the office politics. He was cluey. He was a real journalist. And he was a gentleman. He was everything Ripley and his cronies were not. Another Sydney mortgage slave, she thought. Just like the rest of us.

The cab stopped in front of a stunning hotel. The Draycott was a magnificent old Edwardian townhouse in the back blocks of Kensington that had been tastefully fashioned into a boutique hotel. Kate made a mental note to pick up a better than average souvenir for the production manager.

'Would you like to go out to eat or are you happy just to order room service and get an early night?' Doug asked.

'It's straight to bed for me. Unless you want company at dinner?'

'Jet lag knocks me around a lot more than it used to. So turning in early sounds good to me.'

Kate headed up to her third-floor suite. The room was quaint and girlish with its cream and white striped wallpaper, pink couch lumpy and comfy with feathered stuffing and Victorian antiques. A giant four-poster bed was made up with crisp damask linen while bookcases stood on either side of a white timber fireplace. A small table offered an assortment of liquor in crystal flasks. Kate poured herself a scotch and opened the French doors. The Juliet balcony overlooked a small, private garden square. This was a room fit for a princess.

Kate checked her watch. It was only seven o'clock. Five in the morning Sydney time. She knew from experience that if she gave in to sleep now, she'd be wide awake at 3 a.m.

She sunk into the lounge and sipped her drink, her contact book mocking her from the coffee table. After another slug of whiskey, she dialled Jonathan McTavish's cell phone.

'Hi Jonathan. It's Kate.' She tried not to sound too tentative. They'd talked on the phone twice since Julia's death. Once in Baghdad, after the tank hit, and again after Kate sent a condolence card. There had been a couple of emails but their messages had always been businesslike. Even a little stilted.

'Kate. How wonderful to hear your voice. Where are you? Please tell me you're here in London.'

'Well, I've just arrived. I was hoping maybe you could update me on what's been happening since I left Sydney. I'm twenty-four hours behind on the latest news. So if you have a spare ten minutes of phone time—'

'Where are you?' Jonathan interrupted.

'Well I'm in my hotel and I—'

'Which hotel?'

'Um, the Draycott. It's in—'

'Look, I'm only ten minutes away. I'll come over,' Jonathan offered.

'You really don't need to . . .'

'For heaven's sake, Kate. I'd really like to see you.'

'Okay. Yeah. Me too. Thanks. Bye.'

As she put down the phone, excitement gave way to panic. God. She looked like absolute shit. Jet lagged. Tired. She raced to the bathroom and turned on the shower. She didn't have time to apply make-up. But she could at least wash off the stale plane air. Then she looked down. Oh crap. It was winter in Sydney so she hadn't shaved her legs in weeks. That settled the question of what she would wear. Jeans were it.

The knock came twenty minutes later as Kate was towelling her hair dry.

She opened the door and her heart skipped a beat.

Jonathan leant casually against the door jamb, arms crossed, as gorgeous as ever. His swimmer's body was still in perfect shape.

'Hi there, stranger.' He grinned.

Kate backed into the room to allow him inside. 'You didn't have to come all the way over here . . .' Kate didn't get to finish her thought. He grabbed her. And kissed her. Passionately.

'*That* was unexpected,' she said as he pulled back and held her face in his hands.

There was that same primal glint in his eyes that had driven her crazy all those years ago. As he carried her to the bed, Kate experienced the most wonderful sense of déjà vu.

The soft London sunlight nudged Kate awake. Stretching, she looked over towards the sideboard where a glorious, naked man was pouring himself a cup of tea.

'Sugar?' he asked with a smile.

'No thanks. Just a touch of milk.'

'One of the many little things I need to learn about you.' Jonathan returned to bed carrying a breakfast tray. She propped herself up against goosedown pillows and tucked into thick toast and jam.

'How can you be so beautiful first thing in the morning?' he asked, stroking her face as he snuggled in beside her.

'I appreciate the sentiment but I know you're just flattering me. I'm very aware that I'm now officially pushing forty.'

'When is your birthday?'

'Next July. And I intend to mark the occasion by completely disappearing for a week or so.'

'Don't be silly. Forty's easy. Now fifty. That's going to hurt,' Jonathan said.

'You're not! You look nothing like fifty. When do you turn fifty?'

'Year, or two, maybe three, depending on who I'm talking to,' he said with a grin.

Other than a few smile lines, Kate couldn't see a single wrinkle on Jonathan's face. He was like one of those Omega watch models with perfect olive features, designer stubble and just a streak of grey at the temples.

'How long are you here for by the way?'

'The plan is to broadcast from Monday to Wednesday and then head home on Wednesday afternoon. And of course, I have to work today. Don't you?'

'Normally I would but I've been busy packing. I've been posted to the INN Middle Eastern bureau in Gaza. I leave on Wednesday too. For once it seems our timing is perfect.'

'Isn't that Max Rogers' post?'

'Yep, but he's had enough. The job came up a month ago. And

really there's nothing for me here in London any more.' Kate heard the sadness in his voice. 'Julia's last year just gutted me. Watching her struggle. It was awful. It's taken me close to a year to figure out what to do next.'

'I'm so sorry, Jonathan.'

They were silent for a few moments.

'But what about you, Kate?' Jonathan tried to lighten the mood. 'No near marriages? How is it a woman of your calibre is still single?' He was fishing, just as Kate had once done in Baghdad. And she liked it.

'Oh, there was someone there for a while I thought about putting a picket fence around. But it didn't work out.' And thank God for that, she thought. Really meaning it for the first time.

'So we're both single.' Jonathan reached over and gently touched her neck. 'I don't suppose your station has a Middle Eastern bureau?'

'Most of the people I work with would be hard pressed to locate the Middle East on a map. Anyway, I have my own show. It's not supposed to get any better than that,' Kate said, trying to ignore the nibbling at her ear. 'Speaking of which, I have to start getting ready.'

'Work can wait,' Jonathan said, pushing the tray aside. 'Just for a little while, anyway.'

'Okay. We have an interview at eleven with John Tullock. He's the bloke you've seen in all the newspapers with the blackened face and tattered suit. He's become the poster boy of terrorism. And get this. He's a media studies professor of all things. Better still, he's also an Aussie.'

Doug kept talking as they climbed into a cab.

'We have a bid in for one victim. But she's in surgery so I'm not expecting her to say yes any time soon. You've got to respect that,' Doug said.

'You and I might respect that, Doug. But our esteemed boss probably doesn't.'

'You let me worry about him. The Melbourne IT man is still in a critical condition. There are seven other survivors and we're still tracking down more. We'll shoot the lot today and cut it all together for tomorrow night's show. Which is live from here at 8.30 a.m. our time. By the way, Kate. You look absolutely terrific. Do you have some secret cure for jet lag?'

'Vitamins,' Kate improvised. Who would have thought a good old-fashioned shag could reconcile time zones?

'Can you give me some when we get back to the hotel?' Doug asked as he flipped open his Motorola and started punching in numbers.

The day was as harrowing as it was hectic. Once again Kate found herself listening to gut-wrenching tales of tragedy and survival. Iraq. Kosovo. And now London. Such different places. And yet forever bound by the terrible legacy of hatred. She remembered Jonathan's words outside that bomb shelter in Baghdad.

'It never gets easier – trying to comprehend what human beings are capable of doing to one another. He had been right. It never did get any easier.

'Never let it be said we're the product of something divine,' Kate commented to Doug as they headed back to the Draycott at the end of the day.

'Definitely proof we're descended from monkeys,' he agreed. 'You up for dinner? I have a date with an edit suite all night. But I'm happy to accompany you if you like.'

'That's okay. I may catch up with an old friend from Baghdad days.'

'Well, you enjoy. I'll take care of today's stuff. See you in the morning. We're going live at 8.30. Hair and make-up is booked at 6.30 at the hotel, so get a good night's sleep.'

Doug gave her a fatherly peck on the cheek. Thank heavens for the good guys, she thought.

Packing for the trip, Kate hadn't given a moment's thought to eveningwear. So when Jonathan had suggested dinner at The Ivy, she'd tried to beg off, explaining that she'd only brought very conservative work clothes and a pair of Sass & Bide jeans. Not only that, but her best shirt was suddenly and most mysteriously missing a couple of buttons.

'Don't worry about that,' he'd said on the phone. 'I'll get it sorted. Size ten, right?'

Kate studied the intriguing white box that sat on the bed before pulling the big gold ribbon and lifting the lid. She gasped. Nestled amid folds of delicate white tissue paper was an exquisite Alexander McQueen cocktail dress. Black silk chiffon plunged midway down her back. The neckline was trimmed with dark crystals. Jonathan had even provided a pair of matching and very strappy Miu Miu sandals. Happily the Draycott offered a razor amongst its free toiletries.

Kate pulled the dress over her head and slipped on the shoes. Strangely enough, she discovered she had absolutely no trouble walking on designer heels. It was almost worth forking out eight hundred or so dollars just to know she wasn't about to fall and twist an ankle.

As she glided down the stairs and into the small bar near the lobby, she felt like Cinderella.

'I knew you'd look beautiful in that,' Jonathan said, jumping out of his chair.

'This dress, it's just gorgeous. Thank you so much!' Kate couldn't think of a single man, or woman for that matter, who could find a dress so perfect for her.

'I didn't want you feeling like you were still at work. And I pulled some major strings to get a table tonight. So the evening has to be perfect. I have a town car out the front,' he said, offering his arm.

'I have to be back and in bed at a reasonable time you know. 6 a.m. roll call.'

'That's fine. I'll have you home by eleven. Asleep by midnight.' Jonathan flashed a wicked smile.

The Ivy was a British dining institution, with its warm wood panels, expensive art work and stained-glass windows. It also happened to serve some of the best food in town.

'Our first official date. Not bad fourteen years down the track.' Kate raised her glass of French chablis as if to toast.

'Don't forget we had a Coke together in the Al-Rashid bar,' Jonathan protested. 'Although you weren't anywhere near so exquisitely dressed on that occasion. I actually realised yesterday I've only ever seen you in jeans and a flak jacket. Or naked, of course. It made me wonder what a little bit of British finery could do.'

Jonathan paused before adding hurriedly, 'Not that you need adornment.'

'So, are you pleased with the results of your little experiment?' Kate asked, knowing what he'd say but wanting to hear him say it anyway.

'You look absolutely stunning.' He leaned forward. 'But I still prefer you naked.'

True to his word, Jonathan had Kate back at the Draycott by eleven and pleasantly ravished by midnight.

'You have such an early start, I'd best head home tonight,' he said reluctantly as he kissed Kate on the forehead.

'Jonathan,' Kate said as he opened the door to leave. 'Thank you. For everything.'

'The pleasure was entirely mine. Sweet dreams.' And with that he was gone.

'In five, Kate.' Doug used his fingers to count down the last four seconds.

'Hello and welcome. We're coming to you live from London, a city reeling from the bomb attack that has claimed more than fifty lives and shattered the belief that terrorists only come from other countries. The four suicide bombers were born and bred British nationals. Tonight on the program we will be analysing this disturbing new development. But first, I've spent the last couple of days here talking with survivors about their experiences.'

Kate threw to the package Doug had been up all night cutting.

'You need some sleep, Doug,' she said. The veteran producer was barely able to keep his eyes open.

'Yeah, I'll sleep the rest of the day. I've lined up another interview for you for tomorrow's show. You can handle it on your own, can't you?'

'I should be offended you even asked me that, Doug. I'm a journalist, remember? Not some spokesmodel or reconstituted soapie star.'

'Thank God for the real deal,' Doug sighed, looking up to the heavens.

'I can't believe its Wednesday already,' Kate said as she lay in Jonathan's arms. They had sacrificed a night's sleep for the intoxicating combination of sex and conversation.

In just over three hours, Kate would be hosting the show again.

She knew she would be impossibly tired by 8.30. But she didn't give a toss how she looked. Stealing a few extra minutes with Jonathan felt more important than anything.

'My flight leaves at noon,' Kate said sadly.

'Mine leaves at one. So at least we can see each other off at the airport.'

'I hate goodbyes,' Kate stated flatly, trying not to sound too whiney.

'Maybe we can plan Christmas together?' Jonathan suggested. 'How about somewhere in the snow? Open fires. Bear rugs. Hot tubs. Mmmm. It's only five months away.'

'I guess we've waited this long. A few more months won't hurt.' Kate was lying. As far as she was concerned, every minute hurt. But there didn't seem to be any other option, short of knocking the bloke over the head and sticking him in her suitcase.

'I'll see how I settle in at the bureau. You never know. If everyone in the Middle East finds it in their hearts to be nice to each other for a while, I might be able to pop down to Sydney in October.'

'A quiet moment in the Middle East. You're hopeful.' Kate shook her head. 'If that's the criteria, then Christmas it is.'

'Well, if I'm going to have to wait that long . . .'

Back in Sydney, Jenni was getting screwed as well. But she wasn't finding the experience anywhere near as pleasurable as her London-based colleague.

'Who's hosting the show tomorrow with Kate en route?' she demanded.

'Well, I thought we'd give Michelle a go. You hosted over summer,' Ripley explained. He loved torturing the fragile egos of television wannabes. It was like pulling the legs off insects, an activity he had always enjoyed as a kid.

'That's fucked. People think of *me* as the fill-in host. Why did I give up my Christmas holidays then?'

Jenni was yelling so loudly that everyone in the main production area stopped working. A dozen or so pairs of eyes were trained on Ripley's office, trying to figure out just what was going on.

'Well, I'm just following your advice. Now what was it? "Give someone else a go." Isn't that what you said, Jenni?' Ripley was enjoying the rush of power.

'This is an attack on my credibility. If Michelle presents, everyone will think I failed over summer. I waited a decade to have a go at hosting. She's been here five fucking minutes. What about my credibility?'

Ripley was wondering what credibility Jenni was talking about exactly. She had a great set of tits, nice hair and had given him a blowjob or two in the early days. But that was pretty much the extent of her professional achievements.

'You hosted all summer. That was six whole weeks. Michelle is hosting one night. And by the way, she has just as much credibility as you.' The 'joke' went sailing right over Jenni's head.

'Well, I'm going home then. Clearly I'm not required here.' Jenni stomped out.

'Suit yourself,' Ripley said, reaching for the phone and pushing one of his speed dial options.

'Hiya, Megan,' he said sweetly. 'I thought you might like to know we have a rising star filling in for Kate tomorrow night.'

'Oh, really? Has Jenni got the flick?'

'She's got a bit of a cold. So Michelle is sitting in the chair. Talented reporter. You might remember she covered Aceh while Kate was in Thailand. A nice little write-up would be great,' Ripley wheedled.

'Oh, come on, Mike. You'll have to give me more if you want me to write that one up.'

'Well, you didn't get it from me, of course. But senior management thinks Michelle may be a younger version of Kate Corish. Watch this space. But for fuck's sake don't source me on that. Okay?'

'You know me better than that, Mike. Consider it done.'

Stupid fat slut doesn't even know she's being played, Ripley thought, hanging up the phone.

'Got anything we can use for a poll tonight?' the unit manager asked as she walked into Ripley's office. 'The bean counters upstairs are hot for them. We made sixty grand on the last one. "Should four-wheel drives be banned from the city?" Who would have thought so many people would have an opinion and pay for the privilege of sharing it.'

'Yeah, mate. We've got a Telstra yarn. It's the usual shit about delays repairing and connecting lines. What about asking if Telstra is the worst company in Australia? That should get the cunts running for their phones.'

'No good. We did that one a few months ago. What else have you got?'

The unit manager stopped and sniffed the air suspiciously. 'Is there a fire under your desk? Where's that smoke coming from?'

'Oh, fuck. That's nothing. Hang on.' Ripley bent down under his desk and poured coffee into the smouldering ashtray.

'Okay. Got that sorted. Now let me check this rundown.' He scrolled down the computer screen. 'Here we go. Perfect. Don't know why I didn't think of it earlier. We're running a piece on Costello's comments about hard-line Muslims. There has to be a poll in that one. Let's ask if the laws should be changed so authorities can send radicals back to their homeland. The punters will go nuts for it. Earn us plenty. Now gotta go. Got a meeting.' Ripley grabbed his car keys.

'Do I have to remind you again about the network rules on smoking in the workplace, Ripley?' the unit manager yelled after him. 'And don't drive if you have too much to drink. You'll get caught one of these days.'

Ripley waved a hand. He wondered how she'd guessed he was off to the pub. He preferred his staff to be a little less observant.

TWENTY-EIGHT

Kate slumped in the back seat of a cab at Kingsford Smith Airport. 'Good flight?' the cabbie asked.

'Yeah, fine,' she lied. She had barely slept. Coupled with the shagging marathon of the previous night, she felt one hundred years old.

She opened the newspaper and started to read. By page thirteen she was wishing she'd used the twenty-minute cab ride for a refreshing power nap instead.

> *The dewy new face that graced the Channel Eight screen last night has been dubbed a young Kate Corish by senior station executives. Perhaps Kate should be watching her back. Michelle looked very much at home anchoring* Australia Tonight. *No doubt management will be watching the ratings figures closely.*

The Megan Halliday exclusive was accompanied by a particularly fetching photo of Michelle sitting smugly in Kate's hosting chair. That girl would dance on my grave, Kate thought.

On the opposite page was a picture of Matthew Keaton, being tipped as the 'young, fresh new face of the 6 p.m. news'. So at forty,

Matthew was a youthful contender for the prime newsreading role. But at thirty-nine, Kate needed to watch her back to avoid losing her job to a younger rival. The television industry really could be crazily inconsistent.

Her mobile rang.

'Ah it's the young, fresh new face of Channel Eight news.' Kate laughed, hoping her friend couldn't detect the bitterness in her voice.

'Only a bloke could be described as young at forty,' Matthew replied. 'And don't worry. You're not going anywhere.'

'I particularly liked the way your story was so nicely juxtaposed with the article on the dewy-faced Michelle. It really is too good of her to keep my chair warm in my absence.'

'It's a silly business, Kate. You shouldn't take it to heart. But here's some interesting scuttlebutt. I heard Ray Martin might be up for the chop soon. The talk is Grimshaw's going to get the gig. But Ellen and Peter's names keep popping up too.'

'No doubt we'll read all about it in the papers when the time comes . . . as will they.'

As did Reg Carter, in the case of Michelle's sudden and unexpected elevation to the role of Kate's understudy and eventual replacement.

'Where the fuck did they get that shit?' Carter roared down the phone at Ripley.

'Mate, you tell me. Senior executives apparently. Is there stuff you guys aren't letting me in on?' Ripley countered.

'I've barely heard of the bloody girl. What's her name again?'

'Michelle. Look, it's good to get some positive press. It's good for her profile as one of our reporters. And it's good that they're talking about us instead of the other lot.' Ripley paused as if he was speaking entirely off the cuff. 'You know we really should consider

Michelle for the next series of *Turning Pointe*. She'd look great in a tutu.'

Turning Pointe was the network's celebrity ballet show, where minor celebrities and famous footballers tried to be graceful and beautiful girls stuck their legs in the air wearing tiny little skirts. It was a ratings juggernaut and a brilliant promotional platform for the network's stars.

'Yeah, maybe. Jenni's already put her hand up for that one. But I don't have to give her the gig if you reckon this Michelle is the goods. In the meantime, we're going to have to hose down Corish. When she reads Fatso's article, she's going to go ballistic. Maybe we should take her out to lunch,' Carter suggested.

'She's already called and told me she's going to catch up on some sleep today and will be in at four for tonight's show. That's if, and I quote, "Michelle can prise herself out of the host's chair",' Ripley said.

'The woman has a sense of humour. Thank God,' Carter said, stroking his balls.

Back home from the airport, Kate collapsed onto her white designer couch. She arranged a couple of cushions behind her head and glanced over at the side table. The red light on her answering machine was blinking insistently. But she was too exhausted even to reach over and push the button.

She let her eyes close. An hour later she woke in the same position. The phone was ringing.

'Hello?'

'Kate. It's your mother.'

'Hi, Mum. I just got home. I was about to call you. How's Bernstein? Thanks for looking after him for me.'

'I'm afraid I have some very sad news. I don't quite know how to tell you this. Dear old Bernie . . . Well, he just didn't wake up yesterday. He's dead. I'm so sorry, Kate.'

'Oh, Mum,' Kate cried. Tears were streaming down her cheeks. 'He's been with me for fifteen years.'

'I know, sweetheart. I buried him in the backyard under the lemon tree. I hope you don't mind, I didn't know what else to do.'

'No, you did the right thing. I'm just sorry you had to deal with it.' Kate snuffled.

'He had a lovely life, Kate.'

'I know. God, I will really miss him,' Kate said, looking around her sparse apartment. 'This place isn't going to feel the same.'

'Why don't you pop round for dinner tonight? We can send him off with a toast.'

'Okay, Mum, that'd be nice. Although I warn you, I may end up falling asleep on you.'

'That will be fine, dear. See you tonight.'

Kate could scarcely keep her eyes open as she hosted her final show for the week. And it wasn't just the jet leg. The stories she was presenting were enough to nudge anyone into a coma. Television audiences were traditionally much smaller on Friday nights. So producers tended to offload material that didn't quite hit the mark.

Kate dutifully watched each story on her studio monitor. She liked to see the reports go to air so she didn't have to resort to the bland back-announces favoured by some hosts.

'Hmmm, interesting story,' was one of the more banal and popular comments amongst her peers. All that meant was that the host had spent the previous four minutes picking the dirt from under his or her fingernails.

Kate liked to try for something a little more insightful. But it wasn't always easy. The Patrick Riley story she was currently watching was a case in point.

Young Patrick had insinuated himself into every single shot as usual. So much so, it was hard to work out what the story was actually about. Kate presumed it was supposed to be a run-of-the-mill star fuck with some visiting Hollywood celebrity. But Patrick was getting vastly more air time than his famous subject. Oh Christ. Now the egotistical prat was teaching the actor how to juggle.

What the hell was she going to say about this self-serving piece of crap? 'Well, there's Patrick proving once again it's possible to be in two places at once. On television. And fair up his own arse.'

Eventually Kate settled on 'Hmmm, interesting story.' She wished she had spent the last four minutes cleaning her fingernails. It would have been a far more productive use of her time.

An hour later, Kate was pulling into the driveway of her childhood home.

'Hi, Mum,' Kate called as she jumped out of the car.

She kissed her mother on the cheek and followed her inside. Dianne Corish had always been a small woman but tonight she seemed suddenly frail as she walked unsteadily along the hallway.

'Are you okay?' Kate asked, pulling up a stool at the breakfast bar.

'Yes, darling. Just a little tired.' All her attention was focused on chopping the vegetables.

Dianne Corish had softened of late. She had finally stopped harping on about grandkids. Kate figured she'd given up on the idea. And their relationship was far less fraught as a result. Her thoughts were interrupted by the clatter of a knife hitting the tiled floor.

'Oh, bugger. I've nicked myself.' Her mother was sucking on her left index finger.

'Here, Mum. Let me finish the onions.' She confiscated the knife and watched closely as her mother struggled to remove a bandaid from its packaging.

'Are you tipsy, Mum?' Kate asked suspiciously.

'Maybe a little. It goes to my head more these days. I had one and a bit while I was waiting for you. It's been a tough forty-eight hours, you know.'

'Yeah, I know. And I do appreciate it. Bernstein was something special.' Kate lifted her glass to toast. 'To Bernie.'

'To my favourite grandcat,' Dianne responded. Kate noticed her words were a little slurred.

To: Kate
From: Jonathan

Dear Kate,

I have settled in quite nicely. Max even stocked the fridge for me and the apartment is comfortable enough. So the transition has been smooth. But I can't begin to tell you how much I miss you already.

I have a trip to Iraq planned next month. Then a trip to Iran on the nuclear issue. So I figure December will be here before we know it. I have an image of Kate in the snow. Wooden chalet. Open fire. Bear-skin rug. Or is that bare on a rug? I must stop this. I'll go blind. But shall we make a date?

The question is Europe or North America? Park City looks nice. It will make this separation more tolerable knowing what is in store for us at Christmas.

I miss you horribly,
Jonathan.

Kate spent the morning on the internet happily researching alpine accommodation over two continents. Eventually she found the perfect place. A classic Utah ski in/ski out lodge with solid timber beams, the colour of maple syrup. The photographs showed fluffy rugs and pillows scattered across the floor in front of a rugged river stone fireplace. The views down the valley across to Bald Mountain were breathtaking. Kate emailed the link to Jonathan.

To: Kate
From: Jonathan

My dear Kate,
It's perfect. I've gone ahead and booked it. I hope you don't mind. Dec 23–January 10. I can't wait to get you on those rugs!
Jonathan xxx

Only three months to go, Kate reminded herself as she worked her way through a week's worth of correspondence. There was a tentative rap on the door.

'Excuse me, Kate. Ripley wants you to do an interview this afternoon to promote Michelle's role on *Turning Pointe*,' the young researcher said nervously.

Kate didn't even know the girl's name. All the juniors were starting to look the same, like Midwich Cuckoos. Every one of them was young, blonde and leggy.

'You are fucking kidding, aren't you?' Kate asked indignantly.

'Um, no, sorry. He says you have to do it.'

'We'll see about that.'

Kate stormed past the terrified girl and into Ripley's office. He was on the phone, talking under the desk, puffs of smoke billowing out of his arse as usual.

Kate listened to the conversation, wishing the bloke would somehow spontaneously combust.

'Megan, she's never done ballet before. She is just talented. So this is just a load of crap spun by those other bastards. I don't care if they have a fucking interview with the former ballet teacher. I'm telling you, she's a novice. Just a very supple one. And yes, quote me on that. Why don't you chase up Naomi's love life? There's plenty of mileage in that for you. Jesus. All right. All right. I gotta go too. Be easy on Michelle, Megan.'

Ripley emerged from beneath his desk to discover Kate standing by the door, arms crossed and a furious expression on her face.

'Fuck me. The opposition is running a story saying that Michelle is cheating on *Turning Pointe* just because she had a few ballet lessons as a child. A bit rich when the other mob passed off Nicky Webster as an amateur. I want you to interview Michelle to refute the claim. We can't have those shits running down our reporters. It's just fucking sour grapes now that the show's rating so well.'

'Ripley, *Australia Tonight* is a current affairs show. Not a promotional vehicle for the network. Come on, we already did the launch of the show with that idiot footballer grabbing me and twirling me in the air. Enough.'

'Mate, mate, mate. I know. But tell it to the fucking cunts upstairs, all right. This is an order from above. Out of my hands.'

'It constitutes editorial interference in my book.'

'Oh Jesus, Corish. It's just station politics not federal fucking parliament. Fuck me. Lighten up. All I'm asking for is a quick studio interview. Five minutes tops.'

'Well, I'm not doing it. No way. Get Jenni to do your dirty work. If she looks after the interview, you might even get yourself a real live catfight. Now there's a ratings winner,' Kate said as she walked out.

'Bitch,' Ripley snorted as he lit another cigarette under the desk.

For the next few months, Kate and Ripley kept a careful distance from one another. The executive producer always preferred to ignore his wilful host. And Kate was in too good a mood to provoke him, despite the plummeting ratings. For once, there was something more important in her life than her career. Her world revolved around her phone calls with Jonathan, their constant emails and the promise of December.

She could scarcely believe it when the day finally arrived. In just three hours, she would be on a plane and heading for America.

The phone rang just as she was about to call a cab for the airport.

'Is this Miss Kate Corish?' The voice on the other end of the line sounded official.

'Speaking,' Kate replied, aware of the knot tightening in her stomach.

'Are you the daughter of Dianne Corish?'

'Yes.' She was really frightened now.

'This is Officer Stephen Marks. I'm sorry to inform you that your mother has been in a car accident.'

Kate could barely recognise the woman lying in the hospital bed. Her face was blackened and bruised. A mask covered her mouth, pushing oxygen into reluctant lungs.

'Ms Corish . . . Kate.' A doctor entered the room. She was in her early thirties at most. When did everyone start being younger than me, Kate wondered?

'I'm so sorry. But there's no good news. Your mum has suffered an acute stroke. It's probably what caused the accident. We're making her as comfortable as possible. But you need to prepare yourself. She's slipping away. She might last into the night but not long past that. There won't be any miracles.'

'Oh, Mum,' Kate cried, stroking her mother's silver hair. Beneath the mask, Dianne's mouth was open, gasping for air.

'She's in a coma and pneumonia has set in. That happens some-times with stroke patients,' the doctor explained. 'You should also know that the blood work showed your mum had been drinking. There was alcohol present. And anti-depressants.'

'Depressed? She didn't tell me. She always had a drink at the end of the day, one or two. But I didn't realise it was anything more than that. Oh God.'

Kate lifted her mother's hands to her lips. She thought of Dianne's need for grandchildren. How lonely she must have been after Kate left home. All of a sudden, so much of her mother's behaviour made sense. She had been sinking and Kate had been too busy with her life to even notice.

She started to cry.

'Kate. It wouldn't have made any difference. The stroke would have killed her whether she was in the car, at home or playing bowls. Maybe over the years, the alcohol increased the likelihood of stroke. But really, there was nothing you could have done.'

Kate only left her mother's side for the few minutes it took to call Jonathan to cancel the trip. The rest of the time, she sat in the little hospital room, her head resting beside her mother's arm. Occasionally nurses came in to administer a shot of morphine. Once they removed the face mask and inserted little tubes in her nostrils instead. Each time they left, her mother's breathing became a little shallower. Kate understood they were easing her mother away, a bit at a time.

Dianne was dying before her eyes.

'I'm sorry, Mum. I'm so sorry. I'm sorry I didn't know you were so sad. I'm sorry I failed you. I'm sorry Dad died,' Kate whispered over and over again.

Just after midnight, Dianne's breathing became erratic. There would be a few moments silence and then a sudden round of deep and desperate gasps. The pattern continued for maybe a quarter of an hour. And then with one loud and terrible intake of breath, she was gone. Kate felt her mother's soul leave the room and she was alone.

A few minutes later, or maybe it was hours, she felt a hand on her shoulder. It was the hospital chaplain.

'It's time, Kate. Can we call someone to come and get you? Or maybe you'd like to sit and talk with me for a while.'

'No, thank you. I have my car.' Kate pulled herself out of the chair. She felt light headed and heavy bodied all at once.

'Walking away isn't easy. But don't worry. They're good people here. They'll look after your mum. And the social worker can help you make other arrangements.'

Kate kissed her mother on the head, her tears falling onto Dianne's now pale and cold cheeks.

'Goodbye, Mum. I love you. I love you so much.'

Kate drove home on autopilot. She had no idea how she got back into the apartment. She must have parked the car. Put the key in the door. Turned on the kettle. She supposed she did all of those things but it was a blur. All she knew was that she had somehow ended up sitting on her balcony clasping a cold cup of coffee in her hands.

There was a knock at the door. Like a sleepwalker, she crossed the apartment and put her eye up to the peephole. Jonathan was standing in the hall, a suitcase in each hand.

Kate pulled the door open and collapsed sobbing into his arms.

'Sweetheart.' He held her face in his hands and kissed her.

'She died. I was with her and she just died.' Kate's entire body was shuddering with grief. 'And now you're here. Thank God you're here.'

'I was already at the airport. It was just a matter of changing flights. I only wanted to see you. I don't care about where or under what circumstances.' He gently pushed a blond lock out of her eye. 'But you look so tired, Kate. Beautiful but tired. I think I should put you to bed.'

'Only if you hold me till I go to sleep.'

'I can do that.'

As she drifted off, she heard Jonathan whisper, 'I love you, Kate Corish.'

A week went by in a flash.

'I don't know what I would have done without you here,' Kate said as she lay in Jonathan's arms one morning.

'You would have soldiered on, Kate. You're a survivor. Like me.'

'No. I would have crumbled. You walked in and saved me. Again.' She rolled over to look at him. 'But what are we going to do about us?'

'We'll work something out this year. Don't worry, Kate. Everything will turn out just fine.'

Their conversation was interrupted by the ringing of Jonathan's mobile phone. He leapt out of bed to answer it,

'What? Brain haemorrhage. In a coma. Shit. Okay. Okay. But I'm twenty-four hours away.'

Kate stared at her lover, already knowing the effect if not the details of what he had to say.

'Ariel Sharon's had a brain haemorrhage.'

'You have to go back,' she said flatly.

'Will you be okay?'

'I hate that the world has reached into my bedroom and is taking you away from me. But I understand. You have to go. And yes. I will be okay.'

At the airport, Kate gave Jonathan a final goodbye kiss. As he started to walk towards the departure gates, she caught him by the elbow.

'Jonathan? I love you too.'

TWENTY-NINE

'I think Matthew Keaton should take over the 6 p.m. bulletin,' Reg Carter announced as a batch of fresh, warm muffins were laid out on the boardroom table.

'Reg, I know I'm new to this game. But is it wise to suddenly switch to a younger man like that?' Billy Simpson was the network's new chief executive. He'd slashed and burned his way to the top of the corporate ladder in telecommunications. And now, after an extraordinarily generous golden handshake, he'd bobbed up in television. The fact he knew nothing about the industry was beside the point. He understood how to make a profit.

'Don't viewers prefer a bit of experience and consistency? My instinct is to stick with the bloke we've got. Or at least fabricate some kind of health scare to make his departure more publicly acceptable.'

'We can certainly arrange something like that.' Reg wiped some errant poppy seeds from the side of his mouth. 'But let's look at the options. Nine has gone with a younger bloke. And Ray has been replaced by Tracey. The jury's still out on those changes. Seven has made huge headway going with an experienced head. So it can go either way. But our viewers know Matt. He's been reading the late news and afternoon bulletins for years now. The research says women love him. And his Q score is up there with Jules Lund and Grant Denyer.'

'What the fuck is a Q score?'

Billy talked like a TV man with his short, angry, expletive-charged sentences. But he was an outsider. And an odd one at that. He had the physique of a jockey. And according to station gossip, his secretary booked him in for a pedicure every month. Network executives didn't know quite what to make of him.

'Basically it measures the bond between viewers and our stars. It rates their credibility and tells us how recognisable they are.' Mike Ripley joined the conversation. He was keen to position himself favourably within the new power structure. Someone had to school the new CEO in the art of television. Ripley had decided he was the man for the job. 'Some clever bastard charges a fortune for the fucking survey. But the advertisers want to know the results. So we have to cough up the bucks and pay some attention.'

'What's the Q score for our current anchor?' Simpson asked.

'Well, it's slipped over the last year. The viewers reckon he's past his prime. "Out of touch" was the phrase that kept coming up,' Reg explained.

'And the dip in news ratings is affecting the lead in for *Australia Tonight*. It's hurting our numbers,' Ripley added. It was his latest excuse for the show's declining audience and he was keen to float it with upper management.

'What about Kate's Q score?' Simpson asked.

'She's highly regarded although some women said they don't trust her. She's single with no kids. That doesn't go down well with a lot of our female viewers.' In reality, Ripley's sole source for that snippet was his wife. But he reckoned she was pretty bloody typical.

'Can we commission our own viewer research on Matt and Kate?'

'Good idea. When Michelle hosted over summer, we pulled some of the best ratings we've had for quite a while.'

'Be fair, Ripper. Michelle did flop a magnificent bare tit out of her frock at Carols in the Park. That had to be a factor.' Reg laughed as his hand headed under the boardroom table.

'That was an accident. Albeit a fortuitous one. That pic in the *Daily Mail* certainly piqued interest in the show. But maybe the viewers find Michelle more user-friendly. She's nowhere near as threatening as Corish.'

'That courier certainly took a shine to the lovely Michelle,' Reg added, snickering.

'What?' Simpson grunted.

'Oh. Security caught a delivery guy with his pants down in wardrobe making a rather intimate deposit into her shoes,' Ripley explained.

'And that's supposed to convince me that Michelle has what it takes to lift us out of the ratings doldrums? Advertising revenue is down. And that's the issue here. I don't care how popular the girl is among voyeurs and fetishists. Let's commission the research,' Simpson ordered.

Ripley smiled to himself as he reached for his third muffin. He'd have that soft cock Billy Simpson in his back pocket by the end of the month. Corish would be lucky to last the year.

'Someone just took our photo,' Kate noted to Matthew three weeks later as she tucked into a cholesterol-laden plate of bacon and eggs. 'No doubt we'll be a "hot item in love tryst" in the paper tomorrow.'

'Two of Channel Eight's stars were seen sharing an intimate brunch on Sunday morning,' Matt mimicked, putting down the newspaper. 'Actually, for once I think they've got better things to write about. Can you believe this Jessica Rowe business?'

'What the hell does "bone" mean exactly anyway?'

'I presume Eddie planned to fuck her over,' Matthew said. 'Although he's denying he ever said it, of course.'

'Charming term. But it's nice to finally have a word for how they do it in this business. Speaking of which, how's our erstwhile newsreader? I was surprised to hear about his heart condition. Quite extraordinary given he's been competing in triathlons for years. Just as well you were on hand to step into the breach. Hey, Matt?'

'Come on. It's not like I planned it. Anyway, our day will come. We'll both get boned sooner or later. Everyone does.'

'Not me. I'm way too good at my job,' Kate said, only half joking. 'And what do I care anyway? I'm on holidays.'

Actually Kate cared quite a lot. Even in a notoriously cutthroat industry, the supposed plot to bone Jessica Rowe represented a new low. And there had been all kinds of catty comments in the press recently about other female presenters. To describe Naomi as a dominatrix was just appalling. And from what she had heard, Tracey would be wise to hurry back from maternity leave as well.

That Kate had been left alone so far was probably just luck. And her luck would almost certainly run out while she was out of the country and working on her tan.

Staring down at the Indian Ocean from her first-class seat, she was starting to wonder about her decision to take the week off. She'd always planned to skip town rather than endure any big fortieth celebrations. Still, an overseas holiday right in the middle of ratings? It was absolute bloody madness.

But there was Jonathan, of course, and he was just the tonic she needed on the eve of a 'significant' birthday. It was seven months since they'd seen one another. They had planned to meet up back in

April but a couple of survivors buried deep within the Beaconsfield mine took care of that.

And what a miserable bloody assignment that had been, Kate remembered. She'd hosted the show from the mine site for two wretched weeks, suffering through every wet and bitterly cold Tasmanian day. All the time knowing that between Kochie's antics and Eddie's backslapping, *Australia Tonight* was next to no chance of landing the exclusive.

'Football and money. The knockout combo,' Kate commented when Nine announced it had brokered a deal.

'What's the bloody CEO doing shouting drinks in some shithole pub in the middle of fucking nowhere anyway?' Ripley grumbled.

'If we'd wanted the exclusive that badly, our CEO would have been down here pulling beers with the rest of them.'

'What and get his fucking manicured feet dirty?'

'Pedicure, Ripley. Manicure is for the hands,' Kate had corrected.

As the plane straightened up to land in the Maldives, Kate understood why the brochures called Male International the island airport. The entire runway looked like it was floating on water. It was an extraordinary sight. Trust Jonathan to come up with a destination so spectacular and so exotic.

Kate strode into the arrivals lounge and spotted a dark-skinned man holding a sign with her name on it.

'Hi, I'm Kate.'

'Hello. My name is Samir. I will be escorting you to your villa. Please come.'

'Where are we going exactly?' she asked as they crossed the tarmac and headed towards a gleaming new sea plane.

'It's a surprise, Miss Corish, but you will be very pleased.'

The short flight north was spectacular. And so was their destination. Kate had never seen anything quite as blue as the water or as inviting as this long, crescent-shaped island with its endless white sandy beaches.

The sea plane circled once then landed, stopping in front of a beautiful two-storey white villa with a thatched roof.

'Welcome to Dhonakulh,' her guide and pilot announced.

Samir helped Kate with her bags and led her along the jetty to the back of the villa. He pushed open the double timber doors and stepped aside, signalling for her to go through.

'I will leave your bags here, Miss Corish. Your companion is waiting for you on the terrace.'

Kate surveyed the villa's cool, light-filled interior. It was luxury on a scale she'd never experienced before. Fresh orchids filled opulent metre-high urns. An antique dining table was positioned next to enormous glass doors, offering an uninterrupted view of the Indian Ocean.

Kate walked outside. Jonathan was standing on the far side of the terrace, dressed in a loose, white cotton shirt and long khaki shorts. He spotted her straightaway and raised one hand, flashing the laconic, lopsided grin she loved.

Kate had always thought that going weak at the knees was just a figure of speech. But as Jonathan walked towards her, she felt her body tremble. She pinched her thigh. For once, the old reporters' trick didn't work.

Without a word, Jonathan slid his hands around her waist and pulled her in for a kiss. Kate let her hands map the muscles in his back as she inhaled his scent.

Jonathan's feel. His cologne. The sound of the sea. The magnificent view. It was a sensual cocktail and an intoxicating one.

Finally, he leaned back and took a long look at the woman in front of him.

'Happy birthday, Kate,' he whispered. 'I've missed you terribly.'

I can't tell you the number of times I've nearly jumped on a plane to be with you. I wish I had now. You're even more beautiful than I remember.'

'Now you're just trying to make me feel better about turning forty.'

'You're the same woman I fell for back in '91. Actually . . . no you're not. You're even more wonderful.' Jonathan's eyes left hers and swept over her body. Soon he was kissing her again, pressing his body into hers.

Kate loosened the straps on her sundress. Only for the briefest moment did she consider if they were alone.

That night they ate dinner out on the terrace.

As they sipped champagne, a waiter ducked in and out serving oysters, baked reef fish and island salads. A light ocean breeze brushed Kate's skin as she looked over at the man across from her. So perfect. So handsome. So kind.

'I've never been happier than I am right now,' she said. 'Don't you wish you could snap-freeze happy moments like this and just pull them out of the freezer on a shitty day?'

'Yes. But I'd rather my memories were fresh every day.'

Jonathan took her hand.

'Kate,' he said as he reached into his pocket. 'I want those happy moments today, tomorrow, always.'

He slid a dark-blue velvet box across the table. Kate opened it and stared at an enormous diamond solitaire ring.

The only sounds were the little waves lapping at the seawall.

Jonathan got down on one knee and cleared his throat.

'Kate Corish. I have loved you since the day I met you. And I've had to live without you for too long. Will you marry me?' His eyes never left Kate's face.

All Kate managed was a squeaky 'But—'.

'No buts. I'm moving to Australia. INN is setting up an Australian bureau and you're looking at him.

Jonathan slipped the ring onto Kate's finger. It was a perfect fit.

THIRTY

Ripley gave the cigarette lighter an impatient shove and waited for Jenni to stop wailing. He'd invited her to dinner to hose her down. And now, at the arse end of the evening, he was getting waterworks instead. Stupid bloody woman. As if he didn't get enough of this crap at home.

'Why is Michelle hosting the show again?' Jenni sobbed drunkenly, great highways of mascara streaking her cheeks. She buried her face into the bucket seat of his company-leased BMW. Fuck he'd be pissed if any of that black shit ended up on his upholstery.

'I'm supposed to be next in line. You always told me I was next in line.'

'Look, I know I told you that. But upstairs decided Michelle should have another crack at it.' It was a lie of course. Ripley called the shots. Only Jenni seemed unaware of the fact.

'Can't you do something?'

'Look, I'll talk to Carter and Simpson. Try to convince them to give you another go.'

'You will?' she stammered, wiping away her tears.

'Yes. I will, Jenni.' He pushed a lock of damp hair out of her eyes. In the dull light of a suburban back street, she almost looked as attractive as she had in her twenties. Christ, he'd had the hots for her then.

Jenni placed a hand on his knee.

'You have always been good to me, Mike,' she purred, her fingers edging up to his fly.

Mate. You're about to get lucky again, he thought. The woman might be near-certifiable but she always did do a good blowjob. Ripley lowered the car seat and pressed Jenni's head down into his crotch. As she wrapped her lips around his flaccid member, he let out a gasp of anticipation. Then nothing.

Minutes ticked by as he became embarrassingly aware that his body did not share his mind's enthusiasm for this encounter.

After a while, Jenni sat up and burst into tears again. 'I can't even get you hard. It's because I'm old. An old has-been!'

'You said it,' Ripley spat as he yanked at his zipper. 'I don't usually have any trouble getting it up. As you well know.'

But the truth was Ripley hadn't managed an erection in months. He had figured the problem was motivation. His wife was a fucking harridan. No one could get excited screwing that. But now not even the usually reliable Jenni could make him respond. Fucking bitches, all of them he thought.

He was still in a bad mood when he checked the wire services the next morning. One story in particular grabbed his attention: *Latest impotence research*, it read.

Ripley checked the area outside his office. There was no one lurking around. He clicked to open the piece.

Researchers have found that one in three men who are still smoking after the age of forty will become irreversibly impotent.

Irreversibly fucking impotent! Fuck that. He ducked under the desk to take a drag on his sixth cigarette for the day.

'Gidday, Ripper,' Tubby beamed as he walked in waving a computer printout.

'Mate. I just got this off the wires. Piece on smoking and impotence. Maybe they should put a picture of a limp dick on the packets, eh? That'd make people think twice before they lit up. Reckon everyone will be onto this story like a fucking seagull on a hot chip. Waddaya reckon?'

'I reckon it's fucking crap. Haven't you got anything fucking better to chase. Find a real fucking story. Not some fucking crap off the wires!'

'All right, all right. Keep your hair on. Might be time to give up the fags though, mate.' Tubby exited, unaware that he'd just kicked his boss squarely in his now-redundant balls.

Ripley glanced up at the clock. 8.30. Time to check the previous night's ratings. Legs crossed, he appraised the figures that ruled all their lives. They were up. Marginally. But *Australia Tonight* was still being soundly beaten by both opposition shows. The computer sure had it in for him today.

His phone rang right on cue.

'Fucking hell. We're going down the gurgler, Ripley. Thank God Kate's back on Monday,' Carter boomed.

'Mate, look at the trend over the last few months. I reckon once viewers get used to Michelle, the numbers will build.'

Carter paused. The figures were disappointing. Again. But Ripley could be right. 'Well, that research we commissioned on Kate is due in three weeks time. We'll make some decisions then.'

Three weeks and one day later, the results of Channel Eight's highly confidential research were splashed across the front page of the *Daily Mail* headlined, NOT TONIGHT, KATE.

Sitting in her office with the door locked, Kate thought back over the last few weeks. Ever since she'd returned from the Maldives, her emails had gone unanswered. Ripley, Tubby and Carter were barely acknowledging her while Michelle had been constantly and nauseatingly pleasant. Jenni, on the other hand, had been acting plain weird. But that probably didn't mean anything. The girl had seemed a little unhinged for a while now.

Now it all suddenly made sense. Kate was being boned.

This had to be Ripley's doing. The photograph in the newspaper was all the evidence she needed. The treacherous bastard had been snapped heading off to the football with Billy Simpson. When did Mike Ripley get so buddy-buddy with the CEO, she wondered?

Kate got up from her desk for the third time that morning, grateful that her office included an en suite. This was one hell of a hangover. And atrociously timed. But maybe that's what happened when you overindulged in your forties.

At the other end of the corridor, Ripley's door was also firmly closed.

'We'll have to deny any movement just yet,' he whispered on the phone to Carter. 'We need to time this for the start of 2007. Kate can host until the end of November. That leaves just over three months to go.'

'We'll have to think of something to offer her. Set up a documentary unit or something. I know she misses being out on the road. Maybe we push that angle?'

'Do you think she'll buy it? What about special projects? That has the odd big story to cover. That could be the way to go.'

'Yeah, well, with fucking Mawson at the opposition now, he's likely to fucking swoop on her. We'll have to do this gently. Mind you that fucking horse has bolted thanks to the *Mail* article. Who the fuck is that fat slut's source?'

'Mate. The place leaks like a fucking sieve. I reckon it's some-one on your floor. No one else has access to the research.' Ripley shuffled his feet.

'Heard from Kate yet?' Carter asked.

'Called her and left a message. Now she's holed up in her office sulking.' Ripley tapped a cigarette out of the packet, twisting it so he didn't have to look at the picture of gangrenous feet. 'Sorry, mate. Gotta go. There are people waiting at the door.'

Patrick Riley swaggered into the room.

'G'day, Ripper.'

'How's it going, mate?' Ripley replied through a mouthful of smoke. He was quite fond of Patrick. The kid reminded him a little of himself when he was young. Good looking. A bit of a stud.

'Bad luck about Kate . . . if what I'm reading is more than just rumour, of course.' Patrick flopped down into a chair and assumed the alpha male position. Hands behind his head. Legs apart and fully extended. 'Look, I don't know if you've seen the viewer com-ments lately. But plenty of people are asking why I'm not hosting. I just thought I'd throw my hat into the ring, if you were thinking about going left of field.'

'Patrick, I can guarantee you'll be the face of the network one day. But not yet. You've gotta be seen to pay your dues, mate. Just be patient. Okay?'

Patrick had expected this response. But it didn't hurt to plant the seed. He moved smoothly onto the real reason for his morning visit. 'Just bought a new car. Hate the fact it's sitting in the sun all day.'

Ripley laughed at the kid's audacity. He'd already had five emails that morning angling for Kate's prime car spot. But he liked Patrick. And he wanted Patrick to like him. One of these days it might prove a handy alliance.

'Okay, okay. If – and that's a big if – Kate leaves, you can have her car spot. Happy?'

'You're a champion, mate.' Patrick slapped his boss on the back. He'd have to score the guy some tickets to the members.

'Just a sparkling mineral water, thanks.' Kate handed the wine list back to the hovering waiter. She wondered if he'd seen the newspaper that morning. Probably. But he was too well trained to let his curiosity show.

She loved Catalina for its harbour views and discreet staff.

'You're not drinking?' Gillian asked in horror. 'I've put aside a whole night to cheer you up. And you're not even drinking? This is worse than I thought.'

'Sorry, Gill. I've just had one too many I-miss-Jonathan-inspired hangovers since I've been back. It must be my age finally catching up with me.'

'I doubt that. You can drink anyone under the table . . . except me. And speaking of celebrating with your nearest and dearest, have you told anyone at work about your engagement yet?'

Kate instinctively touched the solitaire hanging around her neck. 'No, they're the last people I want knowing my business. And I feel like if I tell them I might jinx everything. What if INN changes its mind about opening a bureau here? Anyway, I haven't been given the chance. Everyone at work has been avoiding me, funnily enough. I've never been on the outer like this before. Never thought I'd be candidate for a "boning" as they say.'

'It's a fine television tradition, my love. You're not the first. You won't be the last.'

'Right now, I feel like telling them to shove their fucking job. But I don't want them to win.'

'That's my girl. Now I'm having steak. How about you?'

'Ugh. Can't you order something else?'

'What are you talking about, Kate?'

'Smells seem to be setting me off for some reason. Just the thought of sharing the table with a slab of charred meat makes me want to throw up.'

'Hmmm. Not drinking . . . smells making you queasy . . . I suppose your periods are late too. Hellooooo, Kate.'

Kate stared at her friend as the bleedingly obvious finally registered. Work had been brutal lately. She'd scarcely drawn breath since coming back from holidays. Everything was a blur off the back of that one blissful, sex-filled week. One blissful, *unprotected* sex-filled week, she corrected.

'Oh my God,' Kate breathed. 'Surely not.'

'I think I'm pregnant,' Kate blurted to her doctor, a plump, middle-aged woman with hairy underarms and a prickly disposition.

'Congratulations,' she stated flatly, her eyes never leaving the computer screen. God help anyone who wanted a medical certificate off the woman.

'I took a test and it, well, it was positive,' Kate stammered, 'So, I'm here to see if it's true.'

'Kate.' The doctor's tone suggested she was speaking to someone half Kate's age and intelligence. 'The tests are ninety-nine per cent accurate these days. So unless you managed to have someone else pee on the stick, you *are* pregnant. You've also obviously missed a period and are probably throwing up every morning. It's not a hard one to diagnose.'

'Oh, fuck,' she said, tears threatening. 'At my age. I can't believe it.'

'I think we can say you're approximately seven weeks.' The doctor peered at Kate over the top of her spectacles. 'So no drinking, no cigarettes, no smoked salmon, camembert, pate. I'm sure you know the drill.'

'That's how I knew,' Kate volunteered, momentarily forgetting who she was talking to. 'I just knew something was up when the cigarettes, coffee and wine made me feel sick.'

'I'm going to pretend I didn't hear that. That kind of behaviour stops right here. Now get home and take care of that baby. I'll see you in a few weeks.'

Kate floated out of the surgery. The world around her seemed somehow unreal, as if she had disconnected from it. She wasn't sure how she felt exactly. Excited. Terrified. Elated. Confused. All of the above, probably. Who would've thought? At forty! She had always wanted a baby. But she'd given up on motherhood a long time ago.

She flipped open her phone. She had to tell Jonathan. God, what would she say? What would he say? She laughed out loud at the whole crazy situation. They hadn't even discussed kids. A one-night stand in a dusty war zone sixteen years ago. A few nights of passion in London. An explosive week in the Maldives. An engagement that seemed so right at the time. But now, a baby?

'This is insane,' she muttered as the phone rang. Her nerves jangled.

'Hello,' the familiar voice crackled from somewhere in Lebanon.

'Jonathan, it's me. Can you hear me?'

'Yes, hang on. I'll just get off the street.'

Kate heard gunshots in the background. 'What's happening?' She felt scared. 'I thought you were covering the ceasefire.'

'I'm afraid not everyone here got the press release.'

'You have to get out of there right now. I need you here.'

'Kate? What's wrong?'

'We're having a baby.' Kate held her breath, waiting for his response.

'What baby? What?' Jonathan was straining to hear her.

'I'm pregnant. Our child is due in mid-April,' Kate shouted, loving the sound of the words and praying he did too.

'Oh my God. Oh my God, Kate.'

'Jonathan, are you okay?'

'Bloody hell. I'm going to be a father.' He laughed.

Kate heard a large explosion. It sounded close.

'Are you okay with it? You're not . . . upset?'

'Okay? Upset? This is amazing, Kate. It's fantastic. I love you. Oh shit.'

Kate heard the loud boom.

'Come home, Jonathan,' she pleaded.

'I will. I just have to wrap up this assignment. Then I'm heading over to Basra to cover a British troop changeover. Don't worry. It's as safe as houses. I'll be with the military the whole time. And that will be my last official story from the region. So all going to plan, I'll be in Australia the following week.'

'Can't you come home straight away?' she yelled.

'Can't hear you now, my love. The ceasefire is getting louder. I'll be in touch soon. Take care of yourself. Love you, my little mother to be.' The line went dead.

'You missed your calling, Dr Gillian,' Kate observed over Sunday brunch.

'It wasn't hard to diagnose, Kate. Year 10 biology covers the basics. What I can't believe is that you missed it.'

'I don't know. I thought it took a test tube, several thousands of dollars and the planets to align to get knocked up at my age.'

'Sometimes you really can be clueless, Kate. Which reminds

me, in a roundabout way. I have a present for you.' Gillian handed over a thick paperback. *Up the Duff* it screamed from the cover. 'This book looked more your style than the pregnancy guide with the smock-cloaked fat chick in the rocking chair on the cover.'

'Thanks. I think. I'll be keeping that one in a brown paper bag for a while yet.'

'Keeping mum so to speak? That's probably a good idea in the current climate. How was J-Mac with the news by the way?'

'Well, he sounded delighted . . . in between bombs going off. I guess it's hard to shock a man in that situation.'

'I think a baby is pretty good ammunition. But hey, that's wonderful. Of course, if he wasn't delighted I'd have to go over to the Middle East and kill him myself.' Gillian shoved the last bit of spinach omelette into her mouth. 'When will you drop the bombshell at work do you think?'

'I'll wait till I get through the danger period. Another three weeks and I'll have made it to the second trimester. At my age the miscarriage rate is fifty per cent or something, which is completely freaking me. And if anything does go wrong, I'd prefer to deal with it without Ripley knowing.'

'So are you excited yet – or just worried?'

'A bit of both, I guess. I lie in bed at night and I can scarcely believe I'm carrying a child. I feel warm and fuzzy but weird too. Kind of hard to explain. But I just know it's what I really want . . . this baby, and Jonathan back here and safe.'

'Well, not long now.'

'Easy for you to say,' Kate replied. The next couple of weeks were going to feel like a lifetime.

THIRTY-ONE

Kate nervously counted down the days until Jonathan was out of Iraq. It was another week before she heard from him again and she had to settle for a message. But it was the news she'd been waiting to hear.

'Hello, my darling. I can't wait to see you. Drove out of Iraq via Kuwait and just landed back at the Gaza office. Still got a bit of work to do here. But I'll speak to you tonight when I get home. Love you.'

Thank God for that, Kate thought. Iraq was lawless. And the rest of the region wasn't too much better. As a fiancée and mother-to-be, she wanted her man out of the Middle East.

But Jonathan didn't call. By Sunday morning, twenty hours later, Kate was panicking. She tried to tell herself there was nothing to worry about, that he'd probably just been sent out on another story. But he would have told her, surely?

First she tried his apartment. It was eleven in the morning in Sydney. That made it 5 a.m. in Gaza. The phone went to voicemail. Next she tried his cell phone. But it didn't even ring.

She paced anxiously until it was late enough to call the office in Gaza. The bureau chief answered.

'Hi there, it's Kate. Is Jonathan there, please?'

'I haven't seen him yet this morning. But it's still early. You should catch him at home.'

'Yeah. Thanks,' Kate replied. She felt ill. And it wasn't morning sickness. A car accident perhaps? A confrontation between Palestinian and Israeli forces? A bomb? He said he would ring. What could possibly have stopped him? After a few more hours of worry and countless calls to Jonathan's cell and home number, Kate finally rang INN's foreign-affairs desk in London. But they hadn't heard from their star reporter either.

Kate spent the rest of the day on the computer, trawling news services for any hint of trouble in Gaza. As the hours passed without word, Kate became more and more certain that something terrible had happened.

No amount of chamomile tea could coax her to sleep. So she was on the internet when the news broke at 3 a.m.

'Gaza Abduction', Kate read, her mind battling the words in front of her.

AAP. Sunday 21.42 pm. Gaza.
Palestinian Security Forces say they cannot yet confirm reports that INN reporter Jonathan McTavish has been kidnapped. It's believed McTavish was seized at gunpoint yesterday as he returned home from his Gaza office. A group claiming to be affiliated with al Qaeda said it will kill the foreign journalist to raise international awareness of the thousands of Palestinian prisoners held in Israeli jails.

Kate stared at the screen in horror. Please God let this be a mistake, she thought, as she reached for the phone. It was Sunday in London but news was a seven-day-a-week business. There would be someone on the INN foreign desk.

'Kate, I was just about to call you.' It was Elliott Smythe, INN's foreign editor. 'We've only known for about an hour. We don't have many details yet. But the Gaza office has received a video of Jonathan from his captors. So yes. It's confirmed. I'm so sorry.'

'Kidnapped in Gaza? That doesn't happen. It's impossible,' Kate argued.

'No. It doesn't happen. And because of that we're reasonably optimistic of sorting this mess out quite quickly. No foreign journalists or aid workers have been harmed since the Intifad. The President is sure to step in. Public sympathy for the Palestinian cause comes via the correspondents on the ground. So this abduction is a political nightmare for them. They'll want Jonathan returned safely as much as we do.'

'What can we do? Can we give them money? Who are these people? What do they want?' Kate's head was spinning.

'They're some new group called the Brigades of Holy War. But don't worry. We're onto this and so is the Foreign Office. They've already set up a meeting with Abbass. And we will pay for his release. Of course that's off the record.'

'Oh Jesus, what if they kill him?' Kate cried.

'We can't think like that now. And there is no reason that should happen. Try to stay calm, Kate. We'll get him out of there, I know it.'

Kate put down the phone and switched on the BBC world news service. She was shaking. No mother. No father. Even Bernie was gone. The thought of losing Jonathan terrified her.

At six, the BBC picked up the story. The kidnappers had sent a tape to Al Jazeera. With the telepathic speed of electronic news gathering, her lover's image had been beamed around the world and now into her apartment. Jonathan appeared on the screen, slump shouldered, blindfolded and kneeling in a bare room. Two masked men with guns stood on either side of him.

'If they blindfold you, they probably won't kill you,' Kate remembered her instructor saying during her 'working in a hostile environment' training. It was reason for hope.

The phone rang the moment the BBC report was over.

'It's me, Gillian. Oh, Kate. Are you okay?'

'You saw it?'

'Yeah. I watch the BBC first thing every morning. How are you holding up?'

'God, I don't even know. The people at INN are certain they'll have him out sooner rather than later. I'm just grateful I haven't told too many people about Jonathan and me or I'd have the whole media catastrophe camped out on my doorstep right now. Maybe that's what I deserve. A dose of my own medicine.' Kate's voice started to shake.

'Sweetheart, stop it. You did not bring this on yourself.'

'But that's what it feels like. Gill, I have to go. I've just realised. I have to be there!'

'Kate. Kate. Calm down. Think this through. You need to give it a day or two. INN seems confident they'll get him out. So is the British Foreign Office. I just don't think heading off to Gaza in your condition is a good idea. At least promise me you'll see your doctor before you go flying to the other side of the world.'

The doctor sided with Gillian. 'You've had some spotting. The baby looks fine but there's no sense taking any chances. So there will be no flights anywhere. And I'm ordering you to take a week off work. You're exhausted and you need to slow down. You don't want to risk a miscarriage.'

Kate didn't want to endanger the baby. But, trapped at home, it felt like the walls were closing in on her. Partly out of habit and mostly to keep sane, she immersed herself in research, spending hours on the internet and on the phone to experts all over the world. Days and days went by without any word from the kidnappers. No one knew if Jonathan was alive or dead.

Then exactly one week after the abduction the phone rang. It was the INN foreign editor.

'We've received a wire.' Elliott's voice was unsteady. 'The terrorist group . . . Brigades of Holy War . . . They claim they've killed him.'

There was silence.

'Are you there, Kate?'

'It's not true,' Kate said. 'If Jonathan was dead I would know it. He's not dead, Elliott. You have to believe me. He's not dead.'

Kate kept repeating the mantra to herself throughout the morning. 'He's not dead. Jonathan is not dead.'

She wished now she hadn't invited Sandra Cook for lunch. It had seemed a good idea when she'd picked up the *Mail* that morning and read Megan Halliday's latest outpouring of venom.

Kate Corish hasn't reacted at all well to that research suggesting she's losing ground with viewers. The anchor known to her colleagues as the ice maiden has taken to her bed with the flu this week. Colleagues say it's a classic case of a dummy spit-inspired lurgy.

Kate had laughed like a madwoman after reading the piece. Ripley just didn't know when to back off.

Talking shop with Sandra would have been a good distraction. But that was when everyone believed Jonathan would be released at any moment. Before some obscure terrorist group claimed he was dead.

Sandra arrived at Kate's apartment right on the dot of one o'clock. She was wearing a cool white linen shirt, her devastatingly long legs encased in crisp khakis. Even at sixty, she had the most amazing bone structure. The woman belonged in television.

Sandra settled into the feathered cushions of the white lounge and gazed out over the harbour.

'Any news on Jonathan?' she asked.

Sandra was one of the few people Kate trusted enough to take into her confidence. Sandra knew about the engagement and the baby . . . and the medical problems that had stopped Kate from making a mad dash halfway across the world. But this report from the Middle East that Jonathan was dead . . . Kate wasn't ready to share that news with anybody. It was as if the mere telling of it might make it true.

She shook her head. 'Nothing concrete, I'm afraid.'

'Prefer to talk about something else for a bit?' Sandra asked. Something about Kate's expression told her all was not well.

'Yeah. That would be good. I'd love to hear your take on that viewer survey they're using to shaft me.' Kate struggled to make small talk.

'Ah yes. Bloody audience sampling,' Sandra said, shaking her head in disgust. 'You're too cold. Women are suspicious of you. Men are intimidated. Christ, it's the same shit they threw at me two decades ago.'

Sandra glanced down at the coffee table where *The Telegraph* lay open on page three.

'And look at this, the women of Willoughby aren't allowed to wear empire-line dresses now for fear they might be mistaken as pregnant. Can you believe this crap? You'd think it was the fifties.'

'To be honest, Sandra, I just don't care any more. I'm too tired to fight.' Kate's drawn face underscored her words. She'd spent the morning hunched over the toilet bowl. And it had been weeks since she'd had a decent night's sleep.

'It's gone crazy out there, hasn't it? First Jessica. Judging from all the leaks I'm guessing Jana will be the next to go. And today, you get lumped with the ice-maiden tag.'

Sandra was on a roll. 'How stupid are these people? You'd think they were in enough trouble already over the Jessica Rowe incident. And that was one well-timed pregnancy you'd have to say. She'll get a lot of money out of them if they do decide to get rid of her.'

As Sandra chatted away, tears started streaming down Kate's face. She couldn't pretend a moment longer.

'What is it? What's happened?' Sandra pulled Kate into her chest and let her sob.

'They say they've killed him,' Kate cried, her shoulders heaving. 'I was told today the bastards are claiming they've already done it.'

Sandra soothed and waited for Kate to catch her breath.

'Kate, we've both reported on these things for long enough to know that every extremist group in the region will be keen to get a few lines of publicity out of Jonathan's abduction. This is a claim and that's all it is.'

Sandra's good sense and even tone calmed Kate. She felt hopeful again for the first time since Elliott's phone call.

'I know you're right. But it's so hard . . . especially with all of this work stuff as well. Although at the moment, I don't give a shit about my job.'

'Kate, you can't give up now. You still have a future. You have hope. And you have to provide for your baby no matter what happens.' She held Kate by the shoulders and looked into her eyes. 'I can't help you get Jonathan back. But I'm not going to let those pricks at Eight beat you down. There has to be a way of turning this around.'

Sandra jumped up and began pacing around the apartment, eyes narrowed in concentration. After a few minutes, she stopped and turned to her friend. 'I think I might just have a plan.'

THIRTY-TWO

Three weeks later, Kate was back in the office when a newsflash appeared on the wires.

A Palestinian government spokesman says kidnapped British journalist Jonathan McTavish is alive and well and could soon be released.

Speaking at a literary festival in Wales late yesterday, Hamas government spokesman Ghazi Hamad said he was in contact with the group holding INN's Middle East correspondent and is personally involved in negotiations to free him.

Hamad told journalists he knows McTavish is well and healthy, saying no one has tried to harm him or hurt him and he hopes to see his release very soon.

She immediately rang Elliott Smythe.

'Kate, Abbass says his intelligence officials have evidence Jonathan is still alive. So hold on, girl. We have to hold on.'

It was just the boost Kate needed to tackle the Channel Eight boys' club. She'd called this mid-morning meeting herself, selecting the date in careful consultation with Sandra.

'The rumours have gone on long enough,' she'd told Carter over the phone, relieved to finally be in control of some small part of her life. 'I think it's time we got together to talk about my future. How does next week sound?'

'I think that's a fabulous idea, Katie. I was actually just about to ring you.'

'Sure. BYO bone?'

'What?'

'Nothing. See you there.'

Kate sat at one end of the long wooden table. Carter, Ripley and Simpson hunkered together at the other.

'Maybe I should get the ball rolling,' Kate started. 'I'm pregnant. Isn't that fantastic news?'

The three men stared back at her as if she had just rolled a grenade down the length of the table.

Ripley was the first to recover. 'Congratulations, Kate, um, that's fantastic news.' He jumped up and kissed her on the cheek. Kate fought off a wave of nausea that wasn't entirely associated with her pregnancy.

'Well, this will all work out well then,' Billy announced cheerfully. 'Next year we'd like Michelle to host *Australia Tonight*. She did well when she stepped up to the plate two weeks ago. And given your family commitments with bub, we'll organise a flexible work arrangement for you to contribute to special projects.'

'What if I want to keep my job?' Kate replied calmly.

'Come on. You know the deal, Katie,' Carter observed. His voice had a steel edge. 'You've seen it time and time again. It's why hosts get paid ten times more than anyone else. They have a limited shelf life.'

'You're a huge asset to this network, Kate. You are part of a very successful team. We'll renegotiate your salary for next year now that your circumstances have changed.' Billy was still grinning, refusing to acknowledge the tension in the room.

'So, as they say over at Nine, you want me to eat a shit sandwich?' Kate got up, hands on her hips. 'I'll think about it.'

Carter waited for Kate to leave the room before continuing the conversation.

'None of these chicks want to come back after they have a kid anyway. This is the perfect out for us. Makes it look like she just went on maternity leave and didn't come back.'

'But what if Corish does want to come back? I mean, we're fucked then, aren't we?' Ripley asked.

'As that new bloke over at Nine so eloquently noted: television is just a bucket of contracts. And Kate's contract is up next month,' Carter replied. 'We've got her cold.'

The next morning, Carter was still congratulating himself for his deft handling of the Corish dilemma. Kate had been good in her day. But she'd reached her use-by date. And given her pregnancy and soon to be publicised desire to stay at home with her baby, no one would be able to accuse Channel Eight of boning her.

He took a sip of coffee. Black. Four sugars. Life was sweet.

The latest magazines were piled neatly at one corner of his desk. Carter pushed *The Bulletin* to one side. He preferred to start the day with something easier. He reached over and grabbed *Women's World* instead.

One glance at the front cover and Carter spat out his coffee. Dark brown puddles formed on top of Kate's beautiful Madonna-like face.

'Brave Kate' proclaimed the front cover of the October edition of Australia's most popular women's magazine. The cover shot showed

Kate in a strapless cream silk gown. The material skimmed her body, offering the merest hint of a swollen belly.

Now he knew why Kate had been so adamant about the date for their meeting. The cunning bitch.

Carter raced through the story. It detailed Kate's grief for her missing fiancé. What the fuck? Then there were her hopes for their unborn child. And, oh Christ. Kate also described how Channel Eight had abandoned her in her darkest hour. Pregnant, grieving and boned. It was a public-relations nightmare.

Three decades in television told Carter that *Australia Tonight*'s ratings were about to go ballistic. And for once that was not good news. Not only was the architect of the show's impending resurgence coming off contract, but they'd also managed to piss her off big time.

'Fuck,' Carter yelled as he reached for the phone. 'Ripley, have you fucking seen *Women's World* yet? We're fucking screwed.'

A month later, Ripley sat in the boardroom with Billy Simpson waiting for Kate to arrive. Carter had ducked out to check on the progress of the muffins.

'What do you think of Carter as head of news and current affairs?' Simpson asked.

'Well, his decision to get rid of Kate has been a disaster that I'm not sure we're going to be able to dig ourselves out from. He's a mate. I'm his biggest fan. And I've gone along with his ideas. But the bloke really has no idea about television.'

'Really?'

'Put it this way, if he fell into a barrel full of tits he'd come up sucking his thumb. Fair dinkum. Shit, Billy. We can't afford this kind of fuck-up.'

And it had been a fuck-up of the highest order. The October

issue of *Women's World* had sold more copies than the Princess Mary wedding edition. *Australia Tonight* had returned to the top of the ratings. Kate was now the hottest property on television. And she was about to walk out the Channel Eight gates for the last time.

'Of all the stupid fucking decisions,' Simpson said as Carter returned to the boardroom, Kate trailing behind him.

'Please take a seat, Kate,' Billy Simpson started. 'We've had a rethink and we would be honoured if you hosted the show again next year.'

'After a few months off with the bub, of course,' Carter added, for once refraining from scratching his balls. It seemed inappropriate in front of a pregnant lady.

'We consider you family, Kate. And right now you need our support,' Simpson said.

'We're backing you all the way,' Ripley added.

Kate stared at the three men at the other end of the boardroom table. They were unbelievable.

'Thank you, gentlemen. But I won't be renewing my contract with Channel Eight,' she said, engaging the dramatic pause she had used to such excellent effect as an interviewer.

The blokes changed butt cheeks in their chairs and glanced at each other nervously.

Kate had always planned to knock back any new offer from Simpson and his cronies. But her decision had been made much easier thanks to a phone call from Bruce Mawson offering her the hosting job on a quality weekly program at his new network. And the position came with more money and child-friendly hours. It was the Holy Grail for women in television. Kate had snapped it up.

'Whatever you want. We'll accommodate it,' Simpson pleaded.

'And whatever you come up with, I'm going to decline. I have a real family to worry about now. Good day, gentlemen.' Kate rose from her seat and left the room, only just managing to suppress a grin. As she closed the door, she heard the network CEO start to speak.

'Well, gentlemen, this certainly has been a monumental cock-up on both your parts. Security can help you clear your offices.'

The gentlemen stared at Billy Simpson with mouths open.

'You're not telling us . . . ' Ripley swallowed hard.

'I'm telling you to assume the position, gents.'

EPILOGUE

Kate walked onto the set, Prada heels click-clacking on the shiny studio floor. They were her favourite shoes. But nowadays she could only see them when she was sitting down.

She edged her rounded tummy around the kidney-shaped desk. The godawful design was actually ideal for accommodating her expanding girth. A pregnant host. Bet the boys didn't consider that when they were remodelling the set, she thought.

Just five minutes to go before she hosted her last edition of *Australia Tonight*. She didn't feel sad exactly. More nostalgic.

It had been nineteen years since she'd sat in this exact same studio doing her first screen test. She'd been a starry-eyed kid, with a head full of hopes and dreams about a career in television journalism. Well, there had been plenty of disappointments and reality checks along the way. But still, Kate reflected, she'd achieved pretty much every dream she'd had back then. Although back then, she hadn't known there were other dreams that were just as important.

She thought of Jonathan. It was twelve weeks since he'd been abducted. Another video had been released a few days earlier. This time he was wired up to an explosives vest. The blindfold that had given Kate so much hope was gone. Kate shook her head sharply to clear her head of the nightmare image. Would this rollercoaster of hope and fear ever end?

'How long to go?' The floor manager interrupted her thoughts.

'Next April. So I'm halfway home,' Kate replied, grateful for the distraction. 'And I intend to spend the next twenty weeks lounging about in my trackie daks.'

He laughed. 'Half your luck.'

Kate flipped open her laptop and pulled up the latest wires. It might be her last show but she always went to air knowing exactly what was happening in the world.

'Here we go, Kate,' the director said through her ear piece.

The familiar theme music filled the studio.

'Hello and welcome to the program. Tonight, the shock decision that has rocked the swimming world and devastated a nation of fans. Ian Thorpe has announced he's quitting the pool.'

Kate worked her way through the rundown calmly and proficiently. She'd scripted a farewell. Nothing fancy. Just a simple thank you to viewers for their loyalty and support over the years. She'd been tempted to launch into a diatribe about the appalling state of current affairs in Australia. Maybe even remind viewers that only they had the power to change the situation. All they had to do was switch off their televisions. She might even have felt better for taking the moral high ground for a few snatched minutes. But, really, where was the point? She might generate a few headlines but nothing was likely to change.

'More of *Australia Tonight* after the break.'

The show was almost over. As Kate prepared to say her goodbyes, she glanced over to her laptop. An urgent newsflash had appeared on wires. She clicked on the story and immediately felt the air being sucked out of the studio.

A bloody showdown is underway between Hamas gunmen and the kidnappers of INN reporter Jonathan McTavish. The kidnappers had threatened to kill their hostage if a rescue attempt was launched. No word yet on casualties.

Kate couldn't move. But she was aware of her baby kicking wildly.

'Kate. Are you okay? We're on in ten seconds.' The floor manager's voice seemed to come from a million miles away.

The red light flicked on top of camera one, signalling to Kate that she was now on air. She stared blankly into the lens for a moment, completely disorientated. But then twenty years of experience kicked in and she started to speak.

Kate presumed she read the autocue. That she'd followed the script and smiled at the right times. She was vaguely aware of the theme music playing in the background. Did she say goodnight? She wasn't sure.

'Good one, Kate,' she thought she heard the floor manager say.

She sat motionless as the lights were dimmed. She was vaguely aware of her mobile phone vibrating in her jacket pocket.

Like a zombie she answered it. Her whole world rested on this one call.

'Hello?' she said softly.

Then, at the sound of Jonathan's voice, she began to cry.